650

Stories of Life
North & South

Stories of Life North & South

Selections from the Best Short Stories of Erskine Caldwell

Chosen by
Edward Connery Lathem

New York:
Dodd, Mead & Company

ECL:4

Library of Congress Cataloging in Publication Data
Caldwell, Erskine, 1903-
    Stories of life, north & south.
    I. Lathem, Edward Connery.   II. Title.   III. Title:
Stories of life, north and south.
PS3505.A322A6   1983   813'.52   82-19922
ISBN 0-396-08133-9

Contents

On Getting Established as a Writer of Fiction   vii
The Selections   xxiii

The Mating of Marjorie   3
John the Indian and George Hopkins   8
The Automobile That Wouldn't Run   12
Saturday Afternoon   18
The Empty Room   24
Rachel   29
Indian Summer   38
Over the Green Mountains   49
Warm River   55
Yellow Girl   64
The Medicine Man   75
Meddlesome Jack   85
The Grass Fire   97
A Woman in the House   105
Horse Thief   112
Country Full of Swedes   119
Daughter   134
Maud Island   140
The Cold Winter   152
A Day's Wooing   157
Kneel to the Rising Sun   165
The Growing Season   189

The Negro in the Well   194

Return to Lavinia   201

A Small Day   207

Man and Woman   215

The Night My Old Man Came Home   220

Wild Flowers   227

Balm of Gilead   234

The People v. Abe Lathan, Colored   240

Big Buck   248

Handy   259

On Getting Established
as a Writer of Fiction

Prefatory text, condensed and extracted from
the author's autobiography, *Call It Experience*

I ENTERED the University of Virginia in September 1922. The subjects
that interested me most were English and sociology. After field trips to
state hospitals and county old-age homes and similar institutions, I began
writing about what I had seen. At first I wrote strictly factual reports, but
gradually I began using the same material as the inspiration for sketches
and brief stories.

Writing became such an absorbing interest that, in my desire to learn to
write fiction, I frequently changed courses and even dropped out of the
university for long intervals. Finally, in the spring of 1925, still two years
short of graduation, I left Charlottesville and went to Georgia and applied
for a job on *The Atlanta Journal*. I had no ambition to make journalism
my lifework, but newspaper work was writing, and that was what I wanted
to learn to do.

First of all, I had to put aside the wordy way of writing I had got into,
and I had to acquire the skill to write a readable news item. The city editor would begin his copy reading by whisking a soft-lead pencil over a
three- or four-hundred-word story, about a fire or a holdup or an accident,
until there were perhaps a dozen lines left. Then he would hand it back
to me and say he could use it only if I rewrote the story in half as many
lines. This was a realistic course of instruction in writing, completely different from anything I had learned in English courses.

I would go home in the evening and write short stories and mail them
to magazine editors in New York. The stories, no matter how many times

I rewrote them, were always returned, usually without comment. In the midyear of 1926, I decided my next step should be to give up my job and leave Atlanta. I had written perhaps forty or fifty short stories, not one of which had been published. However, during those past twelve months I had been coming to the realization that I wanted to be, above all else, a professional author. (And as I saw it, there was only one authentic kind of writer — a writer who could see his stories in print.) I was going to devote full and exclusive time to the writing of short stories and novels. I put aside the next five years in which to accomplish my ambition, with the reservation that I would take an additional five years if necessary.

After coming to the decision, and after making up my mind not to let anyone talk me into changing it, I then set out to choose some place in which to live. Except for several months spent in Pennsylvania, I had lived all my life in the South, and I wanted to be where I would find a new and different perspective. Going abroad did not appeal to me; I wanted to live somewhere in the United States. In addition to the promise of inexpensive living costs, the State of Maine seemed to be a faraway place on the map. I decided to go "Down East": the Town of Mount Vernon, Kennebec County.

When I had written dozens of short stories, I had the feeling that they were getting better, or at least more readable, all the time. For one thing, I was beginning to be able to form and shape imaginary incidents and events into the kind of story that produced the effect I wanted it to have. I tried to write with only myself in mind as the reader, believing that a writer himself must be pleased with a story before others could be.

I looked for intensity of feeling in a story, weighing its emotional effect on some inner balance. If a story I had written appealed strongly to me, regardless of lack of conformity to the style of traditional fiction, I was amply satisfied with the result. The time would come, I hoped, when others too, not excluding editors, would accept it as being the only possible way that that particular story could have been written, either by me or by anyone else, to produce the sensation it gave.

Equally important to me was my belief that the content of a story was of greater importance, for enduring effectiveness in fiction, than the style in which it was written. Content was the basic material of fiction — the things in life that one told about, the thought and aspiration of men and women everywhere, the true-to-nature quality of fictitious characters who never once lived on earth but who gave the reader the illusion of being real people.

Naturally, all fictional personages are to some extent created from the recollection or observation of living people by the author, for otherwise people in novels and short stories would have slight resemblance to human beings. In my way of writing, I strove to take directly from life those qualities and attributes in men and women that would, under the circumstances I was about to invent, produce in a telling way the ideal characters for the story I wanted to create. Rarely, if ever, was any such fictional character not a composite one.

It was during this period, the year 1927, that I began getting with some frequency short notes from editors, instead of printed rejection slips. Even though no magazine actually accepted and published a story, at least now and then an editor would reject my work with comment. There was always something, however, that prevented the story from being published; it was too long, too brief, too informally written, too grotesque for readers of the particular publication, too realistic in presentation for the tastes of the editorial board. It was surprising how many reasons, logical and farfetched, could be found for not accepting a story.

*   *   *

During the early part of 1929, a little more than six years after I first began trying to write fiction at the University of Virginia, I received the first letter of its kind I had ever found in the mail.

The letter was from Alfred Kreymborg, and it said that he and the other two editors of *The New American Caravan*, Lewis Mumford and Paul Rosenfeld, were accepting for publication in October a short story I had submitted. The title was "Midsummer Passion." It had been written the year before in Mount Vernon, and it had been submitted to ten or twelve experimental magazines within the past twelve months. (*The New American Caravan* was an anthology that appeared once a year; it was not a magazine.)

The amount to be paid for the story was less than twenty-five dollars, but to me that was of little matter; what was of prime importance was the fact that somebody somewhere had at last accepted one of the short stories

I had written. The accumulated disappointment of many years was suddenly and completely erased from memory.

As the result of the good news from Alfred Kreymborg, I began submitting stories to magazines in batches of six and seven at a time. Within six months, stories were accepted for publication in *transition*, *Blues*, *Hound and Horn*, *Nativity*, and *Pagany*. Even though technically I had achieved an aim, all of these were so-called "little magazines," without general circulation, and payment, if any, was even smaller than that offered by *The New American Caravan*.

In the foggy gray autumn I received one morning a briefly worded letter from Maxwell Perkins, the editor-in-chief of Charles Scribner's Sons, in which he said that he had read one or two of my stories in small publications and that he would like me to let *Scribner's Magazine* see some of the unpublished stories I might have on hand. This was the first time anyone had invited me to submit manuscripts for consideration and, since *Scribner's Magazine* could undoubtedly be classified as a commercial magazine of general circulation, to me it meant an even-longer step forward than the actual printing of my work in *The New American Caravan* and the little magazines.

The letter touched off a three-month orgy of writing. To begin with, I sent Max Perkins a short story a day for a week. Each story was promptly declined by return mail, but I was in no mood to accept discouragement. After that, I settled down to a strictly enforced routine of completing two short stories a week, and by the end of February, I thought I detected in Max's letters of rejection a decided softening of attitude toward my work. Stories were being returned less promptly, and his letters were increasingly less formal and more friendly and encouraging.

It was shortly before the March thaw when I received a letter from Max Perkins bringing word that my three-month campaign gave promise of ending in success. Max said that he had decided to accept one of my stories, but at that writing he had not made up his mind which one it would be. By looking at the chart I kept, I could see that Max was holding five stories from which to make the selection. My immediate fear was that he might change his mind.

I went to work at dusk that evening to supply him with enough material to enable him to make his choice without further delay. After two nights and a day I had completed three new stories. These, together with three additional ones, which I selected from the stack on my table, made a total of eleven stories for him to consider. And this time, instead of hurriedly getting the new stories into the mail, I thought it would be wiser to take them to New York in person.

During the overnight bus trip from Portland to New York, I was kept wide awake with forebodings of misfortune. By the time the bus had passed through Hartford, not long after midnight, I was questioning the wisdom of what I was doing. I had never seen Maxwell Perkins, my only contact with him having been through correspondence, and by daybreak I was beginning to visualize him as a fearsome person who would angrily resent the intrusion and become prejudiced against my work.

Clutching the envelope of manuscripts, I spent the time walking up and down Fifth Avenue, in front of the Scribner Building, from about eight until shortly after ten o'clock in the morning. For two hours I tried to think of a reasonable excuse to offer for presenting myself without invitation, but nothing would come to mind that sounded persuasive and effective. When ten o'clock passed, I crossed the street, feeling that what little remaining courage I had was rapidly vanishing, and took the elevator to the editorial offices.

A pleasant young woman immediately asked me what I wanted. Uneasy in the surroundings, and by then thoroughly unnerved, I told her merely that I wished to leave an envelope of manuscripts for Maxwell Perkins. As I was turning to go, she asked if I would like to leave a message with the envelope. I spelled out my name and said that I was going to be at the Manger Hotel for the next two days. Then I hurriedly took the elevator down.

When I got to the hotel, I went to my room and sat down to wait. At nightfall I went to bed and lay tensely awake until past midnight. The next morning it was midmorning when the phone rang. As I remember it, the conversation was like this:

Perkins — "Caldwell? Erskine Caldwell, from Mount Vernon, Maine?" Caldwell — "Yes." Perkins — "Well, how are you, Caldwell? It's Perkins. Max Perkins. Scribner's." Caldwell — "I'm all right, I guess." Perkins — "I got your new manuscripts yesterday, the ones you left at the office. I wish you had asked for me when you were here." Caldwell — "Well—

you did?" Perkins — "By the way, I've read all your stories on hand now, including the new ones you brought yesterday, and I don't think I need to see any more for a while." Caldwell — (Silence).

Perkins — "I think I wrote you some time ago that we want to publish one of your stories in *Scribner's Magazine*." Caldwell — "I received the letter. You haven't changed your mind, have you? I mean, about taking a story." Perkins — "Changed my mind? No. Not at all. The fact is, we're all in agreement here at the office about your things. I guess so much so that we've decided now to take two stories, instead of one, and run them both in the magazine at the same time. We'd like to schedule them for the June issue. One of them is called 'The Mating of Marjorie' and the other one is 'A Very Late Spring.' They're both good Northern New England stories. There's something about them that appeals strongly to me. There's a good feeling about them. It's something I like to find in fiction. So many writers master form and technique, but get so little feeling into their work. I think that's important." Caldwell — "I'm sure glad you like them — both of them." Perkins — "You're going to keep on, aren't you? Writing, I mean. You'll keep it up, won't you? We want to see some more of your work, later." Caldwell — "I'm going to keep on writing — I'm not going to stop." Perkins — "That's good to hear." Caldwell — (Silence).

Perkins — "Now about these two stories. As I said, we want to buy them both. How much do you want for the two together? We always have to talk about money sooner or later. There's no way of getting around that, is there?" Caldwell — "Well, I don't know exactly. I mean, about the money. I hadn't thought much about it." Perkins — "Would two-fifty be all right? For both of them." Caldwell — "Two-fifty? I don't know. I thought maybe I'd receive a little more than that." Perkins — "You did? Well, what would you say to three-fifty then? That's about as much as we can pay, for both of them. In these times magazine circulation is not climbing the way it was, and we have to watch our costs. I don't think times will get any better soon, and maybe worse yet. Economic life isn't very healthy now. That's why we have to figure our costs closely at a time like this." Caldwell — "I guess that'll be all right. I'd thought I'd get a little more than three dollars and a half, though, for both of them." Perkins — "Three dollars and fifty cents? Oh, no! I must have given you the wrong impression, Caldwell. Not three dollars and a half. No. I meant three hundred and fifty dollars." Caldwell — "You did! Well, that's sure different. It sure is. Three hundred and fifty dollars is just fine. I didn't expect that much." . . .

In due time the stories appeared in the June issue of *Scribner's Magazine*. It was a satisfying feeling to know that I had reached the goal I had set out for in the beginning, but, now that it had been attained, I could think of other goals farther in the distance that seemed to be much more important. I thought one of these to strive for should be the writing and publication of one hundred short stories.

*   *   *

Instead of working furiously now to produce a quantity of short stories, I limited myself to the writing of one story a week; and because I could devote more time to an individual story, I found that the things I did were more satisfactory in the end.

Each new story was sent promptly to Max Perkins, but none was taken. After a story was returned, I mailed it to one of the little magazines, and in almost each instance it was published by one of them. At the stage of writing that I was in, I made no attempt to get my work into the mass-circulation periodicals, as I believed that there was more to be gained, in the end, by first being thoroughly schooled by the literary magazines. I now made it a practice, when a story was declined by any six magazines, to destroy it and abandon the idea on which it had been based. I never regretted that I followed this plan.

After the Fourth of July 1930, I received a letter from Max Perkins in which he said that he had been thinking about the stories I had submitted recently and that he now thought it would be a good idea to bring out a collection of them in book form. He suggested that I get together a sufficient number of stories, previously published in magazines and unpublished ones as well.

Fifteen stories had either been published or accepted for publication in various magazines, and to these fifteen I added ten new stories. It so happened that about half of the stories had New England settings and the other half had Southern background. After thinking about it for several days I decided I wanted to call the book *American Earth*.

The following year, 1931, it was during October and November that I had gradually come to realize that I would not be completely satisfied with any of my work until I had written a full-length novel and, moreover, that it was inevitable that the novel was to be concerned with the tenant farmers and sharecropping families I had known in East Georgia. I wanted to tell the story of the people I knew in the manner in which they actually lived their lives from day to day and year to year, and to tell it without regard for fashions in writing and traditional plots.

My mind was made up. I packed my suitcase and went back to Georgia. Day after day into the country I traveled, farther and farther from settlements and highways. In the evenings I wrote about what I had seen during the day, but nothing I put down on paper succeeded in conveying the full meaning of poverty and hopelessness and degradation as I had observed it. Finally, I left and went to New York. Then I destroyed everything I had written while I was in Georgia. When I was ready to start writing, I typed the title I had decided upon while riding on the bus to New York. There was only one possible title for the novel; it was to be called *Tobacco Road*.

The first draft of *Tobacco Road* was finished the first week in April 1931. *American Earth* was published later in the same month, and Max Perkins, after publication of the book of short stories, wrote to ask how I felt about writing a novel. I did not tell him that I had already finished the first draft of one, but I did say that I hoped to be able to send him the completed manuscript of a novel before the end of summer.

By the end of July the second and final draft had been finished, and in less than two weeks after the manuscript had been sent away, I received a briefly worded note from Max Perkins in which he said that *Tobacco Road* was being accepted and would be published in book form by Charles Scribner's Sons early the following year.

With the experience of writing *Tobacco Road* still dominating my mind and thought, I undertook to readjust myself by writing the next novel about life in some part of the country other than the South. The story I then set out to write was about a family in the State of Maine. The novel became progressively more difficult to manage, and I was far from being satisfied with the first draft of it. The second draft, which I began in January and finished in March 1932, was in my opinion a much better novel than the first draft had been.

Under the terms of my contract, Scribner's had an option to publish the next two books I wrote after *Tobacco Road*, but it was nearly a month before Max Perkins said anything about the manuscript of the new novel I had sent him. He wrote then to say that the several readers at Scribner's had failed to reach complete agreement and that, although he was in favor of publishing it, he alone could not accept it under the circumstances. This was distressing news.

Max said he hoped I would not want to seek another publisher, but offer Scribner's my next book even though the rejection of the present novel voided the option clause of the contract and gave me the right to publish elsewhere. I was willing to agree to the proposal, but Harold Guinzburg and Marshall Best at The Viking Press were quick to point out the advantages to be gained by signing a contract with Viking; and after an abundant and leisurely lunch, I was persuaded to submit my next three books to them, leaving Harold and Marshall the manuscript of the novel that had been rejected by Scribner's.

After thinking about it for several days, I wondered if I really wanted to have the Maine novel published at that time. It had served the purpose for which it had been written, it having been undertaken in an effort to clear my mind of the experience of writing *Tobacco Road*, and now I was certain I wanted to continue writing about the South.

The decision was made for me. As it had happened at Scribner's, the editors at Viking did not agree in their opinion of the novel in manuscript; or perhaps they were unanimously opposed to its publication. Anyway, by that time I was certain I wanted the book put aside. I was anxious to get to work at once on the next Southern novel, and early in May I began writing the novel I called *God's Little Acre*.

Until now I had always written two or more drafts of every novel and novelette, and had rewritten and revised my short stories many times. When I began *God's Little Acre*, I wanted the first draft to be such a finished novel that it would be ready for publication as soon as the last page was written. The story of *God's Little Acre* was so close to the surface of my consciousness, and the characters so familiar to my mind, that I was confident it could be accomplished in this manner. When the first page was written, I was certain it could be done that way. I took the sheet of paper from my typewriter, placed it upside down on the floor, and did not look at it again until the final page had been finished.

The writing of the final page, the final paragraph, the final sentence, and then the last word of *God's Little Acre* was the most satisfying experience I had had since I first began writing. I was far more pleased with what I had done than I had been when I finished writing *Tobacco Road*. I had started the new novel with confidence and without the fears and uncertainties about its outcome that had bothered me throughout the writing of the earlier novel. Now I felt for the first time in my life that I could consider myself a professional novelist.

The book was finished late in August, and a few days later I took it to New York. Everyone at The Viking Press seemed to be surprised to hear that I had come with the completed manuscript of a new novel, and when it was given to Harold Guinzburg and Marshall Best, they were not immediately convinced that I had written it during the past three months. A few days later the novel was accepted and scheduled for publication in the early spring of 1933.

Next, what interested me more than anything else was the writing of short stories. I had devoted most of the time during the past two years to the writing of three novels, and most of the stories I had written previously were either already in print or had been accepted for publication. I went to work that fall and wrote one story after another.

It did not occur to me to ask myself what my purpose was in writing short stories and novels, until the question was put to me with increasing frequency. I liked writing fiction, as some men liked raising cattle or playing baseball or practicing law; and, because I was unhappy doing anything else, I wanted to make it my vocation. When I was asked to explain the meaning of a story or novel, I could only say that it meant what it said to the reader. I had no philosophical truths to dispense, no evangelistic urge to change the course of human destiny. All I wanted to do was simply to describe to the best of my ability the aspirations and despair of the people I wrote about. If there were lessons to be learned therein, they were to be found in these descriptions of life, and each reader was free to place his interpretation upon them.

*   *   *

Beginning early in February and ending in mid-December, 1933 was a crowded and eventful year. For the first time in almost a decade I did not write a single short story or novel during a twelve-month period. At the end of that time, however, I had learned what I considered a useful lesson: a writer should set aside ample time for the practice of his profession and guard it zealously.

At the start of the year, Marshall Best had suggested that I select a number of short stories for a volume that Viking wished to bring out. I chose twenty stories, most of them having been published during the past few months or which were scheduled to be published that year. I considered several possible titles and, finally, decided to call the book *We Are the Living*. The manuscript was typed and taken to Marshall when I went to New York for the publication of *God's Little Acre*. From the end of May 1933, I was a junior screenwriter with Metro-Goldwyn-Mayer, but by the first week in September I was back in Mount Vernon. After Labor Day, I received notification, together with a check for one thousand dollars, that I had been given *The Yale Review's* 1933 award for fiction. (The title of the short story, which had been published in *The Yale Review* that spring, was "Country Full of Swedes." Before that, the story had had a dismal experience of rejection; for a year it had been turned down in rapid succession by a dozen or more magazine editors. Shortly before it was accepted by *The Yale Review* it had been returned by the editor of another magazine with a discouraging note saying, "This old nag will never reach the post.")

Casting and rehearsals of *Tobacco Road*, the play, began in November, and Anthony Brown, who was directing it, asked me to come to New York for several days. I attended several rehearsals, but had few suggestions to offer other than a strong insistence on the use of authentic dialect by the cast. I had read Jack Kirkland's script of the play and had approved it, and he had followed the novel so closely that I saw no need for any changes.

The play struggled along for two months with a weekly box-office gross of between two thousand and three thousand dollars. Then, in January 1934, *The Daily News* published a series of editorials praising the play and urging readers to attend it. Box-office receipts doubled immediately. By the end of the first year, the play had become an established institution on Broadway, and when it finally closed, it had had a continuous run in New York of seven and a half years, setting a record for being at that time the play with the longest run in the history of the New York theater.

My steadfast New Year's resolution in 1934 was to return to writing books without delay. A twelve-month leave from the confining and exacting requirements of authorship had been pleasant and profitable while it lasted; but it had been spent far afield, and now I was dissatisfied and miserable. The full realization of failure, at this point, in my scheme of living-to-write brought about such an unhappy state of mind that I set out at once, the first week in January, to get some writing done.

As usual in recent years, I left home to write. (I became disagreeable, morose, short-tempered, and unreasonably moody at such times, and it was asking too much of my family to endure me through such spells.) I went to New York and rented a basement room in a brownstone front in the West Eighties, near Central Park, and began writing short stories from early morning until late in the night.

It was a bitterly cold winter in New York that year, and I was colder than I remembered ever having been in the State of Maine. After a week of futile argument with the janitor about the lack of adequate heat in the room, I began taking bus trips for several days at a time.

A heated Greyhound bus was comfortably warm during the day. On smooth stretches of highway in the open country I wrote with pencil and pad, and at night I stopped at a hotel and wrote on a typewriter. Such trips, once or twice a week, were taken to Philadelphia, Baltimore, Washington, Scranton, Pittsburgh, Cleveland, Chicago, Detroit, and Buffalo.

At the end of six weeks—it was mid-February then—half a dozen satisfactory stories had been completed. One of these was a short novelette or long story called "Kneel to the Rising Sun." It was rejected by numerous magazines for a year before it was accepted by Max Perkins and published in *Scribner's Magazine*. ("Kneel to the Rising Sun" became the title story of a collection which The Viking Press issued the following year.)

I returned to Mount Vernon in February. The title of the novel I was writing was *Journeyman*, and the idea on which the story was based had been in mind most of the past year. It was ready to be put down on paper as fast as I could type. The novel was finished about the middle of May and sent to Harold Guinzburg and Marshall Best for consideration.

Long before any word was received from Viking as to whether or not *Journeyman* would be accepted and published, there was an unexpected communication from Metro-Goldwyn-Mayer asking me to return to California to work on screen stories at the Culver City studio. I decided that I should go for three months, and I arrived in Los Angeles at the end of May.

For many years I had looked forward to the time when I would have the opportunity to travel at leisure through America by automobile, going where I wished and stopping when I pleased, and when I left California in the late summer of 1934, the time at last was at hand. The Viking Press had scheduled the publication of *Journeyman* for January 1935, and I was making a selection for a third volume of short stories for publication in midyear. A volume of non-fiction, which could be classified as travel notes, seemed to be the most desirable type of book to write next.

I made the final selection of stories to be published in *Kneel to the Rising Sun*. There were seventeen short stories in the collection, one of which had been reprinted in *The Best Short Stories of 1934*, another in *The Best Short Stories of 1935*, and a third story was one which had appeared in *The O'Henry Memorial Award Prize Stories of 1934*. Most of these stories had previously appeared in, or were to be published in, *The American Mercury*, *The Anvil*, *Direction*, *Esquire*, *Literary America*, *New Masses*, *Red Book Magazine*, *Scribner's Magazine*, *Story*, *The Sunday Review*, and *Vanity Fair*. The book was brought out by Viking in June 1935.

Viking decided not to publish *Some American People*, the book of non-fiction, and its publication by Robert M. McBride and Company was in October 1935.

I had spent most of the summer in Mount Vernon and had made plans to go back to the West Coast for several months while deciding on the kind of book to write next. There had been few times in recent years when a number of ideas for books were not clamoring for attention, but I wanted to be sure, now, that the book I wrote next was of most importance to me. This time in California I did no motion-picture writing, and lived at a distance from Hollywood, in San Fernando Valley, from December 1935 to April of the next year.

By the beginning of April there was a clear idea in mind of the kind of book I wanted to undertake next: a factual study of people in cotton states, living under current economic stress. It was my intention to show that the fiction I was writing was authentically based on contemporary life in the

South. Furthermore, I felt that such a book should be thoroughly documented with photographs taken on the scene.

I was strongly in favor of having the best obtainable photographer for the book. Margaret Bourke-White, a spirited young woman with an engaging personality, had published a highly regarded volume of industrial photographs. In addition, she was well known for a volume of photographs of Russian industrial and agricultural operations. Margaret agreed to take the pictures.

After spending several weeks in Maine, I went to Georgia in July 1936, to meet Margaret for the trip through the South. The book we were to collaborate on was to be called *You Have Seen Their Faces*. It was ready early in 1937, for publication by The Viking Press. Later in the year an inexpensive, paper-bound, newsstand edition was issued by Modern Age.

Eager by then to return to writing fiction, I began working on short stories in the spring. Seventeen had been written by the end of summer, and Marshall Best told me that Viking wished to publish the collection the following year. The title I chose for the new book, the fourth volume of short stories to be published, was *Southways*.

The manuscript of *Southways* had been delivered for publication in June 1938, and I did not like the prospect of settling down to the six- or eight-month task of writing a novel until first I had taken another trip somewhere. I was thirty-four years old and had never been outside the United States and Canada; under the circumstances it was not difficult to convince myself that the time to go abroad was at hand. I suggested to Margaret Bourke-White that we collaborate on a second book of photographs-and-text. After considering several possibilities, we decided to go to Czechoslovakia and spend about two months gathering material for a travel book. The title that Margaret and I chose for the book was *North of the Danube*. It was published by The Viking Press in April 1939, after the occupation of Czechoslovakia by Germany.

Dogwood was in blossom in Connecticut. *North of the Danube* had been published and I had begun writing a novel in Darien. The novel was to be called *Trouble in July*, and it represented another phase of life in the cycloramic depiction of the South begun with *Tobacco Road* and continued with *God's Little Acre* and *Journeyman*.

I stayed in Darien during the summer of 1939 and finished *Trouble in*

July before Labor Day. Not only was it the first novel I had written since 1935; more than that, it was the first book I had written since 1930 for which I had no publisher.

I probably would have signed a contract with Random House if I had not happened to meet Charles H. Duell at a dinner. Charlie Duell told me of the plans that he, together with Samuel Sloan and Charles A. Pearce, had made to found a new publishing house. I had known Cap Pearce for many years and had much respect for his abilities and his foresightedness as an editor. I told Charlie that I was looking for a new publisher and that perhaps a young and aggressive publishing house was looking for me. He said at once that I could write my own contract with Duell, Sloan and Pearce.

There were few times during the twelve-month period beginning in the spring of 1940, and ending in the spring of 1941, when I was not traveling or writing. After the publication of *Trouble in July* in February 1940, I began the three-month task of selecting, from magazines and from four previously published volumes, the work which I wished to include in a collection containing seventy-five short stories. Cap Pearce and I had already decided to call the book *Jackpot*, and Duell, Sloan and Pearce planned to publish the seven-hundred-and-fifty-six-page collection in the early fall. There were one hundred short stories from which the selection was to be made, that being the number of published stories which I had set in 1930 as a goal for accomplishment.

The Selections

The selections presented within this volume are from the years 1930-1940, a period beginning with the introduction of Erskine Caldwell's work in *Scribner's Magazine* as that of "one of the most talented of the new American writers" and ending, a decade later, with the attainment of the author's self-imposed goal of writing and seeing into published form a full one hundred short stories—which he accomplished in addition to publication, during the same interval, of four novels, three books of nonfiction, and five collections of his short fiction. The stories herein are arranged chronologically, by the time of their initial appearance in print. Choices have been made with a view to achieving both diversity and range of inclusion. The text reproduced is, basically, that of *The Complete Stories of Erskine Caldwell* (1953), plus one short story not included therein, the text of which is reprinted from *Jackpot* (1940).

Stories of Life
North & South

The Mating of Marjorie

HE was coming—he was coming—God bless him! He was coming to marry her—coming all the way from Minnesota!

Trembling, breathless, Marjorie read the letter again and again, holding it desperately in the ten fingers of her hands. Then at last, her eyes so blurred she could no longer see the handwriting, she placed the letter against the bareness of her breasts where she could breathe into it all the happiness of her heart. All the way from Minnesota he was coming—coming all that great distance to marry her!

The letter's every word, every mark of careless punctuation, was burned inerasably on her memory. The thought of the letter was like a poem running through her—like the chill of sudden warmth—fragments of lines repeating themselves like the roar in a furnace pipe.

His letter was not a proposal of marriage, but he did say he liked the way she looked in the picture she sent him. And why would he be coming all the way from Minnesota if he did not intend asking her to be his wife? Surely he wanted her.

Marjorie had his picture, too. She could actually feel the untiring strength of the lean muscles stretching over his face to the chin. Her fingers stole over his face excitedly, filling her with passion for the man with whom she would mate. He was a strong man. He would do with her as he pleased.

Surely he would like her. He was a mature man, and men who are mature seek beauty of soul and body when they marry. Marjorie was beautiful. Her beauty was her youth and charm. He wrote Marjorie that her eyes and her face and her hair were the loveliest he had ever seen. And her body was beautiful, too. He would see that when he came. Her slender limbs were cool and firm like the young pine trees in winter. Her heart was warm and eager. He would like her—surely he would.

Should she please him, and should he want her, and naturally he would when he saw her, Marjorie would give him her soul. Her soul would be her greatest gift to him. First she would give him her love, then her body, and at last her soul. No one had ever possessed her soul. But neither had her body or her love been possessed.

He had written frankly in all his letters. He said he wanted a wife. It was lonely, he said, living alone in Minnesota. Marjorie was lonesome, too. She had lived the long five years since her mother's death, alone. She understood. She had always been lonesome.

Marjorie prepared a room for him and waited his coming. She laundered the linen sheets and pillowcases three times. She dried the linen each time on the limbs of the fir trees and ironed it in the early morning while it was still damp with the pine-scented air.

The day of his coming Marjorie was awake long before the sun rose. The sun rose cool and swift.

Before laying out the new clothes she would wear for him, she ran to the room and patted the pillows and smoothed the coverlet for the last time. Then hurriedly she dressed and drove to the depot nineteen miles away.

He arrived on the noon train from Boston. He was much larger than she had expected him to be, and he was much more handsome than she had hoped.

"Are you Marjorie?" he asked huskily.

"Yes," Marjorie answered eagerly. "I am Marjorie. You are Nels?"

"Yes," he smiled, his eyes meeting hers. "I am Nels."

Marjorie led Nels to the automobile. They got in and drove away. Nels was a silent man, speaking crisply and infrequently. He looked at Marjorie all the time. He looked at her hands and face intently. She was nervous and self-conscious under his noncommittal scrutiny. After they had gone several miles he placed his arm across the back of the seat. Only once or twice did Marjorie feel his arm. The bumpy roads tossed them both as the car sped across country. Nels' arms were as strong and muscular as a woodsman's.

Late that afternoon Marjorie and Nels walked down through the wood to the lake. There was a cold icy wind out of the northeast and the lake rose and tossed as if a storm were upon it. While they stood on a boulder at the lakeside watching the waves, a sudden gust of wind threw her against his shoulder. Nels braced her with his steellike arms and jumped to the ground. Later she showed Nels the icehouse and pointed out to him the shed where the boats were stored in winter. Then they walked home through the pines and firs.

While Marjorie prepared supper Nels sat in the parlor smoking his pipe. Several times Marjorie ran to the open door for a hurried glimpse of the man she was to marry. The only motion about him was the steady flow of tobacco smoke boiling from the bowl of his pipe. When the meal was ready, Marjorie quickly changed her dress and called Nels. Nels enjoyed the meal before him. He liked the way she had prepared the fish. Her skin was so hot she could not bear to press her knees together. Nels ate with full appetite.

After Marjorie had hastily carried the dishes to the kitchen she again changed her dress and went into the room where Nels sat by the fireplace. They sat in silence until she brought him the album and showed him the pictures. He looked at them silently.

All through the evening she sat hoping he would soon take her in his arms and kiss her. He would later, of course, but she wanted now to be in his arms. He did not look at her.

At ten-thirty Nels said he would like to go to bed. Marjorie jumped up and ran to his room. She turned back the pine-scented covers and smoothed the pillows. Bending over the bed, she laid her flushed cheek against the cool soft linen. Tearing herself away, she went back into the room where Nels sat silently by the fire.

After Nels had gone to his room and closed the door behind him, Marjorie went to her own bedroom. She sat down in a rocking chair and looked out upon the lake. It was after midnight when she got up and undressed. Just before retiring she tiptoed to the door of Nels' room. She stood there several minutes listening intensely. Her fingers touched the door softly. He did not hear her. He was asleep.

Marjorie was awake at five. Nels came into the kitchen at seven while she prepared breakfast. He was freshly clean, and under his loose tweed suit she all but felt the great strength of his body.

"Good morning," he said.

"Good morning, Nels," she greeted him eagerly.

After breakfast they sat in the parlor while Nels smoked his pipe. When he finished smoking, he stood up before the fireplace. He took out his watch and glanced at the time. Marjorie sat hushed behind him.

"What time does the train leave for Boston?" he asked.

With stilled breath she told him.

"Will you take me to the train?" he asked her.

She said she would.

Marjorie immediately went into the kitchen and leaned heavily against the table. Nels remained in the parlor refilling his pipe. Marjorie ran toward the parlor several times, but each time she turned back when she reached the door. She wanted to ask Nels if he were coming back. She picked up a plate and it crashed to the floor. It was the first piece of china she had broken since the morning of her mother's death. Trembling, she put on her hat and coat. Of course he was coming back! How foolish it was to think he would not! He was probably going to Boston to get some presents for her. He would come back — of course he would!

When they reached the depot, Nels held out his hand. She placed her hand in his. It was the first time his skin had touched her skin.

"Good-by," he said.

"Good-by, Nels," she smiled at him. "I hope you enjoyed your visit."

Nels picked up his traveling bag and started towards the waiting room.

Marjorie's arms and legs had the numbness of death in them. She started the motor uncertainly. He had not said he would return!

"Nels!" she cried desperately, gripping the door of the automobile with bloodless fingers.

Nels stopped and turned around, facing her.

"Nels, you are welcome to come back any time you want to," she begged unashamedly.

"Thank you," he replied briefly, "but I'm going home to Minnesota and I'll not be back again."

"What!" she cried, her lips quivering so violently she could barely make them speak. "Where are you going — ?"

"To Minnesota," he replied.

Marjorie drove home as fast as her car would take her. As soon as she reached the house she ran to Nels' room.

In Nels' room Marjorie stood by the side of the bed and looked at the crumpled sheets and pillows with tear-blinded eyes. With a sob she threw herself between the sheets where Nels had lain. In her arms she hugged the pillows and dampened them with her tears. She could feel his body against hers. She kissed his face and held her lips for him to kiss.

It was night when she arose from the bed. The sun had gone down and the day was over. Only the cool clear twilight was left to shadow the room.

Throwing a blanket around her shoulders, Marjorie jerked the sheets and pillowcases from the bed and ran blindly to her own room. She opened the cedar chest and tenderly folded the crumpled sheets and pillowcases. She laid the linen in the chest and dragged the chest to the side of her bed.

Marjorie turned out the light and lay down between the sheets of her own bed.

"Good night, Nels," she whispered softly, her fingers touching the smooth lid of the cedar chest at her side.

(First published in *Scribner's Magazine*)

John the Indian and George Hopkins

GEORGE HOPKINS, who was about ninety years old, died just in time to have his grave decorated on Memorial Day. Grace and Jessie, his two daughters, buried him on the hilltop behind the house and had an iron fence put around the plot. Grace Hopkins, who was several years the older, said she wanted the fence painted red. Jessie, the younger one, said it was going to be left just as it was. They argued about the fence for two days, and then Grace lost her temper and called Jessie ugly names and had the iron fence painted red anyway. Jessie took her half of the furniture from the house and moved to another part of town. Grace stayed where she was and had another coat of red paint put on the fence around George Hopkins's grave.

Nobody in the town paid much attention to what the Hopkins girls were doing, because the whole Hopkins family had been raising the devil for the past twenty years or more.

George Hopkins had been a selectman ever since anybody could remember and he had always scrapped with someone over something.

First it was over the question whether the town should buy a snowplow and keep the main roads open in winter. He had said "No!" the first time, and had kept on saying that at every town meeting.

"Let the snow be!" he shouted. "God melts it every spring and don't make no charge for it!"

Another time he was scrapping with one of the boys from the village who wanted to come and sit up evenings with one of his daughters.

"You get the hell away from here, Tom Peck's son," he told the boy, "and don't you come back unless you've got a marriage license in your pocket."

George Hopkins had been a mean old scoundrel.

Friday before Memorial Day, Jessie brought her lawn mower and hand scythe and went up the hill to where they had buried her father. She cut the grass with the mower and trimmed the edges of the plot where the grass grew against the fence. When she finished, she stuck a flag

8

in the center of the mound and tied a wreath around the headstone.

Grace heard about Jessie going to the grave, so she got her lawnmower and grass clippers and went up the hill. The plot was in fine shape, but Grace went to work and mowed the grass over again and clipped around the edges where it grew between the iron palings of the fence. She jerked the wreath from the headstone and put one of her own making in its place. She pulled up Jessie's flag and stuck a larger one near the headstone and a smaller one near the footstone.

By nightfall Jessie had heard about Grace's going to the grave. She went over at once to John the Indian's. John lived by himself and wove baskets for sale.

She told John she wanted him to do some work for her and he agreed to help her by the hour. After supper that night he went over to Jessie's.

She brought John into the house and told him exactly what she wanted him to do. Then they went across the pasture to the hill where George Hopkins was buried. They carried a pick and shovel with them and began to open up the grave as soon as they got there. John worked for nearly two hours before he reached the coffin. George Hopkins had been buried deep so the frost would not reach him that winter.

It was hard work getting at the casket. There was no light to work by and John could not see very well after he had dug three or four feet into the ground. When he did get to the coffin, he said he would have to open it up where it was and lift George Hopkins out. It was the only thing to do. He could not get the casket out of the hole by himself.

John was a strong Indian and he got the body on top of the ground. Then he hoisted it on his shoulder and carried it to Jessie's house. Jessie came behind, bringing the pick and shovel.

Jessie told John to lay the body down by the icehouse while she looked for a place to dig the new grave. She wanted the grave near the house so she could keep watch over it from her window. She stumbled around in the dark several minutes before deciding where the new grave should be.

"Dig it here," Jessie said, standing over the place she had decided upon. "Come here, John, and dig it here."

John spat on his hands and measured off the grave with the pick handle.

"George Hopkins a lot of damn trouble," he grunted, digging away in the dark.

John dug away in the dark. He worked for nearly an hour and then struck a ledge of rock. It was as deep as he could go without blasting. Jessie found another place for the grave and John started all over again. He dug to about the same depth in the ground and struck the same ledge. Jessie made him begin a third time, and he hit the ledge of rock again. By this time it was getting late. John was tired and Jessie said her feet were wet. She said she was afraid of catching cold and pneumonia. John said he was going home.

"What you do with that?" he asked, pointing toward the icehouse. George Hopkins sat propped up against it.

Jessie said she did not know what to do with it. She asked John what could she do with it.

"I take him home with me tonight and bring him back tomorrow night," he suggested.

"All right, John," Jessie said, much relieved. "You take it home with you and bring it back tomorrow evening after supper."

Jessie went into the house and went to bed.

John lifted the body on his shoulder and started home at a trot. The body was not too heavy for him, but it slipped around on his shoulder. It was difficult for him to keep it there. Whenever he grasped it tighter it slid away under the suit of clothes as if the skin were loose.

John got it home though. He laid it on the floor beside his bed and went to sleep.

The next morning, when he got up, he carried it to the kitchen while he cooked his breakfast.

"Want some fried potatoes for eating, George Hopkins?" John asked the body he had propped up against the wood box.

"Huh, huh," John chuckled, "George Hopkins, you don't eat much these days."

He went about getting his breakfast.

"Maybe you want to smoke your pipe, George Hopkins," John said. "Huh, huh, George Hopkins, I got fine tobacco."

Grace went to the hilltop that forenoon to see if Jessie had been back with another wreath of her own. Grace was determined to take them away as fast as Jessie brought them.

When she reached the top of the hill and saw the pile of fresh earth inside the fenced plot, she turned around and ran straight across the town to the village as fast as she could. She went straight for a warrant.

Grace got the warrant and the man to serve it on Jessie. They went in a hurry to Jessie's house. All the doors and windows were locked tightly and they could not get in. Jessie heard them banging on the door, but she would not come out. Grace and the man found the graves Jessie and John the Indian had started, but they could not find George Hopkins in any of them.

Grace came back again the next day and looked for the body but she could not find it anywhere on the place. Jessie still would not come out of the house.

John was becoming tired of waiting for Jessie to come out of the house so they could bury George Hopkins. He did not know what to do about it. He waited another two days for her to come out and by that time he was sorry he had taken the job to dig a new grave for George Hopkins. John's house was beginning to have a bad odor.

Early the next morning he went to Jessie's house and tried to make her open the door and tell him what to do. She did not make a sound. He knew she was inside because once he saw her looking at him from behind a curtain at the window.

John trotted back to his house and carried the body down to the lake and propped it up in a canoe. Then he towed it to the middle of the lake with his other canoe. He had some live bait with him and a fishing-pole.

When he reached the center of the lake he threw the baited fishing-line overboard, tied the pole securely to the canoe George Hopkins was in, and shoved away from it.

John paddled to the shore, leaving George Hopkins sitting up in the canoe salmon-fishing. He looked back just as he reached the shore and saw the canoe shoot down the lake fast as a speedboat. A big bull-headed salmon had hooked the line. The salmon was taking George Hopkins down the lake so fast the wind blew his hat overboard.

John the Indian waited on the shore chuckling to himself until they were out of sight. Then he went home to get himself some breakfast.

(First published in *Pagany*)

The Automobile That Wouldn't Run

MAL ANDERSON made himself comfortable beside his dog on the back seat of the automobile and tuned up his banjo. Signe sat in a rocking chair on the front porch of the Penobscot Hotel listening to the music Mal made. It was midsummer and the weather was hot. It looked as if a thunderstorm might come from the west before the afternoon was over. Occasionally a gust of wind did come from that direction, blowing the dust down the street in balls like little yellow balloons.

Mal had a job in the spool mill in summer but he did not like to work the year 'round. He went into the woods in winter and did not come out until spring. In the summer he wanted to live in his shack with the dog and play his banjo when Signe sat on the hotel porch.

Mal strummed away on his banjo. Signe sat on the porch rocking faster and faster.

Plunkety plunk . . . plunkety plunk . . . plunkety plink!

Mal, who was called by everybody who did not like him "that damn Swede," was a fine woodsman. In the spool mill, though, he was not such a good workman. He did not like to work in the mill in summer. The mill made spools for electric wires, and Mal was supposed to be there now, checking the squares before they went through the turning-machines; but he did not like to work the year 'round.

Signe ran the Penobscot Hotel. It was a woodsman's hotel. The men used it when they came to town to spend the money they made up in the woods. Signe ran the hotel without help. She did not need any.

Plunkety plunk . . . plunkety plunk . . . plunkety plink!

Mal played his banjo for Signe. Neither of them ever spoke to the other. Mal might just as well have been born without the power of speech, for all the use he made of it. A man could talk to him an hour and he would not say a word.

Signe went to the kitchen and brought back a bone for Mal's dog. Mal opened the door and the dog jumped out after the bone and hopped in again. The dog curled up on the seat beside Mal and licked the bone. Mal played a tune on his banjo for Signe.

Plunkety plunk . . . plunkety plunk . . . plunkety plink!

At five o'clock Signe went into the hotel to start supper. Mal laid his banjo on the seat and he and the dog got out and pushed the automobile up the street to the shed beside his shack. The car would not run. One winter while Mal was up in the woods somebody broke into the shed and took the engine out. When Mal came back in the spring, he got into the habit of pushing his automobile to the hotel where he played his banjo for Signe.

Mal pushed his automobile up the street to the shed. His boss was there waiting to see him. Mal did not like him at all.

"Hello there, Mal," Scott, the boss, said. "I got some good news for you."

"I don't want to hear your news."

Mal knew that when Scott came to the shack he wanted to get some more work out of him. Nobody in the woods liked Scott.

"Get your stuff together, Mal. We're pushing up into the woods tomorrow morning at four o'clock."

"To hell with you and the woods and all your damn spools," Mal shouted, slamming shut the shed door. The only way to make Mal talk was to get him angry. But it was dangerous to make him mad. He had run half a dozen boss woodsmen out of the country. They went to Canada before he got a chance to hurt them.

Scott went down the road without looking back once. Scott was a brave boss woodsman.

Mal went into his shack and slammed shut the door behind him. The dog curled up under the table waiting for supper.

Everybody in the woods had heard about Mal Anderson. He was the best banjo player between Rangeley and Caribou, for one thing. And he was one of the best woodsmen ever to lay a tree down in the woods. He could stick a stake in the ground where he wanted the tree to fall and make the tree drive the stake into the earth. He took his two axes and went to work. When one ax became too hot he laid it aside and took up the other one. Give any two men the same start on a tree with a saw, axes, or anything they wanted, and Mal would have his tree on the ground before the other one was ready to fall. That was one reason why Mal was paid for eight days' work a week while the other men were getting paid for six.

It was summertime now and Mal did not want to go into the woods until winter. In summer he liked to stay in town and play his banjo in front of the Penobscot Hotel. The spool mill was running short of squares, however, and Mal had to help get the logs out of the woods. It was a hell of a time of year to make a man work.

Mal went up the river with the crew the next morning and went to work the following day felling trees for squares. He left his dog and banjo at home.

The crew worked in the woods three weeks and then the men began to grumble. When they left town, Scott had said they would be back by the end of two weeks. At the end of the third week Mal got mad. Scott was going to keep them there another month. And long before the end of the fourth week Scott had to watch himself pretty closely. He had to watch himself to keep from getting hurt. For instance, a tree might fall on him.

"Let's sink the son of a bitch in the river," one of the woodsmen suggested.

"Tie him to a stump and let the bobcats have him," another said. "You couldn't drown the yellow-backed bastard; he was born like a bullfrog."

"Mal'll catch him under a tree some of these days," Sanderson, who was the head teamster, said. "Let Mal have him."

Mal sat back on his haunches and said nothing.

Scott had enough sense to go into his shack every night after supper and not show himself until daylight. He could have been finished in five minutes in the dark, and he knew it.

But at the end of six weeks Scott was in as good condition as he had ever been. He watched himself pretty closely in the woods and he did not show himself after dark.

In the meantime two of the men got it into their heads that they were going out of the woods, Scott or no Scott. They said nothing about it and got ready to slip out alone. Scott was in his shack washing up for dinner when they ran down to the river and pushed off in a canoe.

Scott missed them a few minutes later when everybody sat down at the table to eat. Calling Mal and another man, they ran down to the river. The two men who had set their heads on going out of the woods were half a mile downsteam paddling like mad. They were standing up in the canoe on the lookout for submerged logs and rocks. Their arms and paddles waved like a windmill in a cyclone.

"Get a canoe, Mal, and pick out a good man to help you and bring those God-damn Canucks back to me," Scott ordered, swearing and stamping around on the riverbank.

Mal motioned to one of the men nearest him and they shoved off without a word. Mal was the biggest and strongest man in camp. The other man was to help with the canoe.

The river lay in a straight course downstream for two miles or more. It was used for running logs to the spool mill in the spring and summer. In winter it was frozen over to a depth of three or four feet and the logging teams drove over it going and coming to the woods.

Scott sent a man to camp for his field glasses.

Mal and the other woodsman struck out down the river after the two runaway men. In both canoes the men worked frantically with their oars. Mal's canoe shot through the water at a terrific rate of speed. There was no doubt that he would overtake the other canoe within the next mile. He and the man in the stern squatted on their knees so they would be nearer the water. Their canoe shot down the river, leaving a foaming white wake spreading out to the shores behind.

The man came running back from camp with the field glasses for Scott.

"I'll break those God-damn Canucks of wanting to run away from the job," Scott shouted, snatching the glasses from the man's hand.

The two canoes looked only a dozen lengths apart now. The leading canoe was about a mile and a quarter downstream. Mal's canoe closed up on it with every powerful stroke of his blade. Scott thrust the glasses to his eyes and held them there. The woodsmen crowded down to the edge of the water straining their eyes to see Mal overtake the men. It would be a sight worth seeing. What he would probably do would be to hold their heads under the water until they were nearly drowned before hauling them into his canoe and bringing them back to Scott. Scott had already planned enough work to take all the fight out of them.

Mal's canoe closed up on the one that had had the first start. The men in the canoe were still paddling with all their might, but Mal was stroking faster and faster.

The next instant the two canoes were prow-and-prow, only an oar's length apart. And then, before anybody could see what had happened, Mal had passed them and the first canoe was a whole length behind.

"The God-damn son of a bloody—" Scott swore, smashing the field glasses against the rocks. He was so mad he was almost speechless. Mal had double-crossed him. He shouted at the men and kicked savagely at the broken field glasses on the shore. "The God-damn son of a bloody—" he shouted from the depths of his powerful lungs.

Both canoes were completely out of sight now. One canoe was actually half a mile ahead of the other.

Scott ordered the men back to the woods. After they had gone he walked slowly up the hillside to the camp. Mal Anderson had put one over on him.

Mal got home early the next afternoon and opened the door of his shack. His dog was sleeping under the shack and woke up when he sniffed Mal's scent inside. Mal made a fire and cooked something for the dog and himself to eat.

After they had finished eating Mal got his banjo and pushed his automobile out of the shed and down the street as far as the Penobscot Hotel. Signe was sitting on the front porch rocking in her chair. When she saw Mal coming down the street with his automobile, she leaned back in her chair and rocked faster and faster.

Mal pushed the car down the street and stopped it in front of Signe's hotel. He opened the door and he and the dog got into the back seat and sat down. Mal slammed shut the door and picked up his banjo. Then he began playing a tune for Signe.

The dog curled up and went to sleep. Mal strummed away on the banjo. *Plunkety plunk . . . plunkety plunk . . . plunkety plink!*

Signe rocked back and forth, smiling out into the street at Mal sitting in his car and glad he was back in town again.

Mal settled down and propped his feet on the back of the driver's seat. Signe brought a bone for the dog and Mal opened the door. The dog jumped out after the bone and hopped in again and began licking it. Mal slammed shut the automobile door and took up his banjo again.

Plunkety plunk . . . plunkety plunk . . . plunkety plink!
The tune floated to the porch of the Penobscot Hotel and up the street and down it.

(First published in *Hound and Horn*)

Saturday Afternoon

Tom DENNY shoved the hunk of meat out of his way and stretched out on the meat block. He wanted to lie on his back and rest. The meat block was the only comfortable place in the butcher shop where a man could stretch out and Tom just had to rest every once in a while. He could prop his foot on the edge of the block, swing the other leg across his knee and be fairly comfortable with a hunk of rump steak under his head. The meat was nice and cool just after it came from the icehouse. Tom did that. He wanted to rest himself a while and he had to be comfortable on the meat block. He kicked off his shoes so he could wiggle his toes.

Tom's butcher shop did not have a very pleasant smell. Strangers who went in to buy Tom's meat for the first time were always asking him what it was that had died between the walls. The smell got worse and worse year after year.

Tom bit off a chew of tobacco and made himself comfortable on the meat block.

There was a swarm of flies buzzing around the place; those lazy, stinging, fat and greasy flies that lived in Tom's butcher shop. A screen door at the front kept out some of them that tried to get inside, but if they were used to coming in and filling up on the fresh blood on the meat block they knew how to fly around to the back door where there had never been a screen.

Everybody ate Tom's meat, and liked it. There was no other butcher shop in town. You walked in and said, "Hello, Tom. How's everything today?" "Everything's slick as a whistle with me, but my old woman's got the chills and fever again." Then after Tom had finished telling how it felt to have chills and fever, you said, "I want a pound of pork chops, Tom." And Tom said, "By gosh, I'll git it for you right away." While you stood around waiting for the chops Tom turned the hunk of beef over two or three times businesslike and hacked off a pound of pork for you. If you wanted veal it was all the same to Tom. He slammed the hunk of beef around several times making a great to-do, and got the veal for you. He pleased everybody. Ask Tom for any kind of meat you could name, and Tom had it right there on the meat block waiting to be cut off and weighed.

Tom brushed the flies off his face and took a little snooze. It was midday. The country people had not yet got to town. It was laying-by season and everybody was working right up to twelve o'clock sun time, which was half an hour slower than railroad time. There was hardly anybody in town at this time of day, even though it was Saturday. All the town people who had wanted some of Tom's meat for Saturday dinner had already got what they needed, and it was too early in the day to buy Sunday meat. The best time of day to get meat from Tom if it was to be kept over until Sunday was about ten o'clock Saturday night. Then you could take it home and be fairly certain that it would not turn bad before noon the next day — if the weather was not too hot.

The flies buzzed and lit on Tom's mouth and nose and Tom knocked them away with his hand and tried to sleep on the meat block with the cool hunk of rump steak under his head. The tobacco juice kept trying to trickle down his throat and Tom had to keep spitting it out. There was a cigar box half full of sawdust in the corner behind the showcase where livers and brains were kept for display, but he could not quite spit that far from the position he was in. The tobacco juice splattered on the floor midway between the meat block and cigar box. What little of it dripped on the piece of rump steak did not really matter: most people cleaned their meat before they cooked and ate it, and it would all wash off.

But the danged flies! They kept on buzzing and stinging as mean as ever, and there is nothing any meaner than a lazy, well-fed, butcher-shop fly in the summertime, anyway. Tom knocked them off his face and spat them off his mouth the best he could without having to move too much. After a while he let them alone.

Tom was enjoying a good little snooze when Jim Baxter came running through the back door from the barbershop on the corner. Jim was Tom's partner and he came in sometimes on busy days to help out. He was a great big man, almost twice as large as Tom. He always wore a big wide-brimmed black hat and a blue shirt with the sleeves rolled up above his elbows. He had a large egg-shaped belly over which his breeches were always slipping down. When he walked he tugged at his breeches all the time, pulling them up over the top of his belly. But they were always working down until it looked as if they were ready to drop to the ground any minute and trip him. Jim would not wear suspenders. A belt was more sporty-looking.

Tom was snoozing away when Jim ran in the back door and grabbed him by the shoulders. A big handful of flies had gone to sleep on Tom's mouth. Jim shooed them off.

"Hey, Tom, Tom!" Jim shouted breathlessly. "Wake up, Tom! Wake up quick!"

Tom jumped to the floor and pulled on his shoes. He had become so accustomed to people coming in and waking him up to buy a quarter's worth of steak or a quarter's worth of ham that he had mistaken Jim for a customer. He rubbed the back of his hands over his mouth to take away the fly stings.

"What the hell!" he sputtered, looking up and seeing Jim standing there beside him. "What you want?"

"Come on, Tom! Git your gun! We're going after a nigger down the creek a ways."

"God Almighty, Jim!" Tom shouted, now fully awake. He clutched Jim's arm and begged: "You going to git a nigger, sure enough?"

"You're damn right, Tom. You know that gingerbread nigger what used to work on the railroad a long time back? Him's the nigger we're going to git. And we're going to git him good and proper, the yellow-face coon. He said something to Fred Jackson's oldest gal down the road yonder about an hour ago. Fred told us all about it over at the barbershop. Come on, Tom. We got to hurry. I expect we'll jerk him up pretty soon now."

Tom tied on his shoes and ran across the street behind Jim. Tom had his shotgun under his arm, and Jim had pulled the cleaver out of the meat block. They'd get the God-damn nigger all right—God damn his yellow hide to hell!

Tom climbed into an automobile with some other men. Jim jumped on the running board of another car just as it was leaving. There were thirty or forty cars headed for the creek bottom already and more getting ready to start.

They had a place already picked out at the creek. There was a clearing in the woods by the road and there was just enough room to do the job like it should be done. Plenty of dry brushwood nearby and a good-sized sweet-gum tree in the middle of the clearing. The automobiles stopped and the men jumped out in a hurry. Some others had gone for Will Maxie. Will was the gingerbread Negro. They would probably find him at home lay-ing his cotton by. Will could grow good cotton. He cut out all the grass first, and then he banked his rows with earth. Everybody else laid his cotton by without going to the trouble of taking out the grass. But Will was a pretty smart Negro. And he could raise a lot of corn too, to the acre. He always cut out the grass before he laid his corn by. But nobody liked Will. He made too much money by taking out the grass before laying by his cotton and corn. He made more money than Tom and Jim made in the butcher shop selling people meat.

Doc Cromer had sent his boy down from the drugstore with half a dozen cases of Coca-Cola and a piece of ice in a wash tub. The tub had some muddy water put in it from the creek, then the chunk of ice, and then three cases of Coca-Cola. When they were gone the boy would put the other three cases in the tub and give the dopes a chance to cool. Every-body likes to drink a lot of dopes when they are nice and cold.

Tom went out in the woods to take a drink of corn with Jim and Hubert Wells. Hubert always carried a jug of corn with him wherever he hap-pened to be going. He made the whisky himself at his own still and got a fairly good living by selling it around the courthouse and the barbershop. Hubert made the best corn in the county.

Will Maxie was coming up the big road in a hurry. A couple of dozen men were behind him poking him with sticks. Will was getting old. He had a wife and three grown daughters, all married and settled. Will was a pretty good Negro too, minding his own business, stepping out of the road when he met a white man, and otherwise behaving himself. But nobody liked Will. He made too much money by taking the grass out of his cotton before it was laid by.

Will came running up the road and the men steered him into the clear-ing. It was all fixed. There was a big pile of brushwood and a trace chain for his neck and one for his feet. That would hold him. There were two or three cans of gasoline, too.

Doc Cromer's boy was doing a good business with his Coca-Colas. Only five or six bottles of the first three cases were left in the wash tub. He was getting ready to put the other cases in now and give the dopes a chance to get nice and cool. Everybody likes to have a dope every once in a while.

The Cromer boy would probably sell out and have to go back to town and bring back several more cases. And yet there was not such a big crowd today, either. It was the hot weather that made people have to drink a lot of dopes to stay cool. There were only a hundred and fifty or seventy-five there today. There had not been enough time for the word to get passed around. Tom would have missed it if Jim had not run in and told him about it while he was taking a nap on the meat block.

Will Maxie did not drink Coca-Cola. Will never spent his money on anything like that. That was what was wrong with him. He was too damn good for a Negro. He did not drink corn whisky, nor make it; he did not carry a knife, nor a razor; he bared his head when he met a white man, and he lived with his own wife. But they had him now! God damn his ginger-bread hide to hell! They had him where he could not take any more grass out of his cotton before laying it by. They had him tied to a sweet-gum tree in the clearing at the creek with a trace chain around his neck and another around his knees. Yes, sir, they had Will Maxie now, the yellow-face coon! He would not take any more grass out of his cotton before laying it by!

Tom was feeling good. Hubert gave him another drink in the woods. Hubert was all right. He made good corn whisky. Tom liked him for that. And Hubert always took his wife a big piece of meat Saturday night to use over Sunday. Nice meat, too. Tom cut off the meat and Hubert took it home and made a present of it to his wife.

Will Maxie was going up in smoke. When he was just about gone they gave him the lead. Tom stood back and took good aim and fired away at Will with his shotgun as fast as he could breech it and put in a new load. About forty or more of the other men had shotguns too. They filled him so full of lead that his body sagged from his neck where the trace chain held him up.

The Cromer boy had sold completely out. All of his ice and dopes were gone. Doc Cromer would feel pretty good when his boy brought back all that money. Six whole cases he sold, at a dime a bottle. If he had brought along another case or two he could have sold them easily enough. Everybody likes Coca-Cola. There is nothing better to drink on a hot day, if the dopes are nice and cool.

After a while the men got ready to draw the body up in the tree and tie it to a limb so it could hang there, but Tom and Jim could not wait and they went back to town the first chance they got to ride. They were in a big hurry. They had been gone several hours and it was almost four o'clock. A lot of people came downtown early Saturday afternoon to get their Sunday meat before it was picked over by the country people. Tom and Jim had to hurry back and open up the meat market and get to work slicing steaks and chopping soupbones with the cleaver on the meat block. Tom was the butcher. He did all the work with the meat. He went out and killed a cow and quartered her. Then he hauled the meat to the butcher shop and hung it on the hooks in the icehouse. When somebody wanted to buy some meat, he took one of the quarters from the hook and threw it on the meat block and cut what you asked for. You told Tom what you wanted and he gave it to you, no matter what it was you asked for.

Then you stepped over to the counter and paid Jim the money for it. Jim was the cashier. He did all the talking, too. Tom had to do the cutting and weighing. Jim's egg-shaped belly was too big for him to work around the meat block. It got in his way when he tried to slice you a piece of tenderloin steak, so Tom did that and Jim took the money and put it into the cashbox under the counter.

Tom and Jim got back to town just in time. There was a big crowd standing around on the street getting ready to do their weekly trading, and they had to have some meat. You went in the butcher shop and said, "Hello, Tom. I want two pounds and a half of pork chops." Tom said, "Hello, I'll get it for you right away." While you were waiting for Tom to cut the meat off the hunk of rump steak you asked him how was everything.

"Everything's slick as a whistle," he said, "except my old woman's got the chills and fever pretty bad again."

Tom weighed the pork chops and wrapped them up for you and then you stepped over to Jim and paid him the money. Jim was the cashier. His egg-shaped belly was too big for him to work around the meat block. Tom did that part, and Jim took the money and put it into the cashbox under the counter.

(First published in *Nativity*)

The Empty Room

THE first time I saw her was something more than a year after they
had become married. The funeral was over and all the people had left
and we were in the house alone. There was nothing I could say to her,
and she had not spoken since the morning before. She and Finley had
been married only a little more than a year, and she was still far from being twenty. Her body was in the beauty of girlhood, but she was only a
child.

She had sat by the window, looking out at the gathering dusk until
late in the evening, and night was coming. I had not turned on the lights,
and she had not moved from her chair for several hours. From where I
was, I could see her darkly framed profile motionless against the gray
evening like an ebony cameo. It was then that I knew that there could be
beauty even in sorrow.

Finley was the only brother I had ever had, and before his death he
was the only kinsman I had left in the world, and now she was his widow.

Her name was Thomasine, but I had not yet called her by it. I had
not become used to it, and there is something about an unfamiliar name
that guards itself against a stranger's thoughtless intrusion. When the time
came for me to call her by her name, I knew I would be speaking a sound
that was hers alone.

I was a stranger in the house and we had not yet spoken to each other.
Finley had been her husband, and my brother, and I was not then certain
what our relationship became thereby. I knew, though, that we could not
for long stay in the house alone without an understanding of her place and
mine becoming clear.

The twilight was chill, and the dark room was an expanding void, re-
ceding into its wall-less immensity. Her profile was becoming softer as the
gray dusk fell away to the obscurity of night. The walls retreated and the
room became a place made without them. The room was immense and her

24

profile against the gray dusk melted into the growing darkness of the house.

While she sat across the room she had not fully realized her loneliness. The curve of her head and shoulders drooped with the enveloping shadows, but she was not thinking of even her own presence. Finley had been dead such a short time.

When she got up to go, I got up also, and walked across the room towards her. I went to her side and stood at arm's length from her, but the distance between us could only have been measured by the bounds of the room's infinite space. I wished to put my arms around her and comfort her as I would have comforted the one I loved, but she was Finley's widow, and the room with its walls made distance immeasurable. The room in which we stood was hollow and wide, and it swam in the darkness of its vast space. A spark from a flint would have struck us blind with the intensity of its light, and the certain conflagration would have consumed us to ashes.

Before I came to the house I had given no thought to a girl whose name would be Thomasine, and now she was my brother's widow.

Some of the flowers in the room had curled for the night, but petals from the roses fell gently to the floor.

Suddenly she whispered, turning in the darkness towards me.

"Did you feed Finley's rabbits tonight?"

"Yes, I fed them," I told her. "I gave them all they can eat. They have everything they want for the night."

Her hair had fallen over her shoulders, boiling thickly about her head. Her hair was citrus color, and it strangely matched the darkness of the room and the blackness of her clothes. Its color made her sorrow more uncomfortable, because hers was the head that bowed the deepest in the darkness of the immense room. When I stared at the inky blackness of the walls not within sight, I could somehow see the quickness of her citrus hair tousled on my brother's chest while he kissed the smoothness of her profile and caressed the softness of her limbs. The beauty and richness of their year of love was yielding, though slowly, to the expanding darkness. It was in the darkness of the hollow room that I was able to believe in the finality of death, and to believe the sorrow I felt in her heart. Lovers for a year cannot believe the finality of death, and she least among them. I wished to tell her all I knew of it, but my words would have told only the triviality. Her love was not to be confused with death, and she would not have wished to understand it.

It was then to be the beginning of night.

I could not see her go, but I felt her leave the chair by the window. I walked behind her, touching the unfamiliar furniture, and guiding myself through the room and around it time after time by the direction of the citrus scent of her hair.

She stopped then, and I realized that I was in the bedroom. I found myself standing in the doorway knowing only one direction, and that was the fragrant citrus scent which came from her hair. When she went from corner to corner, I stood in the doorway of the room waiting for her to speak, for a word to send me away until morning. If there was anything else she wished, or if there was nothing I could do, she had not told me.

The lonely walk from corner to corner and back again, and the still coldness of her bed, echoed through the hollow room. I could hear her walk across the floor to the bed, touch it with her fingers, and walk back across the carpeted floor to the window. She stood by the window looking out at the nothing of night, the black nothing, while I waited for her to tell me to close the door and go away and leave her alone.

Though she was in the room, and I was in the doorway, and the rabbits were just outside the window, the emptiness about us descended upon the house like the stillness of night without stars and the moon. When I reached out my arms, they stretched to regions unknown, and when I looked with my eyes, they seemed to be searching for light in all corners of the dark heavens.

She knew I was waiting in the doorway for a word to send me away, but she was helpless in her loneliness. She knew she could not bear to be alone in the room whose walls could not be seen at such a great distance. She knew her loneliness could not be dispelled with a word uttered in the hollow darkness, and she knew herself alone could not be propelled from the immensity of the house.

My brother had written to me of her with a feeling of regret because I did not have someone like her to love. He had been with her a year, sharing this house and sharing this bed. Each night they had gone side by side into this room where she was now but for me alone. Then it was that I could feel the loneliness of this night, because he had been taken away from her; while I, who had never known such love, was never to be made a part of it.

Once more she went to the bed and touched it. The room was dark and the bed was still. She knew now that she was to be alone.

She began to cry softly, as a girl cries.

Her slippers dropped from her feet, and the echo was like the throwing of a man's solid-heeled shoes against the floor.

When she touched a comb on the table and it fell to the floor in the darkness, it might have been a man's clumsy hands feeling in the night and knocking clocks and mirrors from their places.

Her knees touched a chair, but the sound was like a man walking blindly in a dark room, stumbling over furniture and cursing hoarsely under his breath.

The clothes she removed were laid on a chest at the foot of the bed, but it was as if a man were tossing his heavy-laden coat and trousers across the room towards a chair.

Noiselessly she raised the window, but it was as if a man had thrown it open, impatient with delay.

She sat on the side of the bed and lay down upon it, but it was like a man hurling himself there and jerking the cover over him.

Softly she turned over and lay her arm across the far pillow, but it sounded in the hollow room as if a man were tossing there, beating the pillows with his fists.

Her body began to tremble with her sobs, faintly shaking the springs of the bed and the mattress, but it was like the ruthless action of a man quick with his uncontrolled strength.

I do not know how long I had stood in the doorway waiting for a word from her to send me away. Time in the pitch blackness of the house of hollow darkness had passed quickly at first, and then slowly. It may have been an hour, it may have been five.

I parted my lips and spoke to her. The sounds of my words seemed to be without an end in their echo.

"Good night, Thomasine," I said, trembling.

She screamed with fright and with pain. Had someone cut her heart with a knife, she could not have screamed more loudly.

Then slowly she turned over in bed and lay on her other side.

"My God! My God! My God!"

The pillow she had been clutching fell from the far side of the bed to the floor, crashing in the darkness like a felled tree deep in a forest.

Evening gave way, and night in the empty room began.

(First published in *Pagany*)

Rachel

EVERY evening she came down through the darkness of the alley, emerging in the bright light of the street like the sudden appearance of a frightened child far from home. I knew that she had never reached the end of the alley before eight o'clock, and yet there were evenings when I ran there two hours early and waited beside the large green and red hydrant until she came. During all those months I had known her, she had been late only two or three times, and then it was only ten or fifteen minutes past eight when she came.

Rachel had never told me where she lived, and she would never let me walk home with her. Where the alley began, at the hydrant, was the door through which she came at eight, and the door which closed behind her at ten. When I had begged her to let me walk with her, she always pleaded with me, saying that her father did not allow her to be with boys and that if he should see us together he would either beat her unmercifully or make her leave home. For that reason I kept the promise I had given, and I never went any farther than the entrance to the alley with her.

"I'll always come down to see you in the evening, Frank," she said; and added hastily, "as long as you wish me to come. But you must remember your promise never to try to find where I live, or to walk home with me."

I promised again and again.

"Perhaps some day you can come to see me," she whispered, touching my arm, "but not now. You must never go beyond the hydrant until I tell you that you may."

Rachel had told me that almost every time I saw her, as if she wished to impress upon me the realization of some sort of danger that lay in the darkness of the alley. I knew there was no physical danger, because around the corner was our house and I was as familiar with the neigh-

borhood as anyone else. And besides, during the day I usually walked
through the alley to our back gate on my way home, because it was a
short cut when I was late for supper. But after dark the alley was Rachel's, and I had never gone home that way at night for fear of what I
might have seen or heard of her. I had promised her from the beginning
that I would never follow her to find out where she lived, and that I
would never attempt to discover her real name. The promise I had made
was kept until the end.

I knew Rachel and her family were poor, because she had been wearing the same dress for nearly a year. It was a worn and fragile thing
of faded blue cotton. I had never seen it soiled, and I knew she washed
it every day. It had been mended time after time, carefully and neatly,
and each evening when I saw her, I was worried because I knew that
the weave of the cloth would not stand much more wear. I was constantly
afraid that almost any day the dress would fall into shreds, and I dreaded
for that time ever to come. I wished to offer to buy her a dress with the
few dollars I had saved in my bank, but I was afraid to even suggest
such a thing to her. I knew she would not have allowed me to give her
the money, and I did not know what we would do when the dress became
completely worn out. I was certain that it would mean the end of my
seeing her. It was only the constant attention that she gave it and the
care with which she laundered it each day that could have kept the dress
whole as long as it had been.

Once Rachel had worn a pair of black silk stockings. From the first
she had come each night to the brightly lighted street in her white cotton stockings, and for a year she had worn no other kind. Then one
evening she had on a pair of black silk ones.

The next evening I expected to see her wearing them again, but when
she came out of the alley, she was wearing the stockings of white cotton.
I did not ask her about it, because I had learned never to say anything
that might hurt her feelings, but I was never able to understand why she
wore black silk stockings just that one time. She may have borrowed
them from her mother or sister, and there were dozens of other ways
she could have got them, and yet none of the reasons I could think of
ever seemed entirely conclusive. If I had asked her, perhaps she would
have laughed, touched my arm as she did when we were together, and

told me. But I was afraid to ask her. There were so many ways of making her feel badly, and of hurting her.

Each evening when she came out of the black alley I met her there, and together we walked down the brightly lighted street to the corner where there was a drugstore. On the opposite corner there was a moving-picture theater. To one or the other we went each evening. I should have liked to have taken her to both the show and to the drugstore, but I was never able to earn enough money for both in the same evening. The twenty cents I received every day for delivering the afternoon paper on a house-to-house route was not enough to buy ice cream at the drugstore and seats at the picture show, too. We had to take our choice between them.

When we stood on the corner across from the drugstore and across from the theater, we could never decide at first whether to see the show or to eat ice cream. The good times we had there on the corner were just as enjoyable, to me, as anything else we did. Rachel would always try to make me tell her which I would rather do before she would commit herself. And of course I wished to do that which would please her the most.

"I'm not going a step in either direction until you tell me which you would rather do," I would say to her. "It doesn't matter to me, because being with you is everything I want."

"I'll tell you what let's do, Frank," she said, touching my arm, and pretending not to be serious; "you go to the drugstore, and I'll go to the movies."

That was Rachel's way of telling me which she preferred, although I didn't believe she ever suspected that I knew. But when she suggested that I go to the movies while she went to the drugstore, I knew it to mean that she would much rather have a dish of ice cream that evening. The enjoyment of the show lasted for nearly two hours, while the ice cream could never be prolonged for more than half an hour, so all but two or three evenings a week we went to the theater across the street.

There was where I always wished to go, because in the semidarkness we sat close together and I held her hand. And if the house was not filled, we always found two seats near the rear, in one of the two corners, and there I kissed her when we were sure no one was looking at us.

After the show was over, we went out into the bright street and walked slowly towards the green and red hydrant in the middle of the block. There at the entrance to the alley we stopped awhile. If there were no other people in the street, I always put my arm around Rachel's waist while we walked slowly to the dark entrance. Neither of us spoke then, but I held her tighter to me, and she squeezed my fingers. When at last, after delaying as long as possible the time for her to go, we walked together a few steps into the darkness of the alley and stood in each other's arms, Rachel kissed me for the first time during the evening, and I kissed her for as long a time as I had wished to in the theater. Still not speaking, we drew apart, our fingers interwoven and warm.

When she was about to disappear into the darkness of the alley, I ran to her and caught her hands in mine.

"I love you, Rachel," I told her, squeezing her fingers tighter and tighter as she withdrew them.

"And I love you, too, Frank," she said, turning and running into the alley out of sight for another day.

After waiting awhile and listening until she had gone beyond hearing distance, I turned and walked slowly up the street towards home. Our house was only a block away: half a block to the corner, and another half block from there. When I had reached my room, I went to the window and stood there looking out into the night and listening for some sound of her. My window faced the alley behind the house, and the street lights cast a dim glow over the house tops, but I could never see down into the darkness of the alley. After waiting at the window for an hour or more I undressed and went to bed. Many times I thought I heard the sound of her voice somewhere in the darkness, but after I had sprung from bed and had listened intently at the window for a long time I knew it was some other sound I had heard.

Near the end of summer I received five dollars as a birthday present from an aunt. As soon as I got it, I began making plans for Rachel and me. I wanted to surprise her that evening with the money, and then to take her downtown on a streetcar. First we would go to a restaurant, and afterward to one of the large theaters. We had never been downtown together, and it was the first time I had ever had more than fifty cents at one time. That afternoon as soon as I could deliver all the papers on my route, I ran home and began thinking about the plans I had made for the evening.

Just before dark I went downstairs from my room to wait on the front porch for the time to come when I could meet Rachel. I sat on the porch steps, not even remembering to tell my mother that I was going downtown. She had never allowed me to go that far away from the house without my first telling her where I was going, with whom, and at what time I would come back.

I had been sitting on the porch steps for nearly an hour when my older sister came to the door and called me.

"We have a job for you, Frank," Nancy said. "Mother wants you to come to the kitchen before you leave the house. Now, don't forget and go away."

I told her I would come right away. I was thinking then how much the surprise would mean to Rachel, and I did forget about the job waiting for me in the kitchen for nearly half an hour. It was then almost time for me to meet Rachel at the hydrant, and I jumped up and ran to the kitchen to finish the task as quickly as I could.

When I reached the kitchen, Nancy handed me a small round box and told me to open it and sprinkle the powder in the garbage can. I had heard my mother talking about the way rats were getting into the garbage, so I went down to the back gate with the box without stopping to talk about it. As soon as I had sprinkled the powder on the refuse, I ran back into the house, found my cap, and ran down the street. I was angry with my sister for causing me to be late in meeting Rachel, even though the fault was my own for not having done the task sooner. I was certain, though, that Rachel would wait for me, even if I was a few minutes late in getting to the hydrant. I could not believe that she would come to the hydrant and leave immediately.

I had gone a dozen yards or more when I heard my mother calling me. I stopped unsteadily in my tracks.

"I'm going to the movies," I told her. "I'll be back soon."

"All right, Frank," she said. "I was afraid you were going downtown or somewhere like that. Come home as soon as you can."

I ran a few steps and stopped. I was so afraid that she would make me stay at home if I told her that I was going downtown that I did not know what to do. I had never told her a lie, and I could not make myself start then. I looked back, and she was standing on the steps looking at me.

"Mother, I am going downtown," I pleaded, "but I'll be back early."

Before she could call me again, I ran with all my might down the street, around the corner, and raced to the hydrant at the alley. Rachel was not within sight until I had reached it and had stood for a moment panting and blowing with excitement and exertion.

She was there though, waiting for me beside the fence, and she said she had just got there the second before. After we had started towards the corner where the drugstore was, I took the money from my watch pocket and showed it to her. She was even more excited than I had been when I first saw it. After she had looked at it awhile, and had felt it in the palm of her hand, I told her what I had planned for us to do that evening.

We heard a streetcar coming, and we ran to the corner just in time to get aboard. The ride downtown was too fast, even though it took us nearly half an hour to get there. We got off near the theaters.

First I had planned for us to go to a small restaurant, and later to a show. Just as we were passing a drugstore Rachel touched my arm.

"Please, Frank," she said, "I'm awfully thirsty. Won't you take me into that drugstore and get me a glass of water?"

"If you must have a drink right away, I will," I said, "but can't you wait a minute more? There's a restaurant a few doors below here, and we can get a glass of water there while we're waiting for our supper to be served. If we lose much time we won't have the chance to see a complete show."

"I'm afraid I can't wait, Frank," she said, clutching my arm. "Please —please get me a glass of water. Quick!"

We went into the drugstore and stood in front of the soda fountain. I asked the clerk for a glass of water. Rachel waited close beside me, clutching my arm tighter and tighter.

In front of us, against the wall, there was a large mirror. I could see ourselves plainly, but there was something about our reflection, especially Rachel's, that I had never been aware of before. It's true that we had never stood before a mirror until then, but I saw there something that had escaped me for a whole year. Rachel's beauty was revealed in a way that only a large mirror can show. The curve of her cheeks and lips was beautiful as ever, and the symmetrical loveliness of her neck and arms was the same beauty I had worshiped hundreds of times before; but now for the first time I saw in the mirror before us a new and unrevealed charm. I strained my eyes once more against the surface of the mirror, and once again I saw there the new sinuous beauty of her body.

"Quick, Frank!" Rachel cried, clutching me desperately. "Water— please!"

I called to the clerk again, not looking, because I was afraid to take my eyes from the new beauty I saw in the mirror. I had never before seen such beauty in a girl. There was some mysterious reflection of light and shadow that had revealed the true loveliness of Rachel. The mirror had revealed in one short moment, like a flash of lightning in a dark room, the sinuous charm that had lain undiscovered and unseen during all the time I had known her. It was almost unbelievable that a woman, that Rachel, could possess such a new, and perhaps unique, beauty. My head reeled when the sensation enveloped me.

She clutched my arm again, breaking as one would a mirror, the reflection of my thoughts. The clerk had filled the glass with water and was handing it to her, but before he could place it in her hands, she had reached for it and had jerked it away from him. He looked as surprised as I was. Rachel had never before acted like that. Everything she did had always been perfect.

She grasped the glass as if she were squeezing it, and she swallowed the water in one gulp. Then she thrust the glass back towards the clerk, holding her throat with one hand, and screamed for more water. Before he could refill the glass, she had screamed again, even louder than before. People passing the door paused, and ran inside to see what was taking place. Others in the store ran up to us and stared at Rachel.

"What's the matter, Rachel?" I begged her, catching her wrists and shaking her. "Rachel, what's the matter?"

Rachel turned and looked at me. Her eyes were turned almost upside down, and her lips were swollen and dark. The expression on her face was horrible to see.

A prescription clerk came running towards us. He looked quickly at Rachel, and ran back to the rear of the store. By that time she had fallen forward against the marble fountain, and I caught her and held her to keep her from falling to the floor.

The prescription clerk again came running towards us, bringing a glass filled with a kind of milk-white fluid. He placed the glass to Rachel's lips, and forced the liquid down her throat.

"I'm afraid it's too late," he said. "If we had known ten minutes sooner we could have saved her."

"Too late?" I asked him. "Too late for what? What's the matter with her?"

"She's poisoned. It looks like rat poison to me. It's probably that, though it may be some other kind."

I could not believe anything that was being said, nor could I believe that what I saw was real.

Rachel did not respond to the antidote. She lay still in my arms, and her face was becoming more contorted and darker each moment.

"Quick! Back here!" the clerk said, shaking me.

Together we lifted her and ran with her to the rear of the store. The clerk had reached for a stomach pump, and was inserting the tube in her throat. Just as he was about to get the pump started, a physician ran between us and quickly examined Rachel. He stood up a moment later, motioning the other man and myself aside.

"It's too late now," he said. "We might have been able to save her half an hour ago, but there is no heart action now, and breathing has stopped. She must have taken a whole box of poison — rat poison, I guess. It has already reached her heart and blood."

The clerk inserted the tube again and began working with the pump. The physician stood beside us all the time, giving instructions, but shaking his head. We forced stimulants down her throat and attempted to revive her by means of artificial respiration. During all of that time the doctor behind us was saying: "No, no. It's of no use. She's too far gone now. She'll never live again. She has enough rat poison in her system to kill ten men."

Some time later the ambulance came and took her away. I did not know where she was taken, and I did not try to find out. I sat in the little brown-paneled room surrounded by white-labeled bottles, looking at the prescription clerk who had tried so hard to save her. When at last I got up to go, the drugstore was empty save for one clerk who looked at me disinterestedly. Outside in the street there was no one except a few taxi drivers who never looked my way.

In a daze I started home through the deserted streets. The way was lonely, and tears blinded my eyes and I could not see the streets I walked on. I could not see the lights and shadows of the streets, but I could see with a painful clarity the picture of Rachel, in a huge mirror, bending over our garbage can, while the reflection of her beauty burned in my brain and in my heart.

(First published in *Clay*)

Indian Summer

THE water was up again. It had been raining for almost two whole days, and the creek was full to the banks. Dawn had broken gray that morning, and for the first time that week the sky was blue and warm.

Les pulled off his shirt and unbuckled his pants. Les never had to bother with underwear, because as soon as it was warm enough in the spring to go barefooted he hid his union suit in a closet and left it there until fall. His mother was not alive, and his father never bothered about the underclothes.

"I wish we had a shovel to dig out some of this muck," he said. "Every time it rains this hole fills up with this stuff. I'd go home and get a shovel, but if they saw me they'd make me stay there and do something."

While Les was hanging his shirt and pants on a bush, I waded out into the yellow water. The muck on the bottom was ankle deep, and there were hundreds of dead limbs stuck in it. I pulled out some of the largest and threw them on the other bank out of the way.

"How's the water, Jack?" Les asked. "How deep is it this time?"

I waded out to the middle of the creek where the current was the strongest. The yellow water came almost up to my shoulders.

"Nearly neck deep," I said. "But there's about a million dead limbs stuck in the bottom. Hurry up and help me throw them out."

Les came splashing in. The muddy water gurgled and sucked around his waist.

"I'll bet somebody comes down here every day and pitches these dead limbs in here," Les said, making a face. "I don't see how else they could get here. Dead tree limbs don't fall into a creek this fast. Somebody is throwing them in, and I'll bet a pretty he doesn't live a million miles away, either."

"Maybe Old Howes does it, Les."

"Sure, he does it. He's the one I'm talking about. I'll bet anything he comes down and throws limbs in every day."

Les stepped on a sharp limb. He held his nose and squeezed his eyes and ducked under and pulled it out.

"You know what?" Les said.

"What?"

"Old Howes told Pa we scared his cows last Saturday. He said we made them run so much he couldn't get them to let down their milk Saturday night.

"This creek bottom isn't his. Old Howes doesn't own anything down here except that pasture on the other side of the fence. We haven't even been on the other side of the fence this year, have we?"

"I haven't seen Old Howes's cows all summer. If I did see them, I wouldn't run them. He just told Pa that because he doesn't want us to come swimming in the creek."

Pieces of dead bark and curled chips suddenly came floating down the creek. Somewhere up there the trash had broken loose from a limb or something across the water. I held my arms V-shaped and caught the bark and chips and threw them out of the way.

Les said something, diving down to pull up a dead limb. The muck on the bottom of the creek was so deep we could not take a step without first pulling our feet out of the sticky mud; otherwise we would have fallen flat on our faces in the water. The muck had a stink like a pig pen.

Les threw the big limb out of sight.

"If Old Howes ever comes down while we're here and tells us to get out of the creek, let's throw muck at him. Are you game, Jack? Wouldn't you like to do that to him just once?"

"That's what we ought to do to him, but we'd better not, Les. He would go straight and tell my folks, and your pa."

"I'm not scared of Old Howes," Les said, making a face. "He hasn't got me buffaloed. He wouldn't do anything. He's scared to tell anybody. He knows we'd catch him some time and mud-cake him."

"I don't know," I said. "He told on me that time I caught his drake and put it in that chicken run of his."

"That was a long time —" Les stopped and listened.

Somebody had stepped on a dead limb behind the bushes. The crack of the wood was loud enough to be heard above the splashing and gurgling of the creek.

"What's that?" both of us said.

"Who's that?" Les asked me.

"Listen!" I said. "Duck down and be quiet."

Behind the bushes we could hear someone walking on dead twigs and dry leaves. Both of us squatted down in the water until only our heads were above it.

"Who is it?" Les whispered to me.

I shook my head, holding my nose under the water.

The yellow water swirled and gurgled through the tree roots beside us. The roots had been washed free of earth by the high waters many years before, and now they were old-looking and covered with bark.

Les squatted lower and lower until only his eyes and the top of his head were showing. He held his nose under the water with both hands. The water was high, and its swiftness and muddy-heaviness made gurgling sounds that echoed up and down the creek.

Suddenly the bushes parted, and Jenny came through. When Les saw her, his eyes popped open and he jerked his head above the water to get his breath. The noise he made when the water bubbled scared all three of us for a moment.

Jenny was Old Howes's daughter. She was about our age, possibly a year or two older.

Les saw her looking at our clothes hanging on the bushes. He nudged me with his elbow.

"What are you doing down here?" Les said gruffly, trying to scare her.

"Can't I come if I want to?"

"You can't come down here when we're in swimming. You're not a boy."

"I can come if I wish to, smarty," Jenny said. "This creek doesn't belong to you."

"It doesn't belong to you, either," Les said, making a face. "What are you going to do about that?"

"All right," Jenny said, "if you are going to be so mean about it,

Leslie Blake, I'll take your clothes and hide them where you'll never find them again as long as you live. What are you going to do about that?"

Jenny reached for the clothes. She grabbed Les's pants and my shirt and union suit.

Les caught my arm and pulled me towards the bank. We couldn't hurry at first, because we had to jerk our feet out of the muck before we could move at all.

"Let's duck her, Jack," Les whispered. "Let's give her a good ducking. Come on."

We crawled up the bank and caught Jenny just as she was starting to run through the bushes with our clothes. Les locked his arms around her waist and I caught her arms and pulled as hard as I could.

"I'll scream!" Jenny said. "If you don't stop, I'll scream at the top of my lungs. Papa is in the pasture, and he'll come right away. You know what he'll do to both of you, don't you?"

"We're not afraid of anybody," Les said, scowling and trying to scare her.

I put my hand over her mouth and held her with one arm locked around her neck. Together we pulled and dragged her back to the bank beside the creek.

"Don't you want to duck her, Jack?" Les said. "Don't you think we ought to? She's been telling Old Howes tales about us. She's a tattletale tit."

"We ought to duck her, all right," I said. "But suppose she goes and tells on us about that?"

"When we get through ducking her, she won't tell any more tales on us. We'll duck her until she promises and crosses her heart never to tell anybody. She's the one who's been throwing dead limbs into the creek every day. I'll bet anything she's the one who's been doing it."

Jenny was helpless while we held her. Les had her around the waist with both arms, and I still held her neck locked in the crook of my left arm. She tried to bite my hand over her mouth, but every time she tried to hurt me, I squeezed her neck so hard she had to stop.

I was a little afraid to duck Jenny, because once we had ducked a colored boy named Bisco, and it had almost drowned him. We ducked Bisco so many times he couldn't breathe, and he became limp all over.

We had to stretch him out on the ground and roll him over and over, and all the time we were doing that, yellow creek water was running out of his mouth. I was afraid we might drown Jenny. I didn't know what would happen to us if we did that.

"I know what let's do to her, Les," I said.

"What?"

"Let's mud-cake her."

"What's the matter with ducking her? It will scare her and make her stop throwing dead limbs into the creek. It'll stop her from telling tales about us, too."

"We'd better not duck her, Les," I said. "Remember the time we ducked Bisco? We nearly drowned him. I don't want anything like that to happen again."

Les thought a while, looking at Jenny's back. She was kicking and scratching all the time, but she couldn't begin to hurt us, and we had her so she couldn't get loose.

"All right," Les said. "We'll mud-cake her then. That's just as good as ducking, and it'll teach her a lesson. It'll make her stop being a tattletale tit."

"She's going to tell on us anyway, so we'd better do a good job of it this time. But it ought to make her stop throwing dead limbs into the swimming hole, anyway."

"She won't tell on us after we get through with her," Les said. "She won't tell anybody. She won't even tell Old Howes. Ducking and mud-caking always stops kids from telling tales. It's the only way to cure it."

"All right," I said, "Let's do it to her. She needs ducking, or mud-caking, or something. Somebody has got to do it to her, and we're the right ones to make a good job of it. I'll bet she won't bother us again after we get through with her."

Les threw Jenny on the ground beside the bank, locking her arms behind her back and holding her face in the earth so she couldn't make any noise. Les had to straddle her neck to keep her still.

"Take off her clothes, Jack," Les said. "I've got her. She can't get away as long as I'm holding her."

I reached down to pull off her dress, and she kicked me full in the stomach with both feet. When I fell backward and tried to sit up, there was no breath left in me. I opened my mouth and tried to yell at Les, but I couldn't even whisper.

"What's the matter, Jack?" Les said, turning his head and looking at me.

I got up on both knees and doubled over, holding my stomach with both arms.

"What's the matter with you, Jack?" he said. "Did she kick you?"

Les's back had been turned and he had not seen what Jenny had done to me.

"Did she kick me!" I said weakly. "It must have been her, but it felt like a mule. She knocked all of the wind out of me."

"Sit on her legs, then," Les said. "She can't kick you if you do that."

I ran down to the side of the creek and came back with a double handful of yellow muck. When I dug it out of the creek, it had made a sucking sound, and the odor was worse than any that ever came out of a pig pen. The muck in the creek stank worse than anything I had ever smelled. It was nothing but rotted leaves and mud, but it smelled like decayed eggs and a lot of other things.

I got Jenny's dress off and tossed it on the bushes so it would not get covered with muck. Les was able to hold her arms and cover her mouth at the same time by then, because she was not nearly so strong as either of us.

"She's got underwear on, Les," I said.

"Sure she has," Les said. "All girls wear underclothes. That's what makes them so sissy."

"You're not talking about me, are you?" I said, looking at him. "Because if you are —"

"I'm talking about her," Les said. "I know you have to wear the stuff because your people make you do it. But girls like to have it on. They don't want to go without it. That's why girls are so sissy."

"All right," I said, "but don't try to get nasty with me, because I'll —"

"You won't do anything, so shut up. Hurry and take her clothes off."

"Are we going to strip her naked?" I said.

"Sure," Les said. "We've got to. We can't mud-cake her if we don't strip her, can we?"

"I know that," I said, "but suppose Old Howes came down and saw us—"

"Old Howes wouldn't do nothing but spit and slip up in it. Who's scared of him, anyway? I'm not."

After we had struggled with Jenny a while longer, and after her underclothes were finally off, Les said he was tired of holding her. He was puffing and blowing as if he had been running five miles without stopping to rest.

I took Jenny's arms and put my hand over her mouth and sat on her neck. Les picked up a big handful of muck and threw it at her. The muck struck her on the stomach, making a sound like slapping water with a plank. He threw another handful. It splattered all over us.

While Les was running to the creek for another load, I turned Jenny over so he could smear some on her back. She did not struggle any more now, but I was afraid to release my grip on her arms or to take my hand off her mouth. When I had turned her over, she lay motionless on the ground, not even kicking her feet any more.

"This'll fix her," Les said, coming back with his hands and arms full of yellow muck. "She's had it coming to her for a long time. Maybe it'll stop her from being a tattletale tit."

He dropped the mass on her back and ran back for some more.

"Rub that in while I'm getting another load, Jack," he said. "That's what she needs to make her stop throwing dead limbs into the creek. She won't tell any more tales about us, either."

I reached over and with one hand smeared the muck up and down Jenny's back, on her legs, and over her arms and shoulders. I tried not to get any of it in her hair, because I knew how hard it was to try to wash it out with yellow creek water.

"Turn her over," Les said, dropping down beside us with a new load of muck. "We're just getting started on her."

I turned Jenny over again, and she did not even try to get loose from me. Les had begun to spread the muck over her, rubbing it into her skin. He took a handful and smeared it over her legs and thighs and stomach. Then he took another handful and rubbed it over her shoulders and breasts. Jenny still did not attempt to move, though she squirmed a little when Les rubbed the most tender parts of her body with the mass of rotted leaves and mud. Most of the time she lay as still as if she had been sound asleep.

"That's funny," I said.

"What's funny?" Les asked, looking up.

"She's not even trying to get loose now."

"That's because she's foxy," Les said. "She's just waiting for a good chance to break away. Here, let me hold her awhile."

Les took my place and I picked up a handful of muck and began spreading it over her. The muck was not sticky any longer, and when I smeared it on her, it felt slick and smooth. When my hands moved over her, I could feel that her body was much softer than mine, and that parts of her were very soft. When I smeared the slick mud over her breasts, it felt so smooth and soft that I was afraid to touch her there again. I glanced at her face, and I saw her looking at me. From the way she looked at me, I could not help thinking that she was not angry with us for treating her like that. I even thought that perhaps if Les had not been there she would have let me mud-cake her as long as I wished to.

"What are you doing, Jack?" Les said. "That's a funny way to spread muck on her."

"We've got enough on her, Les. Let's not put any more on her. Let's let her go home now. She's had enough."

"What's the matter with you?" Les said, scowling. "We're not half finished with her yet. We've got to put another coat of muck on her."

Jenny looked up when Les said that, and her eyes opened wider. She did not have to speak to tell me what she wished to say.

"That's enough, Les," I said. "She's a girl. That's enough for a girl."

I don't know, but somehow I believed that Les felt the same way I did, only he did not want to admit it. Now that we had stripped her and had smeared her all over with muck, neither of us could forget that Jenny was a girl. We had treated her as though she were a boy, but she remained a girl still.

"If we let you up now, will you promise not to tell?" Les asked her.

Jenny nodded her head, and Les dropped his hand from her mouth.

We both expected to hear her say what she was going to do, and what she was going to tell, because of the way we had treated her; but the moment she was freed she sat up quickly and tried to cover herself with her arms, without once speaking.

As soon as we saw that she was not going to call for Old Howes, Les and I ran to the creek and dived head-on into it. We squatted down until only our heads were showing above the water and began scrubbing the muck off us. Jenny looked at us, covering herself as much as she could.

She still had not said anything to us.

"Let's get dressed and run for home," Les said. "Pa would tear me up into little pieces if he caught me down here now, with her like that."

Jenny covered her eyes while we dashed out of the water and grabbed our clothes. We ran behind the bushes to dress. While we were standing there, we could hear Jenny splashing in the creek, scrubbing the muck from her.

Les had only his shirt and pants to put on, and he was ready to go before I could even straighten out my union suit. He buckled his pants and started backing off with his shirt tail hanging out while he tried to find the right buttons for the buttonholes. I had been in such a hurry to jump in the creek when we first came that I had tangled my union suit, and when I would get the arms straight, the legs would be wrong side out. Les kept backing farther and farther away from me.

"What's the matter?" he said. "Why don't you hurry?"

"I can't get this union suit untangled."

"That's what you get for wearing underclothes in summer."

"I can't help it," I said, "and you know it."

"Well it's not my fault, is it?"

"Aren't you going to wait for me?"

"I can't, Jack," he said, backing away faster. He suddenly turned around and began running. "I've got to go home."

"I thought you said you weren't scared of Old Howes, or of anybody else!" I yelled after him, but if he heard me, he pretended not to understand what I had said.

After Les had gone, I took my time. There was no need to hurry, because I was certain that no matter what time I got home, Jenny would tell Old Howes what we had done to her, and he would come and tell my folks all about it. I wished to have plenty of time to think of what I was going to say when I had to face everybody and tell the truth.

Jenny had left the creek by the time I was ready to button my shirt, and she had only to slip her underclothes over her head and to put on her dress to be ready to go home. She came through the bushes while I was still fumbling with my shirt buttons.

"What's the matter, Jack?" she asked, smiling just a little. "Why didn't you run off with Leslie?"

"I couldn't get dressed any quicker," I said.

I was about to tell her how my union suit was so tangled that I had had to spend most of the time struggling with that, but I thought better of saying it.

She came several steps closer, and I started to run from her.

"Where are you going?" she said. "What are you running for?"

I stopped, turned around, and looked at Jenny. Now that she was dressed, she looked the same as she had always looked. She was the same in appearance, but somehow I knew that she was not the same, after what had happened beside the creek. I could not forget the sensation I had felt when my hands, slick with mud, had touched the softness of her body. As I looked at her, I believed I felt it again, because I knew that without the dress and the underclothes she would always remain the same as she was when I had first touched her.

"Why don't you wait for me, Jack?" she said.

I wanted to run away from her, and I wanted to run to her. I stood still while she came closer.

"But you're going to tell, aren't you? Aren't you going to tell what we did to you?"

She had come to where I stood, and I turned and walked beside her, several feet away. We went through the bushes and out through the woods to the road. There was no one in sight, and we walked together until we reached her house.

Just before we got to the gate I felt my hand touch hers. I don't know, but somehow, whether it was true or not, I believed she had taken my hand and held it in hers for a moment. When I suddenly looked to see, because I wanted to know if she really had taken my hand and squeezed it, she turned the other way and went through the gate.

I waited in the middle of the road until she walked up the front steps and crossed the porch. She stopped there a moment and brushed her dress with her hands, as if she wanted to be sure that there was no muck clinging to it. When she opened the door and went inside, I was not certain whether she had glanced at me over her shoulder, or whether I merely imagined she had. Anyway, I believed she had, because I felt her looking at me, just as I was sure that she had held my hand for a moment.

"Jenny won't tell," I said, running up the road towards home. "Jenny won't tell," I kept saying over and over again all the way there.

(First published in *Story*)

Over the Green Mountains

WAS reading a piece in the Boston paper last night about the smartest people in the whole country coming from the State of Maine. Said at the time, and I'm still here to say it: you can take your pick of any ten men in the whole Union, and I'll back one Varmonter of my own choosing against them any day. Take ten men from any of the states you can find them in, and all of them put together won't have the smartness that my lone Varmonter has got. Have lived in the State of Maine all my life, ninety-odd years of it, but I've always said that if you want some smartness you shall have to go to Varmont to get it. Varmont is where it comes from.

Now, you take the farmers. Varmont farmers is that smart they can't keep from making money while the farmers in other places is all losing money. And here is why they are so smart: not so long ago there was a Varmont farmer over here, riding around in his big auto having a good time and laughing at us farmers here because we hadn't made enough money to retire and maybe take a trip to Florida on, in even years. I asked this Varmont farmer how it was he had made so much money running a farm.

And this is what he told me: "Friend," he said, "the secret of making money out of a farm is this: Sell all you can; what you can't sell, feed to the hogs; what the hogs won't eat, eat yourself."

After he finished telling me that, he drove off laughing in his big auto to look at some more Maine farmers working and sweating in the fields because they ain't got sense enough to make money to retire on, and maybe take a winter trip to Florida, in even years.

That sporting farmer wasn't the first Varmonter I'd known, though. I used to know another one when I was a young man on the Penobscot.

This was a young fellow we called Jake Marks, one of them old-time Varmonters who used to come over here to the State of Maine driving teams of oxen before the railroads was built across the mountains. This Jake Marks was a smart one, if there ever was a Varmonter who warn't. He used to

49

drive his oxen over here hauling freight back and forth all the time. It was a long haul in them days, when you stop to think how slow them brutes travel, and Jake had a lot of mountain to cross coming and going. I don't recall how long it took him to make one of his trips, but it was quite a time in them days when there warn't no State roads, only trails wide enough for a yoke of oxen.

Jake was a real young man at that time, I should say about twenty-five, maybe twenty-seven. He warn't married then, neither. But pretty soon he took a liking to a young and handsome filly who cooked his meals for him at the house in Bangor where he put up while he was changing cargo between trips. She was just the kind of young filly that Jake wanted, too. She used to come into the room where he sat waiting for his meal and make herself real frisky in his presence. Jake, he was tormented something awful by the way she cut up in front of him, and he used to have to get up out of his chair sometimes and walk real fast around the house three-four times to get control over himself.

But this Jake Marks was a cautious man, and he never undertook a deal until he had thought it out a lot beforehand and saw that he had everything on his side. Then, when he had thought it all through, he turned loose and went after whatever it was he wanted like a real Varmonter. All them old-time Varmonters was like that, I guess; anyway, the ones who used to drive ox freights over here to the State of Maine was, and Jake was just like all the rest of them.

This young filly of Jake's got so she pestered him about marrying of her all the time he was resting up between trips. Jake, he wanted her, all right. That was one thing he was wanting all the time he was over here. But Jake, he was taking his own good time about it, I'm telling you. He was figuring the thing out like all them Varmonters who drove ox freights did. He had to be real certain that everything was on his side before he made any signs. He took the rest of the season for figuring the thing out, and he didn't make motions of a move toward the young filly that year at all.

The next spring when the frost had thawed out of the ground and when he could make his first trip of the year over the mountains, Jake he called at the house where this young filly stayed and told her to get ready to be married to him when he got back to Bangor on his next trip. That suited the young filly first-rate. She had been uneasy all winter about Jake, taking too much at heart all the gossip that was talked about them Varmont ox freighters. But when Jake told her to get ready for marrying, she knew he would keep his promise right down to the last letter and come and marry her like he said he would.

So, Jake he went back to Varmont with his freight, promising to be ready to marry the young filly the same day he got back to Bangor on his next trip.

And just as he promised, Jake came back to get married to the young filly. He went straight to the house where she stayed, and there she was all waiting for him. Jake told her to get ready right away for the marriage, and then he went out to find a preacher somewhere. When he got back to the house with the preacher, he called her down to the room where all the guests had gathered to see the ceremony performed.

The minute she stepped into the room where Jake and the rest of the people was, Jake took one look at the young filly and told her to go back upstairs to her room and take off her dress. Well, that was all right and proper, because in those days there was a law in the State of Maine to the effect that a man could make what was called a shift-marriage. That was to say, the man could make the woman take off the dress she was wearing while the ceremony was being performed, and in that case he could not be held legally responsible for her past debts and would not have to pay them for her if he didn't have a mind to. Well, Jake he had heard all about this shift-law in Maine, and he was taking full advantage of its benefits. That was what he had been figuring out all the time he was driving them slow-footed oxen back and forth between Bangor and Varmont. Jake, he warn't no man's fool. Jake, he was a Varmonter.

After a while Jake's young filly came downstairs dressed according to this here shift-law. She had on what women wore under their dresses in those days, and that was all she had on. But Jake, he warn't satisfied, not completely. He told her to go back upstairs and take off everything she had on. Jake, he was a hardheaded ox freighter from Varmont, all right. He had figured all this out while he was driving them slow-footed oxen back and forth across the mountains.

In a little while his young filly came into the room again where Jake and the preacher and all the guests was, and she didn't have nothing on, except that she had a bedsheet wrapped around her, which was a good thing, I tell you. She was a handsome-looking filly if there ever was one.

They all got ready again for the ceremony, the preacher telling them where to stand and what to say to the questions he was getting ready to ask them. Then, just when they was beginning to get married, Jake he told his young filly to drop the bedsheet on the floor. Now, Jake he warn't taking no chances over here in the State of Maine. That shift-law said that if a woman was married without her dress on, her husband couldn't be held liable for her past debts, and Jake he figured that if the young filly didn't have nothing at all on her, there wouldn't be a chance in the whole world for to dun him for what she might owe, while if she had clothes on that he didn't know the true and legal names of, a storekeeper might try to say her underclothes was her overdress. Jake, he was thinking that he might by chance get cheated out of his rights to the full benefits of the shift-law if he didn't take care, and Jake he warn't after taking no chances whatsoever over here in the State of Maine when he was so far away from Varmont. He was as cautious where he sat his foot as the next ox freighter from Varmont.

"Drop the bedsheet on the floor," Jake he told the young filly again.

The young filly was getting ready to turn loose the bedsheet and let it drop on the floor like Jake told her to do, when the preacher he grabbed the bedsheet and held to it tight around her so she wouldn't show none of her naked self to him and Jake and the rest of the people in the house.

"No! No! No!" he yelled, getting red in the face and shaking his head at Jake. "That won't do, my man — that won't do at all! That would be indecent here before all of us! That can't be done! I'll never allow it!"

But the preacher he didn't know Jake Marks. Jake was one of them Varmont ox freighters, and he was as hardheaded about what he wanted as the next one to come along. Jake, he told the young filly again to drop the bedsheet on the floor, and to drop it quick if she wanted to get married.

The handsome young filly was getting ready to let go of it like Jake said to, because she was that crazy about Jake she would have stood on her head right then and there if Jake had told her to do it, but just when she was getting ready to let go of it, the preacher he grabbed the bedsheet again and held it fast with both hands.

The preacher started in trying to argue with Jake about it being indecent for the handsome young filly to stand there naked while she was being married, but Jake he had his head set on getting the full benefits of the shift-law and he wouldn't give in an inch.

Then the preacher said he warn't going to perform the ceremony if that was what Jake was set on doing, and Jake he told the preacher he warn't going to get married at all without the bedsheet being dropped on the floor so that none of the cloth was touching the young filly.

Everybody got excited when Jake said that, and the people talked back and forth for an hour or more, arguing first on Jake's side, because they knew the law on the books, and then on the preacher's side, because they realized how it might upset the preacher if the handsome young filly stood there naked like Jake was set on having her do. The young filly didn't care which way the ceremony was done, just so long as Jake married her. She was willing to drop the bedsheet for Jake the minute the preacher let her. She was all excited about getting married, just like Jake had been all the time.

After a while the preacher gave in to Jake just a little. He saw what a fool he was, trying to argue with a Varmont ox freighter.

"If she'll go inside the closet and shut the door so nobody can see her nakedness, I'll perform the ceremony," the preacher told Jake.

"That's all right by me," Jake said, "but I'll be compelled to have some witnesses on my side in case anybody tries to dispute me about us being married under the shift-law or not."

They finally settled that part when the preacher agreed to allow two of the older women to go in the closet with the young filly, just to make sure that everything was done in a legal manner. The preacher he didn't like to have Jake going in a closet with the naked filly, but he was pretty well worn out by that time after arguing for nearly two hours with a Varmont ox freighter, and he said he would have to allow Jake to go in the closet, too.

Jake went in the closet where the filly and the two older women were.

"Now, you just look once, Jake," the preacher said, shaking his head back and forth, "and then you shut your eyes and keep them shut."

Jake was in the closet saying something to the young filly, but nobody in the room could hear what it was. The preacher he reached over and made a bit of a crack in the door while he was marrying them so he could hear their answers to the questions. And all that time Jake he was in there striking matches to make sure that the young filly was not putting the bedsheet on again, and to be certain that he was getting the full benefits of the shift-law.

When it was all done, the preacher he took the money Jake handed him and went off home without waiting to see what shape the young and handsome filly was in when the closet door was opened. When they came out into the room, the bedsheet was all twisted up into a knot; Jake handed it to her, and she didn't lose no time in getting upstairs where her clothes were. Jake he had told her to hurry and get dressed, because he wanted to get started with his ox freight back to Varmont.

They started home to Varmont right away, the handsome young filly all dressed up in her wedding clothes and sitting on top of the freight cargo while Jake he walked along beside the wagon bellowing at the oxen.

When Jake came back to Bangor on his next trip, a storekeeper tried to present him a bill for a hundred and forty dollars. The storekeeper told Jake that the young filly had bought a lot of dresses and things just before she got married, and he wanted to know if Jake had married her under the shift-law.

Jake just laughed a little, and started unloading his cargo.

"Well, was you married that way, or the other way?" the storekeeper asked him.

"You tell me this first," Jake said, "and then I'll answer your question. Does the State of Maine have a shift-law on the books?"

"Well, yes; but the shift-law says that the woman has to — "

"Never mind about explaining it to me," Jake said. "If the shift-law is on the statute books, then that's the law I married her with."

(First published in *Contact*)

Warm River

THE driver stopped at the suspended footbridge and pointed out to me the house across the river. I paid him the quarter fare for the ride from the station two miles away and stepped from the car. After he had gone I was alone with the chill night and the star-pointed lights twinkling in the valley and the broad green river flowing warm below me. All around me the mountains rose like black clouds in the night, and only by looking straight heavenward could I see anything of the dim afterglow of sunset.

The creaking footbridge swayed with the rhythm of my stride and the momentum of its swing soon overcame my pace. Only by walking faster and faster could I cling to the pendulum as it swung in its wide arc over the river. When at last I could see the other side, where the mountain came down abruptly and slid under the warm water, I gripped my handbag tighter and ran with all my might.

Even then, even after my feet had crunched upon the gravel path, I was afraid. I knew that by day I might walk the bridge without fear; but at night, in a strange country, with dark mountains towering all around me and a broad green river flowing beneath me, I could not keep my hands from trembling and my heart from pounding against my chest.

I found the house easily, and laughed at myself for having run from the river. The house was the first one to come upon after leaving the footbridge, and even if I should have missed it, Gretchen would have called me. She was there on the steps of the porch waiting for me. When I heard her familiar voice calling my name, I was ashamed of myself for having been frightened by the mountains and the broad river flowing below.

She ran down the gravel path to meet me.

"Did the footbridge frighten you, Richard?" she asked excitedly, holding my arm with both of her hands and guiding me up the path to the house.

"I think it did, Gretchen," I said; "but I hope I outran it."

"Everyone tries to do that at first, but after going over it once, it's like walking a tightrope. I used to walk tightropes when I was small—didn't you do that, too, Richard? We had a rope stretched across the floor of our barn to practice on."

"I did, too, but it's been so long ago I've forgotten how to do it now."

We reached the steps and went up to the porch. Gretchen took me to the door. Someone inside the house was bringing a lamp into the hall, and with the coming of the light I saw Gretchen's two sisters standing just inside the open door.

"This is my little sister, Anne," Gretchen said. "And this is Mary."

I spoke to them in the semidarkness, and we went on into the hall. Gretchen's father was standing beside a table holding the lamp a little to one side so that he could see my face. I had not met him before.

"This is my father," Gretchen said. "He was afraid you wouldn't be able to find our house in the dark."

"I wanted to bring a light down to the bridge and meet you, but Gretchen said you would get here without any trouble. Did you get lost? I could have brought a lantern down with no trouble at all."

I shook hands with him and told him how easily I had found the place.

"The hack driver pointed out to me the house from the other side of the river, and I never once took my eyes from the light. If I had lost sight of the light, I'd probably be stumbling around somewhere now in the dark down there getting ready to fall into the water."

He laughed at me for being afraid of the river.

"You wouldn't have minded it. The river is warm. Even in winter, when there is ice and snow underfoot, the river is as warm as a comfortable room. All of us here love the water down there."

"No, Richard, you wouldn't have fallen in," Gretchen said, laying her hand in mine. "I saw you the moment you got out of the hack, and if you had gone a step in the wrong direction, I was ready to run to you."

I wished to thank Gretchen for saying that, but already she was going to the stairs to the floor above, and calling me. I went with her, lifting my handbag in front of me. There was a shaded lamp, lighted but turned low, on the table at the end of the upper hall, and she picked it up and went ahead into one of the front rooms.

We stood for a moment looking at each other, and silent.

"There is fresh water in the pitcher, Richard. If there is anything else you would like to have, please tell me. I tried not to overlook anything."

"Don't worry, Gretchen," I told her. "I couldn't wish for anything more. It's enough just to be here with you, anyway. There's nothing else I care for."

She looked at me quickly, and then she lowered her eyes. We stood silently for several minutes, while neither of us could think of anything to say. I wanted to tell her how glad I was to be with her, even if it was only for one night, but I knew I could say that to her later. Gretchen knew why I had come.

"I'll leave the lamp for you, Richard, and I'll wait downstairs for you on the porch. Come as soon as you are ready."

She had left before I could offer to carry the light to the stairhead for her to see the way down. By the time I had picked up the lamp, she was out of sight down the stairs.

I walked back into the room and closed the door and bathed my face and hands, scrubbing the train dust with brush and soap. There was a row of hand-embroidered towels on the rack, and I took one and dried my face and hands. After that I combed my hair, and found a fresh handkerchief in the handbag. Then I opened the door and went downstairs to find Gretchen.

Her father was on the porch with her. When I walked through the doorway, he got up and gave me a chair between them. Gretchen pulled her chair closer to mine, touching my arm with her hand.

"Is this the first time you have been up here in the mountains, Richard?" her father asked me, turning in his chair towards me.

"I've never been within a hundred miles of here before, sir. It's a different country up here, but I suppose you would think the same about the coast, wouldn't you?"

"Oh, but Father used to live in Norfolk," Gretchen said. "Didn't you, Father?"

"I lived there for nearly three years."

There was something else he would say, and both of us waited for him to continue.

"Father is a master mechanic," Gretchen whispered to me. "He works in the railroad shops."

"Yes," he said after a while, "I've lived in many places, but here is where I wish to stay."

My first thought was to ask him why he preferred the mountains to other sections, but suddenly I was aware that both he and Gretchen were strangely silent. Between them, I sat wondering about it.

After a while he spoke again, not to me and not to Gretchen, but as though he were speaking to someone else on the porch, a fourth person whom I had failed to see in the darkness. I waited, tense and excited, for him to continue.

Gretchen moved her chair a few inches closer to mine, her motions gentle and without sound. The warmth of the river came up and covered us like a blanket on a chill night.

"After Gretchen and the other two girls lost their mother," he said, almost inaudibly, bending forward over his knees and gazing out across the broad green river, "after we lost their mother, I came back to the mountains to live. I couldn't stay in Norfolk, and I couldn't stand it in Baltimore. This was the only place on earth where I could find peace. Gretchen remembers her mother, but neither of you can yet understand how it is with me. Her mother and I were born here in the mountains, and we lived here together for almost twenty years. Then after she left us, I moved away, foolishly believing that I could forget. But I was wrong. Of course I was wrong. A man can't forget the mother of his children, even though he knows he will never see her again."

Gretchen leaned closer to me, and I could not keep my eyes from her darkly framed profile beside me. The river below us made no sound; but the warmth of its vapor would not let me forget that it was still there.

Her father had bent farther forward in his chair until his arms were resting on his knees, and he seemed to be trying to see someone on the other side of the river, high on the mountain top above it. His eyes strained, and the shaft of light that came through the open doorway fell upon them and glistened there. Tears fell from his face like fragments of stars, burning into his quivering hands until they were out of sight.

Presently, still in silence, he got up and moved through the doorway. His huge shadow fell upon Gretchen and me as he stood there momentarily before going inside. I turned and looked towards him but, even though he was passing from sight, I could not keep my eyes upon him.

Gretchen leaned closer against me, squeezing her fingers into the hollow of my hand and touching my shoulder with her cheeks as though she were trying to wipe something from them. Her father's footsteps grew fainter, and at last we could no longer hear him.

Somewhere below us, along the bank of the river, an express train crashed down the valley, creaking and screaming through the night. Occasionally its lights flashed through the openings in the darkness, dancing on the broad green river like polar lights in the north, and the metallic echo of its steel rumbled against the high walls of the mountains.

Gretchen clasped her hands tightly over my hand, trembling to her fingertips.

"Richard, why did you come to see me?"

Her voice was mingled with the screaming metallic echo of the train that now seemed far off.

I had expected to find her looking up into my face, but when I turned to her, I saw that she was gazing far down into the valley, down into the warm waters of the river. She knew why I had come, but she did not wish to hear me say why I had.

I did not know why I had come to see her, now. I had liked Gretchen, and I had desired her above anyone else I knew. But I could not tell her that I loved her, after having heard her father speak of love. I was sorry I had come, now after having heard him speak of Gretchen's mother as he did. I knew Gretchen would give herself to me, because she loved me; but I had nothing to give her in return. She was beautiful, very beautiful, and I had desired her. That was before. Now, I knew that I could never again think of her as I had come prepared.

"Why did you come, Richard?"

"Why?"

"Yes, Richard; why?"

My eyes closed, and what I felt was the memory of the star-pointed lights twinkling down in the valley and the warmth of the river flowing below and the caress of her fingers as she touched my arm.

"Richard, please tell me why you came."

"I don't know why I came, Gretchen."

"If you only loved me as I love you, Richard, you would know why."

Her fingers trembled in my hand. I knew she loved me. There had been no doubt in my mind from the first. Gretchen loved me.

"Perhaps I should not have come," I said. "I made a mistake, Gretchen. I should have stayed away."

"But you will be here only for tonight, Richard. You are leaving early in the morning. You aren't sorry that you came for just this short time, are you, Richard?"

"I'm not sorry that I am here, Gretchen, but I should not have come. I didn't know what I was doing. I haven't any right to come here. People who love each other are the only ones—"

"But you do love me just a little, don't you, Richard? You couldn't possibly love me nearly so much as I love you, but can't you tell me that you do love me just a little? I'll feel much happier after you have gone, Richard."

"I don't know," I said, trembling.

"Richard, please—"

With her hands in mine I held her tightly. Suddenly I felt something coming over me, a thing that stabbed my body with its quickness. It was as if the words her father had uttered were becoming clear to me. I had not realized before that there was such a love as he had spoken of. I had believed that men never loved women in the same way that a woman loved a man, but now I knew there could be no difference.

We sat silently, holding each other's hands for a long time. It was long past midnight, because the lights in the valley below were being turned out; but time did not matter.

Gretchen clung softly to me, looking up into my face and laying her cheek against my shoulder. She was as much mine as a woman ever belongs to a man, but I knew then that I could never force myself to take advantage of her love, and to go away knowing that I had not loved her as she loved me. I had not believed any such thing when I came. I had traveled all that distance to hold her in my arms for a few hours, and then to forget her, perhaps forever.

When it was time for us to go into the house, I got up and put my arms around her. She trembled when I touched her, but she clung to me as tightly as I held her, and the hammering of her heart drove into me, stroke after stroke, like an expanding wedge, the spears of her breasts.

"Richard, kiss me before you go," she said.

She ran to the door, holding it open for me. She picked up the lamp from the table and walked ahead up the stairs to the floor above.

At my door she waited until I could light her lamp, and then she handed me mine.

"Good night, Gretchen," I said.

"Good night, Richard."

I turned down the wick of her lamp to keep it from smoking, and then she went across the hall towards her room.

"I'll call you in the morning in time for you to catch your train, Richard."

"All right, Gretchen. Don't let me oversleep, because it leaves the station at seven-thirty."

"I'll wake you in plenty of time, Richard," she said.

The door was closed after her, and I turned and went into my room. I shut the door and slowly began to undress. After I had blown out the lamp and had got into bed, I lay tensely awake. I knew I could never go to sleep, and I sat up in bed and smoked cigarette after cigarette, blowing the smoke through the screen at the window. The house was quiet. Occasionally, I thought I heard the sounds of muffled movements in Gretchen's room across the hall, but I was not certain.

I could not determine how long a time I had sat there on the edge of the bed, stiff and erect, thinking of Gretchen, when suddenly I found myself jumping to my feet. I opened the door and ran across the hall. Gretchen's door was closed, but I knew it would not be locked, and I turned the knob noiselessly. A slender shaft of light broke through the opening I had made. It was not necessary to open the door wider, because I saw Gretchen only a few steps away, almost within arm's reach of me. I closed my eyes tightly for a moment, thinking of her as I had all during the day's ride up from the coast.

Gretchen had not heard me open her door, and she did not know I was there. Her lamp was burning brightly on the table.

I had not expected to find her awake, and I had thought surely she would be in bed. She knelt on the rug beside her bed, her head bowed over her arms and her body shaken with sobs.

Gretchen's hair was lying over her shoulders, tied over the top of her head with a pale blue ribbon. Her nightgown was white silk, hemmed with a delicate lace, and around her neck the collar of lace was thrown open.

I knew how beautiful she was when I saw her then, even though I had always thought her lovely. I had never seen a girl so beautiful as Gretchen.

She had not heard me at her door, and she still did not know I was there. She knelt beside her bed, her hands clenched before her, crying.

When I had first opened the door, I did not know what I was about to do; but now that I had seen her in her room, kneeling in prayer beside her bed, unaware that I was looking upon her and hearing her words and sobs, I was certain that I could never care for anyone else as I did for her. I had not known until then, but in the revelation of a few seconds I knew that I did love her.

I closed the door softly and went back to my room. There I found a chair and placed it beside the window to wait for the coming of day. At the window I sat and looked down into the bottom of the valley where the warm river lay. As my eyes grew more accustomed to the darkness, I felt as if I were coming closer and closer to it, so close that I might have reached out and touched the warm water with my hands.

Later in the night, towards morning, I thought I heard someone in Gretchen's room moving softly over the floor as one who would go from window to window. Once I was certain I heard someone in the hall, close to my door.

When the sun rose over the top of the mountain, I got up and dressed. Later, I heard Gretchen leave her room and go downstairs. I knew she was hurrying to prepare breakfast for me before I left to get on the train. I waited awhile, and after a quarter of an hour I heard her coming back up the stairs. She knocked softly on my door, calling my name several times.

I jerked open the door and faced her. She was so surprised at seeing me there, when she had expected to find me still asleep, that she could not say anything for a moment.

"Gretchen," I said, grasping her hands, "don't hurry to get me off — I'm not going back this morning — I don't know what was the matter with me last night — I know now that I love you —"

"But, Richard — last night you said —"

"I did say last night that I was going back early this morning, Gretchen, but I didn't know what I was talking about. I'm not going back now until you go with me. I'll tell you what I mean as soon as breakfast is over. But first of all I wish you would show me how to get down to the river. I have got to go down there right away and feel the water with my hands."

(First published in *Pagany*)

Yellow Girl

NELL stood at the kitchen window packing the basket of eggs. She arranged eleven white eggs carefully, placing the cottonseed hulls between them and under them so that none would be broken. The last one to be put into the basket was large and brown and a little soiled. She dipped it into the pan of soap and warm water and wiped it dry with a fresh dish towel. Even then she was not pleased with the way it looked, because it was brown; all the other eggs in the basket were as white as September cotton bolls.

Behind her in the room, Myrtie was scouring the two frying pans with soapy water and a cloth dipped in sand. Nell laid down the brown egg and called Myrtie.

"Here's another of those big brown eggs, Myrtie," she said, pointing at the egg. "Do you have any idea where they come from? Have you seen any strange hens in the yard? There must be a visiting hen laying eggs in the chicken house."

Myrtie laid down the frying pan and came over to the little table by the window. She picked up the large brown egg and looked at it. The egg no longer looked brown. Nell looked at the egg again, wondering why in Myrtie's hands it had apparently changed color.

"Where do these brown eggs come from, Myrtie?" she asked. "There was one last week, and now today there's this. It was in the basket Mr. Willis brought in from the chicken house, but he said he forgot to notice which nest he took it from."

Myrtie turned the egg over in her hands, feeling the weight of it and measuring its enormous circumference with her fingers.

"Don't ask me, Miss Nell," Myrtie said, staring at the egg. "I've never seen a flock of Leghorns yet, though, that didn't lay a few brown eggs, sometime or other. Looks like it just can't be helped."

"What do you mean, Myrtie? What on earth are you talking about? Of course Leghorns lay white eggs; this is a brown egg."

"I'm not saying the Leghorns lay them, Miss Nell, and I'm not saying they don't. Those old Buff Orpingtons and Plymouth Rocks and Domineckers lay funny-looking eggs, too, sometimes. I wouldn't take on so much about finding one measly brown egg, though. I've never seen anybody yet, white or colored, who knew how such things happen. But I wouldn't worry about it, Miss Nell. Brown eggs are just as good as white eggs, to my way of tasting."

Nell turned her back on Myrtie and looked out the window until the girl had returned to the other side of the kitchen. Nell disliked to talk to Myrtie, because Myrtie pretended never to know the truth about anything. Even if she did know, she would invariably evade a straightforward answer. Myrtie would begin talking, and talk about everything under the sun from morning to night, but she would never answer a question that she could evade. Nell always forgave her, though; she knew Myrtie was not consciously evading the truth.

While the girl was scouring the pans, Nell picked up the egg again and looked at it closely. Mrs. Farrington had a flock of Dominique chickens, and she gathered in her chicken house eggs of all sizes, shapes, and colors. But that was to be expected, Mrs. Farrington had said, because she had two old roosters that were of no known name or breed. Nell had told Mrs. Farrington that some of her Dominiques were mixed-bred, and consequently they produced eggs of varying sizes, shapes, and colors; but Mrs. Farrington continued to lay all the blame on her two roosters, because, she said, they were a mixture of all breeds.

Once more Nell dipped the brown egg into the pan of water and wiped it with the fresh dish towel, but the egg remained as brown as it was at first. The egg was clean by then, but soap and water would not alter its size or change its color. It was a brown egg, and it would remain brown. Nell gave up, finally; she realized that she could never change it in any way. If she had had another egg to put into the basket in its place, she would have laid it aside and substituted a white one; but she only had a dozen, counting the brown one, and she wished to have enough to make an even exchange with Mrs. Farrington when she went over after some green garden peas.

Before she finally placed the egg in the basket with the others she glanced out the window to see where Willis was. He was sitting in the crib door shelling red seed corn into an old wooden lard pail.

"I'm going over to Mrs. Farrington's now to exchange these eggs for some peas," she told Myrtie. "Keep the fire going good, and put on a pan of water to boil. I'll be back in a little while."

She turned around and looked at Myrtie.

"Suppose you mash the potatoes today, for a change, Myrtie. Mr. Willis likes them that way."

"Are you going to take that big egg, Miss Nell?" Myrtie asked, looking down at it in the basket with the eleven white Leghorns.

"Certainly," she said. "Why?"

"Mrs. Farrington will be surprised to see it in with all those white ones, won't she, Miss Nell?"

"Well, what if she does see it?" Nell asked impatiently.

"Nothing, Miss Nell," Myrtie said. "But she might want to know where it came from. She knows we've got Leghorn hens, and she might think one of her Domineckers laid it."

"I can't help that," Nell said, turning away. "And, besides, she should keep her Dominiques at home if she doesn't want them to lay eggs in somebody else's chicken house."

"That's right, Miss Nell," Myrtie said. "She sure ought to do that. She ought to keep her Domineckers at home."

Nell was annoyed by the girl's comments. It was none of Myrtie's business, anyway. Myrtie was getting to be impertinent, and she was forgetting that she was a hired servant in the house. Nell left the kitchen determined to treat Myrtie more coldly after that. She could not allow a colored cook to tell her what to do and what not to do.

Willis was sitting in the crib door shelling the red seed corn. He glanced up when Nell came down the back steps, and looked at her. He stopped shelling corn for a moment to wipe away the white flakes of husk that clung to his eyes.

"I'm going over to Mrs. Farrington's now and exchange a basket of eggs for some green peas, Willis," she said. "I'll not be gone long."

"Maybe she won't swap with you today," Willis said. He stopped and looked up at her through the thin cloud of flying husk that hovered around him. "How do you know she will want to take eggs for peas today, Nell?"

"Don't be foolish, Willis," she said, smiling at him; "why wouldn't she take eggs in exchange today?"

"She might get to wondering where that big brown egg came from," he said, laughing. "She might think it is an egg one of her hens laid."

Nell stopped, but she did not turn around. She waited, looking towards the house.

"You're as bad as Myrtie, Willis."

"In which way is that?"

The moment he spoke, she turned quickly and looked at him. He was bending over to pick up an ear of seed corn.

"I didn't mean to say that, Willis. Please forget what I said. I didn't mean anything like that."

"Like what?"

"Nothing," she said, relieved. "It wasn't anything; I've even forgotten what it was I said. Good-by."

"Good-by," he said, looking after her, wondering.

Nell turned and walked quickly out of the yard and went around the corner of the house towards the road. The Farrington house was half a mile away, but by taking the path through the cotton field it was two or three hundred yards nearer. She crossed the road and entered the field, walking quickly along the path with the basket of eggs on her arm.

Halfway to the Farringtons' Nell turned around and looked back to see if Willis was still sitting in the crib door shelling seed corn. She did not know why she stopped and looked back, but even though she could not see him there or anywhere else in the yard, she went on towards the Farringtons' without thinking of Willis again.

Mrs. Farrington was sitting on the back porch peeling turnips when Nell turned the corner of the house and walked across the yard. There was a bucket of turnips beside Mrs. Farrington's rocking chair, and long purple peelings were lying scattered on the porch floor around her, twisted into shapes like apple peelings when they were tossed over the shoulder. Nell ran up the steps and picked up the longest peeling she could find; she picked up the peeling even before she spoke to Mrs. Farrington.

"Sakes alive, Nell," Mrs. Farrington said; "why are you throwing turnip peelings over your shoulder? Doesn't that good-for-nothing husband of yours love you any more?"

Nell dropped the turnip peeling, and, picking it up again, tore it into short pieces and threw them into the bucket. She blushed and sat down in the chair beside Mrs. Farrington.

"Of course, he loves me," Nell said. "I suppose I did that so many times when I was a little girl that I still have the habit."

"You mean it's because you haven't grown up yet, Nell," the woman said, chuckling to herself. "I used to be just like that myself; but, sakes alive, it doesn't last, always, girl."

Both of them laughed, and looked away, one from the other. Over across the cotton field a cloud of white dust hung close to the earth. Mr. Farrington and the colored men were planting cotton, and the earth was so dry it rose up in the air when it was disturbed by the mules' hooves and the cotton planters. There was no wind to carry the dust away, and it hung over the men and mules, hiding them from sight.

Presently Mrs. Farrington dropped a peeled turnip into the pan and folded her hands in her lap. She looked at Nell, noting her neatly combed hair and her clean gingham frock and white hands. Mrs. Farrington turned away again after that and gazed once more at the cloud of dust where her husband was at work.

"Maybe you and Willis will always be like that," she said. "Seems like you and Willis are still in love with each other. As long as he stays at home where he belongs and doesn't run off at night, it's a pretty sure sign he isn't getting ready to chase after another woman. Sakes alive, men can't always be depended upon to stay at home at night, though; they go riding off when you are least looking for them to."

Nell sat up, startled by what Mrs. Farrington had said, terrified by the directness of her comments.

"Of course, Willis wouldn't do a thing like that," she said confidently. "I know he wouldn't. Willis wouldn't do a thing like that. That's impossible, Mrs. Farrington."

Mrs. Farrington glanced at Nell, and then once more she looked across the field where the planting was being done. The cloud of white dust followed the men and mules, covering them.

"Seems like men are always saying something about being compelled to go to Macon on business, and even up to Atlanta sometimes," she said, ignoring Nell. "And then there are the times when they say they have to go to town at night. Seems like they are always going off to town at night."

Several Dominique hens came from under the porch and stopped in the yard to scratch on the hard white sand. They scratched listlessly; they went through the motions of scratching as if they knew of nothing else to do. They bent their long necks and looked down at the chicken-scrawls they had made with their claws, and they walked away aimlessly, neither surprised nor angry at not having unearthed a worm to devour. One of them began singing in the heat, drooping her wings until the tips of them dragged on the sand. The other hens paid no attention to her, strolling away without interest in the doleful music.

"You have pretty chickens, Mrs. Farrington," Nell said, watching the Dominiques stroll across the yard and sit down in the shaded dust holes as though they were nests.

"They're nothing but Domineckers," she said; "sakes alive, a body can't call them much of a breed, but they do get around to laying an egg or two once in a while."

Nell glanced down at the basket of eggs in her lap, covering the brown egg with her hand. She looked quickly at Mrs. Farrington to see if she had noticed what she had done.

"How are your Leghorns laying now, Nell?" she asked.

"Very well. Willis gathered sixteen eggs yesterday."

"My Domineckers seem to be taking a spell of resting. I only gathered two eggs yesterday, and that's not enough for a hungry man and a yard full of blacks. Sakes alive, we were saying only last night that we wished you would bring over some eggs in a day or two. And now here you are with them. Half an hour's prayer couldn't have done better."

"I thought you might let me have some green peas for dinner," Nell said, lifting the basket and setting it on the floor. "Willis likes green peas at this time of year, and ours haven't begun to bear yet."

"You're as welcome to as many as you want," Mrs. Farrington said. "Just walk into the kitchen, Nell, and look on the big table and you'll find a bushel basket of them. Help yourself to all you think you and Willis will want. We've got more than we can use. Sakes alive, there'll be another bushel ready for picking tomorrow morning, too."

Nell went into the kitchen and placed the eleven Leghorn eggs and the big brown one in a pan. She filled the basket with green peas and came back to the porch, closing the screen noiselessly behind her.

"Sit down, Nell," Mrs. Farrington said, "and tell me what's been happening. Sakes alive, I sit here all day and never hear a word of what's going on."

"Why, I haven't heard of anything new," Nell said.

"What's Willis doing now?"

"He's getting ready to plant corn. He was shelling the seed when I left home. He should be ready to begin planting this afternoon. The planter broke down yesterday, and he had to send to Macon for a new spoke chain. It should be here in the mail today."

"Myrtie is still there to help you with the house, isn't she?"

"Yes, Myrtie is still there."

The hens lying in the dust holes in the shade of the sycamore tree stood up and flapped their wings violently, beating the dust from their feathers. They stretched, one leg after the other, and flapped their wings a second time. One of them spread her legs, bending her knees as if she were getting ready to squat on the ground, and scratched the hard white sand five or six times in quick succession. The other hens stood and watched her while she stretched her long neck and looked down at the marks she had made; and then, wiping her beak on her leg as one whets a knife blade, she turned and waddled back across the yard and under the porch out of sight. The other hens followed her, singing in the heat.

"Couldn't you find a black woman to help you with the house?" Mrs. Farrington asked.

"A black woman?" Nell said. "Why, Myrtie is colored."

"She's colored all right," Mrs. Farrington said; "but, sakes alive, Nell, she isn't black. Myrtie is yellow."

"Well, that's all right, isn't it?" Nell asked. "Myrtie is yellow, and she is a fairly good cook. I don't know where I could find a better one for the pay."

"I reckon I'd heap rather have a black girl and a poor cook, than to have a yellow girl and the finest cook in the whole country."

Nell glanced quickly at Mrs. Farrington, but her head was turned, and she did not look at Nell.

There was a long silence between them until finally Nell felt that she must know what Mrs. Farrington was talking about.

One of the Dominiques suddenly appeared on the bottom step. She came hopping up to the porch, a step at a time. When she reached the last one, Mrs. Farrington said, "Shoo!" The hen flew to the yard and went back under the porch.

"You don't mean —"

Mrs. Farrington began rocking slowly, backward and forward. She gazed steadily across the field where her husband was planting cotton with the colored men.

"You don't mean Willis and —"

One of the roosters strutted across the yard, his eye first upon the hens under the porch and next upon the two women, and stopped midway in the yard to stand and fix his eye upon Mrs. Farrington and Nell. He stood jerking his head from side to side, his hanging scarlet comb blinding his left eye, while he listened to the squeaking of Mrs. Farrington's chair. After a while he continued across the yard and went out of sight behind the smokehouse.

"Mrs. Farrington, Willis wouldn't do anything like that!" Nell said indignantly.

"Like what?" Mrs. Farrington asked. "Sakes alive, Nell, I didn't say he would do anything."

"I know you didn't say it, Mrs. Farrington, but I thought you said it. I couldn't help thinking that you did say it."

"Well, that's different," she replied, much relieved. "I wouldn't want you to go telling Willis I did say it. Menfolks never understand what a woman means, anyway, and when they are told that a woman says something about them, they sometimes fly off the handle something awful."

Nell got up and stood beside the chair. She wished she could run down the steps and along the path towards home without another second's delay, but she knew she could not jump up and leave Mrs. Farrington like that, after what had been said. She would have to pretend that she was not in such a great hurry to get home.

"You're not going so soon, are you, Nell? Why, sakes alive, it seems like you only got here two or three minutes ago, Nell."

"I know," she said, "but it's getting late, and I've got to go home and get these peas ready for dinner. I'll be back to see you soon."

She walked carelessly down the steps. Mrs. Farrington got up and followed her across the hard yard. When they reached the beginning of the path that led across the field, Mrs. Farrington stopped. She never went any farther than that.

"I'm afraid I must hurry home now and hull the peas in time for dinner," Nell said, backing down the path. "I'll be back again in a few days, Mrs. Farrington. Thank you so much for the peas. Willis has wanted some for the past week or longer."

"It's as fair an exchange as I can offer for the Leghorn eggs," she said, laughing. "Because if there's anything I like better than those white Leghorn eggs, I don't know what it is. I get so tired of eating my old Domineckers brown eggs I sometimes say I hope I may never see another one. Maybe I'll be asking you for a setting of them some day soon."

"Good-by," Nell said, backing farther and farther away. She turned and walked several steps. "I'll bring you another basket soon, Mrs. Farrington."

It seemed as if she would never reach the house, even though it was only half a mile away. She could not run, because Mrs. Farrington was in the yard behind her watching, and she could not walk slowly, because she had to get home as soon as possible. She walked with her eyes on the path in front of her, forcing herself to keep from looking up at the house. She knew that if she did raise her eyes and look at it, she would never be able to keep herself from running. If she did that, Mrs. Farrington would see her.

It was not until she had at last reached the end of the path that she was able to look backward. Mrs. Farrington had left her yard, and Nell ran across the road and around to the back of the house.

Willis was nowhere within sight. She looked first at the crib where she had hoped she would find him, but he was not there, and the crib door was closed and locked. She looked down at the barn, but he was not there, either. When she glanced hastily over the fields, she was still unable to see him anywhere.

She stopped at the bottom step on the back porch. There was no sound within the house that she could hear, and not even the sound of Myrtie's footsteps reached her ears. The place seemed to be entirely deserted, and yet she knew that could not be, because only half an hour before when she left to go to Mrs. Farrington's to exchange eggs, Willis was sitting in the crib door shelling seed corn, and Myrtie was in the kitchen scouring the two frying pans.

Nell's hands went out and searched for the railing that led up the porch steps. Her hands could not find it, and her eyes would not let her see it.

The thought of Mrs. Farrington came back to her again and again. Mrs. Farrington, sitting on her own back porch, talking. Mrs. Farrington, sitting in her rocking chair, looking. Mrs. Farrington, peeling purple-top turnips, talking about yellow girls.

Nell felt deathly sick. She felt as if she had been stricken with an illness that squeezed the core of her body. Deep down within herself, she was deathly ill. A pain that began by piercing her skull struck downward and downward until it became motionless in her stomach. It remained there, gnawing and biting, eating the organs of her body and drinking the flow of her blood. She sank limp and helpless upon the back porch steps. Although she did not know where she was, she could still see Mrs. Farrington. Mrs. Farrington, in her rocking chair, looking. Mrs. Farrington, peeling purple-top turnips, talking about yellow girls.

Nell did not know how much later it was when she opened her eyes. The day was the color of the red seed corn Willis had been shelling when she last saw him sitting in the crib door, and it swam in a sea so wide that she almost cried out in fear when she saw it. Slowly she remembered how she had come to be where she was. She got to her feet weakly, holding to the railing for support.

Stumbling up the steps and across the porch, she flung open the screen door and went into the kitchen. Myrtie was standing beside the table mashing the boiled Irish potatoes with a long fork that had seven tines. Myrtie looked up when Nell ran in, but she did not have an opportunity to speak. Nell ran headlong through the dining room and on into the front room. Myrtie looked surprised to see her running.

Nell paused a moment in the doorway, looking at Willis, at the room, at the daybed, at the floor, at the rugs, at the open door that led into their room. She stood looking at everything she could see. She looked at the pillows on the daybed, at the rugs on the floor, at the chairs against the wall, at the counterpane on their bed. Remembering, she looked at the carpet in their room. Willis sat in front of her reading the *Macon Telegraph* that had just come in the mail, and he was calmly smoking his pipe. She glanced once more at the daybed, at the pillows arranged upon it, and at the rug in front of it. Running, she went to their room and ran her hands over the counterpane of the bed. She picked up the pillows, feeling them, and laid them down again. She ran back into the other room where Willis was.

Willis looked up at her.

Nell ran and fell on her knees in front of him, forcing her body between his legs and locking her arms around him. She pressed her feverish face against his cool cheeks and closed her eyes tightly. She forced herself tightly to him, holding him with all her might.

"Did Mrs. Farrington exchange with you?" he asked. "I'll bet a pretty that she had something to say about that big brown egg in a basketful of Leghorns."

Nell felt her body shake convulsively, as if she were shivering with cold. She knew she had no control over herself now.

"Look here," he said, throwing aside the *Telegraph* and lifting her head and looking into her eyes. "I know where that brown egg came from now. I remember all about it. There was one of Mrs. Farrington's old Dominecker hens over here yesterday morning. I saw her scratching in the yard, and she acted like she didn't give a cuss whether she clawed up a worm or not. She would scratch awhile and then walk off without even looking to see if she had turned up a worm."

Nell felt herself shaking again, but she did not attempt to control herself. If she could only lie there close to Willis with her arms around him, she did not care how much she shivered. As long as she was there, she had Willis; when she got up and walked out of the room, she would never again be that certain.

(First published in *Story*)

The Medicine Man

THERE was nobody in Rawley who believed that Effie Henderson would ever find a man to marry her, and Effie herself had just about given up hope. But that was before the traveling herb doctor came to town.

Professor Eaton was a tall gaunt-looking man with permanent, sewn-in creases in his trousers and a high celluloid collar around his neck. He may have been ten years older than Effie, or he may have been ten years younger; it was no more easy to judge his age than it was to determine by the accent of his speech from what section of the country he had originally come.

He drove into Rawley one hot dusty morning in mid-August, selling Indian Root Tonic. Indian Root Tonic was a beady, licorice-tasting cure-all in a fancy green-blown bottle. The bottle was wrapped in a black and white label, on which the most prominent feature was the photographic reproduction of a beefy man exhibiting his expanded chest and muscles and his postage-stamp wrestler's trunks. Professor Eaton declared, and challenged any man alive to deny his statement, that his Indian Root Tonic would cure any ailment known to man, and quite a few known only to women.

Effie Henderson was the first person in town to give him a dollar for a bottle, and the first to come back for the second one.

The stand that Professor Eaton had opened up was the back seat of his mud-spattered touring car. He had paid the mayor ten ragged one-dollar bills for a permit to do business in Rawley, and he had parked his automobile in the middle of the weed-grown vacant lot behind the depot. He sold his medicine over the back seat of his car, lifting the green-blown bottles from a box at his feet as fast as the customers came up and laid down their dollars.

There had been a big crowd standing around in the weed-grown lot the evening before, but there were only a few people standing around him

75

listening to his talk when Effie came back in the morning for her second bottle. Most of the persons there then were Negroes who did not have a dollar among them, but who had been attracted to the lot by the alcoholic fumes around the mud-caked automobile and who were willing to be convinced of Indian Root Tonic's marvelous curative powers. When Effie came up, the Negroes stepped aside, and stood at a distance watching Professor Eaton get ready to make another sale.

Effie walked up to the folded-down top in front of Professor Eaton and laid down a worn dollar bill that was as limp as a piece of wet cheesecloth.

"I just had to come back this morning for another bottle," Effie said, smiling up at Professor Eaton. "The one I took last night made me feel better than I have ever felt before in all my life. There's not another medicine in the whole country like it, and I've tried them all, I reckon."

"Pardon me, madam," Professor Eaton said. "There are hundreds of preparations on the market today, but there is only one Indian Root Tonic. You will be doing me a great favor if you will hereafter refer to my aid-to-human-life by its true and trade-marked name. Indian Root Tonic is the name of the one and only cure for ailments of any nature. It is particularly good for the mature woman, madam."

"You shouldn't call me 'madam,' Professor Eaton," Effie said, lowering her head. "I'm just a young and foolish girl, and I'm not married yet, either."

Professor Eaton wiped the perspiration from his upper lip and looked down at Effie.

"How utterly stupid of me, my dear young lady," he said. "Anyone can see by looking at your fresh young face that you are a mere girl. Indian Root Tonic is particularly good for the young maiden."

Effie turned around to see if any of the Negroes were close enough to hear what Professor Eaton had said. She hoped that some of the women who lived on her street would walk past the corner in time to hear Professor Eaton talk like that about her.

"I never like to talk about myself, but don't you think I am too young yet to get married, Professor Eaton?"

"My dear young lady," he continued after having paused long enough to relight his dead cigar, "Indian Root Tonic is particularly good for the unmarried girl. It is the greatest discovery known to medical science since the beginning of mankind. I personally secured the formula for this marvelous medicine from an old Indian chief out in our great and glorious West, and I was compelled to promise him on my bended knee that I would devote the remainder of my life to traveling over this great nation of ours offering Indian Root Tonic to men and women like you who would be helpless invalids without it."

He had to pause for a moment's breath. It was then that he looked down over the folded top and for the first time looked at Effie face to face. The evening before in the glare of the gasoline torch, when the lot was crowded with people pushing and shoving to get to the medicine stand before the special introductory offer was withdrawn, he had not had time to look at everyone who came up to hand him a dollar for a bottle. But now when he looked down and saw Effie, he leaned forward to stare at her.

"Oh, Professor Eaton," Effie said, "you are such a wonderful man! Just to think that you are doing such a great work in the world!"

Professor Eaton continued to stare at Effie. She was as good-looking as the next girl in town, not over thirty, and when she fixed herself up, as she had done for nearly two hours that morning before leaving home, she usually had all the drummers in town for the day staring at her and asking the storekeepers who she was.

After a while Professor Eaton climbed out of the back seat of his car and came around to the rear where she was. He relit his cold cigar, and inspected Effie more closely.

"You know, Professor Eaton, you shouldn't talk like that to me," she said, evading his eyes. "You really don't know me well enough yet to call me 'dear girl.' This is the first time we have been alone together, and—"

"Why! I didn't think that a beautiful young girl like you would seriously object to my honorable admiration," he said, looking her up and down and screwing up his mouth when she plucked at her blouse. "It's so seldom that I have the opportunity of seeing such a charming young girl that I must have lost momentarily all sense of discretion. But, now that we are fully acquainted with each other, I'm sure you won't object to my devoted admiration. Will you?"

"Oh, Professor Eaton," Effie said excitedly, "do you really and truly think I am beautiful? So many men have told me that before, I'm accustomed to hearing it frequently, but you are the first man to say it so thrillingly!"

She tried to step backward, but she was already standing against the rear of the car. Professor Eaton moved another step closer, and there was no way for her to turn. She would not have minded that if she had not been so anxious to have a moment to look down at her blouse. She knew there must be something wrong, surely something had slipped under the waist, because Professor Eaton had not raised his eyes from her bosom since he got out of the car and came down beside her. She wondered then if she should not have confined herself when she dressed that morning, putting on all the undergarments she wore to church on Sunday morning.

"My dear girl, there is not the slightest doubt in my mind concerning your beauty. In fact, I think you are the most charming young girl it has been my good fortune to encounter during my many travels over this great country of ours—from coast to coast, from the Lakes to the Gulf."

"You make me feel so young and foolish, Professor Eaton!" Effie said, smoothing her shirtwaist over her bosom. "You make me feel like—"

Professor Eaton turned abruptly and reached into the back seat for a bottle of Indian Root Tonic. He closed his teeth over the cork stopper and popped it out, and, with no further loss of time, handed it to Effie.

"Have this one on me, my dear girl," he said. "Just drink it down, and then see if it doesn't make you feel even better still."

Effie took the green-blown bottle, looking at the picture of the strong young man in wrestler's trunks.

"I drank the whole bottle I bought last night," she said. "I drank it just before going to bed, and it made me feel so good I just couldn't lie still. I had to get up and sit on the back porch and sing awhile."

"There was never a more beneficial—"

"What particular ailment is the medicine good for, Professor Eaton?"

"Indian Root Tonic is good for whatever ails you. In fact, merely as a general conditioner it is supreme in its field. And then on the other hand, there is no complaint known to medical science that it has yet failed to allevi—— to help."

Effie turned up the bottle and drank down the beady, licorice-tasting fluid, all eight ounces of it. The Negroes standing around the car looked on wistfully while the alcoholic fumes from the opened bottle drifted over the lot. Effie handed the empty bottle to Professor Eaton, after taking one last look at the picture on the label.

"Oh, Professor Eaton," she said, coming closer, "it makes me feel better already. I feel just like I was going to rise off the ground and fly away somewhere."

"Perhaps you would allow me —"

"To do what, Professor Eaton? What?"

He flicked the ashes from his cigar with the tip of his little finger.

"Perhaps you would allow me to escort you to your home," he said. "Now, it's almost dinnertime, and I was just getting ready to close up my stand until the afternoon, so if you will permit me, I'll be very glad to drive you home in my automobile. Just tell me how to get there, and we'll start right away."

"You talk so romantic, Professor Eaton," Effie said, touching his arm with her hand. "You make me feel just like a foolish young girl around you."

"Then you will permit me to see you home?"

"Of course, I will."

"Step this way, please," he said, holding open the door and taking her arm firmly in his grasp.

After they had settled themselves in the front seat, Effie turned around and looked at Professor Eaton.

"I'll bet you have had just lots and lots of love affairs with young girls like me all over the country."

"On the contrary," he said, starting the motor, "this is the first time I have ever given my serious consideration to one of your sex. You see, I apply myself faithfully to the promotion, distribution, and sale of Indian Root Tonic. But this occasion, of course, draws me willingly from the cares of business. In fact, I consider your presence in my car a great honor. I have often wished that I might —"

"And am I the first young girl — the first woman you ever courted?"

"Absolutely," he said. "Absolutely."

Professor Eaton drove out of the vacant weed-grown lot and turned the car up the street toward Effie's house. She lived only two blocks away, and during the time it took them to drive that distance neither of them spoke. Effie was busy looking out to see if people were watching her ride with Professor Eaton in his automobile, and he was busily engaged in steering through the deep white sand in the street. When they got there, Effie told him to park the machine in front of the gate where they could step out and walk directly into the house.

They got out and Effie led the way through the front door and into the parlor. She raised one of the shades a few inches and dusted off the sofa.

Professor Eaton stood near the middle of the room, looking uneasily through the small opening under the shade, and listening intently for sounds elsewhere in the house.

"Just sit down here on the sofa beside me," Effie said. "I know I am perfectly safe alone with you, Professor Eaton."

Effie closed her eyes and allowed herself the pleasure of feeling scared to death of Professor Eaton. It was an even nicer feeling than the one she had had the night before when she drank the first bottle of Indian Root Tonic and got into bed.

"And this is the ancestral home?" he asked.

"Don't let's talk about anything but you — and me," Effie said. "Wouldn't you just like to talk about us?"

Professor Eaton began to feel more at ease, now that it was evident that they were alone in the house.

"Perhaps," Professor Eaton said, sitting closer to Effie and looking down once more at her blouse, "perhaps you will permit me to diagnose your complaint. You see, I am well versed in the medical science, and I can tell you how many bottles of Indian Root Tonic you should use in your particular case. Naturally, some people require a greater number of bottles than others do."

Effie glanced out the window for a second, and then she turned to Professor Eaton.

"I won't have to—"

"Oh, no," he said, "that won't be at all necessary, though you may do as you like about it. I can just—"

"Are you sure it's perfectly all right, Professor Eaton?"

"Absolutely," he said. "Absolutely."

Effie smoothed her shirtwaist with her hands and pushed her shoulders forward. Professor Eaton bent towards her, reaching for her hand.

He held her hand for a few seconds, feeling her pulse, and then dropped it to press his ear against her bosom to listen to her heartbeat. While he listened, Effie tucked up a few loose strands of hair that had fallen over her temples.

"Perhaps," he said, raising his head momentarily, "perhaps if you will merely —"

"Of course, Professor Eaton," Effie said excitedly.

He bent closer after she had fumbled nervously with the blouse and pressed his head against her breasts. Her heartbeat jarred his eardrum.

After a while Professor Eaton sat up and loosened the knot in his necktie and wiped the perspiration from his upper lip with the back of his hand. It was warm in the room, and there was no ventilation with the door closed.

"Perhaps I have already told you —"

"Oh, no! You haven't told me!" she said eagerly, holding her hands tightly clasped and looking down at herself with bated breath. "Please go ahead and tell me, Professor Eaton!"

"Perhaps," he said, fingering the open needlework in her blouse, "perhaps you would like to know that Indian Root Tonic is the only complete aid for general health on the market today. And in addition to its general curative properties, Indian Root Tonic possesses the virtues most women find themselves in need of during the middle and later stages of life. In other words, it imparts a vital force to the glands that are in most need of new vitality. I am sure that once you discover for yourself the marvelous power of rejuvenation that Indian Root Tonic possesses, you will never again be alone in the house without it. In fact, I can say without fear of successful contradiction that —"

Effie laid her blouse aside.

"Do you want me to take —"

"Oh, yes; by all means," he replied hastily. "Now, as I was saying —"

"And this, too, Professor Eaton? This, too?"

Professor Eaton reached over and pinched her lightly. Effie giggled and passed her hands over her bosom as though she were smoothing her shirt-waist.

"I don't suppose you happen to have another bottle of that tonic in your pocket, do you, Professor Eaton?"

"I'm afraid I haven't," he said, "but just outside in my car there are several cases full. If you'll let me, I'll step out and —"

"Oh, no!" Effie cried, clutching at his arms and pulling him back beside her. "Oh, Professor Eaton, don't leave me now!"

"Very well," he said, sitting down beside her once more. "And now as I was saying, Indian Root Tonic's supernatural powers of re——"

"Professor Eaton, do you want me to take off all of this — like this?"

"Absolutely," he said. "And Indian Root Tonic has never been known to fail, whereas in so many —"

"You don't want me to leave anything —"

"Of course not. Being a doctor of the medical science, in addition to my many other activities, I need absolute freedom. Now, if you feel that you cannot place yourself entirely in my hands, perhaps it would be better if I —"

"Oh, please don't go!" Effie cried, pulling him back to the sofa beside her. "You know I have complete confidence in your abilities, Professor Eaton. I know you wouldn't —"

"Wouldn't do what?" he asked, looking down at her again.

"Oh, Professor Eaton! I'm just a young girl!"

"Well," he said, "if you are ready to place yourself entirely in my hands, I can proceed with my diagnosis. Otherwise —"

"I was only teasing you, Professor Eaton!" Effie said, squeezing his hand. "Of course I trust you. You are such a strong man, and I know you wouldn't take advantage of a weak young girl like me. If you didn't take care of me, I'd more than likely run away with myself."

"Absolutely," he said. "Now, if you will continue removing the —"

"There is only this left, Professor Eaton," Effie said. "Are you sure it will be all right?"

"Absolutely."

"But I feel so — so bare, Professor Eaton."

" 'Tis only natural to feel like that," he said, comforting her. "A young girl who has never before experienced the —"

"Experienced the what?"

"Well — as I was saying —"

"You make me feel so funny, Professor Eaton. And are you sure —"

"Absolutely," he said. "Absolutely."

"I've never felt like this before. It feels like—"

"Just place yourself completely in my hands, my dear young girl, and I promise nothing will—"

Without warning the parlor door was thrown open and Effie's brother, Burke, came in. Burke was the town marshal.

"Is dinner ready, Effie?" Burke asked, standing in the doorway and trying to accustom his eyes to the near-darkness of the parlor. "It's a quarter after twelve and—"

Burke stopped in the midst of what he was saying and stared at Effie and Professor Eaton. Effie screamed and pushed Professor Eaton away from her. He got up and stood beside Effie and the sofa, looking first at Burke and then at Effie. He did not know what to do. Effie reached for the things she had thrown aside. Professor Eaton bent down and picked up something and threw it at her.

The room suddenly appeared to Professor Eaton to be as bright as day.

"Well, I'll be damned!" Burke said, coming slowly across the floor. His holster hung from his right hip, and it swung heavily as he swayed from step to step. "I'll be damned!"

Professor Eaton stood first on one foot and then on the other. He was between Effie and her brother, and he knew of no way by which he could change his position in the room. He wished to get as far away from Effie as he possibly could. Until she had dressed herself, he hoped he would not be forced to look at her.

Burke stepped forward and pushed Professor Eaton aside. He looked at Effie and at the herb doctor, but he gave no indication of what he intended doing.

Professor Eaton shifted the weight of his body to his other foot, and Burke's hand dropped to the top of the holster, his fingers feeling for the pearl handle that protruded from it.

Effie snapped a safety pin and ran between Burke and Professor Eaton. She was still not completely dressed, but she was fully covered.

"What are you going to do, Burke?" she cried.

"That all depends on what the Professor is going to do," Burke said, still fingering the pearl handle on the pistol. "What is the Professor going to do?"

"Why, Professor Eaton and I are going to be married, Burke," she said. "Aren't we, Professor Eaton?"

"I had not intended making known the announcement of our engagement and forthcoming marriage at this time," he said, "but since we are to be married very shortly, Effie's brother should by all means be the first to know of our intentions."

"Thanks for telling me, Professor," Burke said. "It had better by a damn sight be forthcoming."

Effie ran to Professor Eaton and locked her arms around his neck.

"Oh, do you really mean it, Professor Eaton? I'm so happy I don't know what to do! But why didn't you tell me sooner that you really wanted to marry me? Do you really and truly mean it, Professor Eaton?"

"Sure," Burke said; "he means it."

"I'm the happiest girl in the whole town of Rawley," Effie cried, pressing her face against Professor Eaton's celluloid collar. "It was all so unexpected! I had never dreamed of it happening to me so soon!"

Burke backed across the room, one hand still around the pearl handle that protruded from the cowhide holster. He backed across the room and reached for the telephone receiver on the wall. He rang the central office and took the receiver from the hook.

"Hello, Janie," he said into the mouthpiece. "Ring up Reverend Edwards for me, will you, right away."

Burke leaned against the wall, looking at Effie and Professor Eaton while Janie at the central office was ringing the Reverend Edwards's number.

"Just to think that I'm going to marry a traveling herb doctor!" Effie said. "Why! all the girls in town will be so envious of me they won't speak for a month!"

"Absolutely," Professor Eaton said, pulling tight the loosened knot in his tie and adjusting it in the opening of his celluloid collar. "Absolutely. Indian Root Tonic has unlimited powers. It is undoubtedly the medical and scientific marvel of the age. Indian Root Tonic has been known to produce the most astounding results in the annals of medical history."

Effie pinned up a strand of hair that had fallen over her forehead and looked proudly upon Professor Eaton.

(First published in *We Are the Living*)

Meddlesome Jack

HOD SHEPPARD was in the kitchen eating breakfast when he heard one of the colored boys yell for him. Before he could get up and look out the window to see what the trouble was, Daisy came running into the room from the garden house in the field looking as if she had been scared out of her wits.

"Hod! Hod!" she screamed at him. "Did you hear it?"

He shook her loose from him and got up from the table. Daisy fell down on the kitchen floor, holding on to his legs with all her might.

"Hear what?" he said. "I heard one of the niggers yelling for me. That's all I heard. What's the matter with you, Daisy?"

Just then Sam, the colored boy, called Hod again louder than ever. Both Hod and Daisy ran to the back door and looked out across the field. The only thing out there they could see was the yellow broom sedge and the dead-leafed blackjack.

"What's all this fuss and racket about, anyway?" Hod said, looking at Daisy.

"I heard something, Hod," she said, trembling.

"Heard what? What did you hear?"

"I don't know what it was, but I heard it."

"What did it sound like — wind, or something?"

"It sounded like — like somebody calling me, Hod."

"Somebody calling you?"

She nodded her head, holding him tightly.

"Who's calling you! If I ever find anybody around here calling you out of the house, I'll butcher him. You'd better not let me see anybody around here after you. I'll kill him so quick — "

Sam came running around the corner of the house, his overall jumper flying out behind, and his crinkly hair jumping like a boxful of little black springs let loose. His eyes were turning white.

"Hey there, you Sam!" Hod yelled at him. "Quit your running around and come back here!"

"Sam heard him, too," Daisy said, standing beside Hod and trembling as if she would fall apart. "Sam's running away from him."

"Heard what — heard who! What's the matter with you, Daisy?"

Daisy held Hod tighter, looking out across the broom sedge. Hod pushed her away and walked out into the back yard. He stood there only a minute before the sound of Sam's pounding feet on the hard white sand grew louder and louder. Sam turned the corner of the house a second later, running even faster than he had before. His eyes were all white by that time, and it looked as if his hair had grown several inches since Hod had last seen him.

Hod reached out and caught Sam's jumper. There was a ripping sound, and Hod looked down to find that he was holding a piece of Sam's overall. Sam was around the house out of sight before Hod could yell at him to stop and come back.

"That nigger is scared of something," Hod said, looking in the doorway at Daisy.

"Sam heard him," Daisy said, trembling.

Hod ran to Daisy and put both hands on her shoulders and shook her violently.

"Heard who!" he yelled at her. "If you don't tell me who it was around here calling you, I'll choke the life out of you. Who was around here calling you? If I catch him, I'll kill him so quick — "

"You're choking me, Hod!" Daisy screamed. "Let me loose! I don't know who it was — honest to God, I don't know who it was, Hod!"

Hod released her and ran out into the yard. Sam had turned and was running down the road towards the lumber mill a mile away. The town of Folger was down there. Two stores, the post office, the lumber mill, and the bank were scorching day after day in an oval of baked clay and sand. Sam was halfway to Folger by then.

"So help me!" Daisy screamed. "There he is, Hod!"

She ran into the kitchen, slamming and bolting the door.

Out behind the barn Amos Whittle, Sam's father, was coming through the broom sedge and blackjack with his feet flying behind him so fast that they looked like the paddles on a water mill. He had both hands gripped around the end of a rope, and the rope was being jerked by the biggest, the ugliest, and the meanest-looking jack that Hod had ever seen in his whole life. The jack was loping through the broom sedge like a hoop snake, jerking Amos from side to side as if he had been the cracker on the end of a rawhide whip.

"Head him, Mr. Hod!" Amos yelled. "Head him! Please, sir, head him!"

Hod stood looking at Amos and the jack while they loped past him. He turned and watched them with mouth agape while they made a wide circle in the broom sedge and started back towards the house and barn again.

"Head him, Mr. Hod!" Amos begged. "Please, Mr. Hod, head him!"

Hod picked up a piece of mule collar and threw it at the jack's head. The jack stopped dead in his tracks, throwing out his front feet and dragging his hind feet on the hard white sand. The animal had stopped so suddenly that Amos found himself wedged between his two hind legs.

Hod walked towards them and pulled Amos out, but Amos was up and on his feet before there was any danger of his being kicked.

"Where'd you get that jack, Amos?" Hod said.

"I don't know where I got him, but I sure wish I'd never seen him. I been all night trying to hold him, Mr. Hod. I ain't slept a wink, and my old woman's taken to the tall bushes. She and the girls heard him, and they must have thought I don't know exactly what, because they went off yelling about being scared to hear a sound like that jack makes."

The jack walked leisurely over to the barn door and began eating some nubbins that Hod had dropped between the crib and the stalls. One ear stood straight up, and the other one lay flat on his neck. He was the meanest-looking jackass that had ever been in that part of the country. Hod had never seen anything like him before.

"Get him away from here, Amos," Hod said. "I don't want no jack around here."

"Mr. Hod," Amos said, "I wish I could get him away somewhere where I'd never see him again. I sure wish I could accommodate you, Mr. Hod. He's the troublesomest jack I ever seen."

"Where'd you get him, Amos? What are you doing with him, anyway?"

Amos glanced at Hod, but only for a moment. He kept both eyes on the jack.

"I traded that old dollar watch of mine for him yesterday, Mr. Hod, but that jack ain't worth even four bits to me. I don't know what them things are made for, anyhow."

"I'll give you fifty cents for him," Hod said.

"You will!" Amos shouted. "Lord mercy, Mr. Hod, give it here! I'll sure be glad to get rid of that jack for four bits. He done drove my wife and grown girls crazy, and I don't know what mischief he'll be up to next. If you'll give me fifty cents for him, I'll sure be much obliged to you, Mr. Hod. I don't want to have nothing more to do with that jackass."

"I don't want him around, either," Hod said, turning to look through the kitchen window, "but I figure on making me some money with him. How old is that jack, Amos?"

"The man said he was three years old, but I don't know no way of telling a jack's age, and I don't aim to find out."

"He looks like he might be three or four. I'm going to buy him from you, Amos. I figure on making me a lot of money out of that jack. I don't know any other way to make money these days. I can't seem to get it out of the ground."

"Sure, sure, Mr. Hod. You're welcome to that jack. You're mighty much welcome to him. I don't want to have nothing more to do with no jackass. I wish now I had my watch back, but I reckon it's stopped running by now, anyhow. It was three years old, and it never did keep accurate time for me. I'll sure be tickled to get four bits for that jack, Mr. Hod."

Hod counted out fifty cents in nickels and dimes and handed the money to Amos.

"Now, you've got to help me halter that jack, Amos," Hod said. "Get yourself a good piece of stout rope. Plow lines won't be no good on him."

"I don't know about haltering that jack, Mr. Hod. Looks like to me he's never been halterbroke. If it's all the same to you, Mr. Hod, I'd just as lief go on home now. I've got some stovewood to chop, and I got to—"

"Wait a minute," Hod said. "I'll get the rope to halter him with. You go in the house and wake up Shaw. He's in the bed asleep. You go in there and get him up and tell him to come out here and help us halter the jack. Ain't no sense in him sleeping all morning. I'm damned tired of seeing him do it. When he comes home, he ought to get out and help do some work about the place."

Shaw was Hod's brother who had been at home seven or eight days on leave from the Navy. He was getting ready to go back to his ship in Norfolk in a day or two. Shaw was two years younger than Hod, and only a few years older than Daisy. Daisy was nineteen then.

"I'd sure like to accommodate you, Mr. Hod," Amos said, "but the last time you sent me in to wake up Mr. Shaw, Mr. Shaw he jumped out of bed on top of me and near about twisted my neck off. He said for me never to wake him up again as long as I live. Mr. Hod, you'd better go wake up Mr. Shaw your own self."

Hod reached down and picked up a piece of stovewood. He walked towards Amos swinging the stick in his hand.

"I said go in the house and get him up," Hod told Amos again. "That sailor had better stop coming here to stay in bed half the day and be all the time telling Daisy tales."

Amos opened the kitchen door and went into the house. Hod walked towards the barn where the jack was calmly eating red nubbins by the crib door.

When Hod reached the barnyard gate, the jack lifted his head and looked at him. He had two or three nubbins of red corn in his jaws, and he stopped chewing and crunching the grains and cobs while he looked at Hod. One of the jack's ears lay flat against the top of his head and neck, and the other one stood straight up in the air, as stiff as a cow's horn. The jack's ears were about fourteen or sixteen inches long, and they were as rigid as bones.

Hod tossed the piece of stovewood aside and walked to the opened gate for a piece of rope. He believed he could halter the jack by himself.

He started into the barnyard, but he had gone no farther than a few steps when boards began to fly off the side of the barn. The mare in the stall was kicking like a pump gun. One after the other, the boards flew off, the mare whinnied, and the jack stood listening to the pounding of the mare's hooves against the pine boards.

When Hod saw what was happening to his barn, he ran towards the jack, yelling and waving his arms and trying to get him to the leeward side of the barn.

"Howie! Howie!" he yelled at the jack.

As long as the mare got wind of the jack, nothing could make her stop kicking the boards off the barn from the inside. Hod jumped at the jack, waving his arms and shouting at him.

"Howie! Howie!"

He continued throwing up his arms to scare the jack away, but the jack just turned and looked at Hod with one ear up and one ear down.

"Howie! You ugly-looking son of a bitch! Howie!"

Hod turned around to look towards the house to see if Shaw and Amos were coming. He turned just in time to see Amos jumping out the window.

"Hey there, Amos!" Hod yelled. "Where's Shaw?"

"Mr. Shaw says he ain't going to get up till he gets ready to. Mr. Shaw cussed pretty bad and made me jump out the window."

The jack began to paw the ground. Hard clods of stableyard sand and manure flew behind him in all directions. Hod yelled at him again.

"Howie! Howie! You flop-eared bastard!"

The jack stopped and turned his head to look at Amos on the other side of the fence.

"Mr. Hod," Amos said, "if you don't mind, I'd like to have a word with you."

Hod yelled at Amos and at the jack at the same time.

"Mr. Hod," Amos said, "if I don't go home now and chop that stovewood, me and my folks won't have no dinner at all."

"Come back here!" Hod shouted at him.

Amos came as far as the gate, but he would not come any farther.

Suddenly the jack lifted his head high in the air and brayed. It sounded as if someone were blowing a trumpet in the ear.

The bray had no more than died out when the mare began pounding the boards with both hind hooves, the boards flying off the side of the barn faster than Hod could count them. He turned and looked to see what Amos was doing, and over his head he saw Daisy at the window. She looked as if she had completely lost her mind.

The jack brayed again, louder than ever, and then he leaped for the open barnyard gate. Hod threw the rope at him, but the rope missed him by six feet. The jack was through the gate and out around the house faster than Hod could yell. Amos stood as if his legs had been fence posts four feet deep in the ground.

The jack stopped at the open bedroom window, turned his head towards the house, and brayed as if he were calling all the mares in the entire county. Daisy ran to the window and looked out, and when she saw the jack no more than arm's length from her, she screamed and fell backward on the floor.

"Head him, Amos! Head him!" Hod yelled, running towards the jack.

Amos's feet were more than ever like fence posts. He was shaking like a tumbleweed, but his legs and feet were as stiff as if they had been set in concrete.

"Where in hell is that God damn sailor!" Hod yelled. "Why in hell don't he get up and help me some around here! If I had the time now, I'd go in there with a piece of cordwood and break every bone in his head. The son of a bitch comes home here on leave once a year and lays up in bed all day and stays out all night running after women. If that seagoing son of a bitch comes here again, I'll kill him!"

"Yonder goes your jack, Mr. Hod," Amos said.

Daisy stuck her head out of the window again. She was looking to see where the jack was, and she did not look at Hod. She was standing there pulling at herself, and getting more wild-eyed every second. She disappeared from sight as quickly as she had first appeared.

"Come on, you black bastard," Hod said; "let's go after him. I ought to pick up a stick and break your neck for bringing that God damn jack here to raise the devil. He's got the mare kicking down the barn, and Daisy is in there acting crazy as hell."

They started out across the broom sedge after the loping jack. The jack was headed for Folger, a mile away.

"If I ever get my hands on that jack, I'll twist his neck till it looks like a corkscrew," Hod panted, running and leaping over the yellow broom sedge. "Ain't no female safe around a sailor or a jack, and here I am running off after one, and leaving the other in the house."

They lost sight of the jackass in a short while. The beast had begun to circle the town, and he was now headed down the side of the railroad tracks behind the row of Negro cabins. They soon saw him again, though, when the jack slowed down at a pasture where some horses were grazing.

A hundred yards from the cabins they had to run down into a gully. Just as they were crawling up the other side, a Negro girl suddenly appeared in front of them, springing up from nowhere. She was standing waist-high in the broom sedge, and she was as naked as a pickaninny.

Hod stopped and looked at her.

"Did you see a jack?" he said to her.

"White-folks, I saw that jack, and he brayed right in my face. I just jumped up and started running. I can't sit still when I hear a jackass bray."

Hod started off again, but he stopped and came back to look at the girl.

"Put your clothes back on," he said. "You'll get raped running around in the sedge this close to town like that."

"White-captain," she said, "I ain't hard to rape. I done heard that jackass bray."

Hod turned and looked at Amos for a moment. Amos was walking around in a circle with his hands in his pockets.

"Come on," Hod told him, breaking through the broom sedge. "Let's get that jack, Amos."

They started towards the pasture where the jack had stopped. When the jack saw them coming, he turned and bolted over the railroad tracks and started jogging up the far side of the right-of-way towards Folger. Hod cut across to head him off and Amos was right behind to help.

There were very few men in town at that time of day. Several store-keepers sat on Coca-Cola crates on the sidewalk under the shade of the water-oak trees, and several man were whittling white pine and chewing tobacco. The bank was open, and RB, the cashier, was standing in the door looking out across the railroad tracks and dusty street. Down at the lumber mill, the saws whined hour after hour.

The jack slowed down and ran into the hitching yard behind the brick bank. When Hod saw that the jack had stopped, he stopped running and tried to regain his breath. Both he and Amos were panting and sweating. The August sun shone down on the dry baked clay in the oval where the town was and remained there until sunset.

Hod and Amos sat down in the shade of the depot and fanned themselves with their hats. The jack was standing calmly behind the bank, switching flies with his tail.

"Give me back my fifty cents, Amos," Hod said. "You can have that God-damn jack. I don't want him."

"I couldn't do that, Mr. Hod," Amos pleaded. "We done made the trade, and I can't break it now. You'll just have to keep that jack. He's yours now. If you want to get shed of him, go sell him to somebody else. I don't want that jack. I'd heap rather have my old dollar watch back again. I wish I'd never seen that jack in all my life. I can do without him."

Hod said nothing. He looked at the brick bank and saw RB looking out across the railroad tracks towards the stores where the men were sitting on upturned Coca-Cola crates in the water-oak shade.

"Sit here and wait," Hod said, getting up. "I've just thought of something. You sit here and keep your eyes on that jack till I come back."

"You won't be gone long, will you, Mr. Hod? I don't mind watching your animal for you, but I'd sure hate to have to look at that jack any more than I'm compelled to. He don't like my looks, and I sure don't like his. That's the ugliest-looking creature that's ever been in this country."

"Wait here till I get back," Hod said, crossing the tracks and walking towards the brick bank.

RB saw Hod coming, and he went back inside and stood behind his cashier's cage.

Hod walked in, took off his hat and leaned his arm on the little shelf in front of the cage.

"Hello, RB," he said. "It's hot today, ain't it?"

"Do you want to deposit money, or make a loan?"

Hod fanned himself and spat into the cuspidor.

"Miss it?" RB asked, trying to see through the grill.

"Not quite," Hod said.

RB spat into his own cuspidor at his feet.

"What can I do for you?" he said.

"Well, I'll tell you, RB," Hod said. "It's like this. You've got all this money here in the bank and it ain't doing you much good where it is. And here I come with all my money tied up in livestock. There ain't but one answer to that, is there?"

"When did you get some livestock, Hod?" he asked. "I didn't know you had anything but that old mare and that gray mule."

"I made a trade today," Hod said, "and now just when my money is all tied up in livestock, I find a man who's willing to let me in on a timber deal. I need fifty dollars to swing my share. There ain't no use trying to farm these days, RB. That's why I'm going in for livestock and timber."

"How many head of stock do you own?"

"Well, I've got that mare, Ida, out there at my place, but I ain't counting her. And likewise that old mule."

"How many others do you own?"

"I purchased a high-class stud animal this morning, RB, and I paid out all my ready cash in the deal."

"A bull?"

"No, not exactly a bull, RB."

"What was it then?"

"A jackass, RB."

"A jackass!"

"That's right."

"Who in hell wants to own a jackass, Hod? I can't lend the bank's money on a jackass."

"You're in the money-lending business, RB, and I've got an animal to mortgage. What else do you want? I'm putting up my jack, and you're putting up your money. That's business, RB. That's good business."

"Yes, but suppose you force me to foreclose the mortgage — I'd have the jack, and then maybe I couldn't find a buyer. Jackass buyers are pretty scarce customers, Hod. I don't recall ever seeing one."

"Anybody would give you a hundred dollars for a good high-class jack, RB. If you knew as much about farming and stock-raising as you do about banking, you'd recognize that without me having to tell you."

"What does a jackass look like?"

"A jack don't look so good to the eye, RB, but that's not a jack's high point. When a jack brays — "

RB came running around from behind his cage and caught Hod by the arm. He was so excited that he was trembling.

"Is that what I heard last night, Hod?"

"What?"

"A jackass braying."

"Wouldn't be surprised if you did. Amos was out exercising him last night, and he said the jack brayed almost all night long."

"Come back here with me," RB said, still shaking. "I'm going to let you have that loan, and take a mortgage on that jack. I want to have a hand in it. If I'll let you have the loan, will you let me take the jack home and keep him at my house for about a week, Hod?"

"You're more than welcome to him, RB. You can keep him all the time if you want to. But why do you want to keep a jack at your house? You don't breed mules, do you?"

RB had Hod sign the papers before he replied. He then counted out five ten-dollar bills and put them into Hod's hand.

"This is just between me and you, Hod," he said. "Me and my wife haven't been on speaking terms for more than a month now. She cooks my meals and does her housework, but she's been mad at me about something and she won't say a word or have anything to do with me. But last night, sometime after midnight, we were lying there in the bed, she as far on her side as she could get without falling out, and all at once I heard the damnedest yell I ever heard in all my life. It was that jackass braying. I know now what it was, but I didn't know then. That jack was somewhere out in the sedge, and when he brayed, the first thing I knew, my wife was all over me, she was that scared, or some-thing. That sounds like a lie, after I have told you about her not speaking to me for more than a month, and sleeping as far on her side of the bed as she could get without falling on the floor, but it's the truth if I know what the truth is. That jack brayed just once, and the first thing I knew, my wife was all over me, hugging me and begging me not to leave her. This morning she took up her old ways again, and that's why I want to stable that jack at my house for a week or two. He'll break up that streak of not talking and not having anything to do with me. That jack is what I am in need of, Hod."

Hod took the money and walked out of the bank towards the depot where Amos was.

"Where's the jack, Hod?" RB said, running after him.

"Out there behind your bank," Hod said. "You can take him home with you tonight when you close up."

Amos got up to meet Hod.

"Come on, Amos," Hod said. "We're going home."

Amos looked back over his shoulder at the jack behind the bank, watching him until he was out of sight. They walked through the broom sedge, circling the big gully, on the way home.

When they reached the front yard, Hod saw Sam sitting under a chinaberry tree. Sam got up and stood leaning against the trunk.

"What are you doing here?" Hod asked him. "What are you hanging around here for? Go on home, Sam."

Sam came forward a step, and stepped backward two.

"Miss Daisy told me to tell you something for her," Sam said, chewing the words.

"She said what?"

"Mr. Hod, Miss Daisy and Mr. Shaw went off down the road while you was chasing that jack. Mr. Shaw said he was taking Miss Daisy with him back to the navy yard, and Miss Daisy said she was going off and never coming back."

Hod went to the front porch and sat down in the shade. His feet hung over the edge of the porch, almost touching the ground.

Amos walked across the yard and sat down on the steps. He looked at Hod for several minutes before he said anything.

"Mr. Hod," he said, chewing the words worse than his son had before him, "I reckon you'd better go back to Folger and get your jack. Looks like that jack has a powerful way of fretting the womenfolks, and you'd better get him to turn one in your direction."

(First published in *We Are the Living*)

The Grass Fire

DURING the last week of April nobody with any sense at all would have gone out and deliberately set fire to a hayfield. There had been no rainfall since the March thaw and the country was as dry as road dust in midsummer. The farmers who had fields that needed burning over were waiting for a heavy shower of rain to come and soak the ground thoroughly before they dared begin the spring firing.

Carl Abbott had been in the habit of burning over his fields the last week of April for the past thirty years and he said that he was not going to start that late in his life letting his new crop hay be ruined by raspberry bushes and gray-birch seedlings if he knew anything about it. The people in the town thought he was merely talking to himself again to make himself heard, and that he really had the good sense to keep fire away from dry grass until a hard rain had come. Carl was always talking about the way he stuck to his lifelong habits, and people never paid much attention to him any more, anyway.

It was late in the afternoon when Carl got ready to fire the field on the north side of his farm. He carried two buckets of water with him, and a broom, and went up the side road to the north field.

When he reached the gate, he saw Jake Thompson come driving down the backroad. Carl tried to get through the gate and behind the stone wall before Jake saw him, but he could not hide himself quickly enough because of the two buckets of water he was carrying, and his wooden leg.

"Hey there!" Jake called, whipping up his horse. "What you doing in that hayfield?"

Carl waited until Jake drove up to the gap in the wall. He put the buckets down and leaned against the broom handle.

"I'm standing here looking at you," Carl told him. "But I'm already tired of doing that, and so now I'm going in here and fire my hayfield."

"Why! you damned old fool," Jake said, "don't you know that you'll burn up your whole farm if you do that now? Feel that wind — it'll carry flame down across that meadow and into that wood lot before you know which way to look. Nobody with any sense would fire a hayfield until after a good heavy rain comes and soaks the ground."

"I didn't ask for the loan of any of your advice," Carl said.

"And I don't generally pass it around to every damn fool I meet, either," Jake said, "but I hate to have to sit here and see a man burn up all he's got and ever will have. The town's not going to raise money to waste on supporting you. There's too many just like you living on the town already."

"Guess I can live on the town if I've a mind to. Been paying taxes for thirty years and more."

"If it was left up to me," Jake said, "I'd dig a big hole in the ground and cover you up in it. And I'm man enough left to do it, too."

Carl stooped over and picked up the water buckets.

"Didn't you hear about that grass fire over in the east part of town day before yesterday?" Jake asked. "A man over there set fire to his hayfield and it got loose from him and burned up his wife."

"That's nothing to concern me," Carl said. "Haven't got a wife, and never felt the need for one. It's people with wives who do all the fool things in the world, anyway."

"Guess you're right about that," Jake said. "I was about to let it slip my mind that your daddy had a wife."

Carl turned around with the water buckets and walked a dozen yards out into the field. The dead grass was almost waist high, and it cracked and waved in the wind like chaff in a hay barn. Each time Carl took a step in the dead grass a puff of dust rose up behind him and blew away in the wind. Carl was beginning to believe that Jake was right after all. He had not realized how dry the country really was.

Jake drove his horse and buggy to the side of the road and crossed his legs. He sat back to wait and see how big a fool Carl Abbott really was.

"If you go and fire that hayfield, you'd better go take out some insurance on your stock and buildings. They won't be worth a dime otherwise; though I guess if I was hard put to it, I could give you a dollar for the ashes, including yours. They'd make the finest kind of top dressing for my potato field this year."

"If you've got any business of your own, why don't you go and attend to it?" Carl said. "Didn't invite you to stay here."

"By God, I pay just as many taxes for the upkeep of the town's roads as you do, Carl Abbott. Shall stand here until I get good and ready to go somewhere else."

Carl always said something or did something to make Jake angry whenever they got within sight or hearing distance of each other.

Jake crossed his legs again and snapped the leaves off a birch seedling with his horsewhip.

The wind was coming down from the northeast, but it shifted so frequently that nobody could have determined its true direction. In the month of April there was no way of finding out which way the wind was blowing. Jake had said that in April the wind came in all directions, except straight up, and that if man were to dig a hole in the ground it would come that way, too.

Carl stooped over in the grass and struck a match on the seat of his pants. He held the flame close to a tuft of grass and weathered it with his hands.

The flame flared up so quickly and so suddenly that it jumped up through his arms and singed his whiskers before he could get out of the way. The wind was true in the east just then, and it was blowing at about thirty miles an hour. The flame died down almost as suddenly as it had flared up, and a column of white smoke coiled straight upward for a few feet before it was caught in the wind and carried down over the meadow. The fire was smoldering in the dead grass, and the white smoke showed that it was feeding on the crisp dry tufts that grew around the stems like powder puffs. A hayfield could never be burned over completely if it were not for the small coils of grass that curled in tufts close to the ground. When the tufts blazed, the long waist-high stems caught and burned through. Then the tall grass fell over as if it were being mown with a scythe, and the fire would be under way, feeding itself far faster than any number of men could have done.

Jake Thompson watched the white smoke boil and curl in the air. He saw Carl walk over to one of the buckets and souse the broom in the water, taking all the time he wished. Then he went back to the fire and stood looking at it smolder in the tufts.

A fairly new, well-sewn house broom and a pail or two of water was the finest kind of fire-fighting equipment in a hayfield. But farmers who burned over hayfields rarely undertook such a task without having three or four men to help keep the fire under control. Six men who knew how to souse a broom in a bucket of water at the proper time, keeping it sufficiently wet so the broom-straw would not catch on fire, could burn over the largest hayfield in the state. Water alone would not even begin to put out a grass fire; it was the smothering of the flame with the broad side of the broom that kept it from spreading. But nobody with any sense at all would have thought of firing a field that year until a rain had come and made the ground moist and dampened the grass tufts. Under those conditions a field would have burned so slowly that one man could have kept it under control.

Jake knew that Carl did not have a chance in the world of being able to check that fire once it had got under way.

The white smoke was boiling upward in a column the size of a barrelhead by that time. The wind had shifted again, circling around Carl's back and blowing down across the meadow from a new angle. The grass tops bowed under the force of the wind, and the wind was changing so frequently that it kept the field waving first in one and then in some other direction. Carl looked around and overhead as if by that he were doing something that would cause the wind to die down into a breeze.

Jake crossed his legs again and waited to see what was going to happen next. Carl Abbott was without doubt the biggest fool he had ever known.

Suddenly the flames shot into the air higher than Carl's head and began leaping across the field towards the meadow like a pack of red foxes let loose. Carl jumped backward, stumbling, and overturning one of the buckets of water. The flames bent over under the force of the wind until they looked as if they were lying flat on top of the grass. That made the field burn even faster still, the leaping flame setting fire to the grass quicker than the eye could follow. It had been burning no longer than two or three minutes, but in that short time it had spread out into the shape of a quarter cut of pie, and it was growing larger and larger each second. Carl ran around in circles, his wooden leg sticking into the ground and tripping him with nearly every step. He would have to stop every step or two and take both hands to pull the wooden peg out of the ground.

"Hey there, Carl Abbott!" Jake shouted at him above the roar of the burning grass. "What in hell are you doing out there! Get away from that fire!"

Carl heard Jake but he paid no attention to what he said. He was trying to beat out the fire with his wet broom, but his work was not checking the flames in any direction. He was so excited that, instead of beating at the flames, most of the time he was holding the broom in the fire, and hitting the water buckets with his wooden leg. The broom caught on fire, and then he did not know which way to turn. When he did succeed in hitting at the fire with the broom, as fast as he smothered one tuft of grass it caught fire again almost immediately. In the meantime two or three fresh ones blazed up beside it.

"Come out of there, you damn fool!" Jake shouted at him. "You'll be cooked and ready to eat if you don't get out of that fire!"

Carl's hat had fallen off and had already burned into a handful of gray ashes. His whiskers were singed close to his face, making him appear at a distance as if he had had a shave, and his peg leg was charred. If he had stood still all the time he would not have been hurt, because the fire would have burned away from him; but Carl ran right into the hottest part of it, almost out of sight in the smoke and flame. His woolen pants were smoking, his coat was dropping off in smoking pieces, and a big black circle was spreading on his shirt where a spark had ignited the blue cotton cloth.

Jake jumped out of his buggy and ran into the hayfield calling Carl. He could not sit there and see a man burn himself alive, even if the man was Carl Abbott.

He grabbed Carl and dragged him away from the flame and threw him down on the ground where the grass had already burned over. Carl's wooden leg was burned completely through, and as he fell to the ground it broke off in half. All that was left of it was a charred pointed stub about six or eight inches long. Carl had made the peg himself, and, instead of using oak as Jake had advised him to do, he had made it out of white pine because, he said, it would be lighter to carry around. Jake dragged him by the collar to the gap in the stone wall and dumped him in the road. Carl tried to stand up, forgetting the burned-off peg, and he tumbled over into the drain ditch and lay there helplessly.

"You would go ahead and act like a damn fool, after all, wouldn't you?" Jake said. "It's a pity I didn't let you stay out there and make ashes. They would have been worth more than you are alive. Meat ashes make the finest kind of dressing for any kind of crop."

Carl sat up and looked through the gap in the stone wall at the smoking hayfield. The fire line had already reached the wood lot, and flame was beginning to shoot from the top of the pines and hemlocks. Two hundred yards farther away were Carl's buildings. He had a team of horses in the barn, and a cow. There would be no way in the world to save them once the fire had reached the barn and caught the dry hay.

Jake tossed Carl a stick and watched him hobble the best he could down the road towards his house and buildings.

"What are we going to do?" he begged Jake. "We can't let my stock and buildings burn up, too."

"What we?" Jake said. "You and who else? You're not talking to me, because I'm having nothing to do with all this mess. I told you what not to do when you came up here a little while ago, but you were so damn smart I couldn't get anything through your head. That's why I'm having nothing at all to do with all this mess."

Carl protested feebly. He tried to get up and run down the road, but he fell each time he attempted to stand up.

"Why! do you think I'd have people saying that they passed your place and saw me helping you put out a grass fire when nobody with any sense at all would ever have started one in this kind of weather? People in this town know I don't associate with crazy men. They know me better than that. That's why I don't want them to think I've lost my mind and gone plumb crazy with you."

Carl opened his mouth, but Jake had not finished.

"I wouldn't even spit on a blade of witch grass now if I thought it would help check that fire you started. Why! the townspeople would think I had a hand in starting it, if I went and helped you check it. Nobody would believe me if I tried to tell them I begged you not to fire your field in the beginning, and then went right out and helped you fight it. The townspeople have got better sense than to believe a tale like that. They know I wouldn't do a fool thing like you went and did. They know that I have better sense than to go out and start a fire in a hayfield when it hasn't rained yet this spring. I'm no fool, Carl Abbott, even if it does appear that I'm associating with one now."

"But you can't let my stock and buildings burn up," Carl said. "You wouldn't do that, would you, Jake? I've been a fair and honest friend of yours all my life, haven't I, Jake? And didn't I cast my vote for you when you wanted to be road commissioner?"

"So I can't, can't I? Well, you just stand there and watch me try to save your stock and buildings! And this is no time to be talking politics, either. Wouldn't help you, anyway, not after the way you did there in that hayfield. I told you not to go and fire that field, and you went right ahead like a damn fool and struck a match to it, just as if I had been talking to myself away over in another part of town. No! I'm not going to do anything about it—except talk. When the townspeople ask me how your farm and buildings came to catch on fire and burn up your stock and wood lot, I'll tell them you fired it."

Carl found a heavier stick and hobbled down the road towards his house and buildings. The fire had already run through the wood lot by that time, and, as they came around the bend in the road, flame was licking at the house and barn.

Jake walked behind Carl, coming down the road, and led his horse instead of riding in the buggy. He watched Carl try to run, and he thought once of putting him into the buggy, but he did not like the idea of doing that. Townspeople would say he was riding Carl around in his horse and buggy while the stock and buildings burned up.

When they got closer to the house, the roof was ablaze, and the barn was smoking. The hay in there was dry, and it looked as if it would burst into flame any second. Carl hobbled faster when he saw his buildings burning.

"Help me get my stock out, Jake," he begged. "You won't let my stock burn up, will you, Jake?"

Jake tied his horse to a tree beside the road and ran across the yard to the barn. He could not stand there and see a team of horses and a cow burn alive, even if they did belong to Carl Abbott. He ran to the barn and jerked open the stall doors.

An explosion of smoke, dust, and flame burst into his face, but the two horses and the cow bounded out the moment the stall doors were thrown open. The horses and cow ran across the yard and leaped over the brush by the roadside and disappeared into the field on the other side.

Jake knew it was a stroke of chance that enabled him to save the stock, because if the horses and cow had been farther in the barn, nothing could have induced them to leave it. The only way they could have been saved would have been to blindfold them and lead them out, and there would have been no time for that. The flame had already begun to reach the stalls.

Carl realized by that time that there was no chance of saving anything else. He saw the smoke and flame leap through the roof of the barn the moment that Jake had opened the stall doors. He felt terribly sick all over.

Jake went over to the tree and untied his horse. He climbed into the buggy and sat down. Carl stood looking at his burning buildings, and he was trying to lean on the big stick he had found up the backroad.

Jake whipped up his horse and started home. Carl turned around and saw him leave, but he had nothing to say.

"Whoa!" Jake said to his horse, pulling on the reins. He turned around in the buggy seat and called to Carl. "Well, I guess you'll have better sense than to do a thing like that again, won't you? Next time maybe you will be anxious to take some advice."

Carl glared at Jake, and turned with nothing to say to stand and watch the fire. Then suddenly he shouted at Jake.

"By God, the hayfield is burned over, ain't it?" he said, hobbling away. "Well, that's what I set out to do at the start."

Jake whipped up his horse and started for home. When he looked back for the last time, he saw Carl whittling on a pole. Carl had cut down a young pine and he was trimming it to replace the peg that had burned off in the hayfield. He wished to make the new one out of oak, but oak was the kind of wood that Jake had told him to use in the first place.

(First published in *We Are the Living*)

A Woman in the House

MAX CLOUGH was getting along well enough until Elam went away over the week end. Max had his winter's wood in, his house was sawdust-banked against the frost, and there was a good supply of pumpkin wine in the cellar. He had settled himself for a good three months' rest and he thought Elam had done the same. Both of them knew that winter was coming, as the ground was frozen every morning, and the sun was already beginning to set in the intervale by two o'clock.

But Elam went away over the week end. He went off without coming to tell Max about it, and he left early Saturday morning before it was light enough for Max to see him go.

Only a few days before, Max had gone across the road and talked for an hour or longer, but Elam had not said a word about going away. He had not even said that he was thinking of taking a short trip. They had talked about how dear money was getting to be, and how much improved the mail delivery was since Cliff Stone had taken over the route through the intervale, and about the propects for a new State highroad through the town. But Elam had said nothing about his going away over the week end. That was the reason why Max was upset Saturday morning when he went across the road to see Elam a moment, and found that the house was locked and that the shades were drawn.

"When a man gets to be thirty-six years old," Max said, looking sharply at the closed dwelling, "he ought to have sense enough to stay at home, instead of going off for week ends in Lewiston and throwing away dear money for lodging and what-not. Elam might possess a little sense about minor things, but he hasn't got the sense he was born with when it comes to throwing away dear money in Lewiston. Nobody but a plain fool would go to Lewiston and give a woman five-ten dollars for her bed."

He went back across the road and up the slope to his own house, glancing up the intervale and down it, as if he expected to see Elam coming home. But he knew Elam would not come home until Sunday afternoon. He had gone away before like that, and each time he had stayed the two whole days. He knew Elam would not return until the next afternoon.

Max's farm and buildings were on the eastern slope of the intervale, and Elam Stairs' were on the western slope. Between them was the Yorkfield town road. The only advantage Elam had, Max admitted, was longer sunlight in winter. The sun set on Max's house by two o'clock in midwinter, while Elam had an hour's longer sun. But Max was well enough pleased with his place, because he knew that his eastern slope grew better green peas. His land was well watered the year around; in midsummer, Elam's fields became dry.

For the rest of the afternoon and far into the evening, Max could not get off his mind Elam's trip. He did not envy him the week end in Lewiston, because he knew exactly how much it would cost, but he did not wish for Elam to slip off as he did three or four times a year. It upset his carefully planned living. He could do nothing while Elam was absent from home. He had become accustomed to seeing Elam somewhere about his farm at almost any hour of the day when he looked over at the western slope, and when Elam was not there, Max was at a loss to know how to continue doing his work. And, besides that, when Elam was away, there was always the possibility that he would not come back alone. He knew he could never get over Elam's bringing home somebody with him.

They had talked such things over many times. Each time Elam went to Lewiston, he came home talking about the women he had seen on the streets and in the lodginghouses. That was one reason why Max did not like for Elam to go there. Sooner or later, he knew Elam would bring home a woman.

"The women aren't suited to our lives, Elam," Max told him once. "You on your western slope, and me on my eastern slope, live as people ought to live. Just as soon as a man brings home a woman, his house is too small a space for him to live in, eight rooms or twelve rooms. Married, or housekeeper, there's no difference. It's a woman, and there's always trouble under a roof when you mix the two sexes. I wish to stay just as I am. I wish to live peacefully, and my wish is to die the same way."

"Can't somehow always agree with you, Max," Elam said, shaking his head. "You've got a lot of sense; good, sane, horse sense, Max. But God was required to make woman. Why! do you know that before there were any women, the men were fixing to tear the world to pieces unless women were provided?"

"Why?" Max asked.

"Why?" Elam said. "Why! because the men wouldn't stand for it any longer, that's why. They had to have housekeepers, or if they couldn't be had, just wives. There's a world of difference between the two, but at bottom they both are women, and that's what man had to have. Otherwise, us men would have to do all the sewing and cooking."

"Have always got along fairly well doing my own labor," Max said. "Never had a woman to do my work for me. I don't wish to have one in the house to cause trouble."

"Well," Elam said, "they may cause some trouble. I'm willing to grant you that. But taking all in all, their good points pretty well overbalance the bad ones. God was compelled to make them, and I don't aim to disuse anything that is provided. Guess I wish to get all there is in this life to make use of. No sense in letting it go to waste, or to have somebody else take my share, and his too. I wish to have all of everything that's due me."

Max was not convinced then, and he was still firm in his belief that a man could live more happily and peacefully in his house alone. None of the times when Elam tried to make Max admit that women were a necessary part of existence did he succeed. Max was steadfast in his determination to live his life apart from women.

Now that Elam had gone away on another of his quarterly trips to Lewiston, Max was afraid once again that he would bring home a housekeeper. On each occasion before, he had been on edge the whole time Elam was away, and he was never able to calm himself until he could go over and see that Elam had not brought back a housekeeper. He would not even take Elam's word for it. He would first ask Elam if he came home alone, and then he would go from room to room, looking behind doors and into closets, until he was satisfied in his own mind that there was no woman in the house. After that, he would feel better. He could then go back to his own house with a calm mind.

But Elam was away again for the week end, and Max could not sit still. He could not eat his meals, and he could not sleep. He sat beside his window looking across to the western slope, his window raised several inches in case there should be the sound of an automobile in the intervale. He sat by the window all day Saturday, Saturday evening, and Sunday.

Late Sunday afternoon, when Max knew it was time for Elam to come back home, he heard Elam's automobile coming up the intervale. He knew it was Elam's car, and he knew he could not sit there another minute. He jumped up and found his hat and coat and started down the front doorstep.

The road was not within sight of Max's house, as there was a grove of birch trees down there, and he could not see the automobile. He heard Elam drive into his lane, however, and he waited and listened until the sound of the motor stopped abruptly in the barn.

There was something about the abruptness of the sound's stopping that caused him to pause on the doorstep. The motor was shut off the moment the car entered the barn, and then there was complete silence again in the intervale. Not even the rumbling sound of Elam closing the barn doors could be heard. Max wondered if Elam could be in such a hurry to get into his house that he had not waited to close the barn doors. He could not think of any reason to explain that. A man who was in such a great hurry to get into his house would certainly have something of importance coming up. Max thought about that, but he could think of no reason why a man would fail to close the barn doors.

He sat down on the doorstep and waited. He turned his head from side to side, allowing each ear to try to detect some sound in the intervale. Surely, he thought to himself, Elam had not gone and lost his mind. But he could think of no other reason for Elam's failure to close the barn doors. A man who drove his automobile into the barn and then left the doors open would certainly be foolish, and Elam had not been known theretofore as a foolish man. Elam knew better than to leave the barn doors open when evening was coming.

The sun in the intervale was dim and gray. A bank of gray clouds had risen in the northwest, and before long there would be no more sunshine. It was after three o'clock then, and the sun had already set on the western slope. Max had become accustomed to two o'clock sunsets on the eastern slope of the intervale, but when it set before three o'clock on the western slope, he was unprepared for it.

During all the time that he had been sitting on his doorstep, Max had hoped that Elam would come over to see him and tell him about the trip to Lewiston. Elam had always done that. Each time Elam had gone away for the week end in Lewiston, he had come home Sunday afternoon, had slammed shut the barn doors, and then had walked down the lane and up the slope and told Max what he had seen and what he had done in Lewiston. It was long past the time for him to come, and he had not even closed the barn doors. Max could not sit still and wait for Elam any longer. He got up and started down the slope towards the road.

When he reached the road, he stopped a moment and looked up towards Elam's farm and buildings. The barn door was wide open, and the automobile stood there exposed to the weather. There was no one to be seen about the house, but the shades had been opened, and the entrance door was ajar. Something was wrong, Max thought. Something had happened to Elam this time on his trip to Lewiston.

Standing beside Elam's mail box, Max looked up the slope towards the house. It was only a few hundred yards away, and he could see everything as plainly as if he had been standing on the doorstep. The white paint was whiter than ever in the gray twilight of the intervale, and the green trim was brighter than the grass in midsummer. Max stood looking at the place, waiting.

He had been staring at the house for ten minutes without seeing a single sign of Elam, when suddenly Elam appeared at one of the windows. He raised the window with a single thrust of his arm, and stuck out his head. Immediately another window was raised, on the opposite corner of the house, and a woman stuck out her head. They looked at each other for a moment, and then both withdrew their heads and the windows were lowered so quickly that Max was certain that the glass had been cracked. For a few seconds he did not believe what his eyes had seen. He would not believe that he had actually seen a woman in Elam's house. But slowly the realization came to him that he had seen a woman there, a young woman with a full body and yellow hair, and he stepped backward off Elam's land into the public road.

After what he had seen, Max did not know whether to stand there looking at the house, or whether to turn and go back up the slope to his own place. He knew he would never again set foot on Elam's land, however; he had already made up his mind never to have anything more to do with Elam Stairs. He did not even wish to speak to him again. He could never forgive Elam for having brought home a woman from Lewiston.

While he stood in the road trying to make up his mind about what he was going to do, the woman he had first seen in the window came running around the corner of the house. Max stared unbelievingly. Then a moment later came Elam, running faster than Max thought it possible for anyone to run. He was overtaking the yellow-haired young woman, two strides to her one, and if they had not turned the other corner of the house at that moment, he would have seen Elam grab her. Elam had his coat off, and the woman's dress was open down her back all the way to her waist. The woman was laughing, but Elam was not.

Max waited another five minutes, wishing to be there in case they again ran around the house. Then he turned and walked slowly up the eastern slope of the intervale. The sight of a woman at Elam's house made him wish to go over there and drive her out of the intervale, but he knew he could never do that. Elam would not allow him to run her away. Elam would protect her, and send him back across the road.

By the time that Max had reached his own house, he had definitely made up his mind about what he was going to do. He was going to take a trip himself the following week end. He was going down to Lewiston Saturday morning and stay there until Sunday afternoon. And while he was there he would do the same things that Elam had done.

"Elam Stairs isn't the only man in the intervale who can bring home a woman," he said, taking his seat beside the window and looking over at the western slope where the sun had set. He raised the window several inches so that he might hear any sound that was audible in the intervale. "Will hire me a housekeeper in Lewiston and bring her back here, too. Elam Stairs has an hour's more sunshine because his farm and buildings are on the western slope, and he thinks he can have even more advantage with a housekeeper. But he shan't. I'll show him that I can go to Lewiston and maybe get a finer-looking housekeeper than he's got."

Max hitched his chair closer to the window.

"Guess I'll chase mine thrice around the house when I bring her here," he said. "And it might be a good plan to wait till she gets right in the middle of changing her clothes to start chasing her, instead of starting after her like Elam did when she only had her dress unfastened down her back. Guess Elam Stairs will see as how I made a pretty smart deal, when he looks out his window some fine day and sees me chasing a naked housekeeper, and gaining on her three strides to her one. He chased his woman once around the house, so I'll chase mine thrice around, with maybe an extra time to show him what I can do when I get good and started."

Max paused to look out across the intervale. While he watched Elam's house, he began going through the motions of washing his hands.

"Don't guess Elam's idea was so bad, after all. Can't think of much to quarrel about with a Lewiston young woman in the house, and not having to pay her five-ten dollars for her bed over the week end."

(First published in *We Are the Living*)

Horse Thief

I DIDN'T steal Lud Moseley's calico horse.

People all over have been trying to make me out a thief, but anybody who knows me at all will tell you that I've never been in trouble like this before in all my life. Mr. John Turner will tell you all about me. I've worked for him, off and on, for I don't know exactly how many years. I reckon I've worked for him just about all my life, since I was a boy. Mr. John knows I wouldn't steal a horse. That's why I say I didn't steal Lud Moseley's, like he swore I did. I didn't grow up just to turn out to be a horse thief.

Night before last, Mr. John told me to ride his mare, Betsy. I said I wanted to go off a little way after something, and he told me to go ahead and ride Betsy, like I have been doing every Sunday night for going on two years now. Mr. John told me to take the Texas saddle, but I told him I didn't care about riding saddle. I like to ride with a bridle and reins, and nothing else. That's the best way to ride, anyway. And where I was going I didn't want to have a squeaking saddle under me. I wasn't up to no mischief. It was just a little private business of my own that nobody has got a right to call me down about. I nearly always rode saddle Sunday nights, but night before last was Thursday night, and that's why I didn't have a saddle when I went.

Mr. John Turner will tell you I'm not the kind to go off and get into trouble. Ask Mr. John about me. He has known me all my life, and I've never given him or anybody else trouble.

When I took Betsy out of the stable that night after supper, Mr. John came out to the barnyard and asked me over again if I didn't want to take the Texas saddle. That mare, Betsy, is a little rawboned, but I didn't mind that. I told Mr. John I'd just as lief ride bareback. He said it was all right with him if I wanted to get sawn in two, and for me to go ahead and do like I pleased about it. He was standing right there all the time, rubbing

Betsy's mane, and trying to find out where I was going, without coming right out and asking me. But he knew all the time where I was going, because he knows all about me. I reckon he just wanted to have a laugh at me, but he couldn't do that if I didn't let on where I was headed. So he told me it was all right to ride his mare without a saddle if I didn't want to be bothered with one, and I opened the gate and rode off down the road towards Bishop's crossroads.

That was night before last — Thursday night. It was a little after dark then, but I could see Mr. John standing at the barnyard gate, leaning on it a little, and watching me ride off. I'd been plowing that day, over in the new ground, and I was dog-tired. That's one reason why I didn't gallop off like I always did on Sunday nights. I rode away slow, letting Betsy take her own good time, because I wasn't in such a big hurry, after all. I had about two hours' time to kill, and only a little over three miles to go. That's why I went off like that.

II

Everybody knows I've been going to see Lud Moseley's youngest daughter, Naomi. I was going to see her again that night. But I couldn't show up there till about nine-thirty. Lud Moseley wouldn't let me come to see her but once a week, on Sunday nights, and night before last was Thursday. I'd been there to see her three or four times before on Thursday nights that Lud Moseley didn't know about. Naomi told me to come to see her on Thursday night. That's why I had been going there when Lud Moseley said I couldn't come to his house but once a week. Naomi told me to come anyway, and she had been coming out to the swing under the trees in the front yard to meet me.

I haven't got a thing in the world against Lud Moseley. Mr. John Turner will tell you I haven't. I don't especially like him, but that's to be expected, and he knows why. Once a week isn't enough to go to see a girl you like a lot, like I do Naomi. And I reckon she likes me a little, or she wouldn't tell me to come to see her on Thursday nights, when Lud Moseley told me not to come. Lud Moseley thinks if I go to see her more than once a week that maybe we'll take it into our heads to go get married without giving him a chance to catch on. That's why he said I couldn't come to his house but once a week, on Sunday nights.

He's fixing to have me sent to the penitentiary for twenty years for steal-ing his calico horse, Lightfoot. I reckon he knows good and well I didn't steal the horse, but he figures he's got a good chance to put me out of the way till he can get Naomi married to somebody else. That's the way I figure it all out, because everybody in this part of the country who ever heard tell of me knows I'm not a horse thief. Mr. John Turner will tell you that about me. Mr. John knows me better than that. I've worked for him so long he even tried once to make me out as one of the family, but I wouldn't let him do that.

So, night before last, Thursday night, I rode off from home bareback, on Betsy. I killed a little time down at the creek, about a mile down the road from where we live, and when I looked at my watch again, it was nine o'clock sharp. I got on Betsy and rode off towards Lud Moseley's place. Everything was still and quiet around the house and barn. It was just about Lud's bedtime then. I rode right up to the barnyard gate, like I always did on Thursday nights. I could see a light up in Naomi's room, where she slept with her older sister, Mary Lee. We had always figured on Mary Lee's being out with somebody else, or maybe being ready to go to sleep by nine-thirty. When I looked up at their window, I could see Naomi lying across her bed, and Mary Lee was standing beside the bed talking to her about something. That looked bad, because when Mary Lee tried to make Naomi undress and go to bed before she did, it always meant that it would take Naomi another hour or more to get out of the room, because she had to wait for Mary Lee to go to sleep before she could leave. She had to wait for Mary Lee to go to sleep, and then she had to get up and dress in the dark before she could come down to the front yard and meet me in the swing under the trees.

III

I sat there on Betsy for ten or fifteen minutes, waiting to see how Naomi was going to come out with her sister. I reckon if we had let Mary Lee in on the secret she would have behaved all right about it, but on some account or other Naomi couldn't make up her mind to run the risk of it. There was a mighty chance that she would have misbehaved about it and gone straight and told Lud Moseley, and we didn't want to run that risk.

After a while I saw Naomi get up and start to undress. I knew right away that that meant waiting another hour or longer for her to be able to come and meet me. The moon was starting to rise, and it was getting to be as bright as day out there in the barnyard. I'd been in the habit of opening the gate and turning Betsy loose in the yard, but I was scared to do it night before last. If Lud Moseley should get up for a drink of water or something, and happen to look out toward the barn and see a horse standing there, he would either think it was one of his and come out and lock it in the stalls, or else he would catch on it was me out there. Anyway, as soon as he saw Betsy, he would have known it wasn't his mare, and there would have been the mischief to pay right there and then. So I opened the barn door and led Betsy inside and put her in the first empty stall I could find in the dark. I was scared to strike a light, because I didn't know but what Lud Moseley would be looking out the window just at that time and see the flare of the match. I put Betsy in the stall, closed the door, and came back outside to wait for Naomi to find a chance to come out and meet me in the swing in the yard.

It was about twelve-thirty or one o'clock when I got ready to leave for home. The moon had been clouded, and it was darker than everything in the barn. I couldn't see my hand in front of me, it was that dark. I was scared to strike a light that time, too, and I felt my way in and opened the stall door and stepped inside to lead Betsy out. I couldn't see a thing, and when I found her neck, I thought she must have slipped her bridle like she was always doing when she had to stand too long to suit her. I was afraid to try to ride her home without a lead of some kind, because I was scared she might shy in the barnyard and start tearing around out there and wake up Lud Moseley. I felt around on the ground for the bridle, but I couldn't find it anywhere. Then I went back to the stall door and felt on it, thinking I might have taken it off myself when I was all excited at the start, and there was a halter hanging up. I slipped it over her head and led her out. It was still so dark I couldn't see a thing, and I had to feel my way outside and through the barnyard gate. When I got to the road, I threw a leg over her, and started for home without wasting any more time around Lud Moseley's place. I thought she trotted a little funny, because she had a swaying swing that made me slide from side to side, and I didn't have a saddle pommel to hold on to. I was all wrought up about getting away from there without getting caught up with, and I didn't think a thing about it. But I got home all right and slipped the halter off and put her in her stall. It was around one or two o'clock in the morning then.

The next morning after breakfast, when I was getting ready to catch the mules and gear them up to start plowing in the new ground again, Lud Moseley and three or four other men, including the sheriff, came riding lickety-split up the road from town and hitched at the rack. Mr. John came out and slapped the sheriff on the back and told him a funny story. They carried on like that for nearly half an hour, and then the sheriff asked Mr. John where I was. Mr. John told him I was getting ready to go off to the new ground, where we had planted a crop of corn that spring, and then the sheriff said he had a warrant for me. Mr. John asked him what for, a joke or something? And the sheriff told him it was for stealing Lud Moseley's calico horse, Lightfoot. Mr. John laughed at him, because he still thought it just a joke, but the sheriff pulled out the paper and showed it to him. Mr. John still wouldn't believe it, and he told them there was a mix-up somewhere, because, he told them, I wouldn't steal a horse. Mr. John knows I'm not a horse thief. I've never been in any kind of trouble before in all my life.

They brought me to town right away and put me in the cellroom at the sheriff's jail. I knew I hadn't stole Lud Moseley's horse, and I wasn't scared a bit about it. But right after they brought me to town, they all rode back and the sheriff looked in the barn and found Lud Moseley's calico horse, Lightfoot, in Betsy's stall. Mr. John said things were all mixed up, because he knew I didn't steal the horse, and he knew I wouldn't do it. But the horse was there, the calico one, Lightfoot, and his halter was hanging on the stall door. After that they went back to Lud Moseley's and measured my foot tracks in the barnyard, and then they found Betsy's bridle. Lud Moseley said I had rode Mr. John's mare over there, turned her loose, and put the bridle on his Lightfoot and rode him off. They never did say how come the halter came to get to Mr. John's stable, then. Lud Moseley's stall door was not locked, and it wasn't broken down. It looks now like I forgot to shut it tight when I put Betsy in, because she got out someway and came home of her own accord sometime that night.

Lud Moseley says he's going to send me away for twenty years where I won't have a chance to worry him over his youngest daughter, Naomi. He wants her to marry a widowed farmer over beyond Bishop's crossroads who runs twenty plows and who's got a big white house with fifteen rooms in it. Mr. John Turner says he'll hire the best lawyer in town to take up my case, but it don't look like it will do much good, because my footprints are all over Lud Moseley's barnyard, and his Lightfoot was in Mr. John's stable.

I reckon I could worm out of it someway, if I made up my mind to do it. But I don't like to do things like that. It would put Naomi in a bad way, because if I said I was there seeing her, and had put Betsy in the stall to keep her quiet, and took Lightfoot out by mistake in the dark when I got ready to leave — well, it would just look bad, that's all. She would just have to say she was in the habit of slipping out of the house to see me after everybody had gone to sleep, on Thursday nights, and it would just look bad all around. She might take it into her head some day that she'd rather marry somebody else than me, and by that time she'd have a bad name for having been mixed up with me — and slipping out of the house to meet me after bedtime.

Naomi knows I'm no horse thief. She knows how it all happened — that I rode Lud Moseley's calico horse, Lightfoot, off by mistake in the dark, and left the stall door unfastened, and Betsy got out and came home of her own accord.

Lud Moseley has been telling people all around the courthouse as how he is going to send me away for twenty years so he can get Naomi married to that widowed farmer who runs twenty plows. Lud Moseley is right proud of it, it looks like to me, because he's got me cornered in a trap, and maybe he will get me sent away sure enough before Naomi gets a chance to tell what she knows is true.

But, somehow, I don't know if she'll say it if she does get the chance. Everybody knows I'm nothing but a hired man at Mr. John Turner's, and I've been thinking that maybe Naomi might not come right out and tell what she knows, after all.

I'd come right out and explain to the sheriff how the mix-up happened, but I sort of hate to mention Naomi's name in the mess. If it had been a Sunday night, instead of night before last, a Thursday, I could — well, it would just sound too bad, that's all.

If Naomi comes to town and tells what she knows, I won't say a word to stop her, because that'll mean she's willing to say it and marry me.

But if she stays at home, and lets Lud Moseley and that widowed farmer send me away for twenty years, I'll just have to go, that's all.

I always told Naomi I'd do anything in the world for her, and I reckon this will be the time when I've got to prove whether I'm a man of my word, or not.

(First published in *Vanity Fair*)

Country Full of Swedes

THERE I was, standing in the middle of the chamber, trembling like I was coming down with the flu, and still not knowing what God-awful something had happened. In all my days in the Back Kingdom, I never heard such noises so early in the forenoon.

It was about half an hour after sunrise, and a gun went off like a coffer-dam breaking up under ice at twenty below, and I'd swear it sounded like it wasn't any farther away than my feet are from my head. That gun shot off, pitching me six-seven inches off the bed, and, before I could come down out of the air, there was another roar like somebody coughing through a megaphone, with a two-weeks cold, right in my ear. God-helping, I hope I never get waked up like that again until I can get myself home to the Back Kingdom where I rightfully belong to stay.

I must have stood there ten-fifteen minutes shivering in my nightshirt, my heart pounding inside of me like a ramrod working on a plugged-up bore, and listening for that gun again, if it was going to shoot some more. A man never knows what's going to happen next in the State of Maine; that's why I wish sometimes I'd never left the Back Kingdom to begin with. I was making sixty a month, with the best of bed and board, back there in the intervale; but like a God-damn fool I had to jerk loose and came down here near the Bay. I'm going back where I came from, God-helping; I've never had a purely calm and peaceful day since I got here three-four years ago. This is the damnedest country for the unexpected raising of all kinds of unlooked-for hell a man is apt to run across in a lifetime of travel-ing. If a man's born and raised in the Back Kingdom, he ought to stay there where he belongs; that's what I'd done if I'd had the sense to stay out of this down-country near the Bay, where you don't ever know, God-helping, what's going to happen next, where, or when.

But there I was, standing in the middle of the upstairs chamber, shaking like a ragweed in an August windstorm, and not knowing what minute, maybe right at me, that gun was going to shoot off again, for all I knew. Just then, though, I heard Jim and Mrs. Frost trip-trapping around downstairs in their bare feet. Even if I didn't know what God-awful something had happened, I knew things around the place weren't calm and peaceful, like they generally were of a Sunday morning in May, because it took a stiff mixture of heaven and hell to get Jim and Mrs. Frost up and out of a warm bed before six of a forenoon, any of the days of the week.

I ran to the window and stuck my head out as far as I could get it, to hear what the trouble was. Everything out there was as quiet and peaceful as midnight on a back road in middlemost winter. But I knew something was up, because Jim and Mrs. Frost didn't make a practice of getting up and out of a warm bed that time of forenoon in the chillish Maytime.

There wasn't any sense in me standing there in the cold air shivering in my nightshirt, so I put on my clothes, whistling all the time through my teeth to drive away the chill, and trying to figure out what God-damn fool was around so early shooting off a gun of a Sunday morning. Just then I heard the downstairs door open, and up the steps, two at a time, came Jim in his breeches and his shirttail flying out behind him.

He wasn't long in coming up the stairs, for a man sixty-seven, but before he reached the door to my room, that gun went off again: Boom! Just like that; and the echo came rolling back through the open window from the hills: *Boom! Boom!* Like fireworks going off with your eyes shut. Jim had busted through the door already, but when he heard that *Boom!* sound he sort of spun around, like a cockeyed weathervane, five-six times, and ran out of the door again like he had been shot in the hind parts with a moose gun. That *Boom!* so early in the forenoon was enough to scare the daylights out of any man, and Jim wasn't any different from me or anybody else in the town of East Joloppi. He just turned around and jumped through the door to the first tread on the stairway like his mind was made up to go somewhere else in a hurry, and no fooling around at the start.

I'd been hired to Jim and Mrs. Frost for all of three-four years, and I was near about as much of a Frost, excepting name, as Jim himself was. Jim and me got along first-rate together, doing chores and haying and farm work in general, because neither one of us was ever trying to make the other do more of the work. We were hitched to make a fine team, and I never had a kick coming, and Jim said he didn't either. Jim had the name of Frost, to be sure, but I wouldn't ever hold that against a man.

The echo of that gunshot was still rolling around in the hills and coming in through the window, when all at once that God-awful coughlike whoop through a megaphone sounded again right there in the room and everywhere else, like it might have been, in the whole town of East Joloppi. The man or beast or whatever animal he was who hollered like that ought to be locked up to keep him from scaring all the women and children to death, and it wasn't any stomach-comforting sound for a grown man who's used to the peaceful calm of the Back Kingdom all his life to hear so early of a Sunday forenoon, either.

I jumped to the door where Jim, just a minute before, leaped through. He didn't stop till he got clear to the bottom of the stairs. He stood there, looking up at me like a wild-eyed cow moose surprised in the sheriff's corn field.

"Who fired that God-awful shot, Jim?" I yelled at him, leaping down the stairs quicker than a man of my years ought to let himself do.

"Good God!" Jim said, his voice hoarse, and falling all to pieces like a stump of punkwood. "The Swedes! The Swedes are shooting, Stan!"

"What Swedes, Jim — those Swedes who own the farm and buildings across the road over there?" I said, trying to find the buttonholes in my shirt. "Have they come back here to live on that farm?"

"Good God, yes!" he said, his voice croaking deep down in his throat, like he had swallowed too much water. "The Swedes are all over the place. They're everywhere you can see, there's that many of them."

"What's their name, Jim?" I asked him. "You and Mrs. Frost never told me what their name is."

"Good God, I don't know. I never heard them called anything but Swedes, and that's what it is, I guess. It ought to be that, if it ain't."

I ran across the hall to look out a window, but it was on the wrong side of the house, and I couldn't see a thing. Mrs. Frost was stepping around in the downstairs chamber, locking things up in the drawers and closet and forgetting where she was hiding the keys. I could see her through the open door, and she was more scared-looking than Jim was. She was so scared of the Swedes she didn't know what she was doing, none of the time.

"What made those Swedes come back for, Jim?" I said to him. "I thought you said they were gone for good, this time."

"Good God, Stan," he said, "I don't know what they came back for. I guess hard times are bringing everybody back to the land, and the Swedes are always in the front rush of everything. I don't know what brought them back, but they're all over the place, shooting and yelling and raising hell. There are thirty-forty of them, looks like to me, counting everything with heads."

"What are they doing now, Jim, except yelling and shooting?"

"Good God," Jim said, looking behind him to see what Mrs. Frost was doing with his things in the downstairs chamber. "I don't know what they're not doing. But I can hear them, Stan! You hurry out right now and lock up all the tools in the barn and bring in the cows and tie them up in the stalls. I've got to hurry out now and bring in all of those new cedar fence posts across the front of the yard before they start pulling them up and carrying them off. Good God, Stan, the Swedes are everywhere you look outdoors! We've got to make haste, Stan!"

Jim ran to the side door and out the back of the house, but I took my time about going. I wasn't scared of the Swedes, like Jim and Mrs. Frost were, and I didn't aim to have Jim putting me to doing tasks and chores, or anything else, before breakfast and the proper time. I wasn't any more scared of the Swedes than I was of the Finns and Portuguese, anyway. It's a God-awful shame for Americans to let Swedes and Finns and the Portuguese scare the daylights out of them. God-helping, they are no different than us, and you never see a Finn or a Swede scared of an American. But people like Jim and Mrs. Frost are scared to death of Swedes and other people from the old countries; Jim and Mrs. Frost and people like that never stop to think that all of us Americans came over from the old countries, one time or another, to begin with.

But there wasn't any sense in trying to argue with Jim and Mrs. Frost right then, when the Swedes, like a fired nest of yellow-headed bumblebees, were swarming all over the place as far as the eye could see, and when Mrs. Frost was scared to death that they were coming into the house and carry out all of her and Jim's furniture and household goods. So while Mrs. Frost was tying her and Jim's shoes in pillowcases and putting them out of sight in closets and behind beds, I went to the kitchen window and looked out to see what was going on around that tall yellow house across the road.

Jim and Mrs. Frost both were right about there being Swedes all over the place. God-helping, there were Swedes all over the country, near about all over the whole town of East Joloppi, for what I could see out of the window. They were as thick around the barn and pump and the woodpile as if they had been a nest of yellow-headed bumblebees strewn over the countryside. There were Swedes everywhere a man could see, and the ones that couldn't be seen could be heard yelling their heads off inside the yellow clapboarded house across the road. There wasn't any mistake about there being Swedes there, either; because I've never yet seen a man who mistakes a Swede or a Finn for an American. Once you see a Finn or a Swede you know, God-helping, that he is a Swede or a Finn, and not a Portugee or an American.

There was a Swede everywhere a man could look. Some of them were little Swedes, and women Swedes, to be sure; but little Swedes, in the end, and women Swedes too, near about, grow up as big as any of them. When you come right down to it, there's no sense in counting out the little Swedes and the women Swedes.

Out in the road in front of their house were seven-eight autos and trucks loaded down with furniture and household goods. All around, everything was Swedes. The Swedes were yelling and shouting at one another, the little Swedes and the women Swedes just as loud as the big Swedes, and it looked like none of them knew what all the shouting and yelling was for, and when they found out, they didn't give a damn about it. That was because all of them were Swedes. It didn't make any difference what a Swede was yelling about; just as long as he had leave to open his mouth, he was tickled to death about it.

I have never seen the like of so much yelling and shouting anywhere else before; but down here in the State of Maine, in the down-country on the Bay, there's no sense in being taken back at the sights to be seen, because anything on God's green earth is likely and liable to happen between day and night, and the other way around, too.

Now, you take the Finns; there's any God's number of them around in the woods, where you least expect to see them, logging and such. When a Finn crew breaks a woods camp, it looks like there's a Finn for every tree in the whole State, but you don't see them going around making the noise that Swedes do, with all their yelling and shouting and shooting off guns. Finns are quiet about their hell-raising. The Portuguese are quiet, too; you see them tramping around, minding their own business, and working hard on a river dam or something, but you never hear them shouting and yelling and shooting off guns at five-six of a Sunday morning. There's no known likeness to the noise that a houseful of Swedes can make when they get to yelling and shouting at one another early in the forenoon.

I was standing there all that time, looking out the window at the Swedes across the road, when Jim came into the kitchen with an armful of wood and threw it into the wood box behind the range.

"Good God, Stan," Jim said, "the Swedes are everywhere you can look outdoors. They're not going to get that armful of wood, anyway, though."

Mrs. Frost came to the door and stood looking like she didn't know it was her business to cook breakfast for Jim and me. I made a fire in the range and put on a pan of water to boil for the coffee. Jim kept running to the window to look out, and there wasn't much use in expecting Mrs. Frost to start cooking unless somebody set her to it, in the shape she was in, with all the Swedes around the place. She was so upset, it was a downright pity to look at her. But Jim and me had to eat, and I went and took her by the arm and brought her to the range and left her standing there so close she would get burned if she didn't stir around and make breakfast.

"Good God, Stan," Jim said, "those Swedes are into everything. They're in the barn, and in the pasture running the cows, and I don't know what else they've been into since I looked last. They'll take the tools and the horses and cows, and the cedar posts, too, if we don't get out there and put everything under lock and key."

"Now, hold on, Jim," I said, looking out the window. "Them you see are little Swedes out there, and they're not going to make off with anything of yours and Mrs. Frost's. The big Swedes are busy carrying in furniture and household goods. Those Swedes aren't going to tamper with anything of yours and Mrs. Frost's. They're people just like us. They don't go around stealing everything in sight. Now, let's just sit here by the window and watch them while Mrs. Frost is getting breakfast ready."

"Good God, Stan, they're Swedes," Jim said, "and they're moving into the house across the road. I've got to put everything under lock and key before —"

"Hold on, Jim," I told him. "It's their house they're moving into. God-helping, they're not moving into your and Jim's house, are they, Mrs. Frost?"

"Jim," Mrs. Frost said, shaking her finger at him and looking at me wild-eyed and sort of flustered-like, "Jim, don't you sit there and let Stanley stop you from saving the stock and tools. Stanley doesn't know the Swedes like we do. Stanley came down here from the Back Kingdom, and he doesn't know anything about Swedes."

Mrs. Frost was partly right, because I've never seen the things in my whole life that I've seen down here near the Bay; but there wasn't any sense in Americans like Jim and Mrs. Frost being scared of Swedes. I've seen enough Finns and Portuguese in my time in the Back Kingdom, up in the intervale, to know that Americans are no different from the others.

"Now, you hold on a while, Jim," I said. "Swedes are no different than Finns. Finns don't go around stealing another man's stock and tools. Up in the Back Kingdom the Finns are the finest kind of neighbors."

"That may be so up in the Back Kingdom, Stan," Jim said, "but Swedes down here near the Bay are nothing like anything that's ever been before or since. Those Swedes over there across the road work in a pulp mill over to Waterville three-four years, and when they've got enough money saved up, or when they lose it all, as the case may be, they all move back here to East Joloppi on this farm of theirs for two-three years at a time. That's what they do. And they've been doing it for the past thirty-forty years, ever since I can remember, and they haven't changed none in all that time. I can recall the first time they came to East Joloppi; they built that house across the road then, and if you've ever seen a sight like Swedes building a house in a hurry, you haven't got much else to live for. Why! Stan, those Swedes built that house in four-five days — just like that! I've never seen the equal of it. Of course now, Stan, it's the damnedest-looking house a man ever saw, because it's not a farmhouse, and it's not a city house, and it's no kind of a house an American would erect. Why! those Swedes threw that house together in four-five days — just like that! But whoever saw a house like that before, with three stories to it, and only six rooms in the whole building! And painted yellow, too; Good God, Stan, white is the only color to paint a house, and those Swedes went and painted it yellow. Then on top of that, they went and painted the barn red. And of all of the shouting and yelling, at all times of the day and night, a man never saw or heard before. Those Swedes acted like they were purely crazy for the whole of four-five days, and they were, and they still are. But what gets me is the painting of it yellow, and the making of it three stories high, with only six rooms in the whole building. Nobody but Swedes would go and do a thing like that; an American would have built a farmhouse, here in the country, resting square on the ground, with one story, maybe a story and a half, and then painted it lead-white. But Good God, Stan, those fool Swedes had to put up three stories, to hold six rooms, and then went and painted the building yellow."

"Swedes are a little queer, sometimes," I said. "But Finns and Portuguese are too, Jim. And Americans sometimes —"

"A little queer!" Jim said. "Why! Good God, Stan, the Swedes are the queerest people on the earth, if that's the right word for them. You don't know Swedes, Stan. This is the first time you've ever seen those Swedes across the road, and that's why you don't know what they're like after being shut up in a pulpwood mill over to Waterville for four-five years. They're purely wild, I tell you, Stan. They don't stop for anything they set their heads on. If you was to walk out there now and tell them to move their autos and trucks off of the town road so the travelers could get past without having to drive around through the brush, they'd tear you apart, they're that wild, after being shut up in the pulp mill over to Waterville these three-four, maybe four-five, years."

"Finns get that way, too," I tried to tell Jim. "After Finns have been shut up in a woods camp all winter, they make a lot of noise when they get out. Everybody who has to stay close to the job for three-four years likes to act free when he gets out from under the job. Now, Jim, you take the Portuguese —"

"Don't you sit there, Jim, and let Stanley keep you from putting the tools away," Mrs. Frost said. "Stanley doesn't know the Swedes like we do. He's lived up in the Back Kingdom most of his life, tucked away in the intervale, and he's never seen Swedes —"

"Good God, Stan," Jim said, standing up, he was that nervous and upset, "the Swedes are overrunning the whole country. I'll bet there are more Swedes in the town of East Joloppi than there are in the rest of the country. Everybody knows there's more Swedes in the State of Maine than there are in the old country. Why! Jim, they take to this state like potato bugs take to—"

"Don't you sit there and let Stanley keep you back, Jim," Mrs. Frost put in again. "Stanley doesn't know the Swedes like we do. Stanley's lived up there in the Back Kingdom most of his life."

Just then one of the big Swedes started yelling at some of the little Swedes and women Swedes. I'll swear, those big Swedes sounded like a pastureful of hoarse bulls, near the end of May, mad about the black flies. God-helping, they yelled like they were fixing to kill all the little Swedes and women Swedes they could get their hands on. It didn't amount to anything, though; because the little Swedes and the women Swedes yelled right back at them just like they had been big Swedes too. The little Swedes and women Swedes couldn't yell hoarse bull bass, but it was close enough to it to make a man who's lived most of his life up in the Back Kingdom, in the intervale, think that the whole town of East Joloppi was full of big Swedes.

Jim was all for getting out after the tools and stock right away, but I pulled him back to the table. I wasn't going to let Jim and Mrs. Frost set me to doing tasks and chores before breakfast and the regular time. Forty dollars a month isn't much to pay a man for ten-eleven hours' work a day, including Sundays, when the stock has to be attended to like any other day, and I set myself that I wasn't going to work twelve-thirteen hours a day by them, even if I was practically one of the Frosts myself, except in name, by that time.

"Now, hold on awhile, Jim," I said. "Let's just sit here by the window and watch them carry their furniture and household goods inside while Mrs. Frost's getting the cooking ready to eat. If they start taking off any of you and Mrs. Frost's things, we can see them just as good from here by the window as we could out there in the yard and road."

"Now, Jim, I'm telling you," Mrs. Frost said, shaking all over, and not even trying to cook us a meal, "don't you sit there and let Stanley keep you from saving the stock and tools. Stanley doesn't know the Swedes like we do. He thinks they're like everybody else."

Jim wasn't for staying in the house when all of his tools were lying around in the yard, and while his cows were in the pasture unprotected, but he saw how it would be better to wait where we could hurry up Mrs.

Frost with the cooking, if we were ever going to eat breakfast that forenoon. She was so excited and nervous about the Swedes moving back to
East Joloppi from the pulp mill in Waterville that she hadn't got the beans
and brown bread fully heated from the night before, and we had to sit and
eat them cold.

We were sitting there by the window eating the cold beans and brown
bread, and watching the Swedes, when two of the little Swedes started
running across Jim and Mrs. Frost's lawn. They were chasing one of their
big yellow tomcats they had brought with them from Waterville. The yellow tom was as large as an eight-months collie puppy, and he ran like he
was on fire and didn't know how to put it out. His great big bushy tail
stuck straight up in the air behind him, like a flag, and he was leaping over
the lawn like a devilish calf, newborn.

Jim and Mrs. Frost saw the little Swedes and the big yellow tomcat at
the same time I did.

"Good God," Jim shouted, raising himself part out of the chair. "Here
they come now!"

"Hold on now, Jim," I said, pulling him back to the table. "They're
only chasing one of their tomcats. They're not after taking anything that
belongs to you and Mrs. Frost. Let's just sit here and finish eating the
beans, and watch them out the window."

"My crown in heaven!" Mrs. Frost cried out, running to the window and
looking through. "Those Swedes are going to kill every plant on the place.
They'll dig up all the bulbs and pull up all the vines in the flower
bed."

"Now you just sit and calm yourself, Mrs. Frost," I told her. "Those little
Swedes are just chasing a tomcat. They're not after doing hurt to your
flowers."

The big Swedes were unloading the autos and trucks and carrying the
furniture and household goods into their three-story yellow clapboarded
house. None of them was paying any attention to the little Swedes chasing the yellow tom over Jim and Mrs. Frost's lawn.

Just then the kitchen door burst open, and the two little Swedes stood
there looking at us, panting and blowing their heads off.

Mrs. Frost took one look at them, and then she let out a yell, but the kids
didn't notice her at all.

"Hey," one of them shouted, "come out here and help us get the cat. He climbed up in one of your trees."

By that time, Mrs. Frost was all for slamming the door in their faces, but I pushed in front of her and went out into the yard with them. Jim came right behind me, after he had finished calming Mrs. Frost, and telling her we wouldn't let the Swedes come and carry out her furniture and household goods.

The yellow tom was all the way up in one of Jim's young maple shade trees. The maple wasn't strong enough to support even the smallest of the little Swedes, if he should take it into his head to climb to the top after the cat, and neither Jim nor me was hurting ourselves trying to think of a way to get the feline down. We were all for letting the cat stay where he was, till he got ready to come down of his own free will, but the little Swedes couldn't wait for anything. They wanted the tom right away, then and there, and no wasting of time in getting him.

"You boys go home and wait for the cat to come down," Jim told them. "There's no way to make him come down now, till he gets ready to come down of his own mind."

But no, those two boys were little Swedes. They weren't thinking of going back home till they got the yellow tom down from the maple. One of them ran to the tree, before Jim or me could head him off, and started shinnying up it like a popeyed squirrel. In no time, it seemed to me like, he was up amongst the limbs, jumping around up there from one limb to another like he had been brought up in just such a tree.

"Good God, Stan," Jim said, "can't you keep them out of the trees?"

There was no answer for that, and Jim knew there wasn't. There's no way of stopping a Swede from doing what he has set his head on doing.

The boy got almost to the top branch, where the yellow tom was clinging and spitting, when the tree began to bend towards the house. I knew what was coming, if something wasn't done about it pretty quick, and so did Jim. Jim saw his young maple shade tree begin to bend, and he almost had a fit looking at it. He ran to the lumber stack and came back dragging two lengths of two-by-fours. He got them set up against the tree before it had time to do any splitting, and then we stood there, like two damn fools, shoring up the tree and yelling at the little Swede to come down out of there before we broke his neck for being up in it.

The big Swedes across the road heard the fuss we were making, and they came running out of that three-story, six-room house like it had been on fire inside.

"Good God, Stan," Jim shouted at me, "here comes the Swedes!"

"Don't turn and run off, Jim," I cautioned him, yanking him back by his coattail. "They're not wild beasts; we're not scared of them. Hold on where you are, Jim."

I could see Mrs. Frost's head almost breaking through the window glass in the kitchen. She was all for coming out and driving the Swedes off her lawn and out of her flowers, but she was too scared to unlock the kitchen door and open it.

Jim was getting ready to run again, when he saw the Swedes coming towards us like a nest of yellow-headed bumblebees, but I wasn't scared of them, and I held on to Jim's coattail and told him I wasn't. Jim and me were shoring up the young maple, and I knew if one of us let go, the tree would bend to the ground right away and split wide open right up the middle. There was no sense in ruining a young maple shade tree like that, and I told Jim there wasn't.

"Hey," one of the big Swedes shouted at the little Swede up in the top of the maple, "come down out of that tree and go home to your mother."

"Aw, to hell with the Old Lady," the little Swede shouted down. "I'm getting the cat by the tail."

The big Swede looked at Jim and me. Jim was almost ready to run again by that time, but I wasn't, and I held him and told him I wasn't. There was no sense in letting the Swedes scare the daylights out of us.

"What in hell can you do with kids when they get that age?" he asked Jim and me.

Jim was all for telling him to make the boy come down out of the maple before it bent over and split wide open, but I knew there was no sense in trying to make him come down out of there until he got good and ready to come, or else got the yellow tom by the tail.

Just then another big Swede came running out of that three-story, six-room house across the road, holding a double-bladed ax out in front of him, like it was a red-hot poker, and yelling for all he was worth at the other Swedes.

"Good God, Stan," Jim said, "don't let those Swedes cut down my young maple!"

I had lots better sense than to try to make the Swedes stop doing what they had set their heads on doing. A man would be purely a fool to try to stop it from raining from above when it got ready to, even if he was trying to get his corn crop planted.

I looked around again, and there was Mrs. Frost all but popping through the window glass. I could see what she was thinking, but I couldn't hear a word she was saying. It was good and plenty though, whatever it was.

"Come down out of that tree!" the Swede yelled at the boy up in Jim's maple.

Instead of starting to climb down, the little Swede reached up for the big yellow tomcat's tail. The tom reached out a big fat paw and harried the boy five-six times, just like that, quicker than the eye could follow. The kid let out a yell and a shout that must have been heard all the way to the other side of town, sounding like a whole houseful of Swedes up in the maple.

The big Swede covered the distance to the tree in one stride, pushing everything behind him.

"Good God, Stan," Jim shouted at me, "we've got to do something!"

There wasn't anything a man could do, unless he was either a Swede himself, or a man of prayer. Americans like Jim and me had no business getting in a Swede's way, especially when he was swinging a big double-bladed ax, and he just out of a pulp mill after being shut up making paper four-five years.

The big Swede grabbed the ax and let go at the trunk of the maple with it. There was no stopping him then, because he had the ax going, and it was whipping around his shoulders like a cow's tail in a swarm of black flies. The little maple shook all over every time the ax blade struck it, like wind blowing a cornstalk, and then it began to bend on the other side from Jim and me where we were shoring it up with the two-by-fours. Chips as big as dinner plates were flying across the lawn and pelting the house like a gang of boys stoning telephone insulators. One of those big dinner-plate chips crashed through the window where Mrs. Frost was, about that time. Both Jim and me thought at first she had fallen through the window, but when we looked again, we could see that she was still on the inside, and madder than ever at the Swedes.

The two-by-fours weren't any good any longer, because it was too late to get to the other side of the maple in time to keep it from bending in that direction. The Swede with the double-bladed ax took one more swing, and the tree began to bend towards the ground.

The tree came down, the little Swede came down, and the big yellow tom came down on top of everything, holding for all he was worth to the top of the little Swede's head. Long before the tree and the boy struck the ground, the big yellow tom had sprung what looked like thirty feet, and landed in the middle of Mrs. Frost's flowers and bulbs. The little Swede let out a yell and a whoop when he hit the ground that brought out six-seven more Swedes from that three-story, six-room house, piling out into the road like it was the first time they had ever heard a kid bawl. The women Swedes and the little Swedes and the big Swedes piled out on Jim and Mrs. Frost's front lawn like they had been dropped out of a dump truck and didn't know which was straight up from straight down.

I thought Mrs. Frost was going to have a fit right then and there in the kitchen window. When she saw that swarm of Swedes coming across her lawn, and the big yellow tomcat in her flower bed among the tender plants and bulbs, digging up the things she had planted, and the Swedes with their No. 12 heels squashing the green shoots she had been nursing along — well, I guess she just sort of caved in, and fell out of sight for the time being. I didn't have time to run to see what was wrong with her, because Jim and me had to tear out behind the tom and the Swedes to try to save as much as we could.

"Good God, Stan," Jim shouted at me, "go run in the house and ring up all the neighbors on the line, and tell them to hurry over here and help us before the Swedes wreck my farm and buildings. There's no telling what they'll do next. They'll be setting fire to the house and barn the next thing, maybe. Hurry, Stan!"

I didn't have time to waste talking to the neighbors on the telephone line. I was right behind Jim and the Swedes to see what they were going to do next.

"I pay you good pay, Stan," Jim said, "and I want my money's worth. Now, you go ring up the neighbors and tell them to hurry."

The big yellow tom made one more spring when he hit the flower bed, and that leap landed him over the stone wall. He struck out for the deep woods with every Swede on the place behind him. When Jim and me got to the stone wall, I pulled up short and held Jim back.

"Well, Jim," I said, "if you want me to, I'll go down in the woods and raise hell with every Swede on the place for cutting down your young maple and tearing up Mrs. Frost's flower bed."

We turned around and there was Mrs. Frost, right behind us. There was no knowing how she got there so quick after the Swedes had left for the woods.

"My crown in heaven," Mrs. Frost said, running up to Jim and holding on to him. "Jim, don't let Stanley make the Swedes mad. This is the only place we have got to live in, and they'll be here a year now this time, maybe two-three, if the hard times don't get better soon."

"That's right, Stan," he said. "You don't know the Swedes like we do. You would have to be a Swede yourself to know what to tell them. Don't go over there doing anything like that."

"God-helping, Jim," I said, "you and Mrs. Frost ain't scared of the Swedes, are you?"

"Good God, no," he said, his eyes popping out; "but don't go making them mad."

(First published in *The Yale Review*)

Daughter

At sunrise a Negro on his way to the big house to feed the mules had taken the word to Colonel Henry Maxwell, and Colonel Henry phoned the sheriff. The sheriff had hustled Jim into town and locked him up in the jail, and then he went home and ate breakfast.

Jim walked around the empty cellroom while he was buttoning his shirt, and after that he sat down on the bunk and tied his shoelaces. Everything that morning had taken place so quickly that he had not even had time to get a drink of water. He got up and went to the water bucket near the door, but the sheriff had forgotten to put water into it.

By that time there were several men standing in the jailyard. Jim went to the window and looked out when he heard them talking. Just then another automobile drove up, and six or seven men got out. Other men were coming towards the jail from both directions of the street.

"What was the trouble out at your place this morning, Jim?" somebody said.

Jim stuck his chin between the bars and looked at the faces in the crowd. He knew everyone there.

While he was trying to figure out how everybody in town had heard about his being there, somebody else spoke to him.

"It must have been an accident, wasn't it, Jim?"

A colored boy hauling a load of cotton to the gin drove up the street. When the wagon got in front of the jail, the boy whipped up the mules with the ends of the reins and made them trot.

"I hate to see the State have a grudge against you, Jim," somebody said.

The sheriff came down the street swinging a tin dinner pail in his hand. He pushed through the crowd, unlocked the door, and set the pail inside.

Several men came up behind the sheriff and looked over his shoulder into the jail.

"Here's your breakfast my wife fixed up for you, Jim. You'd better eat a little, Jim boy."

Jim looked at the pail, at the sheriff, at the open jail door, and he shook his head.

"I don't feel hungry," he said. "Daughter's been hungry, though — awful hungry."

The sheriff backed out the door, his hand going to the handle of his pistol. He backed out so quickly that he stepped on the toes of the men behind him.

"Now, don't you get careless, Jim boy," he said. "Just sit and calm yourself."

He shut the door and locked it. After he had gone a few steps towards the street, he stopped and looked into the chamber of his pistol to make sure it had been loaded.

The crowd outside the window pressed in closer. Some of the men rapped on the bars until Jim came and looked out. When he saw them, he stuck his chin between the iron and gripped his hands around it.

"How come it to happen, Jim?" somebody asked. "It must have been an accident, wasn't it?"

Jim's long thin face looked as if it would come through the bars. The sheriff came up to the window to see if everything was all right.

"Now, just take it easy, Jim boy," he said.

The man who had asked Jim to tell what had happened elbowed the sheriff out of the way. The other men crowded closer.

"How come, Jim?" the man said. "Was it an accident?"

"No," Jim said, his fingers twisting about the bars. "I picked up my shotgun and done it."

The sheriff pushed towards the window again.

"Go on, Jim, and tell us what it's all about."

Jim's face squeezed between the bars until it looked as though only his ears kept his head from coming through.

"Daughter said she was hungry, and I just couldn't stand it no longer. I just couldn't stand to hear her say it."

"Don't get all excited now, Jim boy," the sheriff said, pushing forward one moment and being elbowed away the next.

"She waked up in the middle of the night again and said she was hungry. I just couldn't stand to hear her say it."

Somebody pushed all the way through the crowd until he got to the window.

"Why, Jim, you could have come and asked me for something for her to eat, and you know I'd have given you all I got in the world."

The sheriff pushed forward once more.

"That wasn't the right thing to do," Jim said. "I've been working all year and I made enough for all of us to eat."

He stopped and looked down into the faces on the other side of the bars.

"I made enough working on shares, but they came and took it all away from me. I couldn't go around begging after I'd made enough to keep us. They just came and took it all off. Then Daughter woke up again this morning saying she was hungry, and I just couldn't stand it no longer."

"You'd better go and get on the bunk now, Jim boy," the sheriff said.

"It don't seem right that the little girl ought to be shot like that," somebody said.

"Daughter said she was hungry," Jim said. "She'd been saying that for all of the past month. Daughter'd wake up in the middle of the night and say it. I just couldn't stand it no longer."

"You ought to have sent her over to my house, Jim. Me and my wife could have fed her something, somehow. It don't look right to kill a little girl like her."

"I'd made enough for all of us," Jim said. "I just couldn't stand it no longer. Daughter'd been hungry all the past month."

"Take it easy, Jim boy," the sheriff said, trying to push forward.

The crowd swayed from side to side.

"And so you just picked up the gun this morning and shot her?" somebody asked.

"When she woke up this morning saying she was hungry, I just couldn't stand it."

The crowd pushed closer. Men were coming towards the jail from all directions, and those who were then arriving pushed forward to hear what Jim had to say.

"The State has got a grudge against you now, Jim," somebody said, "but somehow it don't seem right."

"I can't help it," Jim said. "Daughter woke up again this morning that way."

The jailyard, the street, and the vacant lot on the other side were filled with men and boys. All of them were pushing forward to hear Jim. Word had spread all over town by that time that Jim Carlisle had shot and killed his eight-year-old daughter, Clara.

"Who does Jim sharecrop for?" somebody asked.

"Colonel Henry Maxwell," a man in the crowd said. "Colonel Henry has had Jim out there about nine or ten years."

"Henry Maxwell didn't have no business coming and taking all the shares. He's got plenty of his own. It ain't right for Henry Maxwell to come and take Jim's, too."

The sheriff was pushing forward once more.

"The State's got a grudge against Jim now," somebody said. "Somehow it don't seem right, though."

The sheriff pushed his shoulder into the crowd of men and worked his way in closer.

A man shoved the sheriff away.

"Why did Henry Maxwell come and take your share of the crop, Jim?"

"He said I owed it to him because one of his mules died about a month ago."

The sheriff got in front of the barred window.

"You ought to go to the bunk now and rest some, Jim boy," he said. "Take off your shoes and stretch out, Jim boy."

He was elbowed out of the way.

"You didn't kill the mule, did you, Jim?"

"The mule dropped dead in the barn," Jim said. "I wasn't nowhere around. It just dropped dead."

The crowd was pushing harder. The men in front were jammed against the jail, and the men behind were trying to get within earshot. Those in the middle were squeezed against each other so tightly they could not move in any direction. Everyone was talking louder

Jim's face pressed between the bars and his fingers gripped the iron until the knuckles were white.

The milling crowd was moving across the street to the vacant lot. Somebody was shouting. He climbed up on an automobile and began swearing at the top of his lungs.

A man in the middle of the crowd pushed his way out and went to his automobile. He got in and drove off alone.

Jim stood holding to the bars and looking through the window. The sheriff had his back to the crowd, and he was saying something to Jim. Jim did not hear what he said.

A man on his way to the gin with a load of cotton stopped to find out what the trouble was. He looked at the crowd in the vacant lot for a moment, and then he turned around and looked at Jim behind the bars. The shouting across the street was growing louder.

"What's the trouble, Jim?"

Somebody on the other side of the street came to the wagon. He put his foot on a spoke in the wagon wheel and looked up at the man on the cotton while he talked.

"Daughter woke up this morning again saying she was hungry," Jim said.

The sheriff was the only person who heard him.

The man on the load of cotton jumped to the ground, tied the reins to the wagon wheel, and pushed through the crowd to the car where all the shouting and swearing was being done. After listening for a while, he came back to the street, called a Negro who was standing with several other Negroes on the corner, and handed him the reins. The Negro drove off with the cotton towards the gin, and the man went back into the crowd.

Just then the man who had driven off alone in his car came back. He sat for a moment behind the steering wheel, and then he jumped to the ground. He opened the rear door and took out a crowbar that was as long as he was tall.

"Pry that jail door open and let Jim out," somebody said. "It ain't right for him to be in there."

The crowd in the vacant lot was moving again. The man who had been standing on top of the automobile jumped to the ground, and the men moved towards the street in the direction of the jail.

The first man to reach it jerked the six-foot crowbar out of the soft earth where it had been jabbed.

The sheriff backed off.

"Now, take it easy, Jim boy," he said.

He turned and started walking rapidly up the street towards his house.

(First published in *Anvil*)

Maud Island

UNCLE MARVIN was worried. He got up from the log and walked toward the river.

"I don't like the looks of it, boys," he said, whipping off his hat and wiping his forehead.

The houseboat was drifting downstream at about three miles an hour, and a man in a straw hat and sleeveless undershirt was trying to pole it inshore. The man was wearing cotton pants that had faded from dark brown to light tan.

"It looks bad," Uncle Marvin said, turning to Jim and me. "I don't like the looks of it one whit."

"Maybe they are lost, Uncle Marvin," Jim said. "Maybe they'll just stop to find out where they are, and then go on away again."

"I don't believe it, son," he said, shaking his head and wiping the perspiration from his face. "It looks downright bad to me. That kind of a houseboat never has been out for no good since I can remember."

On a short clothesline that stretched along the starboard side, six or seven pieces of clothing hung waving in the breeze.

"It looks awful bad, son," he said again, looking down at me.

We walked across the mud flat to the river and waited to see what the houseboat was going to do. Uncle Marvin took out his plug and cut off a chew of tobacco with his jackknife. The boat was swinging inshore, and the man with the pole was trying to beach it before the current cut in and carried them back to mid-channel. There was a power launch lying on its side near the stern, and on the launch was a towline that had been used for upstream going.

When the houseboat was two or three lengths from the shore, Uncle Marvin shouted at the man poling it.

"What's your name, and what do you want here?" he said gruffly, trying to scare the man away from the island.

Instead of answering, the man tossed a rope to us. Jim picked it up and started pulling, but Uncle Marvin told him to drop it. Jim dropped it, and the middle of the rope sank into the yellow water.

"What did you throw my rope in for?" the man on the houseboat shouted. "What's the matter with you?"

Uncle Marvin spat some tobacco juice and glared right back at him. The houseboat was ready to run on the beach.

"My name's Graham," the man said. "What's yours?"

"None of your business," Uncle Marvin shouted. "Get that raft away from here."

The houseboat began to beach. Graham dropped the pole on the deck and ran and jumped on the mud flat. He called to somebody inside while he was pulling the rope out of the water.

The stern swung around in the backwash of the current, and Jim grabbed my arm and pointed at the dim lettering on the boat. It said *Mary Jane*, and under that was *St. Louis*.

While we stood watching the man pull in the rope, two girls came out on the deck and looked at us. They were very young. Neither of them looked to be over eighteen or nineteen. When they saw Uncle Marvin, they waved at him and began picking up the boxes and bundles to carry off.

"You can't land that shantyboat on this island," Uncle Marvin said threateningly. "It won't do you no good to unload that stuff, because you'll only have to carry it all back again. No shantyboat's going to tie up on this island."

One of the girls leaned over the rail and looked at Uncle Marvin.

"Do you own this island, Captain?" she asked him.

Uncle Marvin was no river captain. He did not even look like one. He was the kind of man you could see plowing cotton on the steep hillsides beyond Reelfoot Lake. Uncle Marvin glanced at Jim and me for a moment, kicking at a gnarled root on the ground, and looked at the girl again.

"No," he said, pretending to be angry with her. "I don't own it, and I wouldn't claim ownership of anything on the Mississippi, this side of the bluffs."

The other girl came to the rail and leaned over, smiling at Uncle Marvin.

"Hiding out, Captain?" she asked.

Uncle Marvin acted as though he would have had something to say to her if Jim and I had not been there to overhear him. He shook his head at the girl.

Graham began carrying off the boxes and bundles. Both Jim and I wished to help him so we would have a chance to go on board the houseboat, but we knew Uncle Marvin would never let us do that. The boat had been beached on the mud flat, and Graham had tied it up, knotting the rope around a young cypress tree.

When he had finished, he came over to us and held out his hand to Uncle Marvin. Uncle Marvin looked at Graham's hand, but he would not shake with him.

"My name's Harry Graham," he said. "I'm from up the river at Caruthersville. What's your name?"

"Hutchins," Uncle Marvin said, looking him straight in the eyes, "and I ain't hiding out."

The two girls, the dark one and the light one, were carrying their stuff across the island to the other side where the slough was. The island was only two or three hundred feet wide, but it was nearly half a mile long. It had been a sandbar to begin with, but it was already crowded with trees and bushes. The Mississippi was on the western side, and on the eastern side there was a slough that looked bottomless. The bluffs of the Tennessee shore were only half a mile in that direction.

"We're just on a little trip over the week end," Graham said. "The girls thought they would like to come down the river and camp out on an island for a couple of days."

"Which one is your wife?" Uncle Marvin asked him.

Graham looked at Uncle Marvin a little surprised for a minute. After that he laughed a little, and began kicking the ground with the toe of his shoe.

"I didn't quite catch what you said," he told Uncle Marvin.

"I said, which one is your wife?"

"Well, to tell the truth, neither of them. They're just good friends of mine, and we thought it would be a nice trip down the river and back for a couple of days. That's how it is."

"They're old enough to get married," Uncle Marvin told him, nodding at the girls.

"Maybe so," Graham said. "Come on over and I'll introduce you to them.

They're Evansville girls, both of them. I used to work in Indiana, and I met them up there. That's where I got this houseboat. I already had the launch."

Uncle Marvin looked at the lettering on the *Mary Jane,* spelling out *St. Louis* to himself.

"Just a little fun for the week end," Graham said, smiling. "The girls like the river."

Uncle Marvin looked at Jim and me, jerking his head to one side and trying to tell us to go away. We walked down to the edge of the water where the *Mary Jane* was tied up, but we could still hear what they were saying. After a while, Uncle Marvin shook hands with Graham and started along up the shore towards our skiff.

"Come on, son, you and Milt," he said. "It's time to look at that taut line again."

We caught up with Uncle Marvin, and all of us got into the skiff, and Jim and I set the oarlocks. Uncle Marvin turned around so he could watch the people behind us on the island. Graham was carrying the heavy boxes to a clearing, and the two girls were unrolling the bundles and spreading them on the ground to air.

Jim and I rowed to the mouth of the creek and pulled alongside the taut line. Uncle Marvin got out his box of bait and began lifting the hooks and taking off catfish. Every time he found a hook with a catch, he took the cat off, spat over his left shoulder, and dropped it into the bucket and put on a new bait.

There was not much of a catch on the line that morning. After we had rowed across, almost to the current in the middle of the creek mouth, where the outward end of the line had been fastened to a cypress in the water, Uncle Marvin threw the rest of the bait overboard and told us to turn around and row back to Maud Island.

Uncle Marvin was a preacher. Sometimes he preached in the schoolhouse near home, and sometimes he preached in a dwelling. He had never been ordained, and he had never studied for the ministry, and he was not a member of any church. However, he believed in preaching, and he never let his lack of training stop him from delivering a sermon when ever a likely chance offered itself. Back home on the mainland, people called him Preacher Marvin, not so much for the fact that he was a preacher, but because he looked like one. That was one reason why he had begun preaching at the start. People had got into the habit of calling him Preacher Marvin, and before he was forty he had taken up the ministry as a calling. He had never been much of a farmer, anyway — a lot of people said that.

Our camp on Maud Island was the only one on the river for ten or fifteen miles. The island was only half a mile from shore, where we lived in Tennessee, and Uncle Marvin brought us out to spend the week end five or six times during the summer. When we went back and forth between the mainland and the island, we had to make a wide circle, nearly two miles out of the way, in order to keep clear of the slough. The slough was a mass of yellow mud, rotting trees, and whatever drift happened to get caught in it. It was almost impossible to get through it, either on foot or in a flat-bottomed boat, and we kept away from it as far as possible. Sometimes mules and cows started out in it from the mainland to reach the island, but they never got very far before they dropped out of sight. The slough sucked them down and closed over them like quicksand.

Maud Island was a fine place to camp, though. It was the highest ground along the river for ten or fifteen miles, and there was hardly any danger of its being flooded when the high water covered everything else within sight. When the river rose to forty feet, however, the island, like everything else in all directions, was covered with water from the Tennessee bluffs to the Missouri highlands, seven or eight miles apart.

When we got back from baiting the taut line, Uncle Marvin told us to build a good fire while he was cleaning the catch of catfish and cutting them up for frying. Jim went off after an armful of driftwood while I was blowing the coals in the campfire. Jim brought the wood and built the fire, and I watched the pail of water hanging over it until Uncle Marvin was ready to make the coffee.

In the middle of the afternoon Uncle Marvin woke up from his midday nap and said it was too hot to sleep any longer. We sat around for ten or fifteen minutes, nobody saying much, and after a while Uncle Marvin got up and said he thought he would walk over to the other camp and see how the people from Caruthersville, or Evansville, or wherever they came from, were getting along.

Jim and I were up and ready to go along, but he shook his head and told us to stay there. We could not help feeling that there was something unusual about that, because Uncle Marvin had always taken us with him no matter where he went when we were camping on the island. When Jim said something about going along, Uncle Marvin got excited and told us to do as he said, or we would find ourselves being sorry.

"You boys stay here and take it easy," he said. "I've got to find out what kind of people they are before we start in to mix with them. They're from up the river, and there's no telling what they're like till I get to know them. You boys just stay here and take it easy till I get back."

After he had gone, we got up and picked our way through the dry underbrush toward the other camp. Jim kept urging me to hurry so we would not miss seeing anything, but I was afraid we would make so much noise Uncle Marvin would hear us and run back and catch us looking.

"Uncle Marvin didn't tell them he's a preacher," Jim said. "Those girls think he's a river captain, and I'll bet he wants them to keep on thinking so."

"He doesn't look like a river captain. He looks like a preacher. Those girls were just saying that for fun."

"The dark one acted like she's foolish about Uncle Marvin," Jim said. "I could tell."

"That's Jean," I said.

"How do you know what their names are?"

"Didn't you hear Graham talking to them when they were carrying their stuff off that houseboat?"

"Maybe he did," Jim said.

"He called that one Jean, and the light one Marge."

Jim bent down and looked through the bushes.

"Uncle Marvin's not mad at them now for coming here to camp," he said.

"How can you tell he's not?" I asked Jim.

"I can tell by the way he's acting up now."

"He told Graham to get the houseboat away from here, didn't he?"

"Sure he did then," Jim whispered, "but that was before those two girls came outside and leaned over the railing and talked to him. After he saw them a while he didn't try to stop Graham from landing, did he?"

We had crawled as close as we dared go, and fifty feet away we could see everything that was going on in Graham's camp. When Uncle Marvin walked up, Graham was sitting against the trunk of a cypress trying to untangle a fishing line, and the two girls were lying in hammocks that had been hung up between trees. We could not see either of them very well then, because the sides of the hammocks hid them, but the sun was shining down into the clearing and it was easy to see them when they moved or raised their arms.

Five or six cases of drinks were stacked up against one of the trees where the hammocks were, and several bottles had already been opened and tossed aside empty. Graham had a bottle of beer beside him on the ground, and every once in a while he stopped tussling with the tangled fishing line and grabbed the bottle and took several swallows from it. The dark girl, Jean, had a bottle in her hand, half full, and Marge was juggling an empty bottle in the air over her head. Everybody looked as if he was having the best time of his life.

None of them saw Uncle Marvin when he got to the clearing. Graham was busy fooling with the tangled fishing line, and Uncle Marvin stopped and looked at all three of them for almost a minute before he was noticed.

"I'll bet Uncle Marvin takes a bottle," Jim said. "What do you bet?"

"Preachers don't drink beer, do they?"

"Uncle Marvin will, I'll bet anything," Jim said. "You know Uncle Marvin."

Just then Graham raised his head from the line and saw Uncle Marvin standing not ten feet away. Graham jumped up and said something to Uncle Marvin. It was funny to watch them, because Uncle Marvin was not looking at Graham at all. His head was turned in the other direction all the time, and he was looking where the girls lay stretched out in the hammocks. He could not take his eyes off them long enough to glance at Graham. Graham kept on saying something, but Uncle Marvin acted as though he was on the other side of the river beyond earshot.

Jean and Marge pulled the sides of the hammocks over them, but they could not make Uncle Marvin stop looking at them. He started to grin, but he turned red in the face instead.

Graham picked up a bottle and offered it to Uncle Marvin. He took it without even looking at it once, and held it out in front of him as if he did not know he had it in his hand. When Graham saw that he was not making any effort to open it, he took it and put the cap between his teeth and popped it off as easily as he could have done it with a bottle opener.

The beer began to foam then, and Uncle Marvin shoved the neck of the bottle into his mouth and turned it upside down. The foam that had run out on his hand before he could get the bottle into his mouth was dripping down his shirt front and making a dark streak on the blue cloth.

Jean leaned out of her hammock and reached to the ground for another bottle. She popped off the cap with a bottle opener and lay down again.

"Did you see that, Milt?" Jim whispered, squeezing my arm. He whistled a little between his teeth.

"I saw a lot!" I said.

"I didn't know girls ever did like that where everybody could see them," he said.

"They're from up the river," I told him. "Graham said they were from Evansville."

"That don't make any difference," Jim said, shaking his head. "They're girls, aren't they? Well, whoever saw girls lie in hammocks naked like that? I know I never did before!"

"I sure never saw any like those before, either," I told him.

Uncle Marvin had gone to the tree at the foot of one of the hammocks, and he was standing there, leaning against it a little, with the empty bottle in his hand, and looking straight at them.

Graham was trying to talk to him, but Uncle Marvin would not pay attention to what Graham was trying to say. Jean had turned loose the sides of the hammock, and Marge, too, and they were laughing and trying to make Uncle Marvin say something. Uncle Marvin's mouth was hanging open, but his face was not red any more.

"Why doesn't he tell them he's a preacher?" I asked Jim, nudging him with my elbow.

"Maybe he will after a while," Jim said, standing on his toes and trying to see better through the undergrowth.

"It looks to me like he's not going to tell them," I said. "It wouldn't make any difference, anyway, because Uncle Marvin isn't a real preacher. He only preaches when he feels like doing it."

"That doesn't make any difference," Jim said.

"Why doesn't it?"

"It just doesn't, that's why."

"But he calls himself a preacher, just the same."

"He doesn't have to be a preacher now if he doesn't want to be one. If he told them he was a preacher, they'd all jump up and run and hide from him."

Uncle Marvin was still standing against the tree looking at the dark girl, and Graham was a little to one side of him, looking as if he didn't know what to do next.

Presently Uncle Marvin jerked himself erect and turned his head in all directions listening for sounds. He looked towards us, but he could not see us. Jim got down on his hands and knees to be out of sight, and I got behind him.

The three others were laughing and talking, but not Uncle Marvin. He looked at them a while longer, and then he reached down to the top case against the cypress and lifted out another bottle. Graham reached to open it for him, but Uncle Marvin bit his teeth over the cap and popped it off. The beer began to foam right away, but before much of it could run out, Uncle Marvin had turned it up and was drinking it down.

When the bottle was empty, he wiped his mouth with the back of his hand and took three or four steps towards the dark girl in the hammock. Jean kicked her feet into the air and pulled the sides of the hammock around her. The other girl sat up to watch Uncle Marvin.

All at once he stopped and looked towards our camp on the other side of the island. There was not a sound anywhere, except the sucking sound in the slough that went on all the time, and the sharp slap of water against the sides of the houseboat. He listened for another moment, cocking his head like a dog getting ready to jump a rabbit, and broke into a run, headed for our camp. Jim and I just barely got there before Uncle Marvin. We were both puffing and blowing after running so fast, but Uncle Marvin was blowing even harder and he did not notice how short our breath was. He stopped and looked down at the dead fire for a while before he spoke to us.

"Get ready to go home, son, you and Jim," he said. "We've got to leave right now."

He started throwing our stuff into a pile and stamping out the ashes at the same time. He turned around and spat some tobacco juice on the live coals and grabbed up an armful of stuff. He did not wait for us to help him, but started for our skiff on the mud flat right away with a big load of stuff in both arms. Jim and I had to hurry to catch up with him so he would not forget and leave us behind.

He took the oars from us and shoved off without waiting for us to do it for him. When we were out of the mouth of the creek, he took his hat off and threw it on the bottom of the skiff and bent over the oars harder than ever. Jim and I could not do a thing to help, because there were only two oars and he would not turn either one of them loose.

Nobody said a thing while we were rowing around the slough. When we got within a hundred feet of shore, Uncle Marvin started throwing our stuff into a heap in the stern. We had no more than dragged bottom on shore when he picked up the whole lot and threw the stuff on the dried mud. The pans and buckets rolled in every direction.

Both of us were scared to say a word to Uncle Marvin because he had never acted like that before. We stood still and watched him while he shoved off into the river and turned the skiff around and headed around the slough. We were scared to death for a while, because we had never seen anybody cut across so close to the slough. He knew where he was all the time, but he did not seem to care how many chances he took of being sucked down into the slough. The last we saw of him was when he went out of sight around Maud Island.

We picked up our things and started running with them towards home. All the way there we were in too much of a hurry to say anything to each other. It was about a mile and a half home, and upgrade every step of the way, but we ran the whole distance, carrying our heavy stuff on our backs.

When we reached the front gate, Aunt Sophie ran out on the porch to meet us. She had seen us running up the road from the river, and she was surprised to see us back home so soon. When we left with Uncle Marvin early that morning, we thought we were going to stay a week on Maud Island. Aunt Sophie looked down the road to see if she could see anything of Uncle Marvin.

Jim dropped his load of stuff and sank down on the porch steps panting and blowing.

"Where's your Uncle Marvin, Milton?" Aunt Sophie asked us, standing above me and looking down at us with her hands on her hips. "Where's Marvin Hutchins?"

I shook my head the first thing, because I did not know what to say.

"Where's your Uncle Marvin, James?" she asked Jim.

Jim looked at me, and then down again at the steps. He tried to keep Aunt Sophie's eyes from looking straight into his.

Aunt Sophie came between us and shook Jim by the shoulder. She shook him until his hair tumbled over his face, and his teeth rattled until they sounded as if they were loose in his mouth.

"Where is your Uncle Marvin, Milton?" she demanded, coming to me and shaking me worse than she had Jim. "Answer me this minute, Milton!"

When I saw how close she was to me, I jumped up and ran out into the yard out of her reach. I knew how hard she could shake when she wanted to. It was lots worse than getting a whipping with a peach-tree switch.

"Has that good-for-nothing scamp gone and taken up with a shantyboat wench again?" she said, running back and forth between Jim and me.

I had never heard Aunt Sophie talk like that before, and I was so scared I could not make myself say a word. I had never heard her call Uncle Marvin anything like that before, either. As a rule she never paid much attention to him, except when she wanted him to chop some stovewood, or something like that.

Jim sat up and looked at Aunt Sophie. I could see that he was getting ready to say something about the way she talked about Uncle Marvin. Jim was always taking up for him whenever Aunt Sophie started in on him.

Jim opened his mouth to say something, but the words never came out.

"One of you is going to answer me!" Aunt Sophie said. "I'll give you one more chance to talk, Milton."

"He didn't say where he was going or what he was going to do, Aunt Sophie. Honest, he didn't!"

"Milton Hutchins!" she said, stamping her foot.

"Honest, Aunt Sophie!" I said. "Maybe he went off somewhere to preach."

"Preach, my foot!" she cried, jamming her hands on her hips. "Preach! If that good-for-nothing scalawag preached half as many sermons as he makes out like he does, he'd have the whole country saved for God long before now! Preach! Huh! Preach, my foot! That's his excuse for going off from home whenever he gets the notion to cut-up-jack, but he never fools me. And I can make a mighty good guess where he is this very minute, too. He's gone chasing off after some shantyboat wench! Preach, my foot!"

Jim looked at me, and I looked at Jim. To save our life we could not see how Aunt Sophie had found out about the two girls from Evansville on Maud Island.

Aunt Sophie jammed her hands on her hips a little harder and motioned to us with her head. We followed her into the house.

"We're going to have a house cleaning around this place," she said. "James, you bring the brooms. Milton, you go start a fire under the wash-pot in the back yard and heat it full of water. When you get it going good, come in here and sweep down the cobwebs off the ceilings."

Aunt Sophie went from room to room, slamming doors behind her. She began ripping curtains down from the windows and pulling the rugs from the floor. A little later we could hear the swish of her broom, and presently a dense cloud of dust began blowing through the windows.

(First published in the *Brooklyn Eagle*)

The Cold Winter

AFTER I had been in town a week, I began going early in the evening to the room I had rented, to lie awake under the warmth of the blanket.

Out on the streets, when night fell, it was always cold. There was usually a chill wet wind from the river, and from the bare uplands the February winter descended hour after hour, freezing and raw. Even men with overcoats hurried through the icy streets with lowered heads fighting the cold, hurrying towards heated homes.

It was cold in the unheated room I had rented, but the warmth of the blanket was like the clinging arms of a girl.

By the third night of the week I had got accustomed to the unheated house. At first I could not sleep. But on that evening I took off my shoes as soon as I had reached the room and got into bed immediately. For the next five or six hours I lay awake, warm under the blanket, while frost on the windowpanes formed slowly and precisely into fragile designs of cold beauty.

Out in the hall I could hear people passing quickly from room to room, hurrying through the cold corridor while the contracted boards of the floor creaked under their feet.

After a while I became conscious of warm air flowing through the cracks in the wall. A young woman and her small daughter lived in the room next to mine, on the right, and the heat they had was escaping into my room. I could smell the scorched air and the burned gas of their heater. I lay awake then, listening to the movements in the next room, while their slowly formed picture was melted into my memory. Towards midnight I fell asleep, remembering only that in the next room the young woman moved lightly when she walked and that the small girl spoke to her mother softly and lovingly.

After that night I began coming home much earlier in the evening to cover myself with the warmth of the blanket and to lie awake in the darkness listening to all that happened in the next-door room. The young woman prepared supper for the girl and herself, and then they sat at the small table by the window and ate slowly, laughing and talking. The little girl was about eight, and her mother was almost as young as she when they laughed and talked.

The cold of the unheated room was not so hard to bear as it had been before I came to know them.

I knew by the end of that second week how each of them looked even though I had never seen either of them. Through the thin plaster wall I could hear everything they said and did, and I followed the motions of their hands and the expressions on their faces from second to second, hour after hour. The young woman was not working, either; she remained in the room most of the day, going out only in the morning for half an hour to walk with the girl to school, and again in the afternoon to walk home with her. The rest of the day she sat in the room, by the window, looking out over the red-painted tin roof across the way, and waiting for midafternoon to come so she could walk to the school for her daughter.

There were other people in the house, many of them. The three floors of the building were rented, room by room, to men and women who came and went during all hours. Some of them worked during the day, some at night, and many had no jobs at all. But even though there were many people in the house, no one ever came to my door, and no one ever went to the young woman's door next to mine. Sometimes there would be the sound of a man walking heavily, coming hurriedly down the hall, and the young woman would jump from her chair by the window and run frantically to the door, leaning against it while her fingers held the key in the lock and listening to the sound of the man's stride. After he had passed, she went slowly back to her chair and sat down once more to look out over the red-painted tin roof across the way.

Into the month of February it became colder and colder, but I was warm when I lay under the blanket and listened to the sounds that came through the thin plaster wall.

It was not until I had become aware of her running to the door each time the sound of a man's footstep rang through the rooms that I realized something was about to happen. I did not know what the happening was to be, nor when, but each morning before leaving my room I waited and listened for several minutes to hear if she were standing against her door or sitting in her chair. When I came back in the evening, I pressed my ear against the cold wall to listen again.

That evening, after I had listened for nearly half an hour, I knew something was about to happen; and for the first time in my life, while I stood there shivering in the cold, I had the desire to be the father of a child. I did not stop to turn on the light, but climbed straightway into bed without even taking off my shoes. I lay tensely awake upon the bed for a long time listening to the movements on the other side of the wall. The young woman was quick and nervous, and her face was white and drawn. The little girl was put to bed as soon as they had finished eating supper and, without a word being spoken, the young woman went to her chair by the window to sit and wait. She sat silently, not even rocking, for a long time. I had raised my head from the pillow, and my neck was stiff and cold after the strain of holding my head horizontally without support.

It was eleven o'clock before I heard another sound in the room next to mine. During the three hours that I had lain awake on the bed waiting, she had not moved from her chair. But at eleven o'clock she got up and drank a glass of water and covered the girl with another blanket. When she had finished, she moved to her chair for a moment, and then she carried it to the door and sat down. She sat and waited. Before another hour had passed, a man came down the hall, walking heavily on the contracted boards of the floor. We both heard him coming, and we both jumped to our feet. I ran to the wall and pressed my ear against the cold white plaster and waited. The young woman leaned against the door, her fingers gripped around the key, and listened with bated breath. The little girl was sound asleep in bed.

After I had been standing for several minutes I felt the cold of the unheated room wither my hands and feet. Under the warmth of the blanket I had forgotten how cold it was, and the blood had raced through me while I waited still and tense and listened to the sounds in the building. But standing in the unheated room, with my face and ear pressed against the cold white plaster, I was shaking as though with a chill.

The man came to the door next to mine and stopped. I could hear the woman's trembling, and the breathing that jerked her body, and each moment I expected to hear her scream.

He knocked on the door once and waited. She did not open it. He turned the knob and shook it. She pressed with all her strength against the door, and held the key in its place with fingers of steel.

"I know you are in there, Eloise," he said slowly; "open the door and let me in."

She made no reply. I could hear through the thin wall the strain of her body against the frail door.

"I'm coming in," he said.

He had barely finished before there was a sudden thrust of his shoulder against the door that burst the lock and threw him inside. Even then there was no sound from her lips. She ran to the bed and threw herself upon it, hugging desperately in her arms the girl who had slept so soundly.

"I didn't come here to argue with you," the man said. "I came here to put an end to this mess. Get up off the bed."

It was then for the first time that evening that I heard the sound of the young woman's voice. She had sprung to her feet and was facing him. I pressed my face and ear against the cold white plaster and waited.

"She's as much mine as she is yours. You can't take her away from me."

"You took her away from me, didn't you? Well, it's my turn now. I'm her father."

"Henry!" she begged. "Henry, please don't!"

"Shut up," he said.

He strode to the bed and lifted the girl in his arms.

"I'll kill you, Henry, if you take her out of this room," she said slowly. "I mean that, Henry."

He walked with the girl to the door and stopped. He was not excited, and his breath was not even audible through the thin wall. But the woman was frantic, and my hands and feet were numbed with the cold and I could not move the muscles of my lips. The young woman had not begun to cry, but through the plaster wall I could hear her breathe, and I could feel the quick movements of her body.

He turned around.

"You'll do what?" he said.

"I'll kill you, Henry."

There was a moment's silence, complete and still. He stood at the door, the girl lying in his arms waking slowly from sleep, and waited. Each second seemed as though it were an hour long.

"No, you won't do that," he said after a while. "I'm going to beat you to it, Eloise."

Through the thin plaster wall I could hear the smooth slide of his hand into his coat pocket and out again. I could hear everything that was to happen.

When he pointed the pistol at her, she screamed. He waited until she had cried out, and then he pulled the trigger, not taking careful aim, but nevertheless closing one eye as though he were looking down the sights at her.

The echoes of the explosion drowned out the sound of his running down the hall and the creaking of the floor under his feet.

It was several minutes before the ringing in my ears had died out, and by that time there was the sound of people running through the house from top to bottom, flinging open the doors of the heated rooms and of the unheated rooms as they raced towards us on the second floor.

For a long time I lay against the white plastered wall, trembling because I who was the father had allowed without protest the taking away of the girl, and shaking because I was cold in the unheated room.

(First published in *Story*)

A Day's Wooing

When Tuffy Webb woke up that morning, the first thing he saw was his new straw hat hanging on the back of the cane-bottomed chair beside the bed. The red, orange, and blue silk band around the hat looked as bright in the sunshine as the decorations in the store windows in town on circus day. He reached out and felt the rough crown and brim, running his fingers over the stiff brown straw. He would never have to step aside for anybody, in a hat like that. That was all he needed, to get the world by the tail.

"Maybe that won't knock a few eyes out!" Tuffy said, throwing off the covers and leaping to the floor. "They'll all be cross-eyed from looking at it."

He placed the hat carefully on his head and walked over to the mirror on the wall. The new straw hat looked even finer Sunday morning than it had Saturday night, when he tried it on in the store.

"When Nancy sees this lid, she'll come tumbling," Tuffy said, stepping back and tilting the hat a little on one side of his head and winking at himself under the brim.

He walked past the mirror several times, free and easy in his loose knee-length nightshirt, turning his eyes to see himself in passing. It was easy to get up courage in a hat like that.

"I could have all the girls after me now if I wanted them," he said to himself.

Tuffy got dressed in a hurry and made a fire in the cookstove. He pulled the hat down carefully over his head so it would not fall off and hit the floor while he was cooking breakfast.

During all the time he was in the kitchen he kept thinking to himself that he would not have to keep bach much longer after that, not after Nancy saw him in his new hat. She would be tickled to death to marry him now, the first time she saw him walking up to her house with the straw sailor tilted over one ear, sort of like a cock's comb that always looked like it was going to fall off but never did.

After breakfast Tuffy had to drive the cows to the pasture on the other side of the creek because it had become time for them to have a change of feed, and the Johnson grass over there was ready for grazing.

He started off with his hat on his head, but he got to thinking about it and finally decided he ought to leave it at the house. Sometimes a yearling took to heels and bolted off into a thicket, and he did not like to think of taking any chances of having the hat fall off into the briers and mud, and maybe being trampled by the cows. Now that he was thinking about it, he remembered seeing a cow chew up a straw hat once and swallow it.

He hurried back to the house and hung the hat on the cane-bottomed chair beside the bed.

Tuffy got back from the pasture at about eleven o'clock, and he changed his clothes right away, putting on his coat and the hat. After that he still had almost an hour to wait before he could leave home, because he did not wish to get to the Millers' while they were eating dinner. If he did that, one of the Millers would be certain to say that he had got there then to get something to eat.

He walked out on the porch and leaned against the railing for a while. The sun was almost directly overhead, and there was not a cloud in sight. He knew he could not have chosen a finer day to go calling on Nancy in a new straw hat. There was not a single drop of rain in the whole sky above.

"This would be a dandy time to speak to Nancy about us getting married," he said, going out into the yard and walking first around the chinaberry tree and then around the willow. "All I'd have to do would be to ask her, and I know already what Nancy'll say. She's just as willing as I am, and she knows it. It wouldn't do her any good to try to show otherwise."

Tuffy leaned against the willow, picking at the bark with his thumbnail.

"If I go right up to her and say, 'Nancy, how about me and you hitching up together?' she'll say, 'When, Tuffy?' and I'll say, 'The sooner the better suits me.' Then she'll say, 'Nothing would please me more'

That's all there will be to it, and it'll be all planned and settled. All I'll have to do is get a preacher to marry us, and then me and Nancy'll be married for a fare-you-well. Getting married wouldn't take long, maybe no longer than tomorrow noon. We'll probably start right in tomorrow some time. That's none too soon for me, and I know it won't be none too soon for Nancy."

Tuffy went over and sat on the woodpile.

"I'll go over there to old Berry Miller's and walk right up to where they're all sitting on the porch and lose no time about it. Berry'll probably want to know what I came for, all dressed up like this in a coat and a new straw hat, and I'll soon tell him, too. 'Well,' I'll say, 'I came to marry Nancy, Berry. How do you like that? Me and her are getting married right off.' He won't scare me a bit, no matter what he says. He might have some little fault to find to begin with, but there's no objection I know about that's good enough to stop me from going ahead and getting married to Nancy. I'll walk right up to where she's sitting on the porch and put my arm around her and show those Millers I mean business and don't mean maybe."

Tuffy picked up a piece of stovewood and began tearing splinters out of it with his fingernails. He piled the splinters in a little stack between his feet.

"If old Berry Miller makes any show of getting his bristles up, I'll reach right down and kiss her in front of all the Millers, and then pick her up and walk off with her without so much as looking back at them even once. That'll show Berry that when I set out to get married, I don't let nothing in the whole wide world stop me. Those Millers can't put the scare into me."

He hurled the stick of stovewood across the yard. It narrowly missed hitting one of his hens asleep in a dust hole under the chinaberry tree. The hen woke up and ran squawking for her life. The other chickens got scared and followed her under the house.

Tuffy took out his handkerchief and wiped the sweatband of his new straw hat. It was a scorching hot day, especially out in the sun at midday, and the heavy wool coat had never felt so tight before.

"If I had thought to get the license yesterday, me and Nancy could have got married today," he said disgustedly, kicking at the ground.

"Now, why didn't I think about that yesterday? I'll have to wait till to-morrow before I can go to the courthouse now."

He got up and walked to his car. He had not intended getting inside, because it was still about half an hour too soon for him to leave, but he could not wait any longer. He would have to drive around ten or fifteen miles an hour, and maybe stop at the creek and wait awhile, but he was too anxious to be on his way to Nancy's house to wait around home any longer. He started the car and drove off, pushing the new straw hat tightly on his head so the wind could not blow it off.

It was half past twelve o'clock when Tuffy Webb drove up to the Berry Miller place and stopped his car in the shade. He had not got there a minute too soon, because the Millers were at that minute coming out on the porch from the dinner table. It was getting hotter all the time, and Tuffy sat in his car for several minutes trying to cool off before getting out and going up to the house.

Before looking at the Millers on the porch, he took out his handker-chief and tried to wipe off some of the perspiration that trickled down his cheeks and down the back of his neck. When he finished, he took off his hat and wiped the sweatband good and dry.

Old man Berry Miller waved at him from the porch. One of the Miller boys rose up on his elbow from the porch floor to see what Tuffy was doing.

Tuffy got out and walked stiff and erect across the yard to the house. He was uncomfortable all over, and it made his face flush red when he realized what he was doing there. The Millers had a way of staring at him that made him forget what he was doing sometimes.

"Come on in on the porch out of that hot sun and have a slice of watermelon fresh out of the bottom of the well," Berry Miller said. "There's not much left, but what there is, you're welcome to it. It's only the leavings."

Berry brushed away the flies with his hat. They swarmed around the porch for a few moments and then settled back again on the rinds and watermelon seed scattered about on the floor.

"Well, howdy, folks," Tuffy said.

One of the boys waved his arm at Tuffy, and both the girls giggled. Berry's wife rocked back and forth in her chair without saying a thing.

A watermelon seed had stuck to her chin and was drying there. Tuffy wondered why nobody told her to brush it off.

"Mighty hot day today," he said, flushing red again when his eyes swept the porch and saw the two girls.

Their white dresses were starched so stiffly that they looked as if corset stays had been sewn into the cloth.

"Sort of," Berry said. "Can't complain, though. Heat's due us."

The boys on the other end of the porch sat up.

"What are you all dressed up for, Tuffy?" Henry asked him. "Going somewhere?"

Tuffy's eyes dropped and he dug the toe of his shoe into the sandy yard.

Nancy, the oldest girl, giggled again.

Tuffy looked up quickly, hoping to see her plain.

"You're dressed up fit to kill, ain't you, Tuffy?" Henry said.

Berry kicked a piece of watermelon rind off the porch.

"That's a mighty fine-looking straw hat you've got on there, Tuffy," Berry said. "You must have bought that at a big store somewhere, and paid a lot of money for it, in the bargain. A pretty all-colored band like that don't come on everyday hats."

Tuffy nodded his head.

The other Miller boy on the porch, Clyde, scraped up a handful of watermelon seed and began shooting them between his fingers. Presently one of the seed hit Tuffy in the face, making him jump as if somebody had taken a slingshot and hit him in the eye with a hickory nut. Tuffy would not look at Clyde, because he and Clyde never had got along any too well. They had had several fist fights already that summer.

Berry's wife moved to and fro in her rocker, looking disinterestedly at Tuffy. The watermelon seed had dried on her chin and was stuck there for good. He glanced at her, and their eyes met. Whenever she looked at him, it always made Tuffy feel as if she were looking at some object directly behind him. She had never spoken a word to him in all her life.

Nancy smoothed out the skirt of her starched white dress, bending the stiff hem down over her knees. He could still see where her stockings ended on her legs. Nancy's sister looked at Tuffy and giggled.

"I just thought I'd drop by," Tuffy said at last. "I didn't have much else to do today."

"Had any watermelon today so far?" Berry asked him.

"No," Tuffy said.

"If you don't mind eating the leavings," Berry said, waving his hand at the rind-strewn porch, "you're welcome to have some."

Tuffy looked to see what Nancy was doing, but he could not see the expression on her face when his eyes were watching the black and white garter-line on her legs. She bent the starched hem over again, but when she leaned back, it straightened out again and her legs above the stocking tops were as bold as ever.

"Ain't you staying?" Berry asked.

"I don't care if I do," Tuffy said. "I was just riding around, and I thought I'd stop by."

Clyde picked up a piece of rind and threw it at the tree in the yard.

"It's been quite a while since I last saw you all dressed up like that," Berry said. "If I remember correctly, the last time was at the baptizing over at the church about a month ago. Wasn't you all dressed up that day, Tuffy?"

Nancy giggled and hid her face against her sister's shoulder. Tuffy blushed again.

"I didn't have this new hat then, though," he said.

"So you didn't!" Berry said. "That is right, aint it? That hat looks so natural on your head that I forgot all about it. But you did have on a coat that day, didn't you?"

Tuffy nodded, digging the toe of his shoe into the yard.

"I wish you had come by a little sooner," Berry said. "It's pretty late now to get any of the good part of the melons. The leavings ain't much to offer a body. But of course, now, if you ain't particular, just go ahead and help yourself."

One of the boys kicked a piece of rind across the porch and it fell into the yard near Tuffy's feet. He looked at it, all covered with sand.

"Where you going, Tuffy?" Henry asked him.

"Nowhere much," Tuffy said.

"How about me and you going off a piece?" Henry said, winking. "There's some easy pickings on Sunday afternoons over beyond Hardpan."

Tuffy glanced at Nancy. There was a peculiar look on her face that made him uneasy. The garter-line on her legs wavered in his sight when she rocked slightly in her chair. He dropped his eyes to the ground once more.

"I don't reckon I can right now," he told Henry, blushing red all over.

The two girls began whispering to each other. Every once in a while Nancy glanced up at Tuffy, and then she quickly looked the other way.

Tuffy took off his hat and fanned his face with it.

"It's about time to do some thinking about a little fox-hunting, ain't it, Tuffy?" Berry said. "These nights now are beginning to have a little nip in them, along about midnight, and the foxes will be running before you know it. Anyway, it don't hurt none to sort of warm up the hounds. They've been laying around here all summer and have got as lazy as can be. I been thinking lately of going out some night pretty soon and giving them a short run."

Tuffy nodded his head, but he did not say anything.

"I been thinking about making a trade of some kind for a couple more hunters," Berry said. "That Blackie is still a little lame from last year, and that Elsie is weighted down with pups. That Rastus looks like he takes to cold-trailing more and more every year, and I'm a little upset. I don't reckon it would do any harm to make a trade of some kind, if I could find exactly what I'm looking for. I've got a mule that's stove-up pretty bad, and I figure I need hunting dogs a lot more now than I do a blamed stiff-legged mule."

Tuffy glanced up at Nancy, looking as if he were bursting with something to say. He looked at her so desperately that she reached over and bent the starched hem and held it down. He could do no more than swallow hard and flush red all over. It made his skin feel prickly under the heavy coat when she looked at him.

Clyde sat up and slid down to the edge of the porch. He sat swinging his legs over the edge and looking at Tuffy. Tuffy was becoming more and more uncomfortable. He had been standing for half an hour in the hot sun, and he caught himself swaying on his feet.

"I sure admire that new straw hat of yours, Tuffy," Berry said. "Especially that all-colored pretty band around it."

Tuffy looked desperately at Nancy, and then glanced at the rest of the family. Everyone, except Nancy, stared right back at him. Nancy hung her head when their eyes met.

Henry crossed the yard between him and the house, taking something out of his pocket. He began pulling on it, making it snap like elastic. When he stopped in front of Tuffy, Tuffy looked to see what Henry was playing with. It was a girl's garter, bound in pink silk, and tied in a bow with a red rosebud sewn into it. Tuffy jumped as if he had been pricked with a pin.

Tuffy backed off, taking short steps towards his car.

"Not going so soon?" Berry said. "Why, it hardly seems like more than a minute ago when you got here."

Tuffy stopped. Henry had kept up with him, snapping the garter. He put one end against Tuffy's arm, pulled the other end back a foot or two, and turned it loose. Tuffy jumped when the elastic stung him.

"Where you going, Tuffy?" Henry asked him.

Tuffy looked at the porch where Nancy was. She had sat upright in the chair, leaning slightly forward, and stopped rocking. The starched flare of her skirt had straightened out once more, and he was glad she wore yellow garters.

He started backing away again. Henry followed him, springing the elastic rosebud-trimmed garter at him.

"Let's me and you ride over beyond Hardpan, Tuffy," Henry urged. "It won't be no trouble at all to find us a couple of girls, and we can make a lot of headway on a Sunday afternoon. How about it, Tuffy, huh?"

Tuffy backed away faster, shaking his head. When he got to the tree where his car was, he turned around and jumped into the front seat.

Nancy ran into the house. She could be heard crying all the way to the back porch.

When Tuffy got his car started, Berry got up and walked out into the yard. He watched the automobile disappear over the hill, trying to turn his ear away from Henry's cursing.

"I hate to see a man rush off like that," Berry said. "I'd have swore he came here for some purpose to begin with."

He stood with his back to the house while Clyde left the porch and crossed the field to get some more watermelons to cool in the bottom of the well.

(First published in *Redbook*)

Kneel to the Rising Sun

A SHIVER went through Lonnie. He drew his hand away from his sharp chin, remembering what Clem had said. It made him feel now as if he were committing a crime by standing in Arch Gunnard's presence and allowing his face to be seen.

He and Clem had been walking up the road together that afternoon on their way to the filling station when he told Clem how much he needed rations. Clem stopped a moment to kick a rock out of the road, and said that if you worked for Arch Gunnard long enough, your face would be sharp enough to split the boards for your own coffin.

As Lonnie turned away to sit down on an empty box beside the gasoline pump, he could not help wishing that he could be as unafraid of Arch Gunnard as Clem was. Even if Clem was a Negro, he never hesitated to ask for rations when he needed something to eat; and when he and his family did not get enough, Clem came right out and told Arch so. Arch stood for that, but he swore that he was going to run Clem out of the country the first chance he got.

Lonnie knew without turning around that Clem was standing at the corner of the filling station with two or three other Negroes and looking at him, but for some reason he was unable to meet Clem's eyes.

Arch Gunnard was sitting in the sun, honing his jackknife blade on his boot top. He glanced once or twice at Lonnie's hound, Nancy, who was lying in the middle of the road waiting for Lonnie to go home.

"That your dog, Lonnie?"

Jumping with fear, Lonnie's hand went to his chin to hide the lean face that would accuse Arch of short-rationing.

Arch snapped his fingers and the hound stood up, wagging her tail. She waited to be called.

"Mr. Arch, I—"

Arch called the dog. She began crawling towards them on her belly, wagging her tail a little faster each time Arch's fingers snapped. When she was several feet away, she turned over on her back and lay on the ground with her four paws in the air.

Dudley Smith and Jim Weaver, who were lounging around the filling station, laughed. They had been leaning against the side of the building, but they straightened up to see what Arch was up to.

Arch spat some more tobacco juice on his boot top and whetted the jackknife blade some more.

"What kind of a hound dog is that, anyway, Lonnie?" Arch said. "Looks like to me it might be a ketch hound."

Lonnie could feel Clem Henry's eyes boring into the back of his head. He wondered what Clem would do if it had been his dog Arch Gunnard was snapping his fingers at and calling like that.

"His tail's way too long for a coon hound or a bird dog, ain't it, Arch?" somebody behind Lonnie said, laughing out loud.

Everybody laughed then, including Arch. They looked at Lonnie, waiting to hear what he was going to say to Arch.

"Is he a ketch hound, Lonnie?" Arch said, snapping his finger again.

"Mr. Arch, I—"

"Don't be ashamed of him, Lonnie, if he don't show signs of turning out to be a bird dog or a foxhound. Everybody needs a hound around the house that can go out and catch pigs and rabbits when you are in a hurry for them. A ketch hound is a mighty respectable animal. I've known the time when I was mighty proud to own one."

Everybody laughed.

Arch Gunnard was getting ready to grab Nancy by the tail. Lonnie sat up, twisting his neck until he caught a glimpse of Clem Henry at the other corner of the filling station. Clem was staring at him with unmistakable meaning, with the same look in his eyes he had had that afternoon when he said that nobody who worked for Arch Gunnard ought to stand for short-rationing. Lonnie lowered his eyes. He could not figure out how a Negro could be braver than he was. There were a lot of times like that when he would have given anything he had to be able to jump into Clem's shoes and change places with him.

"The trouble with this hound of yours, Lonnie, is that he's too heavy on his feet. Don't you reckon it would be a pretty slick little trick to lighten the load some, being as how he's a ketch hound to begin with?"

Lonnie remembered then what Clem Henry had said he would do if Arch Gunnard ever tried to cut off his dog's tail. Lonnie knew, and Clem knew, and everybody else knew, that that would give Arch the chance he was waiting for. All Arch asked, he had said, was for Clem Henry to overstep his place just one little half inch, or to talk back to him with just one little short word, and he would do the rest. Everybody knew what Arch meant by that, especially if Clem did not turn and run. And Clem had not been known to run from anybody, after fifteen years in the country.

Arch reached down and grabbed Nancy's tail while Lonnie was wondering about Clem. Nancy acted as if she thought Arch were playing some kind of a game with her. She turned her head around until she could reach Arch's hand to lick it. He cracked her on the bridge of the nose with the end of the jackknife.

"He's a mighty playful dog, Lonnie," Arch said, catching up a shorter grip on the tail, "but his wagpole is way too long for a dog his size, especially when he wants to be a ketch hound."

Lonnie swallowed hard.

"Mr. Arch, she's a mighty fine rabbit tracker. I—"

"Shucks, Lonnie," Arch said, whetting the knife blade on the dog's tail, "I ain't ever seen a hound in all my life that needed a tail that long to hunt rabbits with. It's way too long for just a common, ordinary, everyday ketch hound."

Lonnie looked up hopefully at Dudley Smith and the others. None of them offered any help. It was useless for him to try to stop Arch, because Arch Gunnard would let nothing stand in his way when once he had set his head on what he wished to do. Lonnie knew that if he should let himself show any anger or resentment, Arch would drive him off the farm before sundown that night. Clem Henry was the only person there who would help him, but Clem . . .

The white men and the Negroes at both corners of the filling station waited to see what Lonnie was going to do about it. All of them hoped he would put up a fight for his hound. If anyone ever had the nerve to stop Arch Gunnard from cutting off a dog's tail, it might put an end to it. It was plain, though, that Lonnie, who was one of Arch's sharecroppers, was afraid to speak up. Clem Henry might; Clem was the only one who might try to stop Arch, even if it meant trouble. And all of them knew that Arch would insist on running Clem out of the country, or filling him full of lead.

"I reckon it's all right with you, ain't it, Lonnie?" Arch said. "I don't seem to hear no objections."

Clem Henry stepped forward several paces, and stopped.

Arch laughed, watching Lonnie's face, and jerked Nancy to her feet. The hound cried out in pain and surprise, but Arch made her be quiet by kicking her in the belly.

Lonnie winced. He could hardly bear to see anybody kick his dog like that.

"Mr. Arch, I . . ."

A contraction in his throat almost choked him for several moments, and he had to open his mouth wide and fight for breath. The other white men around him were silent. Nobody liked to see a dog kicked in the belly like that.

Lonnie could see the other end of the filling station from the corner of his eye. He saw a couple of Negroes go up behind Clem and grasp his overalls. Clem spat on the ground, between outspread feet, but he did not try to break away from them.

"Being as how I don't hear no objections, I reckon it's all right to go ahead and cut it off," Arch said, spitting.

Lonnie's head went forward and all he could see of Nancy was her hind feet. He had come to ask for a slab of sowbelly and some molasses, or something. Now he did not know if he could ever bring himself to ask for rations, no matter how much hungrier they became at home.

"I always make it a habit of asking a man first," Arch said. "I wouldn't want to go ahead and cut off a tail if a man had any objections. That wouldn't be right. No, sir, it just wouldn't be fair and square."

Arch caught a shorter grip on the hound's tail and placed the knife blade on it two or three inches from the rump. It looked to those who were watching as if his mouth were watering, because tobacco juice began to trickle down the corners of his lips. He brought up the back of his hand and wiped his mouth.

A noisy automobile came plowing down the road through the deep red dust. Everyone looked up as it passed in order to see who was in it.

Lonnie glanced at it, but he could not keep his eyes raised. His head fell downward once more until he could feel his sharp chin cutting into his chest. He wondered then if Arch had noticed how lean his face was.

"I keep two or three ketch hounds around my place," Arch said, honing the blade on the tail of the dog as if it were a razor strop until his actions brought smiles to the faces of the men grouped around him, "but I never could see the sense of a ketch hound having a long tail. It only gets in their way when I send them out to catch a pig or a rabbit for my supper."

Pulling with his left hand and pushing with his right, Arch Gunnard docked the hound's tail as quickly and as easily as if he were cutting a willow switch in the pasture to drive the cows home with. The dog sprang forward with the release of her tail until she was far beyond Arch's reach, and began howling so loud she could be heard half a mile away. Nancy stopped once and looked back at Arch, and then she sprang to the middle of the road and began leaping and twisting in circles. All that time she was yelping and biting at the bleeding stub of her tail.

Arch leaned backward and twirled the severed tail in one hand while he wiped the jackknife blade on his boot sole. He watched Lonnie's dog chasing herself around in circles in the red dust.

Nobody had anything to say then. Lonnie tried not to watch his dog's agony, and he forced himself to keep from looking at Clem Henry. Then, with his eyes shut, he wondered why he had remained on Arch Gunnard's plantation all those past years, sharecropping for a mere living on short rations, and becoming leaner and leaner all the time. He knew then how true it was what Clem had said about Arch's sharecroppers' faces becoming sharp enough to hew their own coffins. His hands went to his chin before he knew what he was doing. His hand dropped when he had felt the bones of jaw and the exposed tendons of his cheeks.

As hungry as he was, he knew that even if Arch did give him some rations then, there would not be nearly enough for them to eat for the following week. Hatty, his wife, was already broken down from hunger and work in the fields, and his father, Mark Newsome, stone-deaf for the past twenty years, was always asking him why there was never enough food in the house for them to have a solid meal. Lonnie's head fell forward a little more, and he could feel his eyes becoming damp.

The pressure of his sharp chin against his chest made him so uncomfortable that he had to raise his head at last in order to ease the pain of it.

The first thing he saw when he looked up was Arch Gunnard twirling Nancy's tail in his left hand. Arch Gunnard had a trunk full of dogs' tails at home. He had been cutting off tails ever since anyone could remember, and during all those years he had accumulated a collection of which he was so proud that he kept the trunk locked and the key tied around his neck on a string. On Sunday afternoons when the preacher came to visit, or when a crowd was there to loll on the front porch and swap stories, Arch showed them off, naming each tail from memory just as well as if he had had a tag on it.

Clem Henry had left the filling station and was walking alone down the road towards the plantation. Clem Henry's house was in a cluster of Negro cabins below Arch's big house, and he had to pass Lonnie's house to get there. Lonnie was on the verge of getting up and leaving when he saw Arch looking at him. He did not know whether Arch was looking at his lean face, or whether he was watching to see if he were going to get up and go down the road with Clem.

The thought of leaving reminded him of his reason for being there. He had to have some rations before suppertime that night, no matter how short they were.

"Mr. Arch, I . . ."

Arch stared at him for a moment, appearing as if he had turned to listen to some strange sound unheard of before that moment.

Lonnie bit his lips, wondering if Arch was going to say anything about how lean and hungry he looked. But Arch was thinking about something else. He slapped his hand on his leg and laughed out loud.

"I sometimes wish niggers had tails," Arch said, coiling Nancy's tail into a ball and putting it into his pocket. "I'd a heap rather cut off nigger tails than dog tails. There'd be more to cut, for one thing."

Dudley Smith and somebody else behind them laughed for a brief moment. The laughter died out almost as suddenly as it had risen.

The Negroes who had heard Arch shuffled their feet in the dust and moved backwards. It was only a few minutes until not one was left at the filling station. They went up the road behind the red wooden building until they were out of sight.

Arch got up and stretched. The sun was getting low, and it was no longer comfortable in the October air. "Well, I reckon I'll be getting on home to get me some supper," he said.

He walked slowly to the middle of the road and stopped to look at Nancy retreating along the ditch.

"Nobody going my way?" he asked. "What's wrong with you, Lonnie? Going home to supper, ain't you?"

"Mr. Arch, I . . ."

Lonnie found himself jumping to his feet. His first thought was to ask for the sowbelly and molasses, and maybe some corn meal; but when he opened his mouth, the words refused to come out. He took several steps forward and shook his head. He did not know what Arch might say or do if he said "No."

"Hatty'll be looking for you," Arch said, turning his back and walking off.

He reached into his hip pocket and took out Nancy's tail. He began twirling it as he walked down the road towards the big house in the distance.

Dudley Smith went inside the filling station, and the others walked away.

After Arch had gone several hundred yards, Lonnie sat down heavily on the box beside the gas pump from which he had got up when Arch spoke to him. He sat down heavily, his shoulders drooping, his arms falling between his outspread legs.

Lonnie did not know how long his eyes had been closed, but when he opened them, he saw Nancy lying between his feet, licking the docked tail. While he watched her, he felt the sharp point of his chin cutting into his chest again. Presently the door behind him was slammed shut, and a minute later he could hear Dudley Smith walking away from the filling station on his way home.

II

Lonnie had been sleeping fitfully for several hours when he suddenly found himself wide awake. Hatty shook him again. He raised himself on his elbow and tried to see into the darkness of the room. Without knowing what time it was, he was able to determine that it was still nearly two hours until sunrise.

"Lonnie," Hatty said again, trembling in the cold night air, "Lonnie, your pa ain't in the house."

Lonnie sat upright in bed.

"How do you know he ain't?" he said.

"I've been lying here wide awake ever since I got in bed, and I heard him when he went out. He's been gone all that time."

"Maybe he just stepped out for a while," Lonnie said, turning and trying to see through the bedroom window.

"I know what I'm saying, Lonnie," Hatty insisted. "Your pa's been gone a heap too long."

Both of them sat without a sound for several minutes while they listened for Mark Newsome.

Lonnie got up and lit a lamp. He shivered while he was putting on his shirt, overalls, and shoes. He tied his shoelaces in hard knots because he couldn't see in the faint light. Outside the window it was almost pitch-dark, and Lonnie could feel the damp October air blowing against his face.

"I'll go help look," Hatty said, throwing the covers off and starting to get up.

Lonnie went to the bed and drew the covers back over her and pushed her back into place.

"You try to get some sleep, Hatty," he said; "you can't stay awake the whole night. I'll go bring Pa back."

He left Hatty, blowing out the lamp, and stumbled through the dark hall, feeling his way to the front porch by touching the wall with his hands. When he got to the porch, he could still barely see any distance ahead, but his eyes were becoming more accustomed to the darkness. He waited a minute, listening.

Feeling his way down the steps into the yard, he walked around the corner of the house and stopped to listen again before calling his father.

"Oh, Pa!" he said loudly. "Oh, Pa!"

He stopped under the bedroom window when he realized what he had been doing.

"Now that's a fool thing for me to be out here doing," he said, scolding himself. "Pa couldn't hear it thunder."

He heard a rustling of the bed.

"He's been gone long enough to get clear to the crossroads, or more," Hatty said, calling through the window.

"Now you lay down and try to get a little sleep, Hatty," Lonnie told her. "I'll bring him back in no time."

He could hear Nancy scratching fleas under the house, but he knew she was in no condition to help look for Mark. It would be several days before she recovered from the shock of losing her tail.

"He's been gone a long time," Hatty said, unable to keep still.

"That don't make no difference," Lonnie said. "I'll find him sooner or later. Now you go on to sleep like I told you, Hatty."

Lonnie walked towards the barn, listening for some sound. Over at the big house he could hear the hogs grunting and squealing, and he wished they would be quiet so he could hear other sounds. Arch Gunnard's dogs were howling occasionally, but they were not making any more noise than they usually did at night, and he was accustomed to their howling.

Lonnie went to the barn, looking inside and out. After walking around the barn, he went into the field as far as the cotton shed. He knew it was useless, but he could not keep from calling his father time after time.

"Oh, Pa!" he said, trying to penetrate the darkness.

He went farther into the field.

"Now, what in the world could have become of Pa?" he said, stopping and wondering where to look next.

After he had gone back to the front yard, he began to feel uneasy for the first time. Mark had not acted any more strangely during the past week than he ordinarily did, but Lonnie knew he was upset over the way Arch Gunnard was giving out short rations. Mark had even said that, at the rate they were being fed, all of them would starve to death inside another three months.

Lonnie left the yard and went down the road towards the Negro cabins. When he got to Clem's house, he turned in and walked up the path to the door. He knocked several times and waited. There was no answer, and he rapped louder.

"Who's that?" he heard Clem say from bed.

"It's me," Lonnie said. "I've got to see you a minute, Clem. I'm out in the front yard."

He sat down and waited for Clem to dress and come outside. While he waited, he strained his ears to catch any sound that might be in the air. Over the fields towards the big house he could hear the fattening hogs grunt and squeal.

Clem came out and shut the door. He stood on the doorsill a moment speaking to his wife in bed, telling her he would be back and not to worry.

"Who's that?" Clem said, coming down into the yard.

Lonnie got up and met Clem halfway.

"What's the trouble?" Clem asked then, buttoning up his overall jumper.

"Pa's not in his bed," Lonnie said, "and Hatty says he's been gone from the house most all night. I went out in the field, and all around the barn, but I couldn't find a trace of him anywhere."

Clem then finished buttoning his jumper and began rolling a cigarette. He walked slowly down the path to the road. It was still dark, and it would be at least an hour before dawn made it any lighter.

"Maybe he was too hungry to stay in bed any longer," Clem said. "When I saw him yesterday, he said he was so shrunk up and weak he didn't know if he could last much longer. He looked like his skin and bones couldn't shrivel much more."

"I asked Arch last night after suppertime for some rations — just a little piece of sowbelly and some molasses. He said he'd get around to letting me have some the first thing this morning."

"Why don't you tell him to give you full rations or none?" Clem said. "If you knew you wasn't going to get none at all, you could move away and find a better man to sharecrop for, couldn't you?"

"I've been loyal to Arch Gunnard for a long time now," Lonnie said. "I'd hate to haul off and leave him like that."

Clem looked at Lonnie, but he did not say anything more just then. They turned up the road towards the driveway that led up to the big house. The fattening hogs were still grunting and squealing in the pen, and one of Arch's hounds came down a cotton row beside the driveway to smell their shoes.

"Them fattening hogs always get enough to eat," Clem said. "There's not a one of them that don't weigh seven hundred pounds right now, and they're getting bigger every day. Besides taking all that's thrown to them, they make a lot of meals off the chickens that get in there to peck around."

Lonnie listened to the grunting of the hogs as they walked up the driveway towards the big house.

"Reckon we'd better get Arch up to help look for Pa?" Lonnie said. "I'd hate to wake him up, but I'm scared Pa might stray off into the swamp and get lost for good. He couldn't hear it thunder, even. I never could find him back there in all that tangle if he got into it."

Clem said something under his breath and went on towards the barn and hog pen. He reached the pen before Lonnie got there.

"You'd better come here quick," Clem said, turning around to see where Lonnie was.

Lonnie ran to the hog pen. He stopped and climbed halfway up the wooden-and-wire sides of the fence. At first he could see nothing, but gradually he was able to see the moving mass of black fattening hogs on the other side of the pen. They were biting and snarling at each other like a pack of hungry hounds turned loose on a dead rabbit.

Lonnie scrambled to the top of the fence, but Clem caught him and pulled him back.

"Don't go in that hog pen that way," he said. "Them hogs will tear you to pieces, they're that wild. They're fighting over something."

Both of them ran around the corner of the pen and got to the side where the hogs were. Down under their feet on the ground Lonnie caught a glimpse of a dark mass splotched with white. He was able to see it for a moment only, because one of the hogs trampled over it.

Clem opened and closed his mouth several times before he was able to say anything at all. He clutched at Lonnie's arm, shaking him.

"That looks like it might be your pa," he said. "I swear before goodness, Lonnie, it does look like it."

Lonnie still could not believe it. He climbed to the top of the fence and began kicking his feet at the hogs, trying to drive them away. They paid no attention to him.

While Lonnie was perched there, Clem had gone to the wagon shed, and he ran back with two singletrees he had somehow managed to find there in the dark. He handed one to Lonnie, poking it at him until Lonnie's attention was drawn from the hogs long enough to take it.

Clem leaped over the fence and began swinging the singletree at the hogs. Lonnie slid down beside him, yelling at them. One hog turned on Lonnie and snapped at him, and Clem struck it over the back of the neck with enough force to drive it off momentarily.

By then Lonnie was able to realize what had happened. He ran to the mass of hogs, kicking them with his heavy stiff shoes and striking them on their heads with the iron-tipped singletree. Once he felt a stinging sensation, and looked down to see one of the hogs biting the calf of his leg. He had just enough time to hit the hog and drive it away before his leg was torn. He knew most of his overall leg had been ripped away, because he could feel the night air on his bare wet calf.

Clem had gone ahead and had driven the hogs back. There was no other way to do anything. They were in a snarling circle around them, and both of them had to keep the singletrees swinging back and forth all the time to keep the hogs off. Finally Lonnie reached down and got a grip on Mark's leg. With Clem helping, Lonnie carried his father to the fence and lifted him over to the other side.

They were too much out of breath for a while to say anything, or to do anything else. The snarling, fattening hogs were at the fence, biting the wood and wire, and making more noise than ever.

While Lonnie was searching in his pockets for a match, Clem struck one. He held the flame close to Mark Newsome's head.

They both stared unbelievingly, and then Clem blew out the match. There was nothing said as they stared at each other in the darkness.

Clem walked several steps away, and turned and came back beside Lonnie.

"It's him, though," Clem said, sitting down on the ground. "It's him, all right."

"I reckon so," Lonnie said. He could think of nothing else to say then.

They sat on the ground, one on each side of Mark, looking at the body. There had been no sign of life in the body beside them since they had first touched it. The face, throat, and stomach had been completely devoured.

"You'd better go wake up Arch Gunnard," Clem said after a while.

"What for?" Lonnie said. "He can't help none now. It's too late for help."

"Makes no difference," Clem insisted. "You'd better go wake him up and let him see what there is to see. If you wait till morning, he might take it into his head to say the hogs didn't do it. Right now is the time to get him up so he can see what his hogs did."

Clem turned around and looked at the big house. The dark outline against the dark sky made him hesitate.

"A man who short-rations tenants ought to have to sit and look at that till it's buried."

Lonnie looked at Clem fearfully. He knew Clem was right, but he was scared to hear a Negro say anything like that about a white man.

"You oughtn't talk like that about Arch," Lonnie said. "He's in bed asleep. He didn't have a thing to do with it. He didn't have no more to do with it than I did."

Clem laughed a little, and threw the singletree on the ground between his feet. After letting it lie there a little while, he picked it up and began beating the ground with it.

Lonnie got to his feet slowly. He had never seen Clem act like that before, and he did not know what to think about it. He left without saying anything and walked stiffly to the house in the darkness to wake up Arch Gunnard.

III

Arch was hard to wake up. And even after he was awake, he was in no hurry to get up. Lonnie was standing outside the bedroom window, and Arch was lying in bed six or eight feet away. Lonnie could hear him toss and grumble.

"Who told you to come and wake me up in the middle of the night?" Arch said.

"Well, Clem Henry's out here, and he said maybe you'd like to know about it."

Arch tossed around on the bed, flailing the pillow with his fists.

"You tell Clem Henry I said that one of these days he's going to find himself turned inside out, like a coat sleeve."

Lonnie waited doggedly. He knew Clem was right in insisting that Arch ought to wake up and come out there to see what had happened. Lonnie was afraid to go back to the barnyard and tell Clem that Arch was not coming. He did not know, but he had a feeling that Clem might go into the bedroom and drag Arch out of bed. He did not like to think of anything like that taking place.

"Are you still out there, Lonnie?" Arch shouted.

"I'm right here, Mr. Arch. I —"

"If I wasn't so sleepy, I'd come out there and take a stick and — I don't know what I wouldn't do!"

Lonnie met Arch at the back step. On the way out to the hog pen Arch did not speak to him. Arch walked heavily ahead, not even waiting to see if Lonnie was coming. The lantern that Arch was carrying cast long flat beams of yellow light over the ground; and when they got to where Clem was waiting beside Mark's body, the Negro's face shone in the night like a highly polished plowshare.

"What was Mark doing in my hog pen at night, anyway?" Arch said, shouting at them both.

Neither Clem nor Lonnie replied. Arch glared at them for not answering. But no matter how many times he looked at them, his eyes returned each time to stare at the torn body of Mark Newsome on the ground at his feet.

"There's nothing to be done now," Arch said finally. "We'll just have to wait till daylight and send for the undertaker." He walked a few steps away. "Looks like you could have waited till morning in the first place. There wasn't no sense in getting me up."

He turned his back and looked sideways at Clem. Clem stood up and looked him straight in the eyes.

"What do you want, Clem Henry?" he said. "Who told you to be coming around my house in the middle of the night? I don't want niggers coming here except when I send for them."

"I couldn't stand to see anybody eaten up by the hogs, and not do anything about it," Clem said.

"You mind your own business," Arch told him. "And when you talk to me, take off your hat, or you'll be sorry for it. It wouldn't take much to make me do you up the way you belong."

Lonnie backed away. There was a feeling of uneasiness around them. That was how trouble between Clem and Arch always began. He had seen it start that way dozens of times before. As long as Clem turned and went away, nothing happened, but sometimes he stayed right where he was and talked up to Arch just as if he had been a white man, too.

Lonnie hoped it would not happen this time. Arch was already mad enough about being waked up in the middle of the night, and Lonnie knew there was no limit to what Arch would do when he got good and mad at a Negro. Nobody had ever seen him kill a Negro, but he had said he had, and he told people that he was not scared to do it again.

"I reckon you know how he came to get eaten up by the hogs like that," Clem said, looking straight at Arch.

Arch whirled around.

"Are you talking to me . . .?"

"I asked you that," Clem stated.

"God damn you, yellow-blooded . . ." Arch yelled.

He swung the lantern at Clem's head. Clem dodged, but the bottom of it hit his shoulder, and it was smashed to pieces. The oil splattered on the ground, igniting in the air from the flaming wick. Clem was lucky not to have it splash on his face and overalls.

"Now, look here . . ." Clem said.

"You yellow-blooded nigger," Arch said, rushing at him. "I'll teach you to talk back to me. You've got too big for your place for the last time. I've been taking too much from you, but I ain't doing it no more."

"Mr. Arch, I . . ." Lonnie said, stepping forward partly between them. No one heard him.

Arch stood back and watched the kerosene flicker out on the ground.

"You know good and well why he got eaten up by the fattening hogs," Clem said, standing his ground. "He was so hungry he had to get up out of bed in the middle of the night and come up here in the dark trying to find something to eat. Maybe he was trying to find the smokehouse. It makes no difference, either way. He's been on short rations like everybody else working on your place, and he was so old he didn't know where else to look for food except in your smokehouse. You know good and well that's how he got lost up here in the dark and fell in the hog pen."

The kerosene had died out completely. In the last faint flare, Arch had reached down and grabbed up the singletree that had been lying on the ground where Lonnie had dropped it.

Arch raised the singletree over his head and struck with all his might at Clem. Clem dodged, but Arch drew back again quickly and landed a blow on his arm just above the elbow before Clem could dodge it. Clem's arm dropped to his side, dangling lifelessly.

"You God-damn yellow-blooded nigger!" Arch shouted. "Now's your time, you black bastard! I've been waiting for the chance to teach you your lesson. And this's going to be one you won't never forget."

Clem felt the ground with his feet until he had located the other singletree. He stooped down and got it. Raising it, he did not try to hit Arch, but held it in front of him so he could ward off Arch's blows at his head. He continued to stand his ground, not giving Arch an inch.

"Drop that singletree," Arch said.

"I won't stand here and let you beat me like that," Clem protested.

"By God, that's all I want to hear," Arch said, his mouth curling. "Nigger, your time has come, by God!"

He swung once more at Clem, but Clem turned and ran towards the barn. Arch went after him a few steps and stopped. He threw aside the singletree and turned and ran back to the house.

Lonnie went to the fence and tried to think what was best for him to do. He knew he could not take sides with a Negro, in the open, even if Clem had helped him, and especially after Clem had talked to Arch in the way he wished he could himself. He was a white man, and to save his life he could not stand to think of turning against Arch, no matter what happened.

Presently a light burst through one of the windows of the house, and he heard Arch shouting at his wife to wake her up.

When he saw Arch's wife go to the telephone, Lonnie realized what was going to happen. She was calling up the neighbors and Arch's friends. They would not mind getting up in the night when they found out what was going to take place.

Out behind the barn he could hear Clem calling him. Leaving the yard, Lonnie felt his way out there in the dark.

"What's the trouble, Clem?" he said.

"I reckon my time has come," Clem said. "Arch Gunnard talks that way when he's good and mad. He talked just like he did that time he carried Jim Moffin off to the swamp—and Jim never came back."

"Arch wouldn't do anything like that to you, Clem," Lonnie said excitedly, but he knew better.

Clem said nothing.

"Maybe you'd better strike out for the swamps till he changes his mind and cools off some," Lonnie said. "You might be right, Clem."

Lonnie could feel Clem's eyes burning into him.

"Wouldn't be no sense in that, if you'd help me," Clem said. "Wouldn't you stand by me?"

Lonnie trembled as the meaning of Clem's suggestion became clear to him. His back was to the side of the barn, and he leaned against it while sheets of black and white passed before his eyes.

"Wouldn't you stand by me?" Clem asked again.

"I don't know what Arch would say to that," Lonnie told him haltingly.

Clem walked away several paces. He stood with his back to Lonnie while he looked across the field towards the quarter where his home was.

"I could go in that little patch of woods out there and stay till they get tired of looking for me," Clem said, turning around to see Lonnie.

"You'd better go somewhere," Lonnie said uneasily. "I know Arch Gunnard. He's hard to handle when he makes up his mind to do something he wants to do. I couldn't stop him an inch. Maybe you'd better get clear out of the country, Clem."

"I couldn't do that, and leave my family down there across the field," Clem said.

"He's going to get you if you don't."

"If you'd only sort of help me out a little, he wouldn't. I would only have to go and hide out in that little patch of woods over there a while. Looks like you could do that for me, being as how I helped you find your pa when he was in the hog pen."

Lonnie nodded, listening for sounds from the big house. He continued to nod at Clem while Clem was waiting to be assured.

"If you're going to stand up for me," Clem said, "I can just go over there in the woods and wait till they get it off their minds. You won't be telling them where I'm at, and you could say I struck out for the swamp. They wouldn't ever find me without bloodhounds."

"That's right," Lonnie said, listening for sounds of Arch's coming out of the house. He did not wish to be found back there behind the barn where Arch could accuse him of talking to Clem.

The moment Lonnie replied, Clem turned and ran off into the night. Lonnie went after him a few steps, as if he had suddenly changed his mind about helping him, but Clem was lost in the darkness by then.

Lonnie waited for a few minutes, listening to Clem crashing through the underbrush in the patch of woods a quarter of a mile away. When he could hear Clem no longer, he went around the barn to meet Arch.

Arch came out of the house carrying his double-barreled shotgun and the lantern he had picked up in the house. His pockets were bulging with shells.

"Where is that damn nigger, Lonnie?" Arch asked him. "Where'd he go to?"

Lonnie opened his mouth, but no words came out.

"You know which way he went, don't you?"

Lonnie again tried to say something, but there were no sounds. He jumped when he found himself nodding his head to Arch.

"Mr. Arch, I—"

"That's all right, then," Arch said. "That's all I need to know now, Dudley Smith and Tom Hawkins and Frank and Dave Howard and the rest will be here in a minute, and you can stay right here so you can show us where he's hiding out."

Frantically Lonnie tried to say something. Then he reached for Arch's sleeve to stop him, but Arch had gone.

Arch ran around the house to the front yard. Soon a car came racing down the road, its headlights lighting up the whole place, hog pen and all. Lonnie knew it was probably Dudley Smith, because his was the first house in that direction, only half a mile away. While he was turning into the driveway, several other automobiles came into sight, both up the road and down it.

Lonnie trembled. He was afraid Arch was going to tell him to point out where Clem had gone to hide. Then he knew Arch would tell him. He had promised Clem he would not do that. But try as he might, he could not make himself believe that Arch Gunnard would do anything more than whip Clem.

Clem had not done anything that called for lynching. He had not raped a white woman, he had not shot at a white man; he had only talked back to Arch, with his hat on. But Arch was mad enough to do anything; he was mad enough at Clem not to stop at anything short of lynching.

The whole crowd of men was swarming around him before he realized it. And there was Arch clutching his arm and shouting into his face.

"Mr. Arch, I—"

Lonnie recognized every man in the feeble dawn. They were excited, and they looked like men on the last lap of an all-night fox-hunting party. Their shotguns and pistols were held at their waist, ready for the kill.

"What's the matter with you, Lonnie?" Arch said, shouting into his ear. "Wake up and say where Clem Henry went to hide out. We're ready to go get him."

Lonnie remembered looking up and seeing Frank Howard dropping yellow twelve-gauge shells into the breech of his gun. Frank bent forward so he could hear Lonnie tell Arch where Clem was hiding.

"You ain't going to kill Clem this time, are you, Mr. Arch?" Lonnie asked.

"Kill him?" Dudley Smith repeated. "What do you reckon I've been waiting all this time for if it wasn't for a chance to get Clem. That nigger has had it coming to him ever since he came to this county. He's a bad nigger, and it's coming to him."

"It wasn't exactly Clem's fault," Lonnie said. "If Pa hadn't come up here and fell in the hog pen, Clem wouldn't have had a thing to do with it. He was helping me, that's all."

"Shut up, Lonnie," somebody shouted at him. "You're so excited you don't know what you're saying. You're taking up for a nigger when you talk like that."

People were crowding around him so tightly he felt as if he were being squeezed to death. He had to get some air, get his breath, get out of the crowd.

"That's right,'" Lonnie said.

He heard himself speak, but he did not know what he was saying.

"But Clem helped me find Pa when he got lost looking around for something to eat."

"Shut up, Lonnie," somebody said again. "You damn fool, shut up!"

Arch grabbed his shoulder and shook him until his teeth rattled. Then Lonnie realized what he had been saying.

"Now, look here, Lonnie," Arch shouted. "You must be out of your head, because you know good and well you wouldn't talk like a nigger-lover in your right mind."

"That's right," Lonnie said, trembling all over. "I sure wouldn't want to talk like that."

He could still feel the grip on his shoulder where Arch's strong fingers had hurt him.

"Did Clem go to the swamp, Lonnie?" Dudley Smith said. "Is that right, Lonnie?"

Lonnie tried to shake his head; he tried to nod his head. Then Arch's fingers squeezed his thin neck. Lonnie looked at the men wild-eyed.

"Where's Clem hiding, Lonnie?" Arch demanded, squeezing.

Lonnie went three or four steps towards the barn. When he stopped, the men behind him pushed forward again. He found himself being rushed behind the barn and beyond it.

"All right, Lonnie," Arch said. "Now which way?"

Lonnie pointed towards the patch of woods where the creek was. The swamp was in the other direction.

"He said he was going to hide out in that little patch of woods along the creek over there, Mr. Arch," Lonnie said. "I reckon he's over there now."

Lonnie felt himself being swept forward, and he stumbled over the rough ground trying to keep from being knocked down and trampled upon. Nobody was talking, and everyone seemed to be walking on tiptoes. The gray light of early dawn was increasing enough both to hide them and to show the way ahead.

Just before they reached the fringe of the woods, the men separated, and Lonnie found himself a part of the circle that was closing in on Clem.

Lonnie was alone, and there was nobody to stop him, but he was unable to move forward or backward. It began to be clear to him what he had done.

Clem was probably up a tree somewhere in the woods ahead, but by that time he had been surrounded on all sides. If he should attempt to break and run, he would be shot down like a rabbit.

Lonnie sat down on a log and tried to think what to do. The sun would be up in a few more minutes, and as soon as it came up, the men would close in on the creek and Clem. He would have no chance at all among all those shotguns and pistols.

Once or twice he saw the flare of a match through the underbrush where some of the men were lying in wait. A whiff of cigarette smoke struck his nostrils, and he found himself wondering if Clem could smell it wherever he was in the woods.

There was still no sound anywhere around him, and he knew that Arch Gunnard and the rest of the men were waiting for the sun, which would in a few minutes come up behind him in the east.

It was light enough by that time to see plainly the rough ground and the tangled underbrush and the curling bark on the pine trees.

The men had already begun to creep forward, guns raised as if stalking a deer. The woods were not large, and the circle of men would be able to cover it in a few minutes at the rate they were going forward. There was still a chance that Clem had slipped through the circle before dawn broke, but Lonnie felt that he was still there. He began to feel then that Clem was there because he himself had placed him there for the men to find more easily.

Lonnie found himself moving forward, drawn into the narrowing circle. Presently he could see the men all around him in dim outline. Their eyes were searching the heavy green pine tops as they went forward from tree to tree.

"Oh, Pa!" he said in a hoarse whisper. "Oh, Pa!"

He went forward a few steps, looking into the bushes and up into the treetops. When he saw the other men again, he realized that it was not Mark Newsome being sought. He did not know what had made him forget like that.

The creeping forward began to work into the movement of Lonnie's body. He found himself springing forward on his toes, and his body was leaning in that direction. It was like creeping up on a rabbit when you did not have a gun to hunt with.

He forgot again what he was doing there. The springing motion in his legs seemed to be growing stronger with each step. He bent forward so far he could almost touch the ground with his fingertips. He could not stop now. He was keeping up with the circle of men.

The fifteen men were drawing closer and closer together. The dawn had broken enough to show the time on the face of a watch. The sun was beginning to color the sky above.

Lonnie was far in advance of anyone else by then. He could not hold himself back. The strength in his legs was more than he could hold in check.

He had for so long been unable to buy shells for his gun that he had forgotten how much he liked to hunt.

The sound of the men's steady creeping had become a rhythm in his ears.

"Here's the bastard!" somebody shouted, and there was a concerted crashing through the dry underbrush. Lonnie dashed forward, reaching the tree almost as quickly as anyone else.

He could see everybody with guns raised, and far into the sky above the sharply outlined face of Clem Henry gleamed in the rising sun. His body was hugging the slender top of the pine.

Lonnie did not know who was the first to fire, but the rest of the men did not hesitate. There was a deafening roar as the shotguns and revolvers flared and smoked around the trunk of the tree.

He closed his eyes; he was afraid to look again at the face above. The firing continued without break. Clem hugged the tree with all his might, and then, with the faraway sound of splintering wood, the top of the tree and Clem came crashing through the lower limbs to the ground. The body, sprawling and torn, landed on the ground with a thud that stopped Lonnie's heart for a moment.

He turned, clutching for the support of a tree, as the firing began once more. The crumpled body was tossed time after time, like a sackful of kittens being killed with an automatic shotgun, as charges of lead were fired into it from all sides. A cloud of dust rose from the ground and drifted overhead with the choking odor of burned powder.

Lonnie did not remember how long the shooting lasted. He found himself running from tree to tree, clutching at the rough pine bark, stumbling wildly towards the cleared ground. The sky had turned from gray to red when he emerged in the open, and as he ran, falling over the hard clods in the plowed field, he tried to keep his eyes on the house ahead.

Once he fell and found it almost impossible to rise again to his feet. He struggled to his knees, facing the round red sun. The warmth gave him the strength to rise to his feet, and he muttered unintelligibly to himself. He tried to say things he had never thought to say before.

When he got home, Hatty was waiting for him in the yard. She had heard the shots in the woods, and she had seen him stumbling over the hard clods in the field, and she had seen him kneeling there looking straight into the face of the sun. Hatty was trembling as she ran to Lonnie to find out what the matter was.

Once in his own yard, Lonnie turned and looked for a second over his shoulder. He saw the men climbing over the fence at Arch Gunnard's. Arch's wife was standing on the back porch, and she was speaking to them.

"Where's your pa, Lonnie?" Hatty said. "And what in the world was all that shooting in the woods for?" Lonnie stumbled forward until he had reached the front porch. He fell upon the steps.

"Lonnie, Lonnie!" Hatty was saying. "Wake up and tell me what in the world is the matter. I've never seen the like of all that's going on."

"Nothing," Lonnie said. "Nothing."

"Well, if there's nothing the matter, can't you go up to the big house and ask for a little piece of streak-of-lean? We ain't got a thing to cook for breakfast. Your pa's going to be hungrier than ever after being up walking around all night."

"What?" Lonnie said, his voice rising to a shout as he jumped to his feet.

"Why, I only said go up to the big house and get a little piece of streak-of-lean, Lonnie. That's all I said."

He grabbed his wife about the shoulders.

"Meat?" he yelled, shaking her roughly.

"Yes," she said, pulling away from him in surprise. "Couldn't you go ask Arch Gunnard for a little bit of streak-of-lean?"

Lonnie slumped down again on the steps, his hands falling between his outspread legs and his chin falling on his chest.

"No," he said almost inaudibly. "No. I ain't hungry."

(First published in *Scribner's Magazine*)

The Growing Season

THE heat was enough to drive anybody crazy.

The wire grass was growing faster than Jesse English could keep it chopped down and covered up. He had been going over the twelve acres of cotton for five days already, and he was just about ready to give up.

At noon when his wife called him to dinner, Jesse unhitched the mule from the scraper and turned him loose. The mule walked unsteadily towards the barn, stumbling over the rows as if he had blindstaggers. Jesse's eyes were bloodshot by the heat, and he was afraid he was going to get a sunstroke. He got to the house, but he could not eat anything. He stretched out on the porch, his straw hat over his face to shut out the glare of the sun, feeling as if he could never get up again as long as he lived.

Lizzie came to the door and told him to get up and eat the meal she had cooked. Jesse did not answer her, and after a while she went back inside out of sight.

The rattling of the trace chain in the yard woke Jesse up. He raised himself on his elbow and looked out under the chinaberry tree at Fiddler. Fiddler crawled around the tree, winding the chain around the trunk of the chinaberry. When Fiddler had wound the chain as far as he could, he lay down again.

Jesse stared at Fiddler with his bloodshot eyes burning into his head until he could not stand it any longer. He dug his knuckles into his eye sockets until the pain had left for a while.

Fiddler got up and made as if to stand. Instead, he pitched forward like a drunken man, falling into a mass. Jesse felt a new rush of blood in his head each time Fiddler rattled the chain. While watching him, he began to wonder what was going to happen to his crop of cotton. It had rained for a solid week just when the cotton was ready to hoe, and before he could catch up with it, the wire grass had got ahead of him. Lizzie had had a sunstroke the year before, and every time she stayed in the sun fifteen or twenty minutes she fainted. She could not help him hoe; there was nobody to help him. There was not even a Negro on the place.

When he looked out over the field, he realized how little he had accomplished since sunup that morning. He did not see how he would ever be able to clear out the grass before the cotton plants got choked out.

The trace chain rattled again. Jesse pushed himself on his hands and feet to the edge of the porch and sat there staring at Fiddler. Lizzie came to the door once more and told him to come and eat his dinner, but he did not hear her.

Fiddler turned over on the ground and lay with his head up against the trunk of the chinaberry tree.

Sitting on the edge of the porch with his feet swinging back and forth, Jesse rubbed his eyes with his knuckles and tried to reason clearly. The heat, even in the shade of the porch roof, was blinding him. His eyes burned like hot chestnuts in his head. When he heard Fiddler rattle the chain again, he tried to stare at him through the heat, but Fiddler was by then no more than a blue patch in the yard.

The crop was going to ruin because there was nobody to help him get the grass out before the cotton plants were choked to death by the wire grass.

Jesse eased himself off the edge of the porch and climbed the steps and went into the hall. His shotgun was standing in the corner behind the door. It was kept loaded all the time, and he did not stop to see if there were any shells in the barrels.

"Your dinner's getting spoiled, Jesse," his wife said somewhere in the house.

He did not answer her.

Outside in the sun and heat once more, Jesse could see the wire grass choking the life out of his crop of cotton. He ran to the far end of the yard and out into the field and began kicking the cotton plants and grass with his feet. Even then the wire grass sprang back like coils in a bedspring. The cotton plants he had kicked from their roots began slowly to wilt in the noonday heat. By the time he had turned away, the plants had shriveled up and died.

He went back into the yard and kicked the trace chain. One end was fastened to the chinaberry tree, and the other end was clamped around Fiddler's neck. He stood the shotgun against the tree and began fumbling with the clamp. While he was stooped over, Lizzie came to the porch again.

"What are you aiming to do with that shotgun, Jesse?" she asked, shading her eyes with her hands.

When he did not answer her, she ran down the steps and raced across the yard to the chinaberry.

The clamp was unfastened then. Jesse grabbed the gun and jerked the chain. He jerked the chain harder the next time, and Fiddler rolled to his feet and went wobbling across the yard like a drunken man trying to walk.

Lizzie tried to jerk the chain out of Jesse's hand. He pushed her aside.

"Jesse!" she screamed at him. "Jesse, what you going to do with Fiddler!"

He pushed her behind him. Fiddler wobbled on his undeveloped legs and Jesse poked him upright with the gunstock each time he looked as if he would fall. Lizzie came screaming after them and fell around her husband's legs. Jesse got away from her before she could lock her arms around his knees.

Fiddler had started running towards the barn. Jesse ran behind, holding the gun ahead so he could prod Fiddler in the direction he wanted him to go.

The crop was ruined. But he had forgotten all about the wire grass choking out the tender cotton plants. The grass had got ahead of him before he could stop it. If Lizzie had not been sunstruck, or if he had had anybody else to help him, he could have saved his cotton. The wire grass on twelve acres was too much for one man, once he fell behind.

His eyes were so bloodshot he could not see Fiddler very well. The heat and the throbbing in his head made him forget everything except that he had to get Fiddler out behind the barn where the gully was. He threw a corncob at the mule to get him out of Fiddler's way. The mule went into the barn.

Fiddler ran off in another direction, but Jesse headed him back to the gully with the butt end of the shotgun. He hit Fiddler again with the stock to keep him from going in the wrong direction.

Lizzie was screaming in the front yard. She did not have her sunbonnet on, and she had already got a touch of heat.

When they got to the gully, Jesse shoved Fiddler down into it. Fiddler lay on the bottom on the wash, digging at the sides and trying to get out.

Jesse raised his gun to sight down the barrels, and all he could see was a wiggling gray mass against the red clay gully-bank. He pulled the trigger anyway, and waited a moment. Without lowering the gun, he fired the second shell at Fiddler.

Fiddler was making more noise than he had ever made before. Jesse sat down on the side of the gully and rubbed his eyes with his knuckles. He felt the dried earth give way under his knees, and he moved back a little to keep from sliding down into the gully where Fiddler was floundering like a fish that had been tossed upon dry land.

"Stop that kicking and squealing, and die, damn you!" Jesse shouted. "Die! Damn you, die!"

He could not sit there any longer. He had waited as long as he could wait for Fiddler to stop thrashing around in the gully. The birdshot in the shells was strong enough to kill a mule at short range, but they had not been strong enough to kill Fiddler.

Lizzie screaming under the chinaberry tree and the heat and the blazing sun overhead sent Jesse running to the woodpile at the back of the house. He grabbed up the ax and came running back to the gully. Fiddler was still thrashing around on the bottom like a chicken with its head cut off. Jesse jumped down the bank and struck at Fiddler three or four times. When he stopped, blood was all over the ax handle and blade, and the bottoms of his overall legs were soaked with it.

After a while Fiddler lay still, and Jesse walked down to the lower end of the gully where the banks were not so steep and climbed to the top. On the way back to the house he could see Lizzie lying on the ground under the chinaberry tree where Fiddler had been kept chained.

He carried the ax to the woodpile and swung the blade into a hickory log. After that he sat down on the woodpile and wiped his face with his hands and tried to stop the burning of his eyeballs by digging at them with his knuckles.

From somewhere a breeze came up, and the wind against his hot face made him feel better all over. He ran his thumb under one overall strap and threw it off. The breeze blowing against his wet shirt and skin felt like a gentle rain.

One of the hounds that had been sleeping under the house got up and walked out to the woodpile and began licking the ax handle. Jesse watched him until he had finished. When the dog started licking his overall legs, Jesse kicked him with all his might. The hound tumbled to his feet and ran yelping back under the house.

Jesse wiped his face with his hands again, and got up. He found the hoe leaning against the side of the house. He carried it to the porch and pulled the rat-tailed file out of the weatherboarding where it had been stuck since the last time he used it.

He thought he heard his wife stumbling through the hall of the house.

Propping the hoe against the porch, Jesse began filing the blade until it was as keen as a corn knife. After that was done, he jabbed the file back into the weatherboarding and walked towards the cotton field, bareheaded in the hot sun, carrying the hoe over his shoulder.

Jesse was not certain, but he felt he might be able to save his crop. The wire grass could not stand up under a sharp hoe blade, and he could go back and file his hoe with the rat-tailed file whenever it wanted sharpening.

(First published in *Kneel to the Rising Sun*)

The Negro in the Well

JULE ROBINSON was lying in bed snoring when his foxhounds struck a live trail a mile away and their baying woke him up with a start. He jumped to the floor, jerked on his shoes, and ran out into the front yard. It was about an hour before dawn.

Holding his hat to the side of his head like a swollen hand, he listened to the trailing on the ridge above the house. With his hat to deflect the sound into his ear, he could hear the dogs treading in the dry underbrush as plainly as his own breathing. It had taken him only a few seconds to determine that the hounds were not cold-trailing, and he put his hat back on his head and stooped over to lace his shoes.

"Papa," a frightened voice said, "please don't go off again now — wait till daybreak, anyway."

Jule turned around and saw the dim outline of his two girls. They were huddled together in the window of their bedroom. Jessie and Clara were old enough to take care of themselves, he thought, but that did not stop them from getting in his way when he wanted to go fox hunting.

"Go on back to bed and sleep, Jessie — you and Clara," he said gruffly. "Those hounds are just up on the ridge. They can't take me much out of hollering distance before sunup."

"We're scared, Papa," Clara said.

"Scared of what?" Jule asked impatiently. "There ain't a thing for two big girls like you and Jessie to be scared of. What's there to be scared of in this big country, anyway?"

The hounds stopped trailing for a moment, and Jule straightened up to listen in the silence. All at once they began again, and he bent down to finish tying his shoes.

Off in the distance he could hear several other packs of trailing hounds, and by looking closely at the horizon he could see the twinkle of campfires where bands of fox hunters had stopped to warm their hands and feet.

"Are you going, anyway, Papa?" Clara asked.

"I'm going, anyway," he answered.

The two girls ran back to bed and pulled the covers over their heads. There was no way to argue with Jule Robinson when he had set his head on following his foxhounds.

The craze must have started anew sometime during the holidays, because by the end of the first week in January it looked and sounded as if everybody in Georgia were trading foxhounds by day and bellowing "Whoo-way-oh!" by night. From the time the sun went down until the next morning when it came up, the woods, fields, pastures, and swamps were crawling with beggar-liced men and yelping hound-dogs. Nobody would have thought of riding horseback after the hounds in a country where there was a barbwire fence every few hundred yards.

Automobiles roared and rattled over the rough country roads all night long. The fox hunters had to travel fast in order to keep up with the pack.

It was not safe for any living thing with four legs to be out after sundown, because the hounds had the hunting fever too, and packs of those rangy half-starved dogs were running down and devouring calves, hogs, and even yellow-furred bobcats. It had got so during the past two weeks that the chickens knew enough to take to their roosts an hour ahead of time, because those packs of gaunt hunt-hungry hounds could not wait for sunset any more.

Jule finished lacing his shoes and went around the house. The path to the ridge began in the back yard and weaved up the hillside like a cow-path through a thicket. Jule passed the well and stopped to feel in his pockets to see if he had enough smoking tobacco to last him until he got back.

While he was standing there he heard behind him a sound like water gurgling through the neck of a demijohn. Jule listened again. The sound came even more plainly while he listened. There was no creek anywhere within hearing distance, and the nearest water was in the well. He went to the edge and listened again. The well did not have a stand or a windlass; it was merely a twenty-foot hole in the ground with boards laid over the top to keep pigs and chickens from falling into it.

"O Lord, help me now!" a voice said.

Jule got down on his hands and knees and looked at the well cover in the darkness. He felt of the boards with his hands. Three of them had been moved, and there was a black oblong hole that was large enough to drop a calf through.

"Who's that?" Jule said, stretching out his neck and cocking his ear.

"O Lord, help me now," the voice said again, weaker than before.

The gurgling sound began again, and Jule knew then that it was the water in the well.

"Who's down there muddying up my well?" Jule said.

There was no sound then. Even the gurgling stopped.

Jule felt on the ground for a pebble and dropped it into the well. He counted until he could hear the *kerplunk* when it struck the water.

"Doggone your hide, whoever you are down there!" Jule said. "Who's down there?"

Nobody answered.

Jule felt in the dark for the water bucket, but he could not find it. Instead, his fingers found a larger pebble, a stone almost as big around as his fist, and he dropped it into the well.

The big rock struck something else before it finally went into the water.

"O Lord, I'm going down and can't help myself," the voice down there said. "O Lord, a big hand is trying to shove me under."

The hounds trailing on the ridge swung around to the east and started back again. The fox they were after was trying to back-trail them, but Jule's hounds were hard to fool. They had got to be almost as smart as a fox.

Jule straightened up and listened to the running.

"Whoo-way-oh!" he called after the dogs.

That sent them on yelping even louder than before.

"Is that you up there, Mr. Jule?" the voice asked.

Jule bent over the well again, keeping one ear on the dogs on the ridge. He did not want to lose track of them when they were on a live trail like that.

"This is me," Jule said. "Who's that?"

"This is only Bokus Bradley, Mr. Jule," the voice said.

"What you doing down in my well, muddying it up like that, Bokus?"

"It was something like this, Mr. Jule," Bokus said. "I was coming down the ridge a while ago, trying to keep up with my hounds, and I stumbled over your well cover. I reckon I must have missed the path, somehow or other. Your well cover wouldn't hold me up, or something, and the first thing I knew, here I was. I've been here ever since I fell in. I reckon I've been down here most of the night. I hope you ain't mad at me, Mr. Jule. I just naturally couldn't help it at all."

"You've muddied up my well water," Jule said. "I ain't so doggone pleased about that."

"I reckon I have, some," Bokus said, "but I just naturally couldn't help it none at all."

"Where'd your dogs go to, Bokus?" Jule asked.

"I don't know, Mr. Jule. I haven't heard a sound out of them since I fell in here. They was headed for the creek when I was coming down the ridge behind them. Can you hear them anywhere now, Mr. Jule?"

Several packs of hounds could be heard. Jule's on the ridge was trailing east, and a pack was trailing down the creek toward town. Over toward the hills several more packs were running, but they were so far away it was not easy to tell to whom they belonged.

"Sounds to me like I hear your dogs down the creek, headed for the swamp," Jule said.

"Whoo-way-oh!" Bokus called.

The sound from the well struck Jule like a blast out of a megaphone.

"Your dogs can't hear you from 'way down there, Bokus," he said.

"I know they can't, Mr. Jule, and that's why I sure enough want to get out of here. My poor dogs don't know which way I want them to trail when they can't hear me talk to them. Whoo-way-oh!" Bokus shouted. "O Lord, help me now!"

Jule's dogs sounded as if they were closing in on a fox, and Jule jumped to his feet.

"Whoo-way-oh!" he shouted, cupping his hands around his mouth. "Whoo-way-oh!"

"Is you still up there, Mr. Jule?" Bokus asked. "Please, Mr. Jule, don't go away and leave me down here in this cold well. I'll do anything for you if you'll just only get me out of here. I've been standing neck-deep in this cold water near about all night long."

Jule threw some of the boards over the well.

"What you doing up there, Mr. Jule?"

Jule took off his hat and held the brim like a fan to the side of his head. He could hear the panting of the dogs while they ran.

"How many foxhounds have you got, Bokus?" Jule asked.

"I got me eight," Bokus said. "They're mighty fine fox trailers, too, Mr. Jule. But I'd like to get me out of this here well before doing much more talking with you."

"You could get along somehow with less than that, couldn't you, Bokus?"

"If I had to, I'd have to," Bokus said, "but I sure enough would hate to have fewer than my eight dogs, though. Eight is just naturally the right-sized pack for me, Mr. Jule."

"How are you figuring on getting out of there?" Jule said.

"I just naturally figured on you helping me out, Mr. Jule," he said. "Leastaways, that's about the only way I know of getting out of this here well. I tried climbing, but the dirt just naturally crumbles away every time I dig my toes into the sides."

"You've got that well so muddied up it won't be fit to drink out of for a week or more," Jule said.

"I'll do what I can to clean it out for you, Mr. Jule, if I ever get up on top of the solid ground again. Can you hear those hounds of mine trailing now, Mr. Jule?"

"They're still down the creek. I reckon I could lower the water bucket, and I could pull a little, and you could climb a little, and maybe you'd get out that way."

"That just naturally would suit me fine, Mr. Jule," Bokus said eagerly. "Here I is. When is you going to lower that water bucket?"

Jule stood up and listened to his dogs trailing on the ridge. From the way they sounded, it would not be long before they treed the fox they were after.

"It's only about an hour till daybreak," Jule said. "I'd better go on up the ridge and see how my hounds are making out. I can't do much here at the well till the sun comes up."

"Don't go away and leave me now, Mr. Jule," Bokus begged. "Mr. Jule, please, sir, just lower that water bucket down here and help me get out. I just naturally got to get out of here, Mr. Jule. My dogs will get all balled up without me following them. Whoo-way-oh! Whoo-way-oh!"

The pack of fox-trailing hounds was coming up from the creek, headed toward the house. Jule took off his hat and held it beside his ear. He listened to them panting and yelping.

"If I had two more hounds, I'd be mighty pleased," Jule said, shouting loud enough for Bokus to hear. "Just two is all I need right now."

"You wouldn't be wanting two of mine, would you, Mr. Jule?" Bokus asked.

"It's a good time to make a trade," Jule said. "It's a mighty good time, being as how you are down in the well and want to get out."

"Two, did you say?"

"Two is what I said."

There was silence in the well for a long time. For nearly five minutes Jule listened to the packs of dogs all around him, some on the ridge, some down the creek, and some in the far-off fields. The barking of the hounds was a sweeter sound to him than anything else in the world. He would lose a night's sleep any time just to stay up and hear a pack of foxhounds live-trailing.

"Whoo-way-oh!" he called.

"Mr. Jule!" Bokus shouted up from the bottom of the well.

Jule went to the edge and leaned over to hear what the Negro had to say.

"How about that there trade now, Bokus?"

"Mr. Jule, I just naturally couldn't swap off two of my hounds, I just sure enough couldn't."

"Why not?" Jule said.

"Because I'd have only just six dogs left, Mr. Jule, and I couldn't do much fox hunting with just that many."

Jule straightened up and kicked the boards over the top of the well.

"You won't be following even so few as one hound for a while," he said, "because I'm going to leave you down in the bottom where you stand now. It's another hour, almost, till daybreak, and I can't be wasting that time staying here talking to you. Maybe when I get back you'll be in a mind to do some trading, Bokus."

Jule kicked the boards on top of the well.

"O Lord, help me now!" Bokus said. "But, O Lord, don't make me swap off no two hounds for the help I'm asking for."

Jule stumbled over the water bucket when he turned and started across the yard toward the path up the ridge. Up there he could hear his dogs running again, and when he took off his hat and held it to the side of his head he could hear Polly pant, and Senator snort, and Mary Jane whine, and Sunshine yelp, and the rest of them barking at the head of the trail. He put on his hat, pulled it down hard all around, and hurried up the path to follow them on the ridge. The fox would not be able to hold out much longer.

"Whoo-way-oh!" he called to his hounds. "Whoo-way-oh!"

The echo was a masterful sound to hear.

(First published in *The Atlantic Monthly*)

Return to Lavinia

At first she did not know what had awakened her. She was not certain whether it had been a noise somewhere about the house, or whether it was the metallike burning of her feverish skin. By the time her eyes were fully open she could hear a bedlam of crowing, the sounds coming from every direction. For an hour at midnight the roosters crowed continually; from the chicken yards in town and from the farms surrounding the town, the sounds filled the flat country with an almost unbearable din.

Lavinia sat up in bed, wide awake after three hours of fitful sleep. She pressed the palms of her hands against her ears to shut out the crowing, but even that did not help any. She could still hear the sounds no matter what she did to stop it.

"I'll never be able to go to sleep again," she said, holding her hands tight to the sides of her head. "I might as well stop trying."

When she looked up, there was a light shining through the rear windows and doors. The illumination spread over the back porch and cast a pale moonlike glow over the walls of her room. She sat tensely awake, holding her breath while she listened.

Presently the screen door at the end of the hall opened, squeaked shrilly, and slammed shut. She shivered while the small electric fan on the edge of her dresser whirred with a monotonous drone. In her excitement she clutched her shoulders in her arms, still shivering while the fan blew a steady stream of sultry air against her face and neck.

The footsteps became inaudible for a moment, then distinct. She would know them no matter where she heard them. For three years she had heard them, night and day since she was fifteen. Some footsteps changed from year to year; strides increased, strides decreased; leather-and-nail heels were changed to rubber, heel-and-toe treads became flat-footed shufflings; most footsteps changed, but his had remained the same during all that time.

Phil Glenn crossed the porch to the kitchen, the room next to hers, and snapped on the light. She shivered convulsively in the fan draft, gasping for breath in the sultry air.

Through the wall she could hear him open the icebox, chip off several chunks of ice, and drop them into a tumbler. When he dropped the lid of the icebox and crossed to the spigot, she could hear the flow of water until the tumbler filled and overflowed. Everything he did, every motion he made, was taking place before her eyes as plainly as if she were standing beside him while he chipped the ice and filled the tumbler to overflowing.

When he had finished, he turned off the light and went back out on the porch. He stood there, his handkerchief in hand, wiping his face and lips spasmodically while he listened as intently as she was listening.

There was a sound of someone else's walking in the front of the house. It was an unfamiliar sound, a sound that both of them heard and listened to for the first time.

When she could bear it no longer, Lavinia threw herself back upon the bed, covering her face with the pillow. No matter how hard she tried, she could not keep from sobbing into the pillow. As regularly as midnight came, she had cried like that every night since he had been away.

The next thing she knew, he was sitting on the edge of her bed trying to say something to her. She could not understand a word he was saying. Even after she had sat up again, she still did not know what it was. Long after he had stopped speaking, she stared at his features in the pale glow of reflected light. She tried to think of something either of them would have to say.

"We just got back," he said.

After he had spoken, she laughed at herself for not having known he would say exactly that.

"We went down to the beach for a few days when we left here," he finished.

Lavinia stared at him while she wondered what he expected her to say by way of comment or reply.

All she could do was nod her head.

"I thought I told you where we were going, but after I left I remembered I hadn't. If we hadn't been halfway there, I'd have turned around and come back to tell you. I wouldn't want you to think—"

She laughed.

"—I wouldn't want you to think—" he said over again.

Lavinia threw her head back and laughed out loud. Her voice sounded soft and deep.

"Well, anyway," he said, "it was a mighty short honeymoon. But it was nice on the beach."

She laughed again, but the sound of her laughter was all but drowned out in the drone of the electric fan.

"It was just what you would expect," he said casually.

The electric fan was blowing her gown against her back with rippling motions. She moved sidewise to the fan so that nothing would prevent her from hearing every word he said. After she had settled down, he crossed his legs.

"I guess it's going to be all right," he said, looking through the window and back again at her. "It'll be all right."

Before he had finished, both of them turned to listen to the sound of footsteps in the front of the house. The sound echoed through the night.

In the closeness of the room, Lavinia could feel his heavy breathing vibrate the air. She wanted to say something to him, but she was afraid. She did not know what she could say. If she said the wrong thing, it would be a lot worse than not saying anything. She held her breath in perplexity.

He got up, went to the window, looked out into the darkness for a moment, and came back to stand beside her. She could feel him looking down at her even though she could not see him distinctly in the shadow he made when his back was to the door. She had to restrain herself from reaching out to feel if he were there beside her.

"Hannah is quite a girl," he said finally, laughing a little to hide his uneasiness.

She knew he would have to say something like that sooner or later. It was the only way to get it over with. After that she waited for him to go on.

"We'll get along all right," he said. "There won't be any trouble."

She shook her hair in the draft of the fan. All at once the fan seemed as if it were going faster than ever. The draft became stronger, the whirring sound rose in volume to an ear-splitting pitch, and her shoulders shook involuntarily in the fan's chill breeze.

"I thought I would have a hard time of it," he said, "but now that it's over, it wasn't half as bad as I thought it was going to be. We'll get along all right."

Lavinia reached out and found his hand in the dark. He sat down on the side of the bed while she tried to think what to say.

"What's the matter, Lavinia?" he asked her. "What's wrong?"

"Let me go, Phil," she begged, beginning to cry in her soft deep voice. "I want to go."

He shook his head unmistakably.

"I couldn't let you go now, Lavinia," he said earnestly. "We agreed about that before this business took place the other day. You promised me. If I hadn't believed you would keep your promise, I wouldn't have gone ahead and done it."

"Please, Phil," she begged, crying brokenly until her soft deep voice filled the room. "Please let me go."

He kept on shaking his head, refusing to listen to her. Suddenly, there rose once more the bedlam of crowing that lasted for an hour in intermittent bursts every midnight. Neither of them tried to say anything while the crowing was at its height.

After several minutes the drone of the fan and the sobs in her breast drowned out the roosters' crowing.

"I've got to go, Phil," she said, holding back her sobs while she spoke.

"I can't let you go," he said. "I just can't let you go, Lavinia."

She stopped crying and sat up more erectly, almost on her knees. He gazed at her wonderingly.

"I'm a nigger, Phil," she said slowly. "I'm a nigger — a cooking, cleaning, washing nigger."

"Shut up, Lavinia!" he said, shaking her until she was in pain. "Shut up, do you hear?"

"I am, and you know I am," she cried. "I'm a nigger — a cooking, cleaning, washing nigger — just like all the rest are."

She brushed the tears from her eyes and tried to look at him clearly in the half-light. She could see his deep, serious expression and she knew he meant every word he had said.

"You'll get over it in a few days," he told her. "Just wait awhile and see if everything doesn't turn out just like I say it will."

"You know what I am, though," she said uncontrollably.

"Shut up, Lavinia!" he said, shaking her some more. "You're not! You're a white girl with colored blood — and little of that. Any of us might be like that. I have colored blood in me, for all I know. Even *she* might have some."

He jerked his head toward the front of the house. Forgetting everything else momentarily, they both listened for a while. There was no sound whatever coming from that part of the building.

"She'll order me around just like she would anybody else," Lavinia said. "She'll treat me like the blackest washwoman you ever saw. She'll be as mean to me as she knows how, just to keep me in my place. She'll even call me 'nigger' sometimes."

"You're just excited now," he said. "It won't be like that tomorrow. You know as well as I do that I don't care what you are. Even if you looked like a colored girl, I wouldn't care. But you don't look like one — you look like a golden girl. That's all there is to it. If she ever says anything different, just don't pay any attention to her."

"She'll keep me in my place," Lavinia said. "I don't mind staying in my place, but I can't live here and have her tell me about it a dozen times a day. I want to go. I am going."

Phil got up, went to the door, and closed it. He came back and stood beside her.

"You're going to stay here, Lavinia," he said firmly. "If anybody goes, she'll have to go. I mean that."

Lavinia lay back on the pillow, closing her eyes and breathing deeply. She would rather have heard him say that than anything else he had said that night. She had been waiting five days and nights to hear him say it, and at last she could relax with the relief he had given her.

"I got married for a pretty good reason," he told her, "but I'm not going to let it ruin everything. I thought you understood all about it before it happened. You even told me to go ahead and marry her, so it would put a stop to all the talk about you living here as my housekeeper. It was hurting business at the store. We had to do something like that. And now you say you are going to leave."

There was silence for a long time after he had finished. Only the drone of the electric fan could be heard, and that for the first time sounded subdued.

"I won't leave," Lavinia said slowly, her voice so low he had to lean closer to her in order to hear. "The only way to make me leave is to throw me out. And I'd come back even if you did that. I want to stay, Phil."

As she lay on her back, she felt herself dropping into unconsciousness. For a while she made no effort to keep herself awake. She lay with her eyes closed and a smile on her lips.

She knew nothing else until he got up from the side of the bed. She opened her eyes as wide as she could in order to see if he was still there.

"I've got to go now," he said.

She sat up, shaking her head from side to side in the breeze of the electric fan. The air that blew through her hair was warm and clinging, and it began making her drowsy once more.

"Phil," she asked, "will you tell me something before you go?"

"Sure," he said, laughing. "What?"

"Phil, did you have a good time on your honeymoon?"

He laughed at her for a moment. After he had stopped there was a pause, and he laughed again.

"I had a great time on the beach," he said hesitatingly.

She laughed at him then, with motions of her head, in her soft deep voice.

"And with that old-maid schoolteacher you married, too?" she said, her words trailing off into soft deep laughter that filled the room.

He did not answer her. He went to the door to open it, but for several moments he did not turn the knob. He turned back to look at her again, her laughter filling his ears.

After a while he jerked open the door, stepped out on the porch, and closed the door as quickly as he could. He waited there for a moment to find out if Hannah had heard the laughter in Lavinia's room. When she did not come out into the hall after that length of time, he walked quickly down the porch to the hall door.

Lavinia's laughter swam through the hot night air, pouring into his ears until he could not hear even the sound of his own footsteps. The soft deep notes followed him like a familiar sound that was so close to him he could not find its source.

(First published in *Esquire*)

A Small Day

GOVERNOR GIL was standing astride the path, knocking heads off the weeds, when Walter Lane came up the hill from the spring. A wide circle of wilted weeds lay on the ground around him, and his walking stick was still swinging. It looked as if he had been waiting there for half an hour or longer.

"It's been mighty hot today," Walter said, stopping and lowering the two pails of water to the ground.

"It's a small day when the sun don't shine," Governor Gil said. "Where's the rest of your family, and the girl?"

"My wife and the young ones went over to visit her folks this afternoon," Walter told him. "They'll be coming home some time tonight after supper." He turned around and looked down the path behind. "Daisy's coming up the path any minute now. She's down at the spring filling a bucket."

Governor Gil looked down the path, but Daisy was not within sight. It was almost a hundred yards from the crown of the slope down to the bottom of the hill, where the spring was.

"I reckon I can wait here," he said, taking a new grip on his walking stick and bending forward to reach the weeds farthest away. "It's a small day when I can't afford to spend a little time waiting."

Walter watched the heads tumble off the stalks of weeds. Governor Gil went about it as if he were determined not to let a weed in the whole county go to seed that year. Every once in a while he shifted his position a little, stamping down the wilted weeds and reaching for new ones to whack at. Sometimes he started out in the morning, after breakfast, on horseback to see how his cotton and cane crops were growing, but before he got out of sight of home he always got off his horse and started whacking away at the weeds with his walking stick. He hated weeds worse than he did boll weevils or screwworms. However, for some reason or other, he never paid any attention to the weeds that grew in the yard around his house; they were so rank there that sometimes his hunting dogs got lost in the growth and had to backtrack their way out.

"Did you want to see me, Governor Gil, or was it Daisy you asked about?" Walter said, wondering.

Instead of answering, Governor Gil stopped a moment and glanced down the path. He nodded his head in that direction, and returned to swinging his stick at the weeds.

Governor Gil Counts had once, for a term, been governor of the state, about twenty-five or thirty years before, and the title suited him so well that nobody ever thought of calling him anything else. He ran his farm with the help of Walter Lane and several other tenants, and never left it. He had not been out of the county since the day he came home from the governor's office, and he had said he would never leave home again. He lived a quarter of a mile up the road in a big three-story mansion, from which the white paint had peeled while he was serving his term in office. The once-white, three-story columns rising from the front porch were now as dark and rough as the bark on a pine tree.

"There's no sense in standing out here in the sun," Walter said. "Come on to my house and take a seat in the porch shade, Governor Gil. Daisy'll be along to the house just about as soon as she'll get here."

"This'll do," he said, stopping and looking down the path. "I haven't got time to sit down now."

He went past Walter and started down the path toward the spring. Walter left his pails and followed behind. Heads of weeds tumbled to the right and left of them.

At the crown of the slope they saw Daisy coming up. She was carrying a pail of water in one hand and fanning herself with a willow branch.

"I may as well tell you now, Walter," Governor Gil said, stopping. "It's time for your girl to marry. It's dangerous business to put it off after they get a certain age."

Walter took half a dozen steps around Governor Gil and stopped where he could see his face.

"Who ought she to marry?" Walter said.

Governor Gil let go at some pigweeds around his knees, whacking his stick at them just under the seed pods. The heads flew in all directions.

"I've arranged for that," he said. "I sent my lawyer a letter today telling him to get a license. It'll be here in a few days."

Walter looked again at Governor Gil, and then down the path. Daisy had come over the crown of the slope.

"That might be all right," Walter said, "but I don't know if she'll be tamed. Right now she's just about as wild as they come. Of course, now, I'm not raising any serious objections. I'm just going over in my mind the drawbacks a man might run into."

"A year from now there might be plenty of drawbacks," Governor Gil said. "Right this minute drawbacks don't count, because she's reached the marrying age, and nothing else matters. If I had a daughter, Walter, I'd want to do the right thing by her. I'd want her to marry before drawbacks had a chance to spoil her. I'm ready to marry her without an argument."

"You damned old fool," Daisy said, dropping her pail, "what put that into your head?"

Governor Gil had drawn back to let go at a clump of weeds swaying in the breeze beside the path, but he never finished the stroke. His stick fell back against his knees and the clump of weeds continued to sway in the wind.

"Now, that's what I was thinking about," Walter said. "I had an idea she wouldn't be willing to be tamed just yet."

"Why, I've been counting on this for a pretty long time," Governor Gil said excitedly. "I've just been biding my time all this while when you were growing up, Daisy. I've had my eyes on you for about three years now, just waiting for you to grow up."

"You damned old fool," Daisy said, stooping down for her pail and starting around them in the path.

Walter did not try to stop her. He looked at Governor Gil to see what he had to say now.

They watched her for a moment.

"She'll tame," Governor Gil said, nodding his head at Walter and following her up the path to the house.

When they got to the back door, Daisy put the pail on the shelf and sat down on the doorstep. She sat and looked at them with her knees drawn up under her elbows and her chin cupped in her hands.

"Maybe if you could just wait —" Walter began. He was waved aside by a sweep of the walking stick.

"I'm going to have the handseling tonight," Governor Gil said, nodding his head at Daisy and flourishing the stick in the air. "The marrying can wait, but the handseling can't. The license will be along from my lawyer in a day or two, and that's just a matter of formality, anyway."

Walter looked at Daisy, but she only stared more sullenly at them.

"I reckon we ought to wait till my wife gets back from visiting her folks," Walter said. "She ought to have a little say-so. For one thing, she'll have to make Daisy some clothes first, because Daisy hasn't got much to wear except what she's got on, and that's so little it wouldn't be decent if we weren't homefolks. Just about all she's got to her name is that little slimsy gingham jumper she's wearing. My wife will want to make her a petticoat, if nothing else. It would be a sin and a shame for her to get married like she is now. If she had something to wear under what she's got on, it might be different, but I won't be in favor of sending her out to get married in just a slimsy jumper between her and the outside world."

Governor Gil shook his walking stick in the air as if to wave away any possible objection Walter might mention.

"That's all right for the marriage," he said, "but that won't be for a few days yet. Your wife will have plenty of time to make up a petticoat for her if she wants to. But she won't even have to do that, because I'll buy her whatever she'll need after the marriage. And what she'll need for the handseling won't be worth mentioning."

He stopped and turned around to look at the sun. It was already setting behind the pine grove in the west.

"Had your supper yet?" he asked, looking at Walter and nodding at Daisy.

"Not yet," Walter said. "We didn't stop work in the cotton until about half an hour ago, and the first thing that needed doing was carrying up the water from the spring. Daisy, you go in the kitchen and start getting something ready to eat. Maybe Governor Gil will stay and eat with us tonight."

"No," he said, waving his stick at Daisy, "don't do that, Daisy. You just come up to my house and get your meal there tonight. There's no sense in you getting all worn out over a hot stove now. There's plenty to eat up there."

He turned to Walter.

"If your wife won't be home until late tonight, you just come up to my house and go around to the kitchen, and the help will set you out a good meal, Walter."

He started walking across the yard toward the road. When he got to the corner of the house, he stopped and found that neither Daisy nor her father had made a move to follow him.

"What's the matter?" he said impatiently.

"Well, now," Walter said, "I can make Daisy go up to your house, Governor Gil, but I can't be held responsible for what she does after she gets there. I wish you would wait till my wife came back tonight before you took Daisy off, but if your mind is made up not to wait, then all I can say is you'll have to charge her yourself after she gets there."

"She won't need any charging," Governor Gil said. "I've yet to know the wildest one of them that wouldn't tame when the time comes to handsel."

He turned around and started walking toward the road that led to his house, a quarter of a mile away.

Walter looked down at the doorstep, where Daisy still sat sullen and motionless.

"You ought to be tickled to death to have the chance to marry Governor Gil," he told her. "Who else is there in the county who'll treat you nice and give you all you want? I'll bet there's many a girl who'd jump at the chance to marry him."

"The damned old fool," Daisy said.

"Well, you'd better," he told her. "I'll bet your mother will make you, if I can't. She's no fool, either. She knows how well off you'll be, not having to go hungry for something to eat, and having enough clothes to cover your nakedness, neither one of which you've got now, or ever will have, if you don't go on up there like you ought to."

Walter sat down on the bottom step and waited for Daisy to say something. The sun had set, and it would be getting dark soon. If she did not go right away, Governor Gil might get mad and change his mind.

Presently he turned around and looked at her.

"What's the matter with you, Daisy? You won't even say anything. What's got into you, anyway?"

"What does he want me to go up there tonight for?" she asked. "He said the license wouldn't be here for two or three days."

"That's just Governor Gil's way, Daisy. He makes up his mind to do something, and nothing stops him once it's made up. He wants to marry you, and he wants to right now. There's no sense in putting it off, anyway. The best thing for you to do is to start right in before he changes his mind. If you don't, you'll live to be sorry, because tomorrow you'll have to go right back to the field again — tomorrow and every day as long as cotton grows."

Daisy got up without saying anything and went into the house. She was in her room for ten or fifteen minutes, and when she came to the door it was dark outside. She could barely see her father sitting on the steps at her feet.

"Now, that's what I call sense," Walter said. "I thought you'd change your mind after you got to thinking about all these hot days in the sun out there in the cotton."

She went down the steps past him and crossed the yard without a word. She started up the road in the direction of Governor Gil's mansion.

After Daisy had gone, Walter began to wonder what his wife would say when she came home. He was certain she would be glad to hear that Governor Gil wanted to marry Daisy, but he was not so sure of what she would say when he told her that the marriage license would not come for another two or three days. He decided it would be best not to say anything about that part to her. Just as long as she knew Governor Gil had come to the house to ask Daisy to marry him, she would be satisfied.

It was pitch-dark when he got up and went into the kitchen, made a light, and looked around for something to eat. He found some bread left over from dinner, and he did not have to build a fire in the cook-stove after all. He sat down at the kitchen table and ate his fill of bread and sorghum.

After he had finished, he blew out the light and went to the front porch to sit and wait for his wife to come home.

Up the road he could see lights in Governor Gil's house. There was a light in the kitchen, as usual, and one in the front part of the house too. Upstairs, two or three rooms were lighted for the first time since he could remember.

Just when he was expecting his wife and children to get there any moment, he heard somebody running down the road. He got up and listened as the sound came closer. It was somebody running fast, because the sound came closer every second.

He ran out to the road to see who it was. At first he thought it might be Daisy, but he soon knew it wasn't, because a boy called out to him.

"Mr. Walter! Mr. Walter!"

"Who's that?" he shouted back.

A Negro houseboy stopped, panting, in the road beside him.

"What's the matter, Lawson?"

"Mr. Walter, Governor said to tell you if you ever raise another hell-cat like Miss Daisy, he'll chop your head off. Now, Mr. Walter, I didn't say it! Please, sir, don't think I said it! It was Governor who told me to tell you that! You know I wouldn't say that myself, don't you, Mr. Walter?"

"What's the matter up there, Lawson?" Walter asked the boy.

"I don't know exactly, Mr. Walter, except that Governor started yelling upstairs a while ago, and he hasn't stopped yet. He told me to tele-phone for the doctor and the lawyer to come in a hurry. He hardly stopped yelling long enough to tell me, either. Soon as I telephoned for them, he told me to run down here as fast as I could and tell you what I told you."

"Was Miss Daisy up there then?" Walter asked.

"I reckon it was Miss Daisy who made him yell," Lawson said hesi-tatingly.

"Why?"

"I don't know if Governor wants me to tell you," Lawson said. "He only told me to tell you what I already told you, Mr. Walter."

"You'd better tell me, Lawson. What was it?"

"Miss Daisy flew into him and pretty near bit the daylights out of him. Governor was yelling and nursing his hurt so much, he didn't have time to say much else."

Walter started back to the porch to sit down and wait for his wife to come home. He could not keep from laughing a little, but he tried to hold himself back so he could laugh all the more with his wife when she got there.

Lawson was still standing outside the yard. He turned around to tell the boy to go on back.

"What else did Governor Gil say, Lawson?" he asked him.

"I didn't hear him say much else, except Governor said it'll be a mighty small day when he tries to handsel a hellcat like Miss Daisy again."

Walter went to the porch and sat down. He leaned back and started to laugh. He could not wait for his wife any longer. He leaned back and laughed until he slid out of the chair.

(First published in *The New Yorker*)

Man and Woman

THEY came slowly up the road through the colorless dawn like shadows left behind by the night. There was no motion in their bodies, and yet their feet scuffed up dust that settled behind them as quickly as it was raised. They lifted their eyes with each step they took, peering toward the horizon for the first red rays of the sun.

The woman held her lower lip clamped tightly between her teeth. It hurt her to do that, but it was the only way she could urge herself forward step after step. There was no other way to drag her feet one behind the other, mile after mile. She whimpered occasionally, but she did not cry out.

"It's time to stop and rest again," Ring said.

She did not answer him.

They kept on.

At the top of the hill, they came face to face with the sun. It was a quarter of the way up, cut like a knife by the treeless horizon. Down below them was a valley lying under a cover of mist that was rising slowly from the earth. They could see several houses and farms, but most of them were so far away they were almost indistinguishable in the mist. There was smoke rising from the chimney of the first house.

Ruth looked at the man beside her. The red rays of the sun had begun to color his pale face like blood. But still his eyes were tired and lifeless. He looked as if he were balancing himself on his two feet with great effort, and as if the next moment he might lose his balance and fall to the ground.

"We'll be able to get a little something to eat at that first house," she said, waiting minute after minute for him to reply.

"We'll get something there," she said, answering for him. "We will."

The sun came up above the horizon, fast and red. Streaks of gray clouds, like layers of woodsmoke, swam across the face of it. Almost as quickly as it

215

had risen, the sun shrank into a small fiery button that seared the eyes until it was impossible to look at it any longer.

"Let's try, anyway," Ruth said.

Ring looked at her in the clear daylight, seeing her for the first time since the sun had set the night before. Her face was paler, her cheeks more sunken.

Without words, he started forward down the hill. He did not turn his head to see if she was following him, but went down the road drawing one foot from behind and hurling it in front of him with all his might. There was no other way he could move himself over the ground.

He had stopped at the front of the house, looking at the smoke that floated overhead, when she caught up with him at last.

"I'll go in and try," she said. "You sit down and rest, Ring."

He opened his mouth to say something, but his throat became choked and no words came. He looked at the house, with its worn doorstep and curtain-filled windows and its smoke-filled chimney, and he did not feel like a stranger in a strange country as long as he kept his eyes upon those things.

Ruth went through the gate, and around the side of the house, and stopped at the kitchen door. She looked behind her and saw Ring coming across the yard from the road.

Someone was watching them from behind a curtain at the window.

"Knock," Ring said.

She placed the knuckles of her right hand against the side of the house and rapped on the clapboards until her hand began to hurt.

She turned around and glanced quickly at Ring, and he nodded his head.

Presently the kitchen door opened a few inches and a woman's head could be seen through the crack. She was middle-aged and brown-faced and had a long, thick scar on her forehead that looked as if it might have been made by a bursting fruit jar.

"Go away," she told them.

"We won't bother you," Ruth said as quickly as she could. "All we wanted was to ask you if you could give us a little something to eat. Just a potato, if you have any, or bread, or something."

"I don't know what you are doing here," the woman said. "I don't like to have strange people around my house."

She almost closed the door, but in a moment the crack widened, and her face could be seen once more.

"I'll feed the girl," she said finally, "but I can't let the man have anything. I don't have enough for both of you, anyway."

Ruth turned quickly around, her heels digging into the sandy earth. She looked at Ring. He nodded his head eagerly.

He could see the word forming on her lips even though he could not hear it. She shook her head.

Ring went several steps toward her.

"We'll try somewhere else," she said.

"No," he said. "You go in and eat what she'll give you. I'll try at the next house we come to."

She still did not wish to go into the house without him. The woman opened the door a foot or more, and waited for her to come up the steps.

Ring sat down on a bench under a tree.

"I'm going to sit here and wait until you go in and get something to eat for yourself," he said.

Ruth went up the steps slowly to the porch and entered the door. When she was inside, the woman pointed out a chair by a table, and Ruth sat down.

There were potatoes, warmed over from the night before, and cold biscuits. These were put on the table in front of her, and then the woman poured a cup of hot coffee and set it beside the plate.

Ruth began to eat as quickly as she could, sipping the hot black coffee and chewing the potatoes and bread while the brown-faced woman stood behind her at the door, where she could watch Ring and her by turns.

Twice Ruth managed to slip pieces of bread into her blouse, and finally she got half a potato into the pocket of her skirt. The woman eyed her suspiciously when she was not watching Ring in the yard outside.

"Going far?" the woman asked.

"Yes," Ruth answered.

"Come far?" the woman asked.

"Yes," Ruth said.

"Who is that man with you?"

"He's my husband," Ruth told her.

The woman looked out into the yard again, then back at Ruth. She did not say anything more for a while.

Ruth tried to put another piece of potato into her skirt pocket, but by then the woman was watching her more closely than ever.

"I don't believe he is your husband," the woman said.

"Well," Ruth answered, "he is."

"I wouldn't call him much of a husband to let you walk through the country begging food like you did just a little while ago."

"He's been sick," Ruth said quickly, turning in the chair to face the woman. "He was sick in bed for five weeks before we started out."

"Why didn't you stay where you were, instead of making tramps out of yourselves? Can't he hold a job, or don't he want to work?"

Ruth got up, dropping the bread in her hand.

"Thank you for the breakfast," she said. "I am going now."

"If you take my advice," the woman said, "you'll leave that man the first chance you get. If he won't work at a job, you'll be a fool —"

"He had a job, but he got sick with a kind of fever."

"I don't believe you. I'd put you down for lying about him."

Ruth went to the door, opened it herself, and went outside. She turned around on the porch and looked at the woman who had given her something to eat.

"If he was sick in bed, like you said," the woman asked, following her past the door, "why did he get up and start tramping like this with nothing for you and him to eat?"

Ruth saw Ring sitting on the bench under the tree, and she was not going to answer the woman, but she could not keep from saying something.

"The reason we started out walking like this was because my sister wrote and told me that our baby had died. When my husband first got sick, I sent the baby to my sister's. Now we're going to see the grave where she's buried."

She ran down the steps and walked across the yard as rapidly as she could. When she reached the corner of the house, Ring got up and followed her to the road. Neither of them said anything, but she could not keep from looking back at the house, where the woman was watching them through the crack in the door.

After they had gone a hundred feet or more, Ruth unfastened her blouse and pulled out the pieces of bread she had carried there. Ring took them from her without a word. When he had eaten all there was, she gave him the potato. He ate it hungrily, talking to her with his eyes while he chewed and swallowed.

They had walked for nearly half an hour before either of them spoke again.

"She was a mean old woman," Ruth said. "If it hadn't been for the food, I'd have got up and left before I ate what she gave me."

Ring did not say anything for a long time. They had reached the bottom of the valley and were beginning to go up the grade on the other side before he spoke again. "Maybe if she had known where we were going, she might not have been so mean to you," Ring said.

Ruth choked back a sob.

"How much farther is it, Ring?"

"About thirty or forty miles."

"Will we get there tomorrow?"

He shook his head.

"The day after?"

"I don't know."

"Maybe if we get a ride, we might get there tonight?" she asked, unable to hold back any longer the sobs that choked her throat and breast.

"Yes," he said. "If we could get a ride, we would get there a lot sooner."

He turned his head and glanced down the road behind them, but there was nothing in sight. Then he looked down at the ground he was walking on, counting the steps he took with his right foot, and then his left.

(First published in *The New Yorker*)

The Night My Old Man Came Home

THE dogs barked at a little before midnight, and Ma got up to look out the window. It was a snowy night about two weeks before Christmas. The wind had died down a little since supper, but not enough to keep it from whistling around the eaves every once in a while. It was just the kind of white winter night when it felt good to be in bed with plenty of covers to keep warm.

The light was burning in the hall, because we always kept one light on all night. Ma did not turn on the light in the room right away. She could see better what was going on outside when the room was dark.

She did not say a word for quite a while. The dogs growled some, and then started in barking again. They were kept chained at the side of the house all night; if they had been allowed to run loose, they would have chewed up a lot of people who came out that way after dark. It was a good thing for my old man, too; they would have chewed him up as quick as they would have somebody they had never smelt before. My old man was away from home so much he was just like a stranger, anyway. The last time he was there was in the summer, and he only stayed about five minutes then. He came back for a pair of pants he had left hanging on a nail in the woodshed the winter before.

"That's him, all right," Ma said, tapping the window-sill with the door key. She was no more mad than usual, but that was enough. When she tapped the woodwork with things like the door key, it was the only sign anybody needed to know how she was feeling.

Presently there was a rumble that sounded like a two-horse wagon crossing a plank bridge. Then a jar shook the house like somebody had taken a sledge hammer and knocked most of the foundation from under it.

That was my old man trying out the front steps and porch in the dark to see if they would hold his weight. He was always afraid somebody was going to set a trap for him when he came home, something like loosening the boards on the porch in such a way that he would fall through and have to lie there until Ma could reach him with the broom or something.

"He's going to come home like this just once too many some of these times," Ma said. "I'm getting sick and tired of it."

"I want to get up and see him," I said. "Please, Ma, let me."

"You stay right where you are, William, and pull those covers up over your head," Ma said, tapping some more on the sill with the door key. "When he gets in here, he's not going to be any fit sight for you to look at."

I got up on my knees and elbows and pulled the covers over my head. When I thought Ma had stopped looking that way, I pulled the covers back just enough so I could see out.

The front door banged open, almost breaking the glass in the top part. My old man never did act like he cared anything about the glass in the door, or about the furniture, or about anything else in the house. He came home once and picked Ma's sewing machine to pieces, and Ma had a dickens of a time saving up enough to get it fixed.

I never knew my old man could make so much racket. It sounded like he was out in the hall jumping up and down to see if he could stomp the floor clear through the ground. All the pictures on the wall shook, and some of them turned cockeyed. Even the big one of Grandpa turned sidewise.

Ma turned the light on and went to the fireplace to kindle the fire. There were lots of embers in the ashes that glowed red when she fanned them with a newspaper and laid some kindling over them. As soon as the kindling began to blaze, she put on two or three chunks of wood and sat down on the hearth with her back to the fire to wait for my old man to come into the room.

He was banging around out in the hall all that time, sounding like he was trying to kick all the chairs down to the far end next to the kitchen. In the middle of it he stopped and said something to somebody he had with him.

Ma got up in a hurry and put her bathrobe on. She looked in the mirror a time or two and straightened her hair. It was a big surprise for him to bring somebody home with him like that.

"You cover up your head and go to sleep like I told you, William," Ma said.

"I want to see him," I begged her.

"Don't argue with me, William," she said, patting her bare foot on the floor. "Go and do like I told you once already."

I pulled the covers up, but slipped them back enough to see out.

The door to the hall opened a couple of inches. I got up on my knees and elbows again so I could see better. Just then my old man kicked the door open with his foot. It flew back against the wall, knocking loose dust that nobody knew was there before.

"What do you want, Morris Stroup?" Ma said, folding her arms and glaring at him. "What do you want this time?"

"Come on in and make yourself comfortably at home," my old man said, turning around and jerking somebody into the room by the arm. "Don't be backward in my own house."

He pulled a girl about half the size of Ma into the room and pushed her around until they were over against Ma's sewing machine. Ma turned on her feet, watching them just like she had been a weathervane following the wind.

It was pretty serious to watch my old man drunk and reeling, and to see Ma so mad she could not get a word out of her mouth.

"Say 'Howdy,'" he told the girl.

She never said a thing.

My old man put his arm around her neck and bent her over. He kept it up, making her bow like that at Ma, and then he got to doing it too, and pretty soon they were keeping time bowing. They did it so much that Ma's head started bobbing up and down, just like she could not help herself.

I guess I must have snickered out loud, because Ma looked kind of silly for a minute, and then she went and sat down by the fire.

"Who's she?" Ma asked, acting like she was pretty anxious to find out. She even stopped looking cross for a little while. "Who is she, Morris?"

My old man sat down heavy enough to break the bottom out of the chair.

"She?" he said. "She's Lucy. She's my helper nowadays."

He turned around in the chair and looked over at me on my knees and elbows under the cover.

"Howdy, son," he said. "How've you been?"

"Pretty well," I said, squeezing down on my knees and trying to think of something to say so I could show him how glad I was to see him.

"Still growing, ain't you, son?" he said.

"A little, I reckon," I told him.

"That's right. That's the thing to do. Just keep it up, son. Some day you'll be a man before you know it."

"Pa, I——"

Ma picked up a piece of kindling and slung it at him. It missed him and hit the wall behind him. My old man jumped up on his feet and danced around like it had hit him instead of the wall. He reeled around like that until he lost his footing, and then he slid down the wall and sat on the floor.

He reached over and got his hands on a straight-back chair. He looked it over carefully, and then he started pulling the rungs out. Every time he got one loose, he pitched it into the fireplace.

When all the rungs and legs were out, he started picking the slats out of the back and throwing them into the fire. Ma never said a word. She just sat and looked at him all the time.

"Let's go, Morris," the girl Lucy said. It was the first thing she had said since she got there. Both Ma and me looked at her sort of surprised, and my old man cut his eyes around too, like he had forgotten she was there. "Morris, let's go," she said.

Lucy looked all but scared to death, it was easy to see. Everybody had stared at her so much, and Ma was acting so mad, that it was no wonder.

"Sit down and make yourself comfortable," my old man told her. "Just sit, Lucy."

She reached for one of the chairs and sat down just like he told her to.

The way she was sitting there, and Ma's mad streak on, and my old man picking the chair to pieces was a funny sight to see. I guess I must have snickered again out loud, because Ma turned around at me and shook her finger and motioned for me to pull the covers up over my head, and to go to sleep too, I guess. But I could never go to sleep while all that was going on, when I had not seen my old man for so long a time, and Ma must have known it. I just squeezed down on my elbows and knees as much as I could, and kept on looking.

"When you get that chair picked to pieces, Morris Stroup, you can just hand me over seven dollars to pay for a new one," Ma said, rocking back and forth.

"Shucks, Martha," my old man said. "Shucks, I don't believe there's a chair in the whole world that I'd give more than a dollar, maybe two, for."

Ma jerked out of her spell like a snapped finger. She jumped up and grabbed the broom from the side of the mantelpiece and started for him. She beat him over the head with it until she saw how much damage she was doing to the broomstraw, and then she stopped. She had beat out so much straw that it was scattered all over the floor. After that she turned the broom around and began poking him with the handle.

My old man got up in a hurry and staggered across the room to the closet, throwing what was left of the chair into the fire as he passed it. He opened the closet door and went inside. He did something to the lock, because no matter how hard Ma tried, she could not make the door open after he had closed it.

By that time Ma was so mad she did not know what she was doing. She sat down on the edge of the bed and pinned her hair up a little.

"This is nice goings-on at this time of night, Morris Stroup!" she yelled at him through the door. "What kind of a child can I raise with things like this going on in the house?"

She did not even wait for my old man to answer her. She just spun around toward Lucy, the girl my old man had brought along with him.

"You can have him," Ma said, "but you've got to keep him away from here."

"He told me he wasn't married," Lucy told Ma. "He said he was a single man all the time."

"Single man!" Ma yelled.

She got red in the face again and ran to the fireplace for the poker. Our poker was about three feet long and made of thick iron. She jabbed it into the crack of the closet and pried with it.

My old man began to yell and kick in the closet. I never heard such a racket as when the dogs started their barking again. People who heard them must have thought robbers were murdering all of us that night.

About then Lucy jumped up, crying.

"Stop that!" she yelled at Ma. "You're hurting him in that closet!"

Ma just turned around, swinging her elbow as she went.

"You leave me be!" Ma told her. "I'll attend to what I'm doing, sister!"

I had to squirm all around to the other side of the bed to keep up with what they were doing at the closet door. I never saw two people carry on so funny before. Both of them were mad, and scared to do much about it. They acted like two young roosters that wanted to fight but did not know how to go about it. They were just flapping around, trying to scare each other.

But Ma was as strong as the next one for her size. All she had to do when she made up her mind was drop the poker, grab Lucy, and give her a shove. Lucy sailed across the room and landed up against the sewing machine. She looked scared out of her wits when she found herself there so quick.

Ma picked up the poker again and she pried with all her might and, *bang!* the door sprang open. There was my old man backed up against the closet wall all tangled up in Ma's clothes, and he looked like he had been taken by surprise and caught red-handed with his fist in the grocer's cash drawer. I never saw my old man look so sheepish before in all my life.

As soon as Ma got him out of the closet and into the room, she went for Lucy.

"I'm going to put you out of my house," Ma told her, "and put a stop to this running around with my husband. That's one thing I won't stand for!"

She grabbed at Lucy, but Lucy ducked out of reach. Then they came back at each other just exactly like two young roosters that had finally got up enough nerve to start pecking. They jumped around on the floor with their arms flapping like wings and Ma's bathrobe and Lucy's skirt flying around like loose feathers. They hopped around in a circle for so long that it looked like they were riding on a merry-go-round. About that time they got their hands in each other's hair and started pulling. I never heard so much screaming before. My old man's eyes had just about got used to the light again, and he could see them, too, every once in a while. His head kept going around and around, and he missed a lot of it.

Ma and Lucy worked across the room and out the door into the hall. Out there they scuffled some more. While it was going on, my old man stumbled across the room, feeling for another chair. He picked up the first one he could put his hands on. It was Ma's high-back rocker, the one she sat in all the time when she was sewing and just resting.

By that time Ma and Lucy were scuffling out on the front porch. My old man shut the door to the hall and locked it. That door was a thick, heavy one with a spring thumb lock as well as a keyhole lock.

"No use talking, son," he said, sitting down on the bed and pulling off his shoes, "there's nothing else in the world like a couple of females at odds. Sometimes——"

He slung his shoes under the bed and turned out the light. He felt his way around the bed, dragging Ma's high-back rocker with him. I could hear the wood creak in the chair when he strained on the rungs. He pulled the covers up, then began picking the chair to pieces and throwing them toward the fire. Once in a while one of the pieces hit the mantelpiece; as often as not one of them struck the wall.

By then Ma and Lucy had got the dogs started again. They must have been out in the front yard scuffling by that time, because I could not hear them on the porch.

"Sometimes, son," my old man said, "sometimes it appears to me like the good Lord ought never put more than one woman in the world at a time."

I snuggled down under the covers, hugging my knees as tight as I could, and hoping he would stay at home all the time, instead of going off again.

My old man broke the back off the rocker and slung it in the dark toward the fireplace. It hit the ceiling first, and then the mantelpiece. He began picking the seat to pieces next.

It sure felt good being there in the dark with him.

(First published in *The New Yorker*)

Wild Flowers

THE mockingbird that had perched on the roof top all night, filling the clear cool air with its music, had flown away when the sun rose. There was silence as deep and mysterious as the flat sandy country that extended mile after mile in every direction. Yesterday's shadows on the white sand began to reassemble under the trees and around the fence posts, spreading on the ground the lacy foliage of the branches and the fuzzy slabs of the wooden fence.

The sun rose in leaps and bounds, jerking itself upward as though it were in a great hurry to rise above the tops of the pines so it could shine down upon the flat country from there to the Gulf.

Inside the house the bedroom was light and warm. Nellie had been awake ever since the mockingbird had left. She lay on her side with one arm under her head. Her other arm was around the head beside her on the pillow. Her eyelids fluttered. Then for a minute at a time they did not move at all. After that they fluttered again, seven or eight or nine times in quick succession. She waited as patiently as she could for Vern to wake up.

When Vern came home sometime late in the night, he did not wake her. She had stayed awake waiting for him as long as she could, but she had become so sleepy her eyes would not stay open until he came.

The dark head on the pillow beside hers looked tired and worn. Vern's forehead, even in sleep, was wrinkled a little over his nose. Around the corners of his eyes the skin was darker than it was anywhere else on his face. She reached over as carefully as possible and kissed the cheek closest to her. She wanted to put both arms around his head and draw him to her, and to kiss him time after time and hold his dark head tight against her face.

Again her eyelids fluttered uncontrollably.

"Vern," she whispered softly. "Vern."

Slowly his eyes opened, then quickly closed again.

"Vern, sweet," she murmured, her heart beating faster and faster.

Vern turned his face toward her, snuggling his head between her arm and breast, and moving until she could feel his breath on her neck.

"Oh, Vern," she said in a whisper.

He could feel her kisses on his eyes and cheek and forehead and mouth. He was comfortably awake by then. He found her with his hands and they drew themselves tightly together.

"What did he say, Vern?" she asked at last, unable to wait any longer. "What, Vern?"

He opened his eyes and looked at her, fully awake at last.

She could read what he had to say on his face.

"When, Vern?" she said.

"Today," he said, closing his eyes and snuggling his head into her warmth once more.

Her lips trembled a little when he said it. She could not help herself.

"Where are we going to move to, Vern?" she asked like a little girl, looking closely to his lips for his answer.

He shook his head, pushing it tightly against her breasts and closing his eyes against her body.

They both lay still for a long time. The sun had warmed the room until it was almost like summer again, instead of early fall. Little waves of heat were beginning to rise from the weatherworn windowsill. There would be a little more of summer before winter came.

"Did you tell him—?" Nellie said. She stopped and looked down at Vern's face. "Did you tell him about me, Vern?"

"Yes."

"What did he say?"

Vern did not answer her. He pushed his head against her breast and held her tighter, as though he were struggling for food that would make his body strong when he got up and stood alone in the bare room.

"Didn't he say anything, Vern?"

"He just said he couldn't help it, or something like that. I don't remember what he said, but I know what he meant."

"Doesn't he care, Vern?"

"I guess he doesn't, Nellie."

Nellie stiffened. She trembled for a moment, but her body stiffened as though she had no control over it.

"But you care what happens to me, don't you, Vern?"

"Oh, God, yes!" he said. "That's all I do care about now. If anything happens—"

For a long time they lay in each other's arms, their minds stirring them wider and wider awake.

Nellie got up first. She was dressed and out of the room before Vern knew how quickly time had passed. He leaped out of bed, dressed, and hurried to the kitchen to make the fire in the cookstove. Nellie was already peeling the potatoes when he got it going.

They did not say much while they ate breakfast. They had to move, and move that day. There was nothing else they could do. The furniture did not belong to them, and they had so few clothes it would not be troublesome to carry them.

Nellie washed the dishes while Vern was getting their things ready. There was nothing to do after that except to tie up his overalls and shirts in a bundle, and Nellie's clothes in another, and to start out.

When they were ready to leave, Nellie stopped at the gate and looked back at the house. She did not mind leaving the place, even though it had been the only home she and Vern had ever had together. The house was so dilapidated that probably it would fall down in a few years more. The roof leaked, one side of the house had slipped off the foundation posts, and the porch sagged all the way to the ground in front.

Vern waited until she was ready to leave. When she turned away from the house, there were tears in her eyes, but she never looked back at it again. After they had gone a mile, they had turned a bend in the road, and the pines hid the place from sight.

"Where are we going, Vern?" she said, looking at him through the tears.

"We'll just have to keep on until we find a place," he said. He knew that she knew as well as he did that in that country of pines and sand the farms and houses were sometimes ten or fifteen miles apart. "I don't know how far that will be."

While she trudged along the sandy road, she could smell the fragrance of the last summer flowers all around her. The weeds and scrub hid most of them from sight, but every chance she got she stopped a moment and looked along the side of the ditches for blossoms. Vern did not stop, and she always ran to catch up with him before she could find any.

In the middle of the afternoon they came to a creek where it was cool and shady. Vern found her a place to lie down and, before taking off her shoes to rest her feet, scraped a pile of dry pine needles for her to lie on and pulled an armful of moss from the trees to put under her head. The water he brought her tasted of the leaves and grasses in the creek, and it was cool and clear. She fell asleep as soon as she had drunk some.

It was late afternoon when Vern woke her up.

"You've been asleep two or three hours, Nellie," he said. "Do you think you could walk a little more before night?"

She sat up and put on her shoes and followed him to the road. She felt a dizziness as soon as she was on her feet. She did not want to say anything to Vern about it, because she did not want him to worry. Every step she took pained her then. It was almost unbearable at times, and she bit her lips and crushed her fingers in her fists, but she walked along behind him, keeping out of his sight so he would not know about it.

At sundown she stopped and sat down by the side of the road. She felt as though she would never be able to take another step again. The pains in her body had drawn the color from her face, and her limbs felt as though they were being pulled from her body. Before she knew it, she had fainted.

When she opened her eyes, Vern was kneeling beside her, fanning her with his hat. She looked up into his face and tried to smile.

"Why didn't you tell me, Nellie?" he said. "I didn't know you were so tired."

"I don't want to be tired," she said. "I just couldn't help it, I guess."

He looked at her for a while, fanning her all the time.

"Do you think it might happen before we get some place?" he asked anxiously. "What do you think, Nellie?"

Nellie closed her eyes and tried not to think. They had not passed a house or farm since they had left that morning. She did not know how much farther it was to a town, and she was afraid to think how far it might be even to the next house. It made her afraid to think about it.

"I thought you said it would be another two weeks . . . ?" Vern said. "Didn't you, Nellie?"

"I thought so," she said. "But it's going to be different now, walking like this all day."

His hat fell from his hand, and he looked all around in confusion. He did not know what to do, but he knew he had to do something for Nellie right away.

"I can't stand this," he said. "I've got to do something."

He picked her up and carried her across the road. He found a place for her to lie under a pine tree, and he put her down there. Then he untied their bundles and put some of their clothes under her head and some over her feet and legs.

The sun had set, and it was becoming dark. Vern did not know what to do next. He was afraid to leave her there all alone in the woods, but he knew he had to get help for her.

"Vern," she said, holding out her hand to touch him.

He grasped it in his, squeezing and stroking her fingers and wrist.

"What is it, Nellie?"

"I'm afraid it is going to happen . . . happen . . . happen right away," she said weakly, closing her eyes before she could finish.

He bent down and saw that her lips were bloodless and that her face was whiter than he had ever seen anyone's face. While he watched her, her body became tense and she bit her mouth to keep from screaming with pain.

Vern jumped up and ran to the road, looking up it and down it. The night had come down so quickly that he could not tell whether there were any fields or cleared ground there as an indication of somebody's living near. There were no signs of a house or people anywhere.

He ran back to Nellie.

"Are you all right?" he asked her.

"If I could go to sleep," she said, "I think I would be all right for a while."

He got down beside her and put his arms around her.

"If I thought you wouldn't be afraid, I'd go up the road until I found a house and get a car or something to carry you. I can't let you stay here all night on the ground."

"You might not get back — in time!" she cried frantically.

"I'd hurry as fast as I could," he said. "I'll run until I find somebody."

"If you'll come back in two or three hours," she said, "I'd be able to stand it, I think. I couldn't stand it any longer than that alone, though."

He got up.

"I'm going," he said.

He ran up the road as fast as he could, remembering how he had pleaded to be allowed to stay in the house a little longer so Nellie would not have to go like that. The only answer he had got, even after he had explained about Nellie, was a shake of the head. There was no use in begging after that. He was being put out, and he could not do anything about it. He was certain there should have been some money due him for his crop that fall, even a few dollars, but he knew there was no use in trying to argue about that, either. He had gone home the night before, knowing they would have to leave. He stumbled, falling heavily, headlong, on the road.

When he picked himself up, he saw a light ahead. It was only a pale ray from a board window that had been closed tightly. But it was a house, and somebody lived in it. He ran toward it as fast as he could.

When he got to the place, a dog under the house barked, but he paid no attention to it. He ran up to the door and pounded on it with both fists.

"Let me in!" he yelled. "Open the door!"

Somebody inside shouted, and several chairs were knocked over. The dog ran out from under the house and began snapping at Vern's legs. He tried to kick the dog away, but the dog was just as determined as he was, and came back at him more savagely than before. Finally he pushed the door open, breaking a button lock.

Several Negroes were hiding in the room. He could see heads and feet under the bed and behind a trunk and under a table.

"Don't be scared of me," he said as calmly as he could. "I came for help. My wife's down the road, sick. I've got to get her into a house somewhere. She's lying on the ground."

The oldest man in the room, a gray-haired Negro who looked about fifty, crawled from under the bed.

"I'll help you, boss," he said. "I didn't know what you wanted when you came shouting and yelling like that. That's why I didn't open the door and let you in."

"Have you got a cart, or something like that?" Vern asked.

"I've got a one-horse cart," the man said. "George, you and Pete go hitch up the mule to the cart. Hurry and do it."

Two Negro boys came from their hiding places and ran out the back door.

"We'll need a mattress, or something like that to put her on," Vern said.

The Negro woman began stripping the covers from the bed, and Vern picked up the mattress and carried it out the front door to the road. While he waited for the boys to drive the cart out, he walked up and down, trying to assure himself that Nellie would be all right.

When the cart was ready, they all got in and drove down the road as fast as the mule could go. It took less than half an hour for them to reach the grove where he had left Nellie, and by then he realized he had been gone three hours or longer.

Vern jumped to the ground, calling her. She did not answer. He ran up the bank and fell on his knees beside her on the ground.

"Nellie!" he said, shaking her. "Wake up, Nellie! This is Vern, Nellie!"

He could not make her answer. Putting his face down against hers, he felt her cold cheek. He put his hands on her forehead, and that was cold, too. Then he found her wrists and held them in his fingers while he pressed his ear tightly against her breast.

The Negro man finally succeeded in pulling him backward. For a while he did not know where he was or what had happened. It seemed as if his mind had gone completely blank.

The Negro was trying to talk to him, but Vern could not hear a word he was saying. He did know that something had happened, and that Nellie's face and hands were cold, and that he could not feel her heart beat. He knew, but he could not make himself believe that it was really true.

He fell down on the ground, his face pressed against the pine needles, while his fingers dug into the soft damp earth. He could hear voices above him, and he could hear the words the voices said, but nothing had any meaning. Sometime—a long time away—he would ask about their baby—about Nellie's—about their baby. He knew it would be a long time before he could ask anything like that, though. It would be a long time before words would have any meaning in them again.

(First published in *Southways*)

Balm of Gilead

BACK in January, about the middle of the first week, Ned Jones received a letter from the fire insurance agent's office in Bangor. The letter said that the company, effective January 1st, last, had discontinued allowing a discount on premiums covering farmhouses and barns which were equipped with lightning rods. Therefore, the letter said, the cost for protection on his buildings would be raised to twenty-two-fifty from twenty-fifty.

However, the letter went on, if the rods were already installed on the building, a lightning-rod expert would call and inspect the terminals, ground wires, brads, and so forth, and if the expert found them in first-class condition, the discount would be reinstated. The charge for all of this, the letter concluded, would be three dollars for the inspector's time.

"Thunderation," Ned said when he had finished reading the letter the third time. "Hell and thunderation!"

It did not take him long to figure out that he would save a dollar by not having the lightning rods inspected, but even so he could see that it was going to cost him two dollars a year more to keep his buildings covered by insurance.

"That's thunderation," he said.

His wife, Betty, was silent about the whole matter. She always froze up inside whenever something came up like that and threatened to cost an extra penny.

The insurance premium was not due and payable until February 1st, but a week before that time Ned got ready to make a trip to Bangor and pay a call at the insurance agent's office.

He and his wife started out to Bangor after breakfast, driving the old car slowly along the black-top road, taking care to stay as far on the right-hand side of the road as possible. The law was that a car owner would not have to carry liability and property-damage insurance as long as he did not have a mishap. Ned was set on not having that first accident on the highways that would force him to pay insurance premiums for the right to drive his car. It was an old car anyway, about twelve years old, and he did not intend buying another one when it was worn out.

They got to Bangor just before ten o'clock in the forenoon, and, after finding a safe place to park and leave the automobile, Ned and his wife went straight to the agent's office.

They sat down on a bench in the hall and waited for several minutes, and then a girl took them to see Mr. Harmsworth.

"Now, about that insurance on my stand of buildings out at Gaylord," Ned said, shaking his head and his finger at the agent.

"I take it you're upset about the new lightning-rod clause, effective January 1st, last," Mr. Harmsworth said, smiling at Ned and his wife. "You see, Mr. Jones, and Mrs. Jones, the company at the home office in New Hampshire rewrites the contracts, and we agents have nothing whatever to do with the terms the company dictates."

"What do people in New Hampshire know about lightning rods anyway?" Ned said. "Now let me tell you. I once knew a man in New Hampshire who —"

"Let's not get off the subject, Mr. Jones, and Mrs. Jones," Mr. Harmsworth said. "After all, both my parents were born and raised in New Hampshire, and I'm sure there is a New Hampshire connection somewhere in your family, too."

He smiled at Mrs. Jones, beaming upon her all the force of what he knew was a sunny smile. Betty refused to be disarmed. She was frozen up inside, and she intended to remain unthawed as long as the insurance company refused to make an adjustment that would not cost them an extra penny.

"Now, I've lived down here in the State of Maine for all my life," Ned said, "and I'm sixty and more right now, and lightning rods are the only things in the world that'll keep lightning from striking and setting fire to the house or barn. All my life I've seen lightning strike a spire and run down the cable into the ground without even so much as smoking up the roof and clapboards. If it wasn't for lightning rods—"

"Are you sure lightning runs down lightning rods, Mr. Jones, and Mrs. Jones?" Mr. Harmsworth said. "I was under the impression it ran up the rods, or rather made contact on the point of the spire. However—"

"Lightning is lightning, whether it runs up or down, or slantwise, if it has a mind to," Ned said, rising up.

"I see you know a lot more about such things than I do," Mr. Harmsworth laughed, beaming upon Mrs. Jones. "I was raised here in the city, and I never had a chance to observe how lightning behaves when it comes in contact with a rod-equipped building. But, just the same, there's nothing either you or I can do about this here clause, because the home office rewrote the contract and sent us the printed forms, and I'm merely their representative. I carry out their orders, but I have no authority to alter a clause in a contract."

Ned looked at his wife, and she shook her head. That was all he wanted to know. No insurance company, with a home office in New Hampshire, run by New Hampshire people, was going to tell him whether they thought lightning rods were protection or not. He looked at his wife again, and shook his head. Betty tightened her mouth, freezing tighter inside, and nodded at Ned.

Mr. Harmsworth shuffled some papers on his desk, and, bringing one out with much crinkling and creasing, laid it before Ned.

"This is your bill for fire-protection coverage, due February 1st," he said, glancing quickly at Ned, but not looking at Mrs. Jones.

Ned pushed it back at him.

"Now, about this Balm of Gilead," Ned said, edging forward in his chair.

"What Balm of Gilead?" Mr. Harmsworth asked, startled. "What's that?"

Ned looked at his wife, and Betty nodded. That was what he wanted to know from her. He pulled his chair closer to the desk.

"My Balm of Gilead," he said. "I've got one in my dooryard, fourteen feet from the west wall of my dwelling house, and twenty-two feet from the east wall of my barn."

"What's a Balm of Gilead?" Mr. Harmsworth asked, still startled.

"Wasn't that something in the Bible? How'd you get something that was in the Bible?"

Ned and Betty looked at each other, but neither of them made any motion of the head.

"Balm of Gilead is a tree," Ned said. "My Balm of Gilead was set out by my father, seventy-seven years ago, and it stands in my dooryard."

"What about it?" Mr. Harmsworth asked, wild-eyed.

"It's a lightning rod," Ned said. "It's the finest lightning rod on earth. After a Balm of Gilead—"

"You want us to give you a discount because you have a tree—" Mr. Harmsworth began, sitting forward in his chair.

"—passes its fiftieth year, it turns into a lightning rod," Ned continued doggedly. "Lightning won't strike any other thing within fifty yards of it. Lightning strikes the Balm of Gilead every time."

"I don't know what you're driving at exactly," Mr. Harmsworth said, "but I wouldn't suppose you expect to get any discount on your fire insurance for having a tree like that."

Betty stiffened her backbone.

"I don't know why not," Ned said. "Why shouldn't I get a discount when I've got a Balm of Gilead located almost halfway between my two buildings, and the farthest is twenty-two feet from it. A tree like that is two or three times more protection than rods on the buildings. Why, it even makes the buildings proof against lightning! I figure I'm due five or six dollars discount for having that tree where it is."

Mr. Harmsworth scratched his head and took a swift look at Mrs. Jones. He had time to see that her mouth was drawn in a tight line across her face. He did not look at her again.

"If you insist upon it," he said, "I'll take it up with the home office in New Hampshire. I won't be able to do a thing until I hear from them. But I shouldn't think they would allow anybody a discount on fire insurance for having a Balm of Gilead tree."

"If they wasn't those New Hampshire people," Ned said, "they'd know how much protection a tree like that is."

"I'll write you a letter and let you know what the home office has to say just as soon as I get their answer," he said, standing up.

Ned and Betty got up and went out into the hall. Mr. Harmsworth followed them trying to shake hands with at least one of them. Betty kept her hands clasped tightly across her waist. Ned outwalked the agent to the street.

"Ignorant young cuss," Ned said. "Associates with New Hampshire people."

Betty nodded her head.

They bought a few things in a store, and then got into their car and drove home. Neither of them mentioned the insurance during the rest of the day.

During the remainder of the week, and through the first three days of the following one, both Ned and his wife watched the mail for the letter from the agent in Bangor. On the third day the letter came.

They went into the kitchen and sat down in the chairs by the window before opening it. Ned first took out his glasses and carefully polished the lenses. Betty put her handkerchief to her nose, and then put it away. Ned read the letter aloud.

DEAR MR. JONES:

I have taken up the matter of the Balm of Gilead tree in your dooryard with the home office in New Hampshire, and I am herewith advising you of their decision. It seems that the company thought it was all a joke or something because, in their own words, they wished to know if your Balm of Gilead tree would "catch mice, scare crows away, and cure painter's colic." Further along in their letter they state most emphatically that under no circumstances would a discount on fire-insurance premiums be allowed for possession of a Balm of Gilead tree. . . .

The letter did not end there, but Ned read no farther. He handed the letter to his wife, and she laid it aside on the table, drawing her mouth into a thin straight line across her face.

"I never did waste any feelings for the people of New Hampshire," Ned said, putting away his glasses, getting his hat, and standing up.

His wife did not say a word when he left the kitchen and went out into the dooryard.

When she saw him come out of the woodshed with the ax and the crosscut saw, she put on her jacket and went out to help him.

First he cut a notch in the Balm of Gilead on the side in order to fell it in the direction where he wanted it to fall. When that was done, he picked up one end of the crosscut, and Betty picked up the other end. They began sawing silently, their faces bright but drawn in tight lines, and both hoping that an electrical storm would come early in the spring, and each of them praying silently that lightning would strike the house and burn it to a heap of ashes on the ground.

(First published in *Story*)

The People *v.* Abe Lathan, Colored

UNCLE ABE was shucking corn in the crib when Luther Bolick came down from the big white house on the hill and told him to pack up his household goods and move off the farm. Uncle Abe had grown a little deaf and he did not hear what Luther said the first time.

"These old ears of mine is bothering me again, Mr. Luther," Uncle Abe said. "I just can't seem to hear as good as I used to."

Luther looked at the Negro and scowled. Uncle Abe had got up and was standing in the crib door where he could hear better.

"I said, I want you and your family to pack up your furniture and anything else that really belongs to you, and move off."

Uncle Abe reached out and clutched at the crib door for support.

"Move off?" Uncle Abe said.

He looked into his landlord's face unbelievingly.

"Mr. Luther, you don't mean that, does you?" Uncle Abe asked, his voice shaking. "You must be joking, ain't you, Mr. Luther?"

"You heard me right, even if you do pretend to be half deaf," Luther said angrily, turning around and walking several steps. "I want you off the place by the end of the week. I'll give you that much time if you don't try to make any trouble. And when you pack up your things, take care you don't pick up anything that belongs to me. Or I'll have the law on you."

Uncle Abe grew weak so quickly that he barely managed to keep from falling. He turned a little and slid down the side of the door and sat on the crib floor. Luther looked around to see what he was doing.

"I'm past sixty," Uncle Abe said slowly, "but me and my family works hard for you, Mr. Luther. We work as hard as anybody on your whole place. You know that's true, Mr. Luther. I've lived here, working for you, and your daddy before you, for all of forty years. I never mentioned to you about the shares, no matter how big the crop was that I raised for you. I've never asked much, just enough to eat and a few clothes, that's all. I raised up a houseful of children to help work, and none of them ever made any trouble for you, did they, Mr. Luther?"

Luther waved his arm impatiently, indicating that he wanted the Negro to stop arguing. He shook his head, showing that he did not want to listen to anything Uncle Abe had to say.

"That's all true enough," Luther said, "but I've got to get rid of half the tenants on my place. I can't afford to keep eight or ten old people like you here any longer. All of you will have to move off and go somewhere else."

"Ain't you going to farm this year, and raise cotton, Mr. Luther?" Uncle Abe asked. "I can still work as good and hard as anybody else. It may take me a little longer sometimes, but I get the work done. Ain't I shucking this corn to feed the mules as good as anybody else could do?"

"I haven't got time to stand here and argue with you," Luther said nervously. "My mind is made up, and that's all there is to it. Now, you go on home as soon as you finish feeding the mules and start packing the things that belong to you like I told you."

Luther turned away and started walking down the path toward the barn. When he got as far as the barnyard gate, he turned around and looked back. Uncle Abe had followed him.

"Where can me and my family move to, Mr. Luther?" Uncle Abe said. "The boys is big enough to take care of themselves. But me and my wife has grown old. You know how hard it is for an old colored man like me to go out and find a house and land to work on shares. It don't cost you much to keep us, and me and my boys raise as much cotton as anybody else. The last time I mentioned the shares has been a long way in the past, thirty years or more. I'm just content to work like I do and get some rations and a few clothes. You know that's true, Mr. Luther. I've lived in my little shanty over there for all of forty years, and it's the only home I've got. Mr. Luther, me and my wife is both old now, and I can't hire out to work by the day, because I don't have the strength any more. But I can still grow cotton as good as any other colored man in the country."

Luther opened the barnyard gate and walked through it. He shook his head as though he was not even going to listen any longer. He turned his back on Uncle Abe and walked away.

Uncle Abe did not know what to say or do after that. When he saw

Luther walk away, he became shaky all over. He clutched at the gate for something to hold on it.

"I just can't move away, Mr. Luther," he said desperately. "I just can't do that. This is the only place I've got to live in the world. I just can't move off, Mr. Luther."

Luther walked out of sight around the corner of the barn. He did not hear Uncle Abe after that.

The next day, at a little after two o'clock in the afternoon, a truck drove up to the door of the three-room house where Uncle Abe, his wife, and their three grown sons lived. Uncle Abe and his wife were sitting by the fire trying to keep warm in the winter cold. They were the only ones at home then.

Uncle Abe heard the truck drive up and stop, but he sat where he was, thinking it was his oldest boy, Henry, who drove a truck sometimes for Luther Bolich.

After several minutes had passed, somebody knocked on the door, and his wife got up right away and went to see who it was.

There were two strange white men on the porch when she opened the door. They did not say anything at first, but looked inside the room to see who was there. Still not saying anything, they came inside and walked to the fireplace where Uncle Abe sat hunched over the hearth.

"Are you Abe Lathan?" one of the men, the oldest, asked.

"Yes, sir, I'm Abe Lathan," he answered, wondering who they were, because he had never seen them before. "Why do you want to know that?"

The man took a bright metal disk out of his pocket and held it in the palm of his hand before Uncle Abe's eyes.

"I'm serving a paper and a warrant on you," he said. "One is an eviction, and the other is for threatening to do bodily harm."

He unfolded the eviction notice and handed it to Uncle Abe. The Negro shook his head bewilderedly, looking first at the paper and finally up at the two strange white men.

"I'm a deputy," the older man said, "and I've come for two things — to evict you from this house and to put you under arrest."

"What does that mean — evict?" Uncle Abe asked.

The two men looked around the room for a moment. Uncle Abe's wife had come up behind his chair and put trembling hands on his shoulder.

"We are going to move your furniture out of this house and carry it off the property of Luther Bolick. Then, besides that, we're going to take you down to the county jail. Now, come on and hurry up, both of you."

Uncle Abe got up, and he and his wife stood on the hearth not knowing what to do.

The two men began gathering up the furniture and carrying it out of the house. They took the beds, tables, chairs, and everything else in the three rooms except the cookstove, which belonged to Luther Bolick. When they got all the things outside, they began piling them into the truck.

Uncle Abe went outside in front of the house as quickly as he could. "White-folks, please don't do that," he begged. "Just wait a minute while I go find Mr. Luther. He'll set things straight. Mr. Luther is my landlord, and he won't let you take all my furniture away like this. Please, sir, just wait while I go find him."

The two men looked at each other.

"Luther Bolick is the one who signed these papers," the deputy said, shaking his head. "He was the one who got these court orders to carry off the furniture and put you in jail. It wouldn't do you a bit of good to try to find him now."

"Put me in jail?" Uncle Abe said. "What did he say to do that for?"

"For threatening bodily harm," the deputy said. "That's for threatening to kill him. Hitting him with a stick or shooting him with a pistol."

The men threw the rest of the household goods into the truck and told Uncle Abe and his wife to climb in the back. When they made no effort to get in, the deputy pushed them to the rear and prodded them until they climbed into the truck.

While the younger man drove the truck, the deputy stood beside them in the body so they could not escape. They drove out the lane, past the other tenant houses, and then down the long road that went over the hill through Luther Bolick's land to the public highway. They passed the big white house where he lived, but he was not within sight.

"I never threatened to harm Mr. Luther," Uncle Abe protested. "I never did a thing like that in my whole life. I never said a mean thing about him either. Mr. Luther is my boss, and I've worked for him ever since I was twenty years old. Yesterday he said he wanted me to move off his farm, and all I did was say that I thought he ought to let me stay. I won't have much longer to live, noway. I told him I didn't want to move off. That's all I said to Mr. Luther. I ain't never said I was going to try to kill him. Mr. Luther knows that as well as I do. You ask Mr. Luther if that ain't so."

They had left Luther Bolick's farm, and had turned down the highway toward the county seat, eleven miles away.

"For forty years I has lived here and worked for Mr. Luther," Uncle Abe said, "and I ain't never said a mean thing to his face or behind his back in all that time. He furnishes me with rations for me and my family, and a few clothes, and me and my family raise cotton for him, and I been doing that ever since I was twenty years old. I moved here and started working on shares for his daddy first, and then when he died, I kept right on like I have up to now. Mr. Luther knows I has worked hard and never answered him back, and only asked for rations and a few clothes all this time. You ask Mr. Luther."

The deputy listened to all that Uncle Abe said, but he did not say anything himself. He felt sorry for the old Negro and his wife, but there was nothing he could do about it. Luther Bolick had driven to the courthouse early that morning and secured the papers for eviction and arrest. It was his job to serve the papers and execute the court orders. But even if it was his job, he could not keep from feeling sorry for the Negroes. He didn't think that Luther Bolick ought to throw them off his farm just because they had grown old.

When they got within sight of town, the deputy told the driver to stop. He drew the truck up beside the highway when they reached the first row of houses. There were fifteen or eighteen Negro houses on both sides of the road.

After they had stopped, the two white men began unloading the furniture and stacking it beside the road. When it was all out of the truck, the deputy told Uncle Abe's wife to get out. Uncle Abe started to get out, too, but the deputy told him to stay where he was. They drove off again, leaving Uncle Abe's wife standing in a dazed state of mind beside the furniture.

"What are you going to do with me now?" Uncle Abe asked, looking back at his wife and furniture in the distance.

"Take you to the county jail and lock you up," the deputy said.

"What's my wife going to do?" he asked.

"The people in one of those houses will probably take her in."

"How long is you going to keep me in jail locked up?"

"Until your case comes up for trial."

They drove through the dusty streets of the town, around the court-house square, and stopped in front of a brick building with iron bars across the windows.

"Here's where we get out," the deputy said.

Uncle Abe was almost too weak to walk by that time, but he managed to move along the path to the door. Another white man opened the door and told him to walk straight down the hall until he was told to stop.

Just before noon Saturday, Uncle Abe's oldest son, Henry, stood in Ramsey Clark's office, hat in hand. The lawyer looked at the Negro and frowned. He chewed his pencil for a while, then swung around in his chair and looked out the window into the courthouse square. Presently he turned around and looked at Uncle Abe's son.

"I don't want the case," he said. "I don't want to touch it."

The boy stared at him helplessly. It was the third lawyer he had gone to see that morning, and all of them had refused to take his father's case.

"There's no money in it," Ramsey Clark said, still frowning. "I'd never get a dime out of you niggers if I took this case. And, besides, I don't want to represent any more niggers at court. Better lawyers than me have been ruined that way. I don't want to get the reputation of being a 'nigger lawyer.' "

Henry shifted the weight of his body from one foot to the other and bit his lips. He did not know what to say. He stood in the middle of the room trying to think of a way to get help for his father.

"My father never said he was going to kill Mr. Luther," Henry protested. "He's always been on friendly terms with Mr. Luther. None of us ever gave Mr. Luther trouble. Anybody will tell you that. All the other tenants on Mr. Luther's place will tell you my father has always stood up for Mr. Luther. He never said he was going to try to hurt Mr. Luther."

The lawyer waved for him to stop. He had heard all he wanted to listen to.

"I told you I wouldn't touch the case," he said angrily, snatching up some papers and slamming them down on his desk. "I don't want to go into court and waste my time arguing a case that won't make any difference one way or the other, anyway. It's a good thing for you niggers to get a turn on the 'gang every once in a while. It doesn't make any difference whether Abe Lathan threatened Mr. Bolick, or whether he didn't threaten him. Abe Lathan said he wasn't going to move off the farm, didn't he? Well, that's enough to convict him in court. When the case comes up for trial, that's all the judge will want to hear. He'll be sent to the 'gang quicker than a flea can hop. No lawyer is going to spend a lot of time preparing a case when he knows how it's going to end. If there was money in it, it might be different. But you niggers don't have a thin dime to pay me with. No, I don't want the case. I wouldn't touch it with a ten-foot pole."

Henry backed out of Ramsey Clark's office and went to the jail. He secured permission to see his father for five minutes.

Uncle Abe was sitting on his bunk in the cage looking through the bars when Henry entered. The jailer came and stood behind him at the cage door.

"Did you see a lawyer and tell him I never said nothing like that to Mr. Luther?" Uncle Abe asked the first thing.

Henry looked at his father, but it was difficult for him to answer. He shook his head, dropping his gaze until he could see only the floor.

"You done tried, didn't you, Henry?" Uncle Abe asked.

Henry nodded.

"But when you told the lawyers how I ain't never said a mean thing about Mr. Luther, or his daddy before him, in all my whole life, didn't they say they was going to help me get out of jail?"

Henry shook his head.

"What did the lawyers say, Henry? When you told them how respectful I've always been to Mr. Luther, and how I've always worked hard for him all my life, and never mentioned the shares, didn't they say they would help me then?"

Henry looked at his father, moving his head sideways in order to see him between the bars of the cage. He had to swallow hard several times before he could speak at all.

"I've already been to see three lawyers," he said finally. "All three of them said they couldn't do nothing about it, and to just go ahead and let it come up for trial. They said there wasn't nothing they could do, because the judge would give you a turn on the 'gang, anyway."

He stopped for a moment, looking down at his father's feet through the bars.

"If you want me to, I'll go see if I can find some other lawyers to take the case. But it won't do much good. They just won't do anything."

Uncle Abe sat down on his bunk and looked at the floor. He could not understand why none of the lawyers would help him. Presently he looked up through the bars at his son. His eyes were fast filling with tears that he could not control.

"Why did the lawyers say the judge would give me a turn on the 'gang, anyway, Henry?" he asked.

Henry gripped the bars, thinking about all the years he had seen his father and mother working in the cotton fields for Luther Bolick and being paid in rations, a few clothes, and a house to live in, and nothing more.

"Why did they say that for, Henry?" his father insisted.

"I reckon because we is just colored folks," Henry said at last. "I don't know why else they would say things like that."

The jailer moved up behind Henry, prodding him with his stick. Henry walked down the hall between the rows of cages toward the door that led to the street. He did not look back.

(First published in *Esquire*)

Big Buck

WHEN the sun went down, there were a heap of people just tramping up and down the dusty road without a care in the whole wide world. It was Saturday night and the cool of the evening was coming on, and that was enough to make a lot of folks happy. There were a few old logging mules plodding along in the dust with a worried look on their faces, but they had a right to look that way, because they had worked hard in the swamp all week and suppertime had come and gone, and they were still a long way from home.

It was the best time of the whole year for colored people, because it was so hot the whites didn't stir around much, and a colored man could walk up and down in the big road as much as he wanted to. The women and girls were all dressed up in starched white dresses and bright silk hair bows, and the men had on their Sunday clothes.

All at once a hound dog somewhere down the road started barking his head off. You could look down that way, but you couldn't see anything much, because the moon hadn't come up yet. The boys stopped in the middle of the road and listened. The old dog just kept on barking. They didn't say much, but they knew good and well those old hound dogs never took the trouble to get up and bark unless it was a stranger they smelled.

"Take care yourself, nigger!" the black boy in the yellow hat yelled. "Stand back and hold your breath, because if you don't, you won't never know what hit you."

"What you talking about, anyhow?" Jimson said.

"I just turned around and looked down the road," Moses said, "and I saw a sight that'll make your eyes pop out of your head."

"What you see, nigger?" Jimson asked, trembling like a quiver bug. "You see something scary?"

"I seen Big Buck," Moses said, his voice weak and thin. "I seen him more than once, too, because I looked back twice to make sure I saw right the first time."

The two Negroes backed off the road into the ditch and pulled the bushes around them. They squatted there a while listening. Farther up the road people were laughing and singing, and talking loud. The old hound dog down the road was barking like he just wouldn't give up.

"Ain't no sense in Big Buck scaring the daylights out of folks the way he does," Jimson said. "It's a sin the way he keeps on doing it."

"Big Buck don't exactly aim to set out to scare folks," Moses said. "People just naturally get the shakes when he comes anywhere around, that's all. It ain't Big Buck's fault none. He's as gentle as a baby."

"Then how come you're sitting here, squatting in these bushes, if he ain't nothing to be scared of?"

Moses didn't say anything. They pulled the bushes back a little and looked down the road. They couldn't see much of Big Buck, because it had been dark ever since sundown; but they could hear his feet flapping in the dusty road as plain as cypress trees falling in the swamp in broad daylight.

"Maybe he once was gentle, when he was a baby himself," Jimson said. "Maybe he is now, when he's asleep in his bed. But last Saturday night down at the crossroads store he didn't act like no baby I ever knew."

"What did he do down there?" Moses asked.

"He said he liked the looks of the striped band on my new straw hat, and then he slapped me so hard on the back I hit the ground smack with my face. That's how like a baby Big Buck is. I know, I do."

"Quit your jabbering," Moses whispered. "Here he comes!"

They pulled the bushes around them and squatted closer to the ground so they wouldn't be seen. They took off their hats and ducked down as far as they could so their heads wouldn't show. They were mighty glad it had got as dark as it was.

"Just look at that courting fool," Jimson whispered. "Ain't he the biggest sport you ever did see? He's all dressed up in yellow shoes and red necktie ready to flash them colors on the first gal he sees. That courting fool can do courting where courting's never been done before. Man alive, don't I wish I was him! I'd get me a high yellow and—"

"Shut your big mouth, nigger!" Moses whispered, slamming Jimson in the ribs with his elbow. "He'll jump us here in these bushes sure, if you don't shut that big mouth of yours."

Big Buck swung up the road like his mind was made up beforehand just exactly where he was headed. He was whistling as loud as a sawmill engine at Saturday afternoon quitting time, and throwing his head back and swinging his arms like he was sitting on top of the world. He was on his way to do some courting, it was plain to see.

The colored boys in the bushes shook until their bones rattled.

Then right square in front of the bushes Big Buck stopped and looked. There wasn't no cat that could see better than him in the dark. His big black face only had to turn toward what he wanted to see, and there it was as plain as day in front of his eyes.

"You niggers is going to shake all the leaves right off them poor bushes," Big Buck said, grinning until his teeth glistened like new tombstones in the moonlight. "Why you boys want to go and do that to them pretty little trees?"

He reached an arm across the ditch and caught hold of a woolly head. He pulled his arm back into the road.

"What's your name, nigger?" he said.

"I'm Jimson, Mr. Big Buck," the colored boy said. "Just Jimson's my name."

Big Buck reached his other arm into the bushes and caught hold of another woolly head. He yanked on it until Moses came hopping out into the road. He and Jimson stood there under Big Buck's arms trembling worse than the leaves on the bushes had done.

"What's your name, black boy?" Big Buck said.

"This is little Moses," he answered.

"Little Moses how-many?"

"Just little Moses March."

"That's a funny name to have in August, boy," Big Buck said, shaking him by the hair until Moses wished he'd never been born. "What you quivering like that for, boy? Ain't nothing to be scared of if you change your name to August."

"Yes, sir, Mr. Big Buck," Moses said. "I'll change it. I'll change my name just like you said. I'll do just like you told me. I sure will, Mr. Big Buck."

Big Buck turned Moses loose and laughed all over. He slapped Jimson on the back between the shoulders and, before Jimson knew what had happened, the ground rose up and smacked him square in the face. Big Buck looked down at Jimson and raised him to his feet by gripping a handful of woolly hair in his hand. He stood back and laughed some more.

"You peewees don't have to act like you is scared out of your mind," Big Buck said. "I ain't going to hurt nobody. You boys is my friends. If it wasn't so late, and if I wasn't on my way to do some courting, I'd stop a while and shoot you some craps."

He hitched up his pants and tightened up his necktie.

The boys couldn't help admiring his bright yellow shoes and red necktie that looked like a red lantern hanging around his neck.

"Which-a-way is it to Singing Sal's house from here?" he asked.

"Whoses house?" Jimson asked, his mouth hanging open. "Whoses house did you say?"

"I said Singing Sal's," Big Buck answered.

"You don't mean Singing Sal, does you, Mr. Big Buck?" Moses asked. "You couldn't mean her, because Singing Sal ain't never took no courting. She's mule-headed—"

"You heard me, peewee," Big Buck said. "I say what I mean, and I mean Singing Sal. Which-a-way does she live from here?"

"Is you fixing to court her, sure enough?" Moses asked.

"That's what I'm headed for," he said, "and I'm in a big hurry to get there. You peewees come on and show me the way to get to where that gal lives."

Jimson and Moses ran along beside him, trotting to keep up with the long strides. They went half a mile before anybody said anything.

Every time they met a knot of people in the road, the folks jumped into the ditches to let Big Buck pass. Big Buck didn't weigh more than two hundred and fifty pounds, and he wasn't much over seven feet tall, but it looked like he took up all the space there was in a road when he swung along it. The women and girls sort of giggled when he went by, but Big Buck didn't turn his head at all. He kept straight up the big road like a hound on a live trail.

It wasn't long before Jimson and Moses were puffing and blowing, and they didn't know how much longer they could keep up with Big Buck if he didn't stop soon and give them a chance to get their breath back. The folks in the road scattered like a covey of quail.

When they got to the fork in the road, Big Buck stopped and asked them which way to go.

"It's over that way, across the creek," Jimson said, breathing hard. "If you didn't have no objection, I'd like to tag along behind you the rest of the way. Me and Moses was going over that way, anyway."

"I don't aim to waste no time knocking on wrong people's doors," Big Buck said, "and I want you boys to lead me straight to the place I want to go. Come on and don't waste no more time standing here."

They swung down the right-hand way. There weren't many houses down there, and they didn't lose any time. Big Buck was away out in front and the boys had a hard time keeping up.

They passed a couple of houses and went up the hill from the bridge over the creek. Big Buck started humming a little tune to himself. He didn't mind climbing a hill any more than walking on level ground.

When they got to the top, Big Buck stopped and hitched up his pants. He wiped the dust off his new yellow shoes with his pants' legs, and then he tightened up the red necktie until it almost choked him.

"That's the place," Jimson said, pointing.

"Then here's where I light," Big Buck said. "Here's where I hang my hat."

He started toward the cabin through the gap in the split-rail fence. He stopped halfway and called back.

"I'm mighty much obliged to you boys," he said.

He dug down into his pants and tossed a bright dime to them. Jimson got it before it was lost in the dark.

"You boys helped me save a lot of time, and I'm mighty much obliged," he said.

"You ain't going to try to court that there Singing Sal, sure enough, is you, Mr. Big Buck?" Jimson asked. He and Moses came as far as the fence and leaned on it. "Everybody says Singing Sal won't take no courting. Some say she ain't never took not even a whiff of it. Folks have even got themselves hurt, just trying to."

"She just ain't never had the right man come along before and give it to her," Big Buck said. "I've heard all that talk about how she won't take no courting, but she'll be singing a different tune when I get through with her."

Big Buck took a few steps toward the cabin door. Moses backed off toward the road. He wasn't taking no chances, because Singing Sal had a habit of shooting off a shotgun when she didn't want to be bothered. Moses backed away. Jimson stayed where he was and tried to get Moses to come closer so they could see what happened when Big Buck started inside.

"There ain't nothing to be scared of, Moses," Jimson said. "Big Buck knows what he's doing, or he wouldn't have come all the way here like he done."

Big Buck hitched up his pants again and picked his way around the woodpile and over an old wash tub full of rusty tin cans. He put one foot on the porch step and tried it with his weight to see how solid it was. The step squeaked and swayed, but it held him up.

Out in the yard by the sagging split-rail fence Jimson and Moses hung onto a post and waited to see. When Big Buck rapped on the door, their breath was stuck tight inside of them. There wasn't time to breathe before a chair fell over backward inside the cabin. Right after that a big tin pan was knocked off a table or shelf or something, and it fell on the floor with a big racket, too. She sure had been taken by surprise.

"Who's that at my door?" Singing Sal said. "What you want, whoever you is?"

Big Buck kicked the door with one of his big yellow shoes. The whole building shook.

"Your man has done come," he said, rattling and twisting the door knob. "Open up and let your good man inside, gal."

"Go away from here, nigger, while you is good and able," Singing Sal said. "I ain't got no time to be wasting on you, whoever you is. Now, just pick up your feet and mosey on away from my house."

"Honey," Big Buck said, getting a good grip on the knob, "I done made up my mind a long time back to start my courting while the victuals is hot. Just set me down a plate and pull me up a chair."

Before he could move an inch, a blast from Singing Sal's shotgun tore through the flimsy door. It didn't come anywhere near Big Buck, but it did sort of set him back on his heels for a minute. Then he hitched up his pants and yanked on the knob.

"Put that plaything down before you hurt yourself, honey," he shouted through the hole in the door. "Them things don't scare me one bit."

He gave the knob a jerk, and it broke off, and the lock with it. The door opened slowly, and the yellow lamplight fell across the porch and yard as far as the woodpile. He strutted inside while Singing Sal stared at him wild-eyed. Nobody had ever come through her door like that before. He acted like he wasn't scared of nothing in the world, not even double-barrel shotguns.

"Who's you?" she asked, her eyes popping.

He started grinning at her, and his whole mouth looked like it was going to split open from one ear to the other.

"I'm your man, honey," he said, "and I've come to do you some courting."

He walked on past her, looking her over from top to bottom while she stood in a daze. He walked around her to get a good look at her from behind. She didn't move an inch, she was that up in the air.

Jimson and Moses crept a little closer, going as far as the woodpile. They stayed behind it so they would have a place to dodge in case Singing Sal got hold of herself and started shooting again.

"I'm Big Buck from the far end of the swamp, honey," he said. "You must have heard of me before, because I've been around this part of the country most all my life. It's too bad I've been this long in getting here for some courting. But here I is, honey. Your good man has done come at last."

He pulled up a chair and sat down at the table. He wiped off the red-and-yellow oilcloth with his coat sleeve and reached to the cookstove for a skillet full of pout-mouthed perch. While he was getting the fish with one hand, he reached the other one over and picked up the coffeepot and poured himself a cupful. When that was done, he reached into the oven and got himself a handful of hot biscuits. All the time he was doing that, Singing Sal just stood and looked like she had just woke up out of a long sleep.

"You sure is a fine cook, honey," Big Buck said. "My, oh, my! I'd go courting every night if I could find good eating like these pout-mouthed perches and them hot biscuits."

After Big Buck had taken a bite of fish in one gulp and a whole biscuit in another, Singing Sal shook herself and reached down on the floor for the shotgun she dropped when she shot it off the first time. She brought it up and leveled it off at Big Buck and squeezed one eye shut. Big Buck cut his eyes around at her and took another big bite of perch.

"Honey, shut that door and keep the chilly night air out," he told her, pouring another cup of coffee. "I don't like to feel a draft down the back of my neck when I'm setting and eating."

Singing Sal raised one ear to hear what he was saying, and then she sighted some more down the barrel of the shotgun, but by then it was waving like she couldn't draw a bead any more. She was shaking so she couldn't hold it at all, and so she stood it on its end. After she had rested a minute, she clicked the hammer until it was uncocked, and put the shotgun back under the bed.

"Where'd you come from, anyhow?" she asked Big Buck.

"Honey, I done told you I come from back in the swamp where I cut them cypress trees all week long," he said. "If I had known how fine it is here, I wouldn't have waited for Saturday to come. I'd have gone and been here a long time back before this, honey."

He took another helping of fish and poured himself some more hot black coffee. All the biscuits were gone, the whole bread pan full. He felt on the oilcloth and tried to find some crumbs with his fingers.

Singing Sal walked behind his chair and looked him over good from head to toe. He didn't pay no attention to her at all. He didn't even say another word until he finished eating all the fried fish he wanted.

Then he pushed the table away from him, wiped his mouth, and swung a long arm around behind him. His arm caught Singing Sal around the middle and brought her up beside him. He spread open his legs and stood her between them. Then he took another good look at her from top to bottom.

"You look as good as them pout-mouthed perch and hot biscuits I done ate, honey," he said to her. "My, oh, my!"

He reached up and set her down on his lap. Then he reached out and kissed her hard on the mouth.

Singing Sal swung her nearest arm, and her hand landed square on Big Buck's face. He laughed right back at her. She swung her other arm, but her fist just bounced off his face like it had been a rubber ball.

He reached out to grab her to him, and she let go with both fists, both knees, and the iron lid cover from the top of the skillet. Big Buck went down on the floor when the iron lid hit him, and Singing Sal landed on top of him swinging both the iron lid and the iron water kettle with all her might. The kettle broke, and pieces of it flew all over the room. Big Buck pushed along the floor, and she hit him with the skillet, the coffeepot, and the top of the table. That looked like it was enough to do him in, but he still had courting on his mind. He reached out to grab her to him, and she hit him over the head with the oven door.

Singing Sal had been stirring around as busy as a cat with fur on fire, and she was out of breath. She sort of wobbled backward and rested against the foot of the bed, all undone.

She was panting and blowing, and she didn't know what to pick up next to hit him with. It looked to her like it didn't do no good to hit him at all, because things bounced off him like they would have against a brick wall. She hadn't ever seen a man like him before in all her life. She didn't know before that there was a man made like him at all.

"Honey," Big Buck said, "you sure is full of fire. You is my kind of gal to court. My, oh, my!"

He reached up and grabbed her. She didn't move much, and he tugged again. She acted like she was a post in a posthole, she was that solid when he tried to budge her. He grabbed her again, and she went down on top of him like a sack of corn. She rolled off on the floor, and her arms and legs thrashed around like she was trying to beat off bees and hornets. Big Buck got a grip on her and she rolled over on her back and lay there quiet, acting like she hadn't ever tussled with him at all.

Her eyes looked up into his, and if she had been a kitten she would have purred.

"How did you like my fried fish and hot biscuits, Big Buck?" she asked, lazy and slow. "How was they, Big Buck?"

"The cooking's mighty good," he said. "I ain't never had nothing as good as that was before."

The wind blew the door almost shut. There was only a little narrow crack left. Jimson and Moses stood up and looked at the yellow lamplight shining through the crack. After that they went to the gap in the fence and made their way to the big road. Every once in a while they could hear Singing Sal laugh out loud. They sat down in the ditch and waited. There wasn't anything else they could do.

They had to wait a long time before Big Buck came out of the house. The moon had come up and moved halfway across the sky, and the dew had settled so heavy on them that they shivered as bad as if they had fallen in the creek.

They jumped up when Big Buck came stumbling over the woodpile and through the gap in the fence.

From the door of the house a long shaft of yellow lamplight shone across the yard. Singing Sal was crouched behind the door with only her head sticking out.

"What you boys hanging around here for?" Big Buck said. "Come on and get going."

They started down the hill, Big Buck striking out in front and Jimson and Moses running along beside him to keep up with him.

They were halfway down the hill, and Big Buck hadn't said a word since they left the front of the house. Jimson and Moses ran along, trying to keep up with him, so they would hear anything he said about courting Singing Sal. Any man who had gone and courted Singing Sal right in her own house ought to be full of things to say.

They hung on, hoping he would say something any minute. It wasn't so bad trying to keep up with him going downhill.

When they got to the bottom of the hill where the road crossed the creek, Big Buck stopped and turned around. He looked back up at the top of the hill where Singing Sal lived, and drew in a long deep breath.

Jimson and Moses crowded around him to hear if he said anything.

"Them was the finest pout-mouthed perches I ever ate in all my life," Big Buck said slowly. "My, oh, my! Them fried fish, and all them hot biscuits was the best eating I ever done. My, oh, my! That colored gal sure can cook!"

Big Buck hitched up his pants and started across the bridge. It was a long way back to the swamp, and the sun was getting ready to come up.

"My, oh, my!" he said, swinging into his stride.

Jimson and Moses ran along beside him, doing their best to keep up.

(First published in *College Humor*)

Handy

NOBODY knew where Handy came from, and nobody knew where he would go if he left, but if he had not killed Grandpa Price, he could have stayed another ten years or more.

Grandpa Price was old, and he was peevish, and he did nothing but fuss and find fault all day long. If he had been let alone, he would not have lived much longer, anyway.

But Handy hit Grandpa Price with a windlass, and the old man died that night. Handy had to pack up the little that belonged to him and get ready to go somewhere else to live.

"You ought to have had better sense," Harry Munford told him.

"It wasn't sense that had to do with it," Handy said.

"Just the same, it wasn't a good thing to do."

"A man oughtn't be an out-and-out troublemaker," Handy said. "People who spend their lives building things don't have time to find fault with others."

"Even so," Harry said, "you shouldn't have done what you did to Grandpa Price."

A whole day could be spent counting up the downright troublemaking things Grandpa Price had said and done during the past ten or fifteen years. When he ran out of the ordinary things to find fault with, such as not enough gravy on the chicken or too much sweetening in the custard, he would go around quarreling about the time of day it happened to be. Sometimes when it was morning, he would say it ought to be afternoon, and when it was noon, he would say it ought to be dawn, and then rant and rave if anybody said noon was as good as anything else for it to be. Only a few days before he died, he got after Harry because the chimney might not be in plumb. That made Harry so mad he almost lost his head. "What if it ain't?" he shouted at the old man. "Because if it ain't, it ought to be," Grandpa Price said. Harry was so mad by then that he went for a plumb line and dropped it on the chimney. The chimney was only an eighth of an inch out of plumb. "That ought to make you shut your mouth from now on!" Harry shouted at him. "I won't shut my mouth, because the chimney is out of plumb and you know it. It ought to be torn down and built up again right," Grandpa Price said. "Over my dead body," Harry told him. Grandpa Price fussed about the chimney being out of plumb all the rest of the day, and even through supper until he went to bed that night. He called Harry and all the Munfords lazy, good for nothing, and slipshod. He followed Harry around the place the next day saying anybody who would take up for an out-of-plumb chimney was not a good citizen.

"The more I think about it, Handy, the more I think you shouldn't have done it," Harry said. "Any number of times I've felt like picking up a brick or a crowbar and doing the thing myself, but a man can't go around the world hitting old men like that, no matter how provoked he is. The law's against it."

"I just couldn't stand it no longer, Mr. Harry," Handy said. "I'm sorry about it now, but it just couldn't be helped at the time."

Handy had lived there ten or twelve years. When he walked into the front yard for the first time, it was in the middle of the cotton-picking season. He came in and said he was looking for something to do. It was at a time when Harry needed cotton pickers if he ever needed them. He was glad to see anybody who came up and said he wanted a job. Harry was all ready to hire Handy. He told Handy he was paying sixty cents a hundred in the fields.

Handy shook his head as though he knew exactly what he wanted. Cotton picking was not it. "No sirree, bob. I don't pick no cotton," Handy said. "I haven't got any need for anybody else these days," Harry told him. "The cotton is falling on the ground, going to waste faster every day, and that's all I'm concerned about now." "You always got need for something new, or something made of something old." "What do you mean?" "I make things," Handy said. "I just take what's thrown away and make it useful. Sometimes I like to make a thing just because it's pretty, though."

He picked up a stick of wood about a foot long and two or three inches thick. Nobody paid much attention to what he was doing, and

Harry was sizing him up to be a tramp. He asked Handy if he had ever worked in the fields, and Handy said he had not. He asked him if he had worked on the river steamers, and Handy said, No. In the cotton mills. Not ever. Railroads. No. Harry shook his head. He put Handy down a tramp. Handy scraped the wood with the knife blade and handed it to Harry. It was the smoothest-whittled wooden spoon anybody had ever seen. It looked as if it had been sandpapered and polished with soapstone. It had taken Handy only the length of time he was standing there to do it, too. Harry turned the spoon over and over in his hands, felt of it, and smiled at Handy. Anybody who could do a thing like that deserved a better jackknife than Handy had. Harry took his own out of his pocket and gave it to him.

Nobody said anything more to him about picking cotton in the fields. Handy walked around the yard looking at things for a while, and then he went around to the back of the house and looked inside the barn, the woodshed, the smokehouse, and the chicken run. He looked in all the hen nests, and then he began carving nest eggs out of some blocks of wood he found in the barn. They were smooth and brown, and the laying hens liked them better than any other kind.

After he had made six or eight nest eggs, he found something else to do. He never asked Harry or anybody if it was all right for him to do a thing, or if they wanted something made; he just went ahead and made whatever he felt like doing. The chairs Handy made were the most comfortable in the house, the plowstocks were the strongest on the farm, and the weather vanes were the prettiest in the country.

"The trouble with Grandpa Price, he wasn't like me and you, Handy," Harry said. "The reason me and you are alike is that I crave to get things growing in the fields, and you to make things with your hands. Grandpa Price didn't have that feeling in him. All he wanted was to find fault with what other people grow or make."

Handy was sad and dejected. He knew it would take him a long time to find another place where the people would let him stay and make things. He would be able to stop along the road now and then, of course, and make a chicken coop for somebody or build a pigpen; but as soon as he finished it, they would give him a leftover meal or a pair of old pants and tell him to go on away. He knew all about the trouble he was going to have finding somebody who would let him stay and just make things. Some of them would offer him a job plowing; in the fields, or working on a river steamer. "I want to make things out of pieces of wood," Handy said. "I want to build things with my fingers." The people were going to back away from him; they would shut the door in his face. He could not sit still. His hands began to tremble.

"What's the matter, Handy?" Harry asked him. "What makes you shake like that? Don't let what happened to Grandpa Price untie you."

"It's not that, it's something else."

"What else?"

"I'm going to find it hard not having a place to live where I can make things."

"I hate like everything to see you go," Harry said. "Somehow or other it don't seem right at all." It hurt him so much to think about Handy's leaving that he tried not to look at him. "But," he said, "the sheriff will make it hard for me if I fail to tell him what happened." It was already the day after Grandpa Price had died, and the sheriff had to be told about it before Grandpa Price could be buried in the cemetery. "But I don't want to do it, just the same," Harry said sadly. "It means driving you off, Handy, and I'd drive you off a dozen times before I'd let the sheriff find you here when he comes."

It hurt Harry so much to think about it he could not sit there and look at Handy. He got up and walked away by himself.

When he came back, Handy was not there. But presently he saw Handy's head bobbing up and down behind the barn fence, and he was relieved. After a while he went into the house to change into clean overalls and shirt. He had to change before he could go into town, anyway. There was nothing to stop him from taking as much time as he wanted, though. He looked at two or three pairs of overalls before deciding which to put on. He liked to have a person like Handy around, because Handy was always making something, or getting ready to make something. That was what he liked about Handy. He was like the children when they came home from school, or on holidays. They were busy at something, play or work, every minute they were awake. He was afraid, though, that when they grew up they would get to be like Grandpa

Price, that they would spend their time finding fault instead of making things.

When Harry finally came out into the yard, it was late in the afternoon.

"I don't like to go to town at this time of the day," he said, looking toward the barn where Handy was, up at the sky, and back again toward the barn. "It would mean coming back long after dark."

Harry walked around the house, to the garden several times, and finally toward the barnyard. He wondered more and more all the time what Handy was spending so much time down there for. Several times he had seen Handy come to the barn door, throw some trash and shavings outside, and then disappear again.

It grew dark soon, and he did not see Handy again until the next morning. Handy was at the table eating breakfast when Harry came in and sat down.

"What's this?" Harry asked, standing up again suddenly.

"A little present for Grandpa Price," Handy said.

"But Grandpa Price is dead —"

"I only made it to hang around his neck in the grave," Handy said. "I always wanted to make something for him, but I thought he'd find so much fault with it if he was alive that I went ahead and made it all wrong just to please him."

It was a wooden chain about two feet long, each link about the size of a fingernail, and each one a different object. Handy had carved it from beginning to end since the afternoon before, sitting up all night to finish it.

"If Grandpa Price was alive, he'd be so tickled to get it he wouldn't want to find any fault with it, Handy. As it is, I don't know that I've ever seen a finer-looking present."

Harry sat down and picked up the chain to look at it more closely. The first link he looked at was a miniature chair with three legs shorter than the fourth one.

"I didn't think anybody but me remembered about that time when Grandpa Price quarreled so much about one of the chairs having one leg shorter than the others. I said one leg was shorter. Grandpa Price said three were short and one was long. Up to that time, that was about the biggest quarrel me and him ever had, wasn't it, Handy?"

Handy nodded.

Harry bent over to see what some of the other objects were. One was carved to look like a piece of the sky with the sun and stars shining at the same time. Another was a picture in a frame that looked upside down no matter which way it was turned.

Handy pushed back his chair and got up.

"This is too fine a thing to put in a grave, Handy," Harry said. "It would be a sin to bury a thing like this in the ground where nobody could ever see it again."

"I made it for a present to hang around Grandpa Price's neck," Handy said. "That's why I made it."

"Well," Harry said, shaking his head, "that being the case — I guess you've got the right to say — But it does seem a shame —"

Handy went out through the kitchen, down the steps, and across the yard to the barn. As soon as he got inside the barn door, he fired the shotgun.

Harry jumped to his feet, carrying the chain for Grandpa Price's neck with him.

"What did Handy shoot for?" he said.

He looked out the window for a minute, then he went down to the barn.

When he came back, he was slow about it. He looked sad, but there was another look on his face at the same time. One moment he felt so good he had to grin about it. "Handy won't have to go now, after all." He grinned all over his face. "If Handy had stayed alive, I'd never have seen him again," he said to himself. He walked up on the porch and began looking at the chain again, picking out a link here and a link there to stare at and feel with his fingers.

"Grandpa Price can be buried in the cemetery if he wants to," he said, aloud, "but Handy is going to be buried right here in the back yard."

He felt the chain with all the fingers of both hands and held it up to gaze at in the sunlight.

"I want to have him around," he said.

(First published in *The New Republic*)